GIRL BEFORE A MIRROR

Also by Liza Palmer

Nowhere but Home

More Like Her

Conversations with the Fat Girl

Seeing Me Naked

A Field Guide to Burying Your Parents

GIRL BEFORE
A MIRROR

Liza **Palmer**

WM

WILLIAM MORROW
An Imprint of HarperCollins*Publishers*

P.S.™ is a trademark of HarperCollins Publishers.

GIRL BEFORE A MIRROR. Copyright © 2015 by Liza Palmer. All rights reserved. Printed in the United States of America. No part of this book may be used or reproduced in any manner whatsoever without written permission except in the case of brief quotations embodied in critical articles and reviews. For information address HarperCollins Publishers, 195 Broadway, New York, NY 10007.

HarperCollins books may be purchased for educational, business, or sales promotional use. For information please e-mail the Special Markets Department at SPsales@harpercollins.com.

FIRST EDITION

Designed by Diahann Sturge

Library of Congress Cataloging-in-Publication Data has been applied for.

ISBN 978-0-06-229724-2

15 16 17 18 19   OV/RRD   10 9 8 7 6 5 4 3 2 1

FOR POET: I WAS HER PERSON AND SHE WAS MY GIRL.

Neither a lofty degree of intelligence nor imagination
nor both together go to the making of genius.
Love, love, love, that is the soul of genius.

—*Wolfgang Amadeus Mozart*

I got a ways to go
And I'm carrying a heavy load
But baby I want you to know
Baby I want you to know
That I never been so sure
and I never wanted nothing more
That you were who my love is for
You were who my love is for.

—*Jill Andrews, "My Love Is For"*

GIRL BEFORE A MIRROR

"I don't understand what Bruce Springsteen has to do with why you haven't been on a date in over a year," Hannah says.

"You haven't heard the 'Thunder Road' story?" Michael laughs.

"Everybody has a 'Thunder Road' story," I say, smiling at the approaching waiter as the single candle flickers in the scoop of very pink gelato. My friends sing me "Happy Birthday" and I can't help but smile. They're off-key and terrible.

"Make a wish!" Allison says.

A moment. I close my eyes and breathe in.

You can wish for anything, Anna. You're forty now.

Forty.

My mind riffles through the wishes I have for this next year as if they're in a virtual photo album: me atop mountains, the breeze blowing my hair back. The pages flip and now we're in Paris, meandering through a farmer's market. Flip. Drinking a pint of Guinness overlooking all of Dublin. Flip. A red gingham tablecloth, a picnic, and the Jefferson Memorial. The flips are growing more manic. A gray-shingled cottage in a small beach town along the California coast. Flip. Fresh, lavendery linens, a perfect Sunday morning with nowhere to go, and a muscular chest beneath my cheek. Flip. I'm dressed to the nines and accepting the Clio. Flip. I'm lying on the grass and covered in squirming golden retriever puppies.

I open my eyes. Everyone is staring at me. Concerned.

"It's just a wish, not an exorcism," Ferdie says, taking a swig of his beer. My mind goes blank and I blow out the candle. I'm forty years old and I have no idea what to wish for.

My friends clap as I pull the candle from the gelato and lick the end. Raspberry. The other desserts arrive and we all dig in.

"So, the 'Thunder Road' story," Allison asks, pulling the chocolate monstrosity she and Michael ordered closer to her.

"I went out to dinner with this guy who worked in my building. He seemed nice enough."

"*Seemed* being the operative word," Nathan adds.

"Never a good sign," Hannah says, taking Nathan's hand in hers. He makes no attempt to hold Hannah's hand back. She smiles and picks up her fork, digging into her tiramisu. We all let her think we didn't see. We've been not seeing Nathan's annoyance at Hannah for years now.

"Dinner is fine. Not terrible. Worthy of a second date, anyway, and as we're driving home, 'Thunder Road' comes on the radio," I say, stopping to take a bite of my gelato.

"That's such a great song," Ferdie says.

"Somehow I don't think that's where the story is headed," Hannah says, laughing. Nathan rolls his eyes.

"I just wanted to put it out there. It's not the song's fault," Ferdie says.

"Always the protective brother," Hannah says.

"He's being protective of the song, not me. So," I say, nudging Ferdie. "So this guy starts singing along—not really knowing the words, but enough. Enough for me to think better of him, you know?"

"Knowing the lyrics to 'Thunder Road' is a definite plus on a first date," Michael adds.

"Right? And it was one of those beautiful D.C. nights right before the summer turns evil and there we are: windows down and singing along with The Boss. Then we get to that part—" Allison pulls her cardigan over her face, attempting to shield herself from what's coming next. Michael barks out a laugh and she continues to cringe as if both I and the story I'm telling are some kind of horror film. "We get to that part, *'you ain't a beauty, but hey you're all right.'*" The table gasps in unison. I continue, "And the bastard motions to me." I raise my eyebrows and hold my hand aloft. *"You ain't a beauty, but hey you're all right."* And then I just sit back and nod.

"Your wedding vows are writing themselves," Michael says, cracking both of us up.

"No. That . . . that didn't happen," Hannah says.

"Oh, yes it did," I say, taking another bite of my gelato.

"And he just . . . he just kept singing?" Hannah asks.

"Like nothing had happened. Like he was just hilariously acting out the song," I say.

"No no no no no," Hannah says, picking up her wineglass.

"And it was right then—and you know I don't care about looks, but I sure as hell know that the person you're dating should think you're the most beautiful woman in the world," I say. I catch Michael gazing at Allison as she finishes off their chocolate cake. Hannah and Nathan can't make eye contact.

Ferdie gives me that sheepish grin of his. I know he hates this story, but telling it helps. "I needed a break. Ever since the divorce, I'd been way too focused on moving on with the wrong kind of men. But in that moment, I knew enough to know I was nowhere near ready for the right one."

"So you put yourself—"

I interrupt Hannah. "On a Time-Out, yes."

"Since when?" she asks.

"It was just before summer last year, so—"

"A year? You've been doing this for over a year?" she asks.

"I needed to take some inventory," I say.

"You needed a training montage. We get it," Michael says.

"A training montage?" I ask, laughing.

"Yeah, you needed to run through North and South Philly while being thrown oranges and then hit sides of beef," Michael says absently. We all just look at him. He finally notices our expressions. "Please tell me you know what I'm talking about."

"Oh, we know," Ferdie says.

"Oh, we got it," I say.

"Thank God, I thought I had to get a new group of friends there for a minute. Who doesn't know about *Rocky*?" Michael asks.

"The question is: Are you at the Philadelphia Museum of Art yet?" Allison asks, clearly more used to Michael's *Rocky* analogy than the rest of us.

"That's the only question?" I ask. She laughs.

"No, I get it. Are you ready for the fight? Ready to step into the ring?" Michael asks.

"I think you're taking this whole *Rocky* thing a bit too far," I say.

"I mean, I don't think *Rocky* analogies can ever be taken too far, but that's just me," he says. I laugh.

"Kids have a way of making personal inventory–taking impossible. Sadly, no training montages for us," Hannah pipes up.

"Unless this is a training montage containing a series of clips where I try to figure out where all our money and sleep went," Nathan says.

"Sense of self, cleanliness, how many elastic-waist pants you now own . . . ," Allison adds.

"Chronicling all the neuroses you've clearly passed on to them as you watch them interact with other kids," Michael says.

Everyone laughs, happy to move on. Hannah's eyes dart to her wineglass, her finished dessert, and Nathan now looking at his phone under the table. She looks back up at me and I smile. Allison excuses herself to the bathroom and Hannah joins her. I take this opportunity to check the time. Ten P.M.

"You got somewhere to be?" Ferdie asks, eyeing me.

"I have a plan," I say.

"You're Marpling someone, aren't you," he says.

"What?" I ask innocently.

"Without question," he says.

I ignore him. And I totally am.

It was in my second year at the local community college that I came up with my Marple Theory.

The Anna Wyatt Marple Theory is named after Agatha Christie's Miss Jane Marple, the elderly lady detective who brought countless criminals to justice. Miss Marple was effective because everyone underestimated her and no one ever noticed her observing, chronicling . . . working. No one ever noticed her at all. Ergo, the Anna Wyatt Marple Theory was born: If people don't perceive you as a threat, how will they see you coming? They won't.

A text from Audrey. It's an address on K Street. From where we are in Adams Morgan, it won't take me long at all to get over there.

"Your boss is texting you at ten P.M. on a Sunday?" Ferdie asks, craning over to see my phone.

"Nosy," I say, tucking my phone back into my purse.

"Marple away, birthday girl, Marple away," he says, finishing his beer.

I smile at Ferdie and let him chastise me. Thing is, my birthday dinner was lovely. There were flowers delivered to my apartment this morning from Michael and Allison, and I had a lovely lunch with a couple of people from work. While I don't regret or second-guess my decision to go on a dating sabbatical for the last year, I do welcome the prospect of not having to go home to an empty house just yet. Michael's words come roaring back. Am I ready to step into the ring yet? Guess that's a resounding no. I check back in just as Nathan is settling the bill, much to everyone's chagrin.

"It's on me. I insist," he says, sending the waiter away. Hannah beams. We are all unfailingly polite and thank Nathan for his generosity. We always do. That's the deal: he buys dinners and we act like he wasn't a complete jerk the whole time.

"We'd better get going. The babysitter is going to think we finally made a run for it," Michael says. Allison nods. We gather our belongings, make our way out of the restaurant, and say our good-byes.

"Happy birthday, Anna," Nathan says. I situate my purse over my shoulder, hold on to my phone with the address to where I'm going, and try to stabilize the beautiful handmade mug Allison made me inside the very elaborate pink gift bag it came in.

"Oh, thank you," I say, reaching out and putting a hand on his arm. He smiles and softens for the slightest of moments, his salt-and-pepper hair ruffling in the summer wind. He says his good-byes to everyone and walks over to his waiting car, beeping it unlocked. Hannah's smile falters as he strides away. Michael and Allison remind me that our book club is reading *Hamlet* and that they're making Danish meatballs for our gathering.

"Don't you mean—"

"We mean Danish meatballs. They're *Danish*," Michael says as he hails a cab.

"Even though they may very closely resemble Swedish meat-balls," Allison adds.

"Let's just say there will be plenty of dill and discussions about what exactly happened in that closet between Gertrude and Hamlet," Michael says, arm held high into the night sky.

"I thought we were reading *Twelfth Night*," Ferdic says, scrolling through his phone.

"Nope, that's next," Allison says.

"Next?" Hannah asks.

"We're reading Shakespeare in order," I say.

"Nerds." Hannah laughs.

"Proudly," Michael says, as a cab slows in front of him. He opens the door and signals to Allison.

"Happy birthday, my darling," she says, giving me a huge hug.

"Thank you," I say, letting her warmth surround me. One

last smile and she walks over to the cab and climbs in. Once she's in, Michael walks back over to me.

"Happy birthday," he says, towering over me one minute, then engulfing me in a hug the next. He bends down just enough to whisper "and the rest is silence" in my ear. I can't help but laugh. A quick squeeze and he's climbing into the cab with Allison. They wave and speed off.

"I'm sorry about . . . ," Hannah says, gesturing over to Nathan waiting in the car. Ferdie walks a few steps away to where his bike is chained to a parking meter.

"Oh, honey, don't worry about it. Birthday dinners for your wife's friends are a scourge to couples everywhere," I say.

"I keep thinking it's a phase, you know?" she says, in a shocking moment of honesty. One I will ask her about later and she will "forget" ever happened. "How did you . . . how did you know it was over with Patrick?" I decide to answer with the truth.

"We were driving home from somewhere and having one of our fights—the same fight, really. Right?" Hannah nods and allows a small smile. "Always the same fight. And then this calm passed over me. Completely out of place. I remember it so vividly. Like I could breathe again. And then this germ of an idea: I could get out. It shouldn't be this hard."

"Marriage is hard."

"But not all the time." Hannah pulls a tissue from her purse and dabs at her eyes. "I'd forgotten what being happy felt like. Happy with him, anyway. I filed for divorce a week later."

"Happy. God, we were so happy," Hannah says.

"I know."

"I was much thinner back then!" Hannah laughs.

"Honey, you're beautiful. Stop with that," I say, watching as Hannah pulls at her clothes, trying to smooth out her growing curves. Curves made from trying to comfort herself in a loveless marriage.

"If I could just lose a little weight, you know? Maybe we could—"

"Hannah—"

"Leave it to me to be the crying girl at your birthday," Hannah says, looking back at Nathan. She gives him the "just a sec" sign and he nods. God, they were so in love. They were the couple you hated because they could never keep their hands off each other. They were scandalous and hot and he was all she thought about and vice versa. Now they can't even look at each other.

"You going to be okay?" I ask, tucking her hair behind her ear.

"Yes. Of course I am. Now. Enough of my histrionics, it's your birthday," Hannah says, giving me a big hug. She was always such a good hugger. "Happy birthday," she whispers in my ear.

"Thank you," I say as we pull apart.

"Don't work too much tonight."

"I won't." Hannah reaches out and squeezes my hand. "Call if you need anything," I say.

"I will. Ferdinand Wyatt, come over here and give me a hug." Ferdie walks over and lets Hannah lunge into him with a hug, idly patting her back with his mitt of a hand. She busts him about getting a real job and walks off to the car.

Tonight's festivities, while lovely in every way, still feel a bit off. In transition. There's been a lot of that "in transition" feeling over the past year. On top of the dating hiatus, my training montage has also been about cleaning house of all the friends in my life whom I've outgrown or who just weren't working anymore. And while that may be empowering in the abstract and feel impressive as I wax rhapsodic about it to my therapist, the truth of it—the daily reality of it—is much quieter. The lack of white noise in my life has been a bit harder to get used to than I thought it would be. Having people around that caused drama was, I'm finding, quite the hobby of mine. Now that it's gone? It's just me. In my apartment. Feeling evolved and valiant as I smugly troll the various social media of ex-friends who look like they're having way more fun than I am.

I haven't been ready to step into the ring, so for right now it just feels lonely.

I watch as Hannah closes the door behind her, pulls the seat belt across her body, and smiles at me. Nathan says something to her and she nods. Then she looks down at her lap, her body utterly deflated. They drive off and all I can do is watch. I'll be very happy when I don't have to act as though I like Nathan anymore.

"I have never been around two people who hated each other more," Ferdie says, pulling his messenger bag over his shoulder and situating the strap across his chest. His wild brown curls are cut into this end-of-summer weird fauxhawk thing that he does. He'll shave it all off within the week. His tall frame, powerful from a lifetime of hockey, is still settling around a knee injury that left him hopeless as he disappeared into a fog of pot smoke, barroom brawls, and nights in the drunk tank. But tonight he's cleaned up and clothed in khaki Dickies and a plain white T-shirt. Nine years my junior and quite the surprise to our parents,

Ferdie looks like every kid you screamed at to get off your lawn.

"They weren't always like that," I say, hailing a cab.

"Well, they're like that now," he says. He wheels his bicycle over and wraps the chain around his waist. "So, where are you meeting Audrey?" I pass him my phone and show him the address. "Here?" he asks.

"Yeah, do you know it?" I ask, waving down a cab.

"Oh, I know it," Ferdie says, handing me back the phone. "I worked as a bouncer for them a coupla times." A cab pulls over and I tell him the address through the open window.

"And?" I climb into the back of the cab and settle in.

"It's The Naughty Kitty," Ferdie says, climbing onto his bike.

"Wait, what?"

"It's a strip joint, Anna."

"I . . . what?"

"Maybe you can make it rain for your fortieth," he says.

"I don't even know what that means," I say, as the cab pulls away from the curb.

"You're about to find out," Ferdie yells after me.

As I ride to The Naughty Kitty, I allow myself to get excited. I got the idea several months ago. I'd just finished pitching an ad campaign for this line of bras and panties—or "intimates," as the client insisted on calling them. They'd been known as the relics your grammy bought you for Christmas. Now, thanks to me, they were going to be the line of bras and panties you—yes, you, working professional—are thinking about buying for their function as well as form. It's a huge account and I nailed it. I've certainly come a long way from when I first started at Holloway/Greene as a file clerk fifteen years ago.

* * *

It was yet another freezing day in New York. I was hailing a cab outside this tiny bakery I treat myself to when I did something I hadn't done in years: I looked around. I was always so focused and set on keeping up with the pace of New York that I never stopped and looked up, looked around, took it all in. On this crisp wintry day I could see my breath puffing in front of me. Bright blue skies hung high above the buildings. The honking horns. The sirens. The beeping of some truck backing up. I looked back down and realized I was standing across the street from the monolith that was the Quincy Pharmaceuticals building in Midtown. It was exactly the sort of imposing high-rise that you imagine when you think of New York. I bit into my *pain au chocolat,* crumbs now all over my power suit, and thought, I should be pitching in that building to Quincy Pharmaceuticals: on the Forbes 500 list, with some 110 subsidiary companies, and sold in over 87 countries worldwide. The Quincy Pharmaceuticals with annual worldwide sales that are upward of $25 billion.

I'd been in the trenches with that inane pop star's new clothing line that looked like it was inspired by cotton candy, and all we needed was artwork on that terrible kombucha that my ad piece assured you "tastes great" even though it resembled pond scum. Pitching to the people who worked in a building like that would mean I could stop being relegated to the pink ghetto of ladies-only products.

I went back to the office in D.C. and started digging. Researching anything and everything about Quincy Pharmaceuticals. I had to find a way in. It wasn't until summer rolled around that I finally found it: Lumineux Shower Gel, a sad little pink sparkly soapy-goo that the company had all but forgotten. No ad agency attached. It was ripe for a rebranding. And I was the woman to do it. Of course, they didn't know that yet.

I'm walking through The Naughty Kitty's dirty, vomit-soaked parking lot when I'm almost hit by a speeding car. It screeches into a parking space, and I'm getting ready to yell at the driver when I realize I know him.

"You almost killed me," I say, my stupid pink gift bag not helping my outrage.

"Anna! You're in a strip club parking lot! Just like me!" Chuck Holloway. Maybe twenty-five years old, looks twelve, acts eight.

"What are you even doing here?" I ask. He shuts the driver's-side door behind him and looks at himself in the side mirror. By the time he gets his blond bangs juuuuuuust right with the precision of a surgeon and tightens his tie, I've waited so long I'm positive I've caught chlamydia from this parking lot. "Chuck. What are you doing here?"

"Pop called me. It's got to be about the car account, right? He called you, too?" My stomach drops. No, "Pop," or the man the rest of us mortals get to call Charlton Holloway IV, current senior partner and part of the Holloway advertising dynasty, didn't call me, and no, it's not about the car account. I'm here trying to finagle approval on a goofy little shower gel no one cares about, thank you very much. We approach the two extremely large bouncers who guard the red velvet curtains that hang over The Naughty Kitty's entrance. My kingdom for a black light.

"IDs," one of the bouncers says.

"Dude," Chuck says, digging his wallet out of his jacket pocket. He produces his ID and hands it over. "Twenty-four. Read 'em and weep." Twenty. Four. I can't . . .

I pull mine from my wallet and hand it to the bouncer. He takes it, looks at it, and then hands it back. I want to kiss him full on the mouth for not making some joke about my age or not even asking for my ID at all.

"What's in the bag?" the other bouncer asks.

"A mug," I say.

"Why a mug?" the bouncer asks.

"It's . . . it's just a mug," I say, pulling it out of its pink depths.

"Why are you bringing a mug into a strip club?" Chuck asks. The bouncers await an answer.

"I'm not." They wait. "It's a gift," I say, putting the mug back into the pink gift bag.

"Who are you going to give a mug to?" the other bouncer asks.

"No one. It's my birthday. This is . . . I got the mug as a gift at a birthday dinner. I just came from there. I took a cab," I say, trying to hide my annoyance.

"So you had to bring it with you," the bouncer finishes.

"Yes," I say.

"So the mug is *for* you," the other bouncer says. A line is now forming behind us.

"Yes."

"Ohhh." They all nod in unison, proud.

"Go on in," the bouncer says, finally pulling the red velvet curtain back.

"Thank you," I say.

"Hey, happy birthday," he says, his attention now on the businessmen queuing up just behind us.

"Thanks." I try not to touch the velvet curtains as I finally walk inside The Naughty Kitty.

The music is loud but not deafening. It takes a second for my eyes to recalibrate to the darkness. I slow my pace, with Chuck right at my heels. Finally I can make out the bar all along the left wall. To my amazement, it looks like any other bar, with men and women sitting and leaning, drinking and flirting.

"I always thought it was weird that women come to strip clubs, you know?" Chuck yells over the din.

"I *do* know," I say, continuing to scan the room for the Holloway/Greene group. I look to the right and that's when I see the long, mirrored runway coming out from the large stage. There are smaller tables all around the runway, crowded with men in various stages of arousal or boredom or drunkenness or all of the above.

"You're here on business, though," Chuck says.

"I think a lot of people here are doing business," I say, watching an ancient man, whom I recognize as a senator, receiving a lap dance. The woman on the runway finishes her dance with a flourish, and the crowd applauds.

"Let's give it up for Titty Titty Bang Bang!" the emcee says, as the woman spins her silver pistols around wearing nothing but a pair of cowboy boots, an American flag G-string, and a holster.

"There. Over in the corner," I say to Chuck. He nods and yells out a *"Hey-O!"* thrusting his arm high in the air. And like any other wildlife, his brethren respond in kind. Hey-Os ring through The Naughty Kitty like roars on the African plains.

Holloway/Greene is in its own VIP section, and we have to go through another set of bouncers to finally make it to the drunken bacchanalia that is whatever is happening with the car account. I always thought my career promised land would have fewer pasties.

"Anna!!" Audrey says, walking over. Audrey Holloway is the kind of woman who, if she deigned to do her own grocery shopping at all, would absolutely leave her cart in the middle of the aisle while she studied the different brands of quinoa with the focus of a diamond cutter. She rarely loses that air of calm that makes her look as though she's in a constant state of smelling cinnamon rolls baking. And then she sees Chuck. Audrey's cinnamon-roll air evaporates immediately. "Oh, Chuck. I . . . didn't see you there."

"Hey, sis," he says, scanning the room. A chill. A forced, polite chill. Audrey Holloway is the eldest child from Charlton Holloway's proper first marriage, with the china patterns and the good families. Chuck Holloway is the eldest male child, but he's from Charlton Holloway's second marriage to a buxom secretary named Stormy.

"Chuck! Get over here, son!" Charlton Holloway IV yells from the corner of the VIP section. Chuck says his good-byes and scrambles over to his father and the stripper who's giving him a lap dance. A Hallmark moment, to be sure.

"Get us another round, huh?" A very drunk car executive grabs Audrey by the arm, pulling her to sit on his lap.

"Easy, tiger," I say, pulling Audrey off his lap and maneuvering a barmaid in front of him. I pass the barmaid a twenty-dollar bill in the process.

"Get us another round, huh?" the man says to the barmaid as if he's just repeating himself to the same woman.

"Thanks. . . . Thank you," Audrey says, straightening her

skirt and gathering herself as the barmaid deftly takes the man's order, unmolested.

"Don't worry about it," I say.

"I didn't know Dad called him," Audrey says. The black tailored suit. The silk blouse. The tasteful accessories. The shampoo-commercial shiny brown hair and the alabaster skin of someone who always, to quote Audrey herself, "wore a hat whenever the family went sailing," which I imagine is much the same thing as trying not to get sunburned while playing in the sprinklers with my younger brother. Audrey Holloway looks like she was bred to christen large seagoing vessels and donate entire hospital wings. But tonight she's spending her evening in The Naughty Kitty trying to draw her father's attention away from a woman in a thong.

"Me either. He pulled up when I did," I say, eyeing Charlton Holloway IV over in the corner.

"Thanks for the heads-up about tonight," I say.

"Oh, no worries. He's plenty distracted, to be sure. Good luck," she says. I nod and stride toward Charlton, practicing my speech. This is familiar territory. I use it to my advantage.

The music kicks in as a woman named Acc Bondage takes the stage wearing way too much black leather for this humidity.

"Mr. Holloway," I say. His face is a tangle of confusion, annoyance, and a side of enraged paused arousal. "I wanted to confirm the status of the pop singer's account and—"

"You're talking business? Here?" Charlton laughs and Chuck joins in, although I'm quite sure Chuck has no idea what he's supposed to think is so funny. I wait. If Charlton weren't creeping out over some stripper right now, you'd just as soon think he was trying to sell you life insurance during your nightly viewing of *Jeopardy*. Charlton Holloway IV looks like every sitcom dad from the nineties.

"Yes, sir," I say.

"Which is why you weren't invited, Diane," Charlton says. I know he knows my name.

"It's Anna."

"Anna?"

"Yes, sir."

"It's a shame you have to be leaving," Charlton says. Chuck laughs.

"I'll make it quick then, sir. Lumineux Shower Gel is shopping around for a new agency. They're taking pitches this week. I want to handle ours," I say. This, of course, is only partially true. Okay. None of this is true. Charlton's eyes move over the woman bending down in front of him.

"Why couldn't this have waited until tomorrow?" he asks.

"Because she thought of it tonight?" Chuck asks.

"Yes, I can see why one would think scrubbing myself clean would be at the forefront of my mind tonight," I say to myself, sidestepping to avoid touching Chardonnay as she finishes her lap dance and lets Chuck tuck a hundred-dollar bill into her G-string before she saunters off. "I wanted to move forward as quickly as possible."

"Will saying yes to you make you stop talking?"

"It will," I say.

"Then yes," Charlton grunts. My heart soars. "And goodbye." And then plummets to the ground. But it doesn't matter. My plan worked. Ask when your boss is clearly not paying attention and he'll just want to get rid of you. I'm sure Warren Buffett gave that advice somewhere in one of his books.

"Thank you," I say, turning to leave.

"Wait." Charlton stops. Sighhhh. I turn back around. "What's in the bag?" Charlton asks, motioning to the bright pink gift bag.

"What?" I ask.

"The bag? What's in the bag? You bring me something?" Charlton asks.

"What? No," I say.

"Are you seriously not going to tell me what's in the bag?" Charlton asks.

"It's a mug," I say, pulling Allison's handmade mug from the bag with a flourish.

"Why'd you bring—" Charlton asks. Audrey walks over and stands next to him.

"It's my birthday. I was at my birthday dinner before coming here. It was a gift," I say, tucking the mug carefully back within the folds of the pink tissue paper.

"I knew it was a mug," Chuck says.

"You did," I say.

"Happy birthday," Charlton says.

"Thank you. So, the pitch is this week—" I say, not knowing why I feel the need to elaborate on a lie.

"You're talking about business again . . . ," Charlton says, trailing off.

"Anna," I offer.

"Anna," he says. "Time for you to go."

"Yes, sir." I turn to walk out again. Charlton continues, "This is forty for you, right?" I turn back around, not mentioning that for someone who acts like he doesn't know my name it's downright sloppy to admit that he remembers how old I am

"I think she looks great for forty," Audrey says. Ace Bondage finishes with a crack of her whip and the crowd applauds or whatever it is that strip joint audiences do when they're—you know what? Let's stick with applauds. A woman in a Catholic schoolgirl's uniform strolls out on stage and I'm happy to learn that her name is The Lori Hole.

"At least you're younger than Audrey over there," Charlton says. Audrey is thirty-eight years old. Just turned, actually. We had an office party. Charlton attended—gave a speech even, as he's wont to do.

I nod and stay quiet, not wanting to take Charlton's bait or be privy to whatever it is that Ms. Hole there does to earn her that moniker. Audrey slinks away without a word.

"You too. Off you go," Charlton says.

"Yes, sir," I say, my eyes flipping from Charlton to Chuck and then to the countless other Holloway/Greene ad agents whose pockets are filled with ones and who sport crooked Ivy League colored neckties around pressed, sweat-stained Brooks Brothers shirts. And then I see Audrey. Old Maid Audrey—according to Charlton—over in the corner buying another round of drinks and lap dances for everyone.

I continue walking.

Little do they know . . .

They've all been Marpled.

2

I plucked the shower gel I used this morning from the grocery store shelf for no discernible reason. Why that shower gel? Was it because it had shea butter in it—do I even know what shea butter is?—or was it because it promised to make me feel younger, more refreshed, or softer to the touch? Was it because the packaging was simple and clean or was it because I was rushing through the store and just needed some G.D. shower gel? As I take the Metro into the office the next morning, these questions haunt me. I have to convince Lumineux— then Quincy—that I am the person who can make it the brand women write down on their grocery lists—not just shower gel, but Lumineux Shower Gel. The one they reach for instead of the hundred other shower gels available to them. So how do I make it stand out? It'd help if the name weren't such a messy mouthful. The first thing on my list, however, has to be getting the pitch meeting.

I get into the office early, and with the go-ahead from Charlton Holloway himself dive into everything Lumineux.

It was Quincy Pharmaceuticals' first product back in 1917: Lumineux Medicated Arsenic Soap Wafers. It was how Quincy got its start, and the company hasn't rebranded it once since 1917 from the looks of it. Nope. Wait. Scratch that. I find some artwork that can only be described as a rainbow-suspender, side-ponytailed explosion when they announced the switch from soap to shower gel. I laugh and shake my head.

"Lumineux is the soap your mom's weird friend uses," I say to myself. As I walk into the break room in search of another mug of tea, I allow that Lumineux isn't actually bad. It smells really good. Old-timey. Like soap. It's odd that that's what's revolutionary about it. I pull a tea bag out of the drawer and drop it into the mug Allison made me for my birthday. I pour in some hot water and let the quiet of the room settle in around me.

I am waiting until 10:15 A.M. to put in my phone call to one Preeti Dayal, the unsuspecting vice president in charge of Lumineux marketing. She will have ingested enough caffeine, handled any emergencies from the weekend, and just started returning e-mails when—blammo—an intriguing phone call from whom? Why, she doesn't have another meeting until eleven A.M. (I checked), sure she'll take the call, and that's when I'll strike. And a year later I'll be handling all of Quincy Pharmaceuticals' ad campaigns and running through a sun-kissed wheat field in a white linen sundress laughing. (Or some version of that . . .)

I walk back to my office just as Audrey hurries through the front door of the agency.

"Surprised to see you here this early," I say, stopping at the door to my office.

"You really shouldn't be," she says. Her voice is sharp.

"No, you're right." A smile. "Have a good one," I say and walk into my office.

"I apologize," she says, appearing at my door.

"For what?" I ask.

"My father is a good man. He's just doing what his father did before him and so on," Audrey says.

"You certainly don't need to explain anything to me," I say.

"It's Chuck," she says.

"Chuck seems harmless enough," I say, finally able to take a sip of my tea.

"To you maybe," Audrey says, her voice sharp again. I can't have this conversation right now. I'm nowhere near focused enough to navigate the shark-infested waters that are Audrey Holloway's gripes with the politics of her family. Maybe I should give her the number of my therapist. But right now? I have a life-changing phone call to make and I need to get ready for it before the office begins to fill up.

"No, you're right," I say, hoping to speed her exit along. Audrey lingers at my door. And lingers. And now it's getting weird. Fine. "Not to you?" Audrey swans into my office, closing the door behind her. Great. This better not take long.

"He's Elizabeth the First," Audrey says, floating into one of the client chairs across from me.

"I'm sorry?"

"He's Elizabeth the First and I'm Bloody Mary," Audrey says.

"I'm not following."

"I am the rightful heir to the throne and yet . . ." She trails off as if that's all it will take to clarify this situation.

"Bloody Mary ruled," I say.

"What?"

"Mary the First ruled England for around five years," I say.

"No, I mean—"

"Are you thinking of Mary, Queen of Scots?" I ask, as the clock ticks ever closer to 10:15 A.M.

"The one Elizabeth had beheaded."

"Mary, Queen of Scots. She's a cousin. It's rumored Mary the First died of cancer."

"Cancer? Wait . . ."

"If anything Chuck is Edward the Sixth."

"You're confusing me," she says. I put my hands up and give her my full focus.

"You fear you will be skipped. That when Charlton retires, he will pass the corner office and all that comes with it to Chuck and not you, just as the throne was given to Edward the Sixth despite Mary being first—solely because he was the male heir," I say, boiling down wildly complicated events in history to fit Audrey's needs.

"And who says community colleges don't teach anything valuable," she says. I am quiet. A beat. "But yes. I'm first."

"Yep."

"Chuck is Charlton Holloway the Fifth and he enjoys strippers and golf and I don't. I went to Princeton, too, you know," she says.

"You're doing the best you can," I say, not wanting to bring up that while Audrey may have her eye on the throne, she hasn't exactly been burning up the track to make her mark in the king-dom, if you will. She has yet to bring in one big account, whereas even Chuck, the village idiot, brought in some terrible energy drink that a couple of his frat brothers at Princeton invented. Maybe instead of eyeing the throne, Audrey should roll up her sleeves and get to work. Still, if Audrey were a man, we wouldn't be having this conversation. Her father would be grooming her to take over Holloway/Greene, and that'd be that.

A knock on my office door. Thank God. I tell whoever it is to come in.

A young woman so extraordinarily beautiful I can think of nothing to say except "Casting is down the hall" walks through the door.

"I'm sorry?" the woman asks.

"You're here for the car commercial, right?" I ask.

"Um . . ." The woman tucks a luxurious black tress behind her ear; her flawless skin is downright dewy. She nervously runs a hand down the length of her perfect figure before letting it rest at her side.

"Anna Wyatt, this is Sasha Merchant. Chuck hired her. We're apparently supposed to find a place for her in our art department." Audrey's voice is cruel. Sasha shifts in the doorway.

"Hi . . . um, hello," Sasha says.

"Nice to meet you," I say, standing and extending my hand to her. She takes it, and instead of shaking it, she uses it to anchor a bizarrely childlike curtsy and becomes immediately mortified. I offer Sasha a seat. She sits. Audrey has yet to look at her.

"Chuck said to put Sasha on whatever account you were going on about last night," Audrey says, making her way out of my office.

"Lumineux?" I ask.

"I'm sure I don't know," Audrey says. I begin to speak, but Audrey cuts me off. "Something wrong?"

"No. Nothing. Please thank him for being so thoughtful," I say.

"I will," she says with a smile, and I'm left alone with Sasha. We are quiet. I take a sip of my tea. Sasha clears her throat.

"I have to make a quick phone call. Is there any way I can come find you after I finish?" I ask.

"Oh . . . oh, sure," she says with a quick nod as she unfolds her nearly six-foot frame out of my client chair and turns for the door.

"I'll be there around ten forty-five?" I say.

"Sure . . . sure," she says, and just before she closes the door behind her she adds, "I can't wait to get to work."

Aaaand I'll deal with that whole thing in due time. Sasha seems like a nice enough kid, but Lumineux and I aren't going to need any help, thank you very much.

A deep breath. A look at the clock. And I dial. And then I'm lost in some maze of press one to speak English and if you know your party's extension just . . . I press zero. And zero. And zero. And scream "Representative" into the phone and when that doesn't work I say "Agent" and then more options and I have no idea how far down the yellow brick road I am, but now I'm being asked if I'm calling from a doctor's office and if this is an emergency and another screamed "Operator!" and finally I get the click and then, "One moment, a Quincy representative will be right with you."

And then I hold. I sip my tea, scroll through e-mails, and dust my computer keyboard with the old napkin I got from the coffeehouse this morning.

"Quincy Pharmaceuticals. How may I direct your call?"

"Preeti Dayal, please," I say.

"One moment."

Ha! *Marpled*. A few clicks.

"Preeti Dayal's office," she says in the silken voice of a woman who answers phones in the expensive high-rises in New York City.

"This is Anna Wyatt for Preeti Dayal," I say as confidently as I can.

"And what is this regarding?"

"Lumineux Shower Gel," I say.

"One moment, I'll see if she's available," she says after a pause. I'm not breathing. Is she going to let me get through or come back and tell me that Ms. Dayal is "in a meeting" or "on a call"? I've been an assistant. I know the tricks. Still not breathing. Still not breathing.

"This is Preeti Dayal," the woman says. *Huzzah!*

"Hello, Ms. Dayal, this is Anna Wyatt from Holloway/Greene," I say.

"I'm not familiar with Holloway/Greene, Ms. Wyatt."

"We are an advertising agency in Washington, D.C."

"Ah. I'm sorry, Ms. Wyatt, but—"

"All I want is a meeting, Ms. Dayal. Lumineux Shower Gel is prime for rebranding. It's retro without being dated. It's traditional without being stuffy. It's in a class by itself," I say.

"Ms. Wyatt—"

"The soap is good, but people have forgotten about it. Whoever is doing your advertising is missing a golden opportunity. All I'm asking for is a meeting. Half an hour of your time," I say.

"I appreciate your enthusiasm, but Lumineux Shower Gel is not looking—"

"Quincy Pharmaceuticals was built from Lumineux. It's been relegated to the shadows for too long, wouldn't you say?"

A long beat.

"It appears I've just had a cancellation." *Woot!* "For tomorrow." *What?* "If you're serious, Ms. Wyatt."

"Oh, yes, I'm quite serious," I say.

"Then I will see you in my office tomorrow morning at eleven A.M.," she says and hangs up without further fanfare.

Shit. Shit. Shit.

Before I can panic, I walk out of my office to look for Sasha. Looks like I'll need that help after all. Sasha is sitting by herself in the bull pen as a pack of men study her from afar. She acts like she doesn't notice as she doodles in her sketchpad. I wave her over. The panic, at this point, is dangerously near. It's in my throat. My brain is still whirlpooling around the information, unable to understand or catch or process the task at hand. It's just this spiral of: Yay! Ugh! Yay! Ugh! Yay! Ugh! Sasha walks into my office and closes the door behind her.

"Good news, bad news," I say.

"Good news first," she says.

"We got a pitch meeting with the vice president over at Lumineux Shower Gel," I say.

"That's great!"

"It's for tomorrow," I say.

"What?"

"It's for tomorrow," I say, leaving out the whole lying, scheming, don't-really-have-an-account, trying-to-take-over-the-world plan of mine.

"I don't . . . wow," she says.

"So, you've never worked in an ad agency before, right?" I ask.

"What?" A look from me. Sasha deflates. "No, but—"

"Oh, I don't care, Ms. Merchant; I just want to know where we stand," I say, sifting through the file I've worked up on all things Lumineux. I look up from the file and across the desk at Sasha. I've upset her.

"I just want a chance, Ms. Wyatt," Sasha says.

"That makes two of us," I say. She smiles and I can see her shoulders relax. She takes out her art supplies and pulls her chair closer to my desk. I reach across for Sasha's sketchpad. "May I?" Sasha is hesitant but finally hands it over. I flip through her sketches and, oh, thank God . . . they're good. Great, actually. Her drawings are modern but nostalgic, if that makes any sense. One after the other after the other. "They're beautiful. You're really good." I hand the sketchpad back to her and I swear she looks as though she's on the verge of tears.

"Thanks," she says.

"Now. Let's get to work."

We spend the next several hours going down the wrong path. We get stuck on trying to advertise Lumineux as some nostalgic trip down memory lane. Use Lumineux, remember your grammy. Use Lumineux and remember when soap smelled like soap. Failed taglines and Sasha's sketches now litter my office. None of it works and we've wasted precious hours. But I know this is the process. We order out for a late lunch and Sasha volunteers to pick it up, which will give me a nice break from realizing that Sasha is too young for every pop culture reference I try to make. This movie? Blank stare. That one TV show and this famous scene? Nothing. How about this oft-quoted line and accompanying swoon? To which she offered that she could "Google it," and then I opened up a hard candy in the middle of a theater and told everyone it was too cold and where was my sweater.

As I wait for Sasha to return, I can hear the bustle of the agency just outside my door. I turn around and face my window, which overlooks Wisconsin Avenue. The brick buildings give way to the lush green of Georgetown Waterfront Park as the bustling pedestrians battle yet another humid D.C. summer.

Okay, Anna. Scrap the last several hours. Go back to this morning. What would have made me choose Lumineux . . . no, what would make both Sasha and me choose Lumineux? How do we market this product so both of us want the same thing, as different as we are? Think about our similarities and stop dwelling on our differences and I'll find it. So what do Sasha and I have in common?

A sigh. A long, weary sigh. #nothing.

I find my mug and take a long sip of the now cold tea as I ask the question millions have asked before me: What do women want? And not just from a shower gel. What do I want? I close my eyes and concentrate. Want feels so gluttonous; need feels far more virtuous. Come on, Anna. What do I want?

I tighten my fingers around my homemade mug and remember my birthday dinner. Allison. Michael. Ferdie. Hannah and Nathan. Pink gelato, training montages, and laughing with friends.

What do I want?

I want to be happy and not feel guilty about it. I want to be curious without being called indulgent. I want to be accepted regardless of what I look like, what I do for a living, my marital status, whether I have kids, or whether you think I'm nice enough, hospitable enough, or humble enough to measure up to your impossible standards. I want purpose. I want contentment. I want to be loved and give love unreservedly in return. I want to be seen. I want to matter. I want freedom.

I take another sip of my cold tea. Great. So all I have to do is encapsulate *that* into a slogan that'll sell some old-timey shower gel and I'll be fine.

I'm screwed.

I turn away from the window and focus on a stack of Sasha's things that she left on my desk. Every single item has a generic alternative, but Sasha has chosen the brand-name versions, proving, once again, that women are intensely loyal to brands. Sasha sought out these particular items, paying way more than she would for the same items without the brand tags or symbols that set them apart. As do I. The tea I buy, the shampoo I use, even the hotels in which I stay—it's a relief when I find a brand that feels good to me. I feel understood. Comforted. The search is over, so to speak.

I put down my mug and walk over to the stack of items. It's a hodgepodge of art supplies and various other digital art things that are way beyond my understanding. She has a Moleskine journal, which I don't dare open, sitting on top of several sketchbooks. At the bottom of the stack is a well-read, dog-eared book. I pick it up.

Be the Heroine, Find Your Hero, by Helen Brubaker.

The cover boasts the usual romance novel fare: a shirtless man and some damsel in distress. He's sporting manly pecs and his flaxen hair blows amorously behind him while she tries to keep the top of her dress from sexily falling down her generous bosom. I flip the book over and read the back cover copy. Helen Brubaker has apparently, according to her publisher, anyway, cracked the code of dating by applying her abundant knowledge gleaned from thirty years of experience as a bestselling romance novelist.

"Learn how to be your own heroine, so you too can find your own hero."

Right, because why would you want to spend time learning how to be your own heroine if not for the sole purpose of ensnaring a hero? I can feel my cheeks flushing. As I set the book down quickly, I feel as I did when I was a teenager. I'm sneaking a read of that one Judy Blume book—the one we all know has the racy bits in it—and I'm positive everyone knows . . . everyone knows what part I'm reading and all of a sudden I'm having to explain my curiosity about sex in some bizarre science fictiony courtroom that's inexplicably peopled only with boys I like and my grandmother. And ever since then I have never been able to do it—I could never read one of those books without feeling that flush, unable to stop being utterly aware of how embarrassed I'd be if someone found out what I was reading. It's never about the romance novels; it's about me. And I've never questioned it. Who these people are that would judge me and what conclusions they'd draw. Nope. Instead, I've just stuck to the classics—where the racy bits were never mentioned, just inferred from knowing glances across crowded rooms, and everything hinged on witty banter during a quadrille.

I sit back down behind my desk with the book in hand, deciding not to dismiss it so quickly. I'm not a teenager anymore. Although I do close my door and tell my assistant not to enter for the next half hour as I'll be "on a call." She is, of course, confused, as I've never done this in the years we've worked together and she knows perfectly well there is no call.

Apparently Ms. Helen Brubaker knows what women want. And I need some answers. From anyone. I Google "Be the Heroine, Find Your Hero" and millions upon millions of entries pop up instantaneously. Helen Brubaker has been on every morning television show; she's been written about in every top magazine, newspaper, website . . . you name it. And there she is meandering through the First Lady's garden deep in conversation. How have I not heard of this book before? I pick up the phone and dial.

"Art room," a student answers.

"Is Mrs. Alvarez there?" I ask. The student puts her hand over the phone.

"This is Mrs. Alvarez," Allison says.

"Have you ever heard of a book called *Be the Heroine, Find Your Hero*?"

"Yeah, why?"

"What?"

"It's everywhere."

"How did I not know about this?"

"Because you live under a rock, my dearie. Oof, my next class will be here in ten minutes. I've still got to get their stuff out of the kiln. Talk later?"

"Sure."

"Love you."

"Love you, too." I set my phone down and continue researching online.

To say the book is a phenomenon is an understatement. It's bigger. Cult big. Religion big. It's the book of the moment . . . it's the everything of the moment. It's way more successful than any other dating book. The hook? It's a dating advice book that uses romance novels as a modern-day guide for women who are searching for their Mr. Right.

Sasha comes back with our lunch to find me fully engrossed in her book.

"I'm so sorry, I saw it there and—" I drop the book. I can feel the flush in my cheeks as the embarrassment settles in the pit of my stomach. This is my teenage nightmare.

"Oh, I don't care. I can't believe you don't have your own copy." Sasha sets down the food and starts pulling out containers, condiment packets, and little utensils.

"Thanks for picking up lunch," I say, scanning the food.

"Don't worry about it. You'll get dinner." The stark reality that we will be stuck in this office overnight hits me. I'll get dinner. Right, because we'll still be right here at dinnertime and breakfast.

"I've never even heard of it," I say, bringing the conversation back to the book. I take my container of sushi, pull my chopsticks out of their wrapper, rub them together to protect myself from splinters, and dive in.

"It's all about how romance novels have it right. First you have to consider yourself the heroine and then you attract the hero. Make your man slay dragons and save the world before he gets to ravish you," Sasha says, settling into the chair across from me with her sashimi.

"Are we saying *ravish* now? Are we ravishing now?" I ask.

"Fingers crossed." Sasha smiles. It's taken her all morning to loosen up, but even then it's still only confined to my office. Whenever Sasha walks out to get coffee or make a copy of something, I can see her purposefully shove her shoulders back with a little shake of the head and a huffed breath. I watch her walk through the bull pen, not actually looking at anyone yet completely aware that they're all looking at her. And then she closes the door to my office and she takes all those airs off like a heavy winter coat.

"But, at its core, the book is about becoming your own heroine, right? It's supposed to be empowering. I mean, isn't the title based on that Nora Ephron quote: 'Be the heroine of your life, not the victim'?" I say, flipping through the pages.

"I mean, maybe—but Brubaker's is better. Be the heroine, so you can find a hero. Be the heroine—"

"Find your hero, yep. Wouldn't want to . . . sure, I got it. But if we used this book as a jumping-off point, we might have something," I say.

"What . . . I mean, how would that work?" Sasha eyes the Chinese takeaway container of rice but takes a long drink of her bottle of water instead.

"Clearly, this book is what women want right now. Whether it's the book itself or the message. If we could tap into that trend . . . that idea of empowering women or seeing ourselves as romance novel heroines or whatever it is. That's it. It's exactly what we're looking for, don't you think?"

"That's brilliant," Sasha says. She smiles and I can see her mind start working.

"What else do we know about this Helen Brubaker?" I ask. I find her website and click around.

"She's kind of a legend," Sasha says.

"Seriously," I say, reading the biography. I click on the tag *Books*. "She must have written over a hundred books."

"That's why she's such an expert," Sasha parrots. I click on *Events* to see if there's one where we can see her speak or if she's into that sort of thing at all. I don't know what I'm looking for yet, but I know it's somewhere down this rabbit hole. I scan through her various speaking engagements, book signings, and *Be the Heroine* retreats, and find an event coming up where Mrs. Brubaker will be.

"What's RomanceCon?" I ask, clicking on the link. I turn the computer screen so Sasha can see it, too.

"It's the annual conference for romance novels in Phoenix," Sasha says, leaning forward.

A click and my entire computer becomes a circus of reds and blacks. Large, flowery script writing announces RomanceCon all along the top of the website. I flick through photos of lines of fans wending their way around hotels, huge romance novel covers blown up and hanging aloft, and beautiful men in various states of undress like some kind of debaucherous slideshow.

"It's a conference about romance novels," I repeat.

"All the famous authors are there. They have tons of panels and workshops. A huge book signing, nightly parties—*theme* parties—and then? They have a pageant for the guys on the covers." Sasha takes the *Be the Heroine* book, closes it up, and points to the ridiculous he-man on the cover. "Him. Those guys. Can you imagine?" Sasha has now draped herself across my desk and is speaking more animatedly than I've yet seen her.

"No, I cannot. I can't imagine what any of that would actually look like outside of my nightmares."

"Is Helen Brubaker going to be at this year's?" Sasha pulls my computer screen toward her, helping herself to my mouse as she ably clicks around the website.

"Do you read these? Romance novels?"

"Of course. I love them!" Sasha finds the schedule of events and begins scrolling through for Helen Brubaker.

"But aren't they . . . I mean, come on," I say, keeping the flush at bay.

"Have you ever read one?"

"No."

"Then you can't say anything."

"I just—"

"What I find is that the people who insult romance novels the most have never tried to actually read one."

"I haven't tried letting a wild dog bite me in the face, either, but—"

"Uh-huh," Sasha says, her eyes narrowed.

"What?"

"What's your favorite movie of all time?" Sasha asks, now sitting on my desk.

"What?"

"Just answer the question. What is your favorite—"

"*Ladyhawke.*" No doubt.

"*Ladyhawke?*"

"It's this 1980s cheesefest with Rutger Hauer, Michelle Pfeiffer, and a very young, adorable Matthew Broderick," I say, my voice now animated.

"I've never even—"

"*Isabeauuu!*" I say, my fist shooting into the sky.

"What now?"

"Oh, that's what Navarre yells. He's the captain of the guard and she's the beauty that the evil guy coveted. But she loves Navarre! So"—I dip down and my voice becomes serious—"the evil guy cursed them. By day she is a hawk and by night he is a wolf."

"She's a ladyhawke. Ah. I see," Sasha says, laughing. I shoot her the side-eye as I try to decide if she's making fun of me or not. *Hmpf.*

"He had this amazing black horse," I say, sighing.

"Did he now," Sasha says, taking a delicate sip of her water.

"And there's this brieeeef moment at sunrise and sunset when they can aaaalmost touch each other, but *no*! It cannot be!" I say, exhausted by it all. I lie back in my office chair, succumbing to the utter brilliance. "I've been waiting for Navarre my entire life. Navarre or Han Solo."

"So, that's what it's like to love romance novels," Sasha says.

"What?"

"What if I told you *Ladyhawke* was stupid?" she says.

"Um, what?"

"Yeah. It's cheesy and lame and who cares," she says.

"But *Isabeauuu*!" I wail. Sasha just looks at me. "Also, you just said you haven't even seen it, so . . ." Sasha arches an eyebrow. She waits.

Oh. Wait.

"Ah," I say. Sasha smugly eats another piece of her sashimi and lets her genius wash over me.

"And before you say it's not, it is exactly the same thing. I've been reading romance novels since I was thirteen. And the way you lit up when you talked about that *Ladyhawke* movie?"

"That *Ladyhawke* masterpiece, you mean," I say.

"I'm just saying." Sasha shrugs. "There's nothing wrong with thinking men should be a bit more like Navarre and a little less like"—she motions to the bull pen—"guys who only want one thing." She looks down at her lap and starts picking at her fingernails. "Nothing wrong with a little honor."

"No, I guess not," I say, unable to look at her.

Sasha hops off my desk and motions for me to get up out of my desk chair. "My turn." I stand, take my sushi, and settle in one of the client chairs on the opposite side of the desk. "Okay,

The Brubaker is going to be there for . . . it looks like a whole one-day workshop. That would be so amazing."

"We're just calling her 'The Brubaker' now?"

"I still don't get what this has to do with Lumineux," Sasha says, her eyes flicking over to me between orgasmic outbursts about something else going on at this year's RomanceCon.

"I don't know, either. I almost have it. It's . . . it's part empowering women. Part seeing yourself as a heroine. Part escapism. Part of it can be that honor you were talking about. Maybe it's a little bit about . . ." My eyes fall on the photos of the men vying for Mr. RomanceCon, the romance novel cover model of the year. "Maybe it's a little bit about them."

"It can be all about them if you want," Sasha says, clicking on last year's winner. "Ryder Grant. Swoon, right?" Sasha says.

"If it's a hero women want, why don't we give it to them?" I ask, motioning at Mr. Ryder Grant.

"I don't—"

"They're having a pageant, right? What if we could impress upon the RomanceCon higher-ups that this year's pageant winner would have the opportunity to be the new Lumineux spokesman? I mean, it wouldn't be guaranteed or anything, but if we land the campaign then—"

"They land the campaign," Sasha interrupts.

"Exactly. And if not—"

"It's still great coverage."

"He'd be every woman's hero, so to speak." I pull over a yellow legal pad and begin furiously writing. "But it's not just that. It's the world. It's that world. There's something . . . The Brubaker tapped into something in romance novels and we can, too. In finding your hero, you . . . you have to believe that you're worthy of being the heroine, right? That the story . . . this life . . . is about you. And what woman ever puts herself first?"

"Not one."

"Right. That's what's—"

"That's why I love reading romance novels. It's where I'm allowed to be . . . I don't know . . . it's where I feel like I get to be the woman of my dreams."

"Right there. That's it. That's what we have to . . . Lumineux Shower Gel takes you to a place where you're the woman of your dreams. Just like romance novels. The pitch would center on women empowering themselves by believing that they can be the heroine of their own stories. Going about their daily grind, but with this thread of that romance novel world. So, coming in from work and having that guy—"

"Navarre," Sasha offers.

"Yes. Navarre. You walk in from work and there's Navarre cooking dinner and the kids are sitting at the table already doing homework. I'm missing something. I . . ." I think back to this morning. My own list of what I really want out of this life. Sasha is quiet.

I want to be happy and not feel guilty about it. I want to be curious without being called indulgent. I want to be accepted regardless of what I look like, what I do for a living, my marital status, whether I have kids, or whether you think I'm nice enough, hospitable enough, or humble enough to measure up to your impossible standards. I want purpose. I want contentment. I want to be loved and give love unreservedly in return. I want to be seen. I want to matter. I want freedom.

And then it comes to me.

I want to be . . . I want to just be.

"We just want to be," I say.

Sasha and I look at each other across the table. That's it.

"I love the idea of these vignettes of a woman's daily grind with some hot guy just amid it all, you know?" Sasha says, motioning for me to switch places with her. I oblige. She picks up her sketchpad and starts drawing. "That we matter. That we're worthy of a hero." Sasha draws as she speaks, her voice growing stronger and stronger. This is what I want to tap into. "No, that we *are* the hero." The change in Sasha even thinking about the prospect of being a heroine is what is at the root of this idea. "That we're human. And sexual. And vital. And equal. Every version of us." Sasha is on the edge of her seat now, pulling different colored pencils from her bag. I wait. She turns the sketchbook to me and I'm blown away.

It's a rough sketch of a woman walking into her kitchen in a business suit to a clearly besotted, gorgeous man looking over at her—he has a dish towel slung over one of his broad shoulders, wears worn-in jeans and an old T-shirt, and is elbow-deep in soapy water. The kids sit around the dining room table with textbooks and school supplies strewn about, and dinner is bubbling on the stovetop. She looks happy.

And in beautiful clean writing, Sasha has written "Just Be" along the top of the picture. The Lumineux logo is on the bottom—nondescript and tasteful.

"Wow," I say.

"Right?" Sasha says, beaming.

"It's perfect."

"Lumineux Shower Gel. Just Be," Sasha says again.

"That's it."

3

We haven't slept. Sasha and I board the Metroliner that will take us into Manhattan for the big pitch at the Quincy Pharmaceutical headquarters—the very high-rise I vowed to return to several months prior. For the last twelve hours, I've subsisted on nothing but romance novels—flushed cheeks be damned—black tea, and these terrible green juices I'm trying to work into my diet. As we settle into our seats, I realize I've fallen into an alternate world where gauzy curtains and hot Sahara nights have become the norm. Is that businessman's shirt going to be ripped from his body, only to hang on his biceps in tatters? Is the man with the bicycle going to growl my name as we reach the apex of our passion as one? I've gone from teenage prude to an adult who can talk and talk about romance novels . . . without actually letting them affect me in any way, of course. I've sped right past flushing cheeks all the way to dissecting overt sexuality as if it were a splayed-out frog smelling of formaldehyde. Regardless, I have at least two and a half hours on this train before the biggest pitch of my career. Sasha and I hunker down and use the time to prep and perfect our pitch. We both know the stakes couldn't be higher—or at least one of us does.

When we arrive in Manhattan, my first hurdle quickly becomes how not to walk into Quincy headquarters looking like a pit-stained wretch who likes getting her hair licked by a cat. We duck into the elaborate, art deco bathroom in the lobby of the Quincy building in Midtown to collect ourselves. It's hard not to compare myself to Sasha as I stand next to her at the mirror, re-applying lipstick and trying to make something of my hair. Pushing six-foot, she's all legs, she has black pin-curly hair, and she actually knows how to put on eye makeup. But then I re-member what it was like to actually *be* in my early twenties and all that envy disappears. The tiny apartments, the paralyzingly low self-esteem, the terrible jobs with a parade of incompetent bosses—wait, that actually doesn't feel as far away as I smugly thought. What I do know is that in my twenties I thought hap-piness was always out there—that job, that man, that body. After my year on Time-Out, I now know that happiness is within—or at least I know it just enough to be pissed off that it's not, despite what I do for a living, something I can buy.

"You ready?" I ask, looking at Sasha in the mirror of the bathroom.

"I feel like I'm going to throw up," Sasha says.

"We'll be fine," I say.

"This is my first pitch," Sasha says, unable to look at me.

"I know," I say.

"Last week I was freelancing whatever art work I could find and paying the bills by working as the coat check girl at a club Chu—Mr. Holloway, I mean—a club Mr. Holloway frequented," she says, bending over the sink. I am quiet. "He caught me doodling once. Said his family owned an ad agency and that they were hiring." She tugs a paper towel from the machine and dries her hands. "Looking back, of course, I should have known. He switched the meeting at the last minute to a dinner." She doesn't look at me. "I didn't know until I got there that the address his assistant gave me was for his apartment." She tosses the balled-up paper towel toward the bin. It bounces off the rim and falls to the floor. A little scornful laugh and she walks over to pick it up. "There I am riding up in the elevator, still trying to make up other possible scenarios, holding my portfolio and practicing the pitches I had for Holloway/Greene clients I'd researched beforehand. I even bought an outfit I couldn't afford." She bends over, picks up the balled-up paper towel, and throws it away. This time, it goes in. "This outfit, actually. Anyway, I figured out pretty quickly that it wasn't my art degree from NYU or the time I spent interning in France or my apprenticeship at *Vogue* or any number of sketches I tried to show him that night that got me that meeting."

"What a douchebag," I say. "Not to mention blatant sexual harassment. You have a pretty good case, should you—"

"I don't need a sexual harassment case, Ms. Wyatt. I need a job."

"But—"

"And I've had much worse." She finally looks over at me. She couldn't be more than twenty-five? Twenty-six maybe? But in that moment she looks ancient. I nod. She continues. "He was nice." A look from me. "In the beginning."

"I'm so sorry you had to go through that." She looks surprised. "That must have been . . . well, you must have felt so alone. Is that it—is that the right—"

"No, that's exactly it. I thought I met a nice guy and was finally going to get a real job. Turns out . . ."

"Yep." A beat.

"I didn't sleep with him that night." She turns to me. "I need you to know that." I nod and she allows a small, relieved smile.

"You don't have to—" I pause as Sasha runs into one of the stalls and throws up. "Explain yourself to me," I say to myself as she retches into the toilet.

"Breathe. There's a cafeteria past the elevators. We'll get you a bubble water. Here's some antacids," I say, pulling a bottle from my purse and dropping two tablets into the palm of her hand. She pops them into her mouth as I throw the bottle back into my purse and am finally ready to go. She takes a big, deep breath. "It'll settle your stomach." Sasha gives her lipstick one more pass and we're out of the bathroom. After a quick stop at the cafeteria we're armed with bubble waters and speeding up to the executive floor within minutes.

"Anna Wyatt and Sasha Merchant from Holloway/Greene to see Preeti Dayal," I say to the receptionist. The entire Manhattan skyline is just behind her. Beautiful.

"Yes. There you are. Have a seat and they'll be right with you," she says. Sasha and I sit down on a long, gray, modern couch along the far wall next to a couple of men. It's quiet in the waiting room. We all keep to ourselves and are either scrolling through our phones, looking over paperwork, or quietly whispering to whomever we arrived with. I let myself stare out onto the Manhattan skyline and go over the pitch. A deep breath.

And over. And over. Like a script. Hand gestures, when to show the artwork, when to smile, when to lean in, when to make that joke, and when to tell a "personal" story. Visualizing Preeti Dayal leaning forward in her chair with a smile or a question as she gets more and more engaged in our vision.

The door to the waiting room opens and the assistant gives us a regal nod. I gather my things and walk toward the door, Sasha at my heels. A deep breath. I open the door and walk through to the inner offices of Quincy Pharmaceuticals. There is an assistant waiting for us outside the conference room about six feet down the hall.

"We've got this. They're going to love us. Just breathe," I say to Sasha, who looks as though she's on the verge of losing it. Upon my urging, she takes her first breath since we left the waiting room.

"I am reaching some dizzying heights over here, Anna. I'm panicking. I can't feel my feet. I—"

"Take your time. Breathe. I'm here and I won't leave you," I say.

"I am seriously about to start crying right now," Sasha says.

"This means a lot to you. That's a good thing. Let's let your art do the talking for you," I say, as we finally stand in front of the assistant. Sasha nods, clearly holding back tears.

"Ms. Wyatt. Ms. Merchant. They're ready for you," the assistant says. Again with the *they*. I thank her and enter the conference room. The full-to-bursting conference room. *They*. The large windows frame the Manhattan skyline once again and it is breathtaking. A long, glossy wooden table stretches down the middle of the room and the entire room is completely walled in with floor-to-ceiling windows. The pitch of my career is going to take place in a glorified goldfish bowl with ten times the number of people I'd prepared for.

"Ms. Wyatt, it's a pleasure to finally meet you. After we spoke yesterday, I did a little digging. I love what you did on the Tyler Sheeran clothing line. Making that little singer's clothes actually palatable was herculean to say the least," a woman at the far end of the table says.

"Thank you," I say, scanning the faces of the other executives in the room. I can actually feel Sasha buzzing from here.

"I'm Preeti Dayal, senior vice president at Quincy Pharmaceuticals, and I'll be spearheading the Lumineux campaign. Your phone pitch was intriguing, Ms. Wyatt. I wanted to see what my colleagues thought of it, if that's okay with you." I nod and smile (or at least that's what I think I'm doing) as Preeti goes around the room introducing various executives. The introductions fade into that single moment of silence I've been waiting for my entire life. The moment before the moment. A deep breath.

"What do women want," I say. The men in the room restrain their eye rolls as Preeti leans forward. The next several minutes are a blur as I wind my way through the pitch. The nodding heads of the Lumineux executives. A shared laugh here and a funny anecdote there. Lumineux Shower Gel. *Be the Heroine, Find Your Hero.* Sasha's artwork garners a real smile from Preeti and in an unguarded moment, another executive actually mutters, "Wow."

The Lumineux Shower Gel spokesman will be none other than the top winner of the Mr. RomanceCon pageant and Helen Brubaker, the woman who wrote *Be the Heroine, Find Your Hero,* will be doing a workshop at the conference. It's the perfect opportunity. We find our hero and the workshop will be free market research, if not an opportunity to try to get Mrs. Brubaker on board with our campaign. After thirteen minutes and twenty-four seconds (I timed it last night), I conclude the pitch with "Lumineux Shower Gel. Just Be."

"My wife's book club is reading that *Be the Heroine* book," an executive says. Several of the other executives concur.

"And the pageant for those guys? That's a real thing?" another executive asks.

"Yes, sir," I say.

"And that . . . Romance whatever . . ." he asks.

"Con," Preeti adds.

"They're okay with us inserting ourselves—" A giggle from one of the younger executives. "You know what I mean. Jesus, Ken." Another stifled giggle from Ken, the guy most likely to chime in with "That's what she said."

"Ms. Wyatt?" Preeti asks.

"We have been in communication with Ginny Barton, the president of the League of Romance Novelists," I say, trying to make a harried e-mail exchange in the wee hours of the morning sound way more substantial.

"Sounds like they're superheroes or something," an executive says.

"Well—"

"Don't even think it, Ken," Preeti says. Everyone laughs. Ken flushes red and checks his phone.

"The League is in charge of the Con. President Barton has been most helpful. She's extremely excited about the prospect of aligning with Lumineux Shower Gel," I say.

"It sounds like you've covered all your bases, Ms. Wyatt," the older executive says.

"I have. Like President Barton, I am extremely excited about the prospect of aligning with Lumineux Shower Gel," I say.

"Well, thank you, Ms. Wyatt. Ms. Merchant. We will let you know," Preeti says, smiling.

"Thank you for this opportunity. It's been our pleasure," I say, gathering my things. The assistant opens the glass door and we are led out of the conference room. We walk down the long hallway, out into the waiting room, and straight out to the elevators. Sasha and I don't say anything as the elevator speeds down. The doors open and we both silently walk out into the ornate Quincy Pharmaceuticals lobby.

"I can't—"

I interrupt, "Not here." Sasha nods and I notice her eyes are rimmed with red. "We did great. Breathe." Sasha nods again, but with the pitch finally behind her she begins to fall apart at a more and more rapid rate. I hail a cab and we are whisked away to Penn Station. We're back on the Metroliner in no time. We find our seats, and it is then and only then that I tell her the truth about the pitch. To say the look on her face is terrified and/or horrified would be an understatement.

"So, they weren't looking for an ad agency?" she finally gasps.

"No."

"And we just . . ."

"Yep."

"There is no way . . . I am so glad . . . you were so right not to tell me that," Sasha says.

"I figured," I say.

"I didn't know you could do stuff like that," she says.

"Well . . ." I trail off.

We walk back through the pitch and relive every moment.

Every word and every reaction. We dissect everything. We order many cocktails and I roll through the junk food I bought in the snack car after forgetting to stop for lunch. Sasha is beginning to calm down as we fall silent for the last hour of the train trip.

The client liked the pitch. I could feel it in the room. I know I nailed it. I know that we deserve that account. And now? I've just got to wait to hear if Lumineux Shower Gel agrees with me.

We get back to Holloway/Greene and I stop by Audrey's office to debrief her.

"Sounds like you guys really went for it," Audrey says. I don't know what that means. Is that good . . . is that . . .

"It was a good day," I say.

"But they didn't buy it in the room, so . . ."

"They didn't *not* buy it in the room, either."

"Oh, absolutely. We do so appreciate the attention you give to even the smallest of accounts," Audrey says.

"Well, thank you for your part in it," I say.

"Oh, it was nothing. I'm always looking for opportunities to support and encourage women in this business," she says, her hands in the prayer gesture and her cinnamon-roll air in full effect. "I'll be sure to keep Dad in the loop on this."

"Well, I'll let you know when I hear something." I turn toward the door before I have to say thank you again.

"Hey, how did Sasha do?" Audrey asks.

"She did great. Her artwork is really something," I say.

"So you're not threatened by her?"

"Why would I be threatened by her?"

"She's twenty-five, beautiful—"

"Oh, no—she's brilliant," I say, not wanting to blurt out no, those are the reasons your half brother tried to get in her pants

(and failed), but I'll be sure to pass along your "support and encourage women" speech. "She just needed a break. Chuck was
right in hiring her."

"So, you're not—"

"Not at all," I say.

"Hm."

"Thank you again and I'll let you know when I hear something," I say, letting myself out. As I'm walking toward my
office, I let the energy of the last several days begin to build. I
make myself a cup of tea and walk into my office and close the
door behind me. I want this. This account should be mine.

I scroll through my phone, anything to get my mind off The
Waiting, and see several texts from Ferdie. I dial his number and
wait as it rings.

"How'd it go?" he asks.

"It went really well," I say, sipping my tea.

"And did they go for it?"

"They said they'd let us know."

"Ouch."

"I know."

"So, I have a thing tonight that I want you to come to," Ferdie
says.

"You have a thing?"

"Yeah."

"You going to tell me any more than that?"

"I'm sending you the address."

"It's not The Naughty Kitty, is it?"

"No, definitely not. It's a rink."

"You skating again?"

"Something like that."

"You okay?"

"Just come. We'll be there until eight, I think," he says.

"Okay. I'll be there." We say our good-byes. I can't worry about Ferdie right now. I've been doing that for the past few years and all the years before that. Ferdinand Wyatt: the King of the Bad Decision. I was so thankful when he found hockey, because it kept him on the straight and narrow or whatever the hockey version of straight and narrow is. He could fight and act out and it was all part of the sport. But when he got injured all bets were off and he was right back to the drugs, the booze, and the terrible women, trying to find part-time work bartending and crashing on people's couches if he came home at all. If he's back at a rink, this is good news.

I find myself just sitting at my desk. Running through the pitch. Thinking about Audrey's reaction. All these accounts—when we're waiting to hear—always feel like a puppy you don't know if you get to take home yet. You're at the pound and your parents are giving you that look like mayyyyybe, so you keep your heart walled up just enough so you're not laid completely bare when the answer turns out to be no. I'd love to work on the Lumineux account. Preeti Dayal seems really great, which just complicates matters. And most of all? The campaign feels . . . important. Which is weird for me. A first. The idea that I could be a part of something significant and make up for some of the less-than-noble campaigns I've done earlier in my career is more than a little appealing. Less-than-noble campaigns that, while not at the root of why girls like Sasha think so poorly of themselves, certainly don't help. Lumineux is different. It feels like it's the manifestation of my Time-Out.

"It's the butterfly," I say aloud to myself in a particularly dramatic moment after I've built an entire narrative about how the last year was about cocooning and . . . well, you get the idea. Michael's *Rocky* analogy was way better, although I'll never tell him that.

Time passes.

Time slows down.

Time stops.

It's 6:47 P.M. when Audrey leans against my now open office door, not that I'm staring at the clock or anything.

"So sorry. Lumineux called a few hours ago," she says. I see Sasha appear just behind her, seemingly from nowhere. "Good Lord . . ." Audrey trails off.

"Sasha," she prompts.

"Uh-huh. You scared me." Sasha apologizes and sneaks past her, settling into one of the client chairs in my office.

"And?" I ask.

"They want to see the campaign you pitched through to fruition and then they'll decide. We'll go back in next Monday with everything we've got," Audrey says.

"So, it's a maybe," I say.

"But this is good, right?" Sasha asks, looking from Audrey to me, then back to Audrey. Who doesn't even look at her.

"It's definitely better than a full pass," I say. Sasha looks back over at me. I struggle out a smile for her and she nods, almost agreeing with herself that this is good news.

"Definitely," Sasha says.

"We'll send the two of you down to that RomanceCon thing. They're sending Preeti, Pretty Somebody, as well," Audrey says.

"Preeti Dayal; she's in charge of the campaign," Sasha says. I shoot her a look. The less information Audrey has the better, young Jedi.

"Oh, really? Well, that's a good sign," Audrey says.

"You'll judge the pageant and see if you can get as close to this Brubaker woman as you can. If she signs off on the campaign? It's a lock for us," Audrey says.

"Judge the pageant?" Sasha asks.

"It's basically casting, so yeah. I'm sure Ginny Barton will be amenable," I say, hoping beyond hope that that's actually true. Sasha nods.

"The business office has your travel arrangements," Audrey says, checking her phone. I nod. Audrey waits.

"Thank you so much," I say.

"Dad was really interested in this when I spoke to him earlier," Audrey says.

"That's nice to hear," I say.

"I didn't know that Lumineux was connected with Quincy Pharmaceuticals," she says.

"Is it?" I ask.

"Hm," Audrey says. She taps the side of my doorjamb a couple of times and heads back down the hall. Ugh.

"Close the door," I say to Sasha.

"I hate that she always forgets my name," Sasha says.

"Oh, she remembers your name," I say.

"What? Well, why—"

"It makes you feel forgettable. It's a power move," I say absently.

"That's terrible," she says.

"It is, isn't it," I say.

"What are you . . . shouldn't we be happy? This is good news, right?" Sasha asks.

"I don't trust her."

"Who . . . Audrey?"

"The whole 'we' thing and 'us' and that last little bit about her dad being into this campaign?" I say.

"Him being interested isn't a good thing?"

"It is if she gave us credit for it, which I will bet my entire year's salary that she did not," I say.

"Why would she do that?" Sasha asks.

"Why?"

"Yeah."

"Why would Audrey take credit for an account that could land this agency one of the largest corporations in the world on the eve of her creepy, sexual harassing little half-brother getting control of the company?"

"Oh . . . now I get it."

"Bloody Mary indeed."

"What?"

"Nothing."

"So what do we do?" Sasha asks.

"We go to RomanceCon and we make ourselves indispensable to the client."

"Make sure they won't forget our names," Sasha says.

"Exactly. So that in the end, it won't matter what Audrey or Charlton want. It's what Preeti Dayal and Lumineux wants. And we have less than a week in Phoenix to make Preeti Dayal want no one but us," I say, thankful that in calming Sasha down I'm also calming myself. Having to be positive for her has kept me from spiraling. That and the pure panic and exhaustion of the last thirty-six hours. Fingers crossed I don't have a moment's peace in the coming days.

"Okay. This is good. We can do this," Sasha says, standing and gathering her things.

"Definitely. Definitely. What are you up to tonight?" I ask.

"I've got a date," Sasha says, standing.

"Nice. Don't stay out too late. We have a plane to catch first thing," I say, swinging my workbag over my shoulder.

"Yep," Sasha says.

"See you tomorrow morning?" I begin walking down the hallway.

"Anna?" I turn around. Sasha continues, "Thanks for today. You were . . . thanks for being nice . . . nice to me."

"You're welcome," I say. A smile. An exhausted, starving, why-did-I-agree-to-go-to-an-ice-rink-tonight-of-all-nights smile.

The cold of the rink feels good. I buy a hot dog at the concession stand along with a soda and some peanut M&M's. I eat the hot dog while I'm waiting for some kid to put relish on his dog and then I go back to buy another one. I'm beyond starving.

I walk toward the bleachers and my entire life with Ferdie comes rushing back. How many hours, days, and lifetimes have I spent in the bleachers of some hockey rink? I settle in and bite into my (second) hot dog, putting my soda and M&M's just next to me on the bleachers. I'm glad to be here and not spinning at home in a haze of to-do lists and travel arrangements.

A gaggle of tiny boys in giant hockey pads moves across the ice in a chaotic, swirling eddy of cracking hockey sticks and shouts for them to slow down and listen. It's a game of epic proportions between the teeny-tiny red team and the teeny-tiny blue team. Despite their attempts at being rough and scary, they are beyond adorable. I scan the bleachers for Ferdie, thinking he's up next in some kind of ornery adult league they've got going on here. My eyes are drawn back to the ice as a ref has to pull one teeny-tiny red player off a teeny-tiny blue player like they're over-excited puppies in a box.

Ferdie.

I lean forward, almost choking on my hot dog. Ferdie's faux-hawked curls creep out from under his helmet as he holds the teeny-tiny red player under one arm with ease, trying not to laugh at the windmilling arms of the teeny-tiny blue player who is after them both. The black-and-white-striped long-sleeved shirt hides most of Ferdie's tattoos from the boys who would definitely think they were way too cool.

"You don't think it's stupid?" Ferdie asks after the game is over.

"Stupid? No way. I think it's amazing." We walk to the Metro, his giant hockey bag swung over his shoulder.

"The pay is nothing, but these other refs are telling me you can really make a lot of money doing this."

"I think it's great," I say, looking up at him. "You look happy."

"Happy." He lights up a cigarette.

"Now if you could just stop smoking," I say.

"But smoking makes me happy," he says with a wink, flicking his lighter off and sliding it into his pocket. We are quiet as we walk. "I haven't been happy for a long time."

"I know."

"Feels scary," he says, not looking at me.

"Absolutely terrifying," I say, unable to look at him, either.

4

So when people say Phoenix is a dry heat, they clearly mean that this is what it feels like to be cremated. For the first few feet outside the airport, I'm in denial. It's not that bad, I keep saying to myself. My sunglasses fog up during the Rental Car Shuttle ride. I can't take a full breath. The sweat is immediate. And then it's just basic survival skills as Sasha and I try to find our rental car. We are like two dying rodents stranded in the heat of the desert and all we want is shelter and water.

We find our rental, load our luggage into the nonexistent trunk, and proceed to silently suffocate as the air-conditioning takes its sweet time. Sasha and I just stare dumbly at the vents. Waiting. Unable to think or do anything else.

Then we're cast out onto various freeways that loop and swing around the sprawl of Phoenix, a city that looks like someone spread out a huge sheet of sandpaper and started setting little Monopoly houses on top of it. We were unable to get into the conference hotel, so I made sure we're staying at the same place as Preeti Dayal—the Arizona Biltmore. Her husband enjoys playing golf, according to her secretary, with whom I have become friendly. When I see her in the lobby, I'll feign surprise.

As we drive through the streets of Phoenix I notice immediately that, although the houses look normal enough, it's as though some giant has come along with his thumb and just smashed them a little bit farther into the ground.

"There aren't any windows," Sasha says, dabbing her face with some cosmetics product I would have no idea how to use.

"What?" I ask.

"Look. The buildings. No windows," she says. She's right. While there are windows, they're definitely not the same kind of windows I'm used to. They're screened and awninged and used sparingly, if at all. It seems as though Phoenix's entire architectural sensibility is simply "batten down the hatches because it is hot as hell."

We pull up to the Arizona Biltmore and everything changes. The beautiful Frank Lloyd Wright–inspired 1929 resort is right out of a picture postcard. The first thing I notice is the green. As with the windows, I realize I hadn't really seen any lawns or flora and fauna. Here at the Biltmore? We're surrounded by golf courses and palm trees and lush gardens. I never knew green was such an extravagance.

The valet takes the keys to the rental and motions for Sasha and me to pull our bags out of the trunk. We fall in behind the so very blond women and their aging husbands.

By the time Sasha and I haul our luggage into the lobby of the hotel, I've never been happier to feel the cool whoosh of air-conditioning in my life. And I've lived in the South. We check in to the hotel and head to our rooms, blissfully surrounded by air-conditioning.

"The kick-off toast starts in an hour," Sasha says as we wait for the elevator.

"Kick-off toast?" I ask.

"Sure. It's right before the Opening Night Bacchanalia."

There's just so much wrong with that sentence.

Sasha continues, "It's all in here." She hands me a printout of the RomanceCon schedule. "We have to be in the Silver Ballroom in an hour."

Once the elevator doors close, I scan the schedule Sasha just gave me. The doors ding open and I gather my stuff just enough to walk the few feet out of the elevator and into the hallway of our floor.

" 'Walk the plank at the Pirate Booty Ball'?" I read in a tone that is half wonder, half fear.

"Isn't it great?" Sasha beams, looking at the arrows posted on the wall, as she gets oriented with where our rooms are.

" 'Get wet down under at the Mermaid Bash,' and finally, lest we forget: 'noir it up, gangsta style' is the theme of this year's pageant."

"I can't wait!" Sasha squeals. All of my belongings are strewn at my feet as I scan the parties over and over.

"That's *gangsta* with an *a*," I say, finally handing the printout back to Sasha. I collect my things and check my room key, and we continue trudging down the hall to our rooms.

"We're right across from each other!" Sasha says, gesturing back and forth at our rooms.

"That we are," I say, sticking my room key into the slot. Green light. "See you in an hour?"

"I'll be right here," Sasha says, standing in her now open doorway with a smile that belies what we've endured already today. I let my door close behind me and the silence surrounds me like a dream.

What I want to do is flop onto my oversized king bed and sleep like the dead. What I do instead is unpack my clothes and hop in the shower before I can think better of it. In what feels like thirty seconds, I'm trudging back down the long hallway, getting our car from the valet, and driving through the dusky streets of Phoenix on the way to something called the Silver Ballroom somewhere in the bowels of the designated Romance-Con hotel for the kick-off toast. This event apparently comes before the Opening Night Bacchanalia. I haven't eaten anything since this morning, except the remainder of the peanut M&M's I found in the bottom of my purse—at which point I sadly reacted as though I'd found a million dollars.

"This kick-off toast better have something to eat on par with this little hole-in-the-wall Mexican place I found online," I say, waiting at a red light. "I haven't had good Mexican food since we lived in San Diego."

"You lived in San Diego?" Sasha asks, her neck damp with sweat after only two minutes in the 112-degree heat.

"We lived everywhere. My dad is in the military," I say.

"Like how many places?" Another red light.

"Seventeen before I graduated from high school," I say.

"Eesh," Sasha says, propelling me back into the land of now, where sharing isn't something I usually do. I was lulled into it from starvation and the thought of good Mexican food.

"It was fine," I say, wanting to stop this line of questioning immediately.

"Brothers or sisters?"

"Ferdie. A brother."

"Ferdie?"

"Ferdinand. My mother's French Canadian."

"Younger or older?" Is this the world's longest car ride?

"Nine years younger."

"That's a lot of time to be on your own before he came along."

The GPS robotically tells me that the RomanceCon hotel—*thank God*—is just up on the right. With all the excitement, I act like I don't hear that last comment. Sasha is right, of course, but she doesn't need to know that. We valet and then run into the hotel so as not to get all sweaty again.

And then all hell breaks loose.

RomanceCon explodes all around us. Romance novel covers are everywhere: on people's room key cards, on the doors to the elevators, and hanging high above the hotel lobby. It's almost shocking to see a man with a shirt on at this point. Packs of women swirl and detonate all around us. Laughter, hugs, and happy reunions inject every inch of the hotel with an air of excitement.

"Ms. Wyatt?" A round woman dressed in full Roman garb approaches me, although she looks like the version of a Roman woman who would festoon a jar of jam.

"Yes?" I ask, startled yet somehow comforted.

"I'm Ginny Barton. I'm the president of the League of Romance Novelists." She looks like she could just as soon offer to help me with my math homework than tell me the lovely story of her heroine's "mossy grotto" and how it "burns from want."

"Of course! Thank you so much for everything you've done to make this possible. We so appreciate it," I say.

"We stuck out that much, did we?" Sasha says with a smile.

"Just a bit," Ginny says.

"Such a pleasure to finally meet you. I'm Anna Wyatt and this is Sasha Merchant. We are looking forward to working with you," I say, switching into work mode. Sasha is breathlessly taking it all in, flashing a huge smile for Mrs. Barton.

"Ginny Barton," she repeats, shaking hands with both Sasha and me. "We at the LRN couldn't be more excited about the prospect of Lumineux soap using one of our heroes. It's just all so thrilling." Ginny has led us to a series of escalators and we follow her up, up, and up.

"We hope it works out. It's an exciting campaign," I say. We come to an upper floor and . . .

"Welcome to RomanceCon, ladies," Ginny says.

All I can do is stand there with my mouth hanging open.

In just one short escalator ride, I've entered an alternate universe that makes Wonderland look sedate.

Hundreds of women thread and weave through this upper lobby area, their salon-ready hair now coiffed with olive branches, togas draped with precision, while historically accurate costumes parade past us. The volume is hovering at near-deafening levels. We are propelled into the thick of it.

"I've just died and gone to heaven," Sasha squeals. I say nothing. There are no words. "Take your time. Breathe. I'm here and I won't leave you." Sasha is throwing my own words back at me. She gives me a wide smile and we enter the fray. As we are herded into the Silver Ballroom, Sasha continues to point out famous author after famous author. They are part of it all, bedecked in their Roman best and taking pictures with fans. I tell her she should go up to them. Say something.

"Oh, no. I couldn't! What would I say?" Sasha asks, as we take flutes of champagne off a silver tray now that we're safely inside. We settle ourselves near the back of the Silver Ballroom—a dimly lit, soon-to-be-unveiled masterpiece, I'm sure. The chandeliers twinkle above us, but I can barely make out the Roman columns on either side of the large stage that anchors the entire ballroom. "Should we have dressed up?" Sasha asks, tugging at her tailored blazer, deciding to unbutton it in a moment of pure abandon.

"We can't be the only ones not dressed up," I say, scanning the ballroom filled with everyone dressed up and not one person—

"What do you think?" Ginny Barton asks.

"We're feeling a tad underdressed," I say.

"Not to worry, the editors and agents don't dress up, either," Ginny says, pointing out the sleek-looking women dressed all in black peppering the otherwise debaucherous festivities. "People will just think you two are in publishing." I see a woman in a beautiful tailored suit approaching us. She's probably trying to flock with her own kind. Then I recognize her. I hear Sasha let out an involuntary gasp as the woman—and the two assistants who trail her—nears.

"Helen! So good to see you," Ginny says, extending her hand to the woman.

"Oh, please." Helen Brubaker pulls Ginny in for a hug. They separate from each other and Ginny resituates her toga.

"This heat is killing me, Barton. You guys ever think about having this thing somewhere other than Phoenix?" Helen Brubaker's smoky rasp harkens back to every diner waitress who called you honey and kept your coffee topped off. Her rough-edged accent contrasts with her designer clothes, and I can't help but gawk at the tasteful yet very expensive jewelry that accessorizes her lithe, yoga-ready figure. Even though Helen Brubaker is clearly in her late sixties, she just looks . . . vital. Alive. Polished. Wildly intimidating. And now I'm staring.

"You know we love it here," Ginny says.

"That's ridiculous. No one has a strong opinion on Phoenix. Although maybe that's its allure." Helen laughs.

"Helen Brubaker, this is Anna Wyatt and Sasha Merchant from that ad agency I was talking to you about," Ginny says. The entire crowd begins to notice that Helen Brubaker is among them. The side-glances, the gossiping behind cupped hands, the selfies that just happen to be standing in front of Helen. She is unfazed.

"Oh sure. You guys are coattailing my book, right?" Helen takes a flute of champagne from a passing tray and downs it.

"I assure you—"

"I'm messing with you, hon. You need to loosen up," Helen says, hitting me on the back as if we're longtime friends at some beerfest.

"I'm a huge fan," Sasha ekes out, her eyes fixed on the floor.

"Aren't you cute. Thank you, sweetheart," Helen says, ruffling Sasha's perfect black ringlets.

The room falls into darkness.

The entire crowd erupts in applause as my fingers tighten around my flute of champagne.

A single spotlight illuminates a huge banner high above the Silver Ballroom. The man pictured is muscular and bedecked in a pair of jeans, cowboy boots, and a worn-in cowboy hat. According to the western typeface emblazoned across the top of the banner, his name is COLT. The crowd goes wild. Another spotlight and this time it's BILLY and he's a gladiator in the arena—a hot gladiator in an oddly sexual arena. Another spotlight and now we've got JAKE, the come-hither fireman. LANTZ, with his tangle of reddish-blond hair and scruff, stands on what looks like a moody moor in just a kilt. He's shirtless, of course. TRISTAN is done up in his steampunk best: top hat, goggles, a tweed vest, and pinstripe pants. JOSH, with his tousle of black hair and piercing blue eyes, is perfect as any woman's Austenian fantasy in his historically accurate garb. And finally, my personal favorite, BLAISE. Blaise's blond hair is swept up and he appears to be sporting some kind of sparkly lotion, vampire fangs, and a brooding stare. The spotlights fall from their banners and circle as the electro music builds and builds. The crowd goes wild.

"Welcome to RomanceCon!" a voice booms over the loud-speaker. The music kicks in and a flood of silver confetti falls from the ceiling as the stage comes to life—all seven men posed like Grecian statues in various stages of undress.

Each man comes forward as the announcer calls his name to applause and catcalls.

"This must seem so strange to you," Helen says, noticing that I have yet to close my mouth, choosing just to let it hang open.

"Every community has their own . . . their own standard of norma—" I say as Tristan steps forward in nothing but a well-placed fig leaf.

"Oh, that's bullshit and you know it, Ms. Wyatt," Helen interrupts.

"I'm sorry?"

"I'm not trying to be mean."

"No, of course. I've always thought the word *bullshit* was an underutilized term of endearment," I say.

"I like you," Helen says, with another blow to my back, spilling my champagne. "What I mean is there's something about this place that forces you to drop the act." Billy comes forward and drops his toga to unveil an even smaller toga as if he's some kind of risqué Russian nesting doll. I raise an eyebrow and look from Helen to Billy and back to Helen. "I know it seems antithetical, but there you are," Helen says.

"Oh, come on. This is all just . . . I mean, you guys are selling a fantasy world," I say, watching the women go crazy as the men hop down from the stage and the party really gets started.

"Takes one to know one, dear," Helen says. "You gonna drink that?" I pass her my flute of champagne and she downs it in one go. She hands me back the empty flute with a wink. A snap of her fingers to her assistants and just like that . . . Helen Brubaker is gone.

"I think I'm in love," I say to Sasha once Helen is out of earshot. Sasha just stands there shaking her head, trying to form some kind of word or sentence, but . . . nothing. I scan the ballroom and notice a table at the very back that looks like it has some kind of food on it. "Food." I point to the table, apparently only able to speak in single-word sentences.

"I'm going to head back to the hotel, if that's okay?" Sasha asks.

"I'll be right behind you. I'm going to see if Preeti is here yet," I say.

"I'll cab it back," Sasha says, pulling her phone from her purse.

"Is that the guy from the date the other night?" I ask.

"Yeah," she says. I'm waiting for something more . . . but nothing.

"Nice. Okay, I'll see you back at the hotel," I say, making my way back to the food. I order a club soda with lime from the bartender and start to dig into the tiny cubes of cheese that are stacked high on a decorative platter.

As I stuff several tiny cheese cubes into my mouth, I see Colt, a blond titan of a man. He's almost as big in person as he appeared on the banner. He's decided to attend tonight's party almost nude and holding a discus, rather than appearing as the shirtless cowboy from the banner. He's an Olympian. An ancient Olympian in designer underpants and a yellow Livestrong rubber bracelet.

And, as if on cue, Colt ambles over to me.

"Hey."

"Hey," I say, swallowing the tiny cubes of cheese.

He doesn't even look real. He's everything women desire. And he knows it. Broad shoulders, blond hair, tanned skin, ice-blue eyes, and a body that looks like it could have been chiseled out of marble. A body that I'm seeing pretty much all of right now because his designer underpants are hardly covering much of his six-foot-four-inch frame.

"So, you want to take a picture of me?" Colt asks, posing.

"Oh, no thank you," I say as politely as I can manage now that Colt stands frozen into place as Myron's famous sculpture, *Discobolus*. He waits expectantly, so I wipe my hands of any cheese remnants and pull out my phone and begin to fumble with the camera settings.

"You want to get in here with me?" he asks, still posing.

"Oh, um . . ."

"We'll take it for you!" a very excited group of women say from just behind me. I thank them and hand over the phone. I walk the few steps over to Colt and stand next to him, my face flushing, hands clasped in front of me, purse still on my shoulder.

"Touch him! Act like you're kissing him! Feel his biceps!" the women chirp and shout. I shuffle closer to Colt with a muttered "okay" and awkwardly hover my arm just above his huge extended discus arm. I want to crack a joke to cut the growing tension that's floating all around Colt and me, but all I can manage is muttering and half-starting sentences like I'm some hapless person meandering down the street with a tinfoil helmet atop my head.

I stand next to Colt and it takes all of my energy not to look at anything below his waist and nope, not the chest, either, and Jesus, the shoulders on this guy could—my face is getting hotter and hotter—I've never seen biceps that big in person. In the fantasy version of this I'd be the cool cucumber who swanned over and made some hilarious joke and the women would snap a photo and they'd all see the chemistry and swap knowing glances as oh, do you want my phone number, Colt? Oh, you're really a philosophy professor over at the local university? No, I didn't even notice you were wildly attractive, you know, I don't objectify people like that. Yes, I do think that's noble of me to love you for your mind, Colt. And I'd throw my head back and my long brown hair would waft behind me as I'd finally hit that pose where you look over your shoulder in photographs and it looks mysterious and sexy instead of bewildered and bloated. Then the music kicks in aaaaand cut to a slow-motion shot of Colt and me dancing at our wedding reception, the haze of lanterns in the distance and all we can see is each other and Colt whispers, "You were always my Isabeau," and I nuzzle him as the camera catches the look in his eye of a besotted adoration he thought he'd never find.

Instead.

"I think I ate too much cheese," I say, still standing a good foot away from Colt and the future we'll never share together.

Then, it's like everyone gets the memo in that moment. She's not one of us. I can feel the chill in the air as the women snap the photo and Colt moves into a standing position again. I thank them. They are polite, but disapproving, as they hand me back my phone. I disentangle myself from Colt and they swarm him. I stand on the fringes of the party, watching the revelry.

I turn back to the cheese and scarf down several more cubes, then move on to the slices of pineapple, strawberries, and grapes. Unable to control myself, I dip cubes of pound cake and brownie bites in the chocolate fountain one after the other. I've gone from starving to nauseated in ten minutes flat. I fix myself a little plate of cut-up vegetables and stand off to the side of the buffet table with my club soda still in hand. I take it all in.

"I think I ate too much cheese?" I say to myself. A shake of the head.

The music is loud and right out of every bad wedding reception. The seven male contestants move and mingle throughout the party, taking pictures, dancing, and vying for votes among the crush of hundreds of adoring women. I see every type of woman on the dance floor—every size, every age, every color— shaking her groove thing, if you will. There are no social strata or cliques. It's a mosh pit of women feeling free to let off steam. Helen Brubaker is over in the corner of the dance floor, shoes off and dancing like no one is watching. I can't help but smile seeing her back up into Jake, the cocoa-skinned god who can only throw his hands up and smile.

I take a bite of a carrot, which tastes terrible after those delectable chocolate-doused goodies. I force it down and throw the rest into the bin, conceding defeat. I take a drink of my club soda.

Women continue to flood the dance floor. Helen Brubaker and her entourage keep dancing. The seven cover model contestants smile and pose. The publishing ladies on the fringes laugh and catch up with one another. And then there's me.

I feel as if one of those spotlights that originally illuminated the cover model banners is now focused squarely on me. I don't belong here. And everyone knows it. Sasha happily chatted up several women before she left, but me? Helen Brubaker calls me out for shoveling bullshit within five minutes of meeting her. In the past I've always been able to rise above the fray—or the dance floor, if you will—and go about my business. I chalk up this hiccup to my yearlong Time-Out. Or maybe I'm just afraid I'll get caught reading that one Judy Blume book under the covers again.

I thought by taking on Lumineux, risking it all, and getting that meeting I was finally done with my training montage and ready to step into the ring. But as I stand here on the fringes, I now realize there's a difference between stepping into the building that houses the ring and stepping into the actual ring itself.

While Rocky's training montage consisted of push-ups and jogging, mine was more about learning to be vulnerable. The key to true happiness, my therapist said, was opening myself up to being imperfect or whatever she was talking about. Something something something transparency and then quiet sobbing as I slid down the wall. So, I championed it. I decided to be the *best at vulnerability*! Look at me! I bragged that I'd figured it out, and hand over that blue ribbon because here is the girl who wins at being imperfect! I'm perfect at being imperfect! No? I've missed the point? Hm. Of course I was ready to be transparent with people . . . *someone*.

But apparently it doesn't work like that.

Standing on the fringes of this party it all comes roaring back. I'm thirteen years old and, once again, I'm the new kid in town. The vague promises my parents made that we'd visit or stay in touch with whatever half friend I'd glommed on to were short-lived, so as I got older I learned to just . . . not. Trust. Invest. Care.

I set down my club soda on the bar and notice my hands are shaking. And I know it's not just this stupid party. It's everything. Forty. The Time-Out. Cleaning house.

My death match with vulnerability rages on. And the ring? I'm nowhere near ready to step into that ring. I can't even let go long enough to take a picture with Colt.

Helen Brubaker is right. It's bullshit.

I need to get out of here. And I need a drink. A proper one. I wind through the revelers and finally make it out into the hallway, down the escalators, through the lobby, *oh my God, the heat,* into the rental car, *oh my God, the heat,* and back to the Biltmore.

I see the bar right away. As I walk toward it, my hands finally stop shaking. I pull my cell phone from my purse and look at the picture of Colt and me. I text the photo to Allison, Michael, and Ferdie back home along with:

Kids? Looks like Momma just got her Christmas card picture.

5

I'm scrolling through various work e-mails as I find a seat at the bar, the blaring televisions with various sports shows drowning out the low, thumping electro music that's soundtracking the rest of the hotel. The angular, hard-lined architecture is softened with the deep dark reds and browns of the lush furnishings. Everything here is breathtaking. Or maybe it's just me happy to be in air-conditioning and away from scantily clad men that I am unable to keep my cool around. I scan the landscape, breathing in the cool air.

Because the Bacchanalia is still in full swing at a hotel far, far away, there are no women from RomanceCon here. The beauty of not staying at the Con hotel. I settle onto a low-backed stool at the bar just as I get the text responses to my fabulous picture with Colt.

Michael: *Are you in Logan Circle right now?*

Allison: *Looks like someone wants to throw a little DICKsus, as well. Hahahahahah.*

Ferdie: *I don't understand what I'm looking at.*

I order an ice-cold Lagunitas beer and whatever they have that's fried on the menu. At the last minute, I tack on a cheese plate and a side salad I probably won't eat. I drink. And I eat. I pull out my copy of Helen Brubaker's *Be the Heroine, Find Your Hero,* taking notes and marking passages or ideas that might work for Lumineux. I go back and forth with Allison and Michael, even sending the picture of Colt and me to Hannah—mostly out of guilt. I can feel myself pulling away from Hannah in a move I like to call the Slow Fade. She doesn't respond to my text. Hm.

As the bar begins to fill up, I catch myself hiding the cover of Helen's book. Old habits. The book makes women feel empowered, sexy, and cherished, and challenges them to be the heroine of their own stories, and I can't even be seen in public with it?

"What are you reading?" asks the man seated two barstools down from me, his British accent noticeable even in this noisy hotel bar.

"A book," I say, positive now that the hits are going to keep coming. And apparently the symbology and prevalence of cheese is going to be something I have to analyze when covering this with my therapist later.

"Oh, is that what those things are?" he asks. I turn to him. He's dressed, as Hannah would say, nattily. A bespoke suit, the jacket of which hangs on the back of his stool. His blue oxford cloth shirt is open at the collar and is being reined in by a tweed vest. His dark blondish hair flips up just behind his ears. The length makes me curious. He looks so hemmed in, literally, but his longish hair and the three-day golden-gray stubble that frames his jaw speak to something . . . else. I try to hide the book under my arm and into an alternate universe, while attempting to avoid too much eye contact with what turn out to be very dark blue eyes. "Lincoln Mallory." He extends his hand to me across the two barstools.

"Anna Wyatt," I say, taking his hand in mine. I'm suspicious. Immediately.

"Pleasure," he says. Grabbing his jacket and drink, he moves to the barstool next to me. I watch him. "It's just for convenience, I assure you."

"Mine or—"

"Oh, mine absolutely," he says, settling in. "I really am best up close."

"Wow, really?"

"I thought I'd simply state the obvious," he says.

"If it's so obvious, one could argue it doesn't need to be stated," I say.

"One could argue that."

"Not you or I, clearly." He motions to the waiter to bring me another drink.

"Clearly." And out of the corner of my eye I begin to see the haze of those lanterns and the slow-motion first dance and . . . no. Anna. Stop. Don't think. How about you try that for a change. How about you unpin that poor dissected frog and just . . . let it go.

"I love a hotel bar," I say.

"Do you now?"

"Yes, and I know that was a little bit sarcastic, but I'm going to tell you why with an earnestness that will make you feel just a twinge of guilt." I laugh and he smiles. That's just . . . he really is better up close. I thank the bartender as he sets another beer down in front of me. I take a sip. Lincoln waits.

"Proceed, Ms. Wyatt," he says.

"It's an odds game. No computer or person in the whole wide world could have predicted that this exact group of people would be sitting at this exact hotel bar on this exact night. All of the flights and the rental cars and the trains and the meetings and the showers and the last-minute decision to throw caution to the wind and come down here and watch the game. It's utterly incalculable. So few things are. I love that."

"So few things are?"

"Incalculable," I say.

"Are they, though?"

"Sure. So much of life is routine and controlled and—"

"You mean, so much of *your* life is routine and controlled."

"No, life in general. Everyone's lives. Life." A look from Lincoln. "What? You don't agree?"

"Well, what do your calculations say I'll say?"

"Ah."

"I think life can be as incalculable as you want it to be, Ms. Wyatt."

"I knew you'd say that," I say. Lincoln is momentarily flustered and it is breathtaking. I watch as he collects himself, his long fingers curling around his drink while he slowly takes another sip. He allows a small smirk before he meets my gaze once more.

"Certainty tends to be a bit . . . deceptive. Or at least that's been my experience," he says.

"No, I can definitely . . . I get that," I say. He smiles and he's a bit elsewhere. I continue, "And it's Anna. Please."

"Anna then." Sighhhhhh. "What brings you to Phoenix?"

"Work. Like everyone else, I expect. You?"

"Same. I own a consulting firm in New York. I travel to Phoenix once or twice a year to meet with a client who lives in one of the Biltmore estates. We golf." He ends with an efficient nod.

"Golf, eh?"

"Yes, it's all so very calculable." He toasts with his glass and takes a long drink.

"A couple more drinks and I'm positive I won't be able to say the word *calculable*."

"Then that shall be our litmus test. Say *calculable*. Now? How about now? That's it, Wyatt, we're cutting you off," he says. I'm smiling. Smiling. Leaning into him and I'm completely unguarded.

"DUI checkpoints around the hotel where they demand you say difficult words. Sorry ma'am, you can't order those five desserts from room service until you've said the word *proselytize*," I say, and Lincoln laughs.

"And what is it you do?" he asks.

"Advertising. We're here on a big campaign—well, it's actually a tiny campaign and I kind of tricked my way into getting the meeting, but . . . I think it's a chance, you know?"

"I do know."

"And it feels important. So much of advertising is . . ." I shake my head thinking about scantily clad women biting into hamburgers and perfect mothers happily cleaning up their family's messes. "Well, isn't."

"And this campaign of yours?"

"It's different. It feels different. And it's mine." A flash of Audrey, and this urgency shudders through me.

"What . . . what was that?"

"You know how when you get an idea . . . not just any idea, *the* idea. . . it's almost like you can actually hear the starter pistol go off, and then it's just this all-out race to get to the finish line before anyone else does?"

"That theory only works if you truly believe you're incapable of having another idea. Is that what you believe?"

"Sometimes."

"Hm."

"What . . . what was that?" I say. Lincoln smiles and puts up his hands. Another started and stopped thought and he defaults to scanning the bar with those dark blue eyes of his. I follow his gaze. The drunken businesswomen to our left prattling on with secrets and complaints they'll definitely regret sharing come morning. The quartet of businesspeople making painful conversation about anything and everything until falling silent as they take comfort in the dim screens of their smartphones. The single men and women who just want a drink and maybe to talk sports with someone before going back to their hotel room alone. Lincoln settles back on me with a sigh. "What?" He shakes his head.

"It's not about the idea; it's about confidence, love," Lincoln says.

"Is it now?" I ask, my walls slamming back up.

"You know the most powerful thing a person can do?"

"Tell a total stranger they have no confidence at some random hotel bar?"

He laughs. "Almost." A smile. He leans in. "To convince someone they'll only have one good idea."

"Hm." Gulp.

"You hate that I'm right."

"I do. Oh my God, I so do."

Lincoln leans back and laughs. Really laughs. "I get that a lot," he says, and then I laugh.

We fall silent.

"It's not often you find the door unlocked, you know? There's your way in. And when you do?"

"You open it," he says. And before I can think better of it, I kiss Lincoln Mallory. Right there. In front of that impossibly incalculable grouping of people seated at that hotel bar.

"I knew you were going to do that," he says, as we finally break apart. I laugh.

"I didn't even know I was going to do that," I say, breathless. Lincoln stands and instructs the bartender to put both checks on his room. I am quiet. He signs the tab, thanks the bartender, and turns back to me. I watch as he takes his jacket from the back of his stool.

"Shall we?"

"Yes," I say, without hesitation.

We're standing at the elevator after Lincoln's pressed the call button when I finally wake up from whatever stepping-into-the-ring haze I was in that made me say yes to following this man to places unknown. As the doors ding open, he motions for me to enter first. I'm expecting him to touch me, whether on the small of my back or the arm, as I glide past him and into the elevator. He doesn't. He steps inside the elevator and just as he's about to press the floor for his room, I press the floor for mine. I turn to him and raise an eyebrow. We are quiet as the elevator ascends.

I find myself just staring at the numbers, trying to calm myself. I take a deep breath and make patterns out of the numbers, multiplying and dividing them as the elevator speeds to my floor. *It's about confidence, love.* And before I can think better of it, I press the red stop button, pulling my hand back like I've just touched an open flame. I stand there for a second, staring at the red button. And then I turn to face him.

I run my hand down the front of his jacket, curling my fingers around the lapel, the material soft and weightless in my hands. The alarm of the stopped elevator muting in my now overheated ears. Lincoln's eyes are everything I need them to be in these moments—surprised, curious, and wanton. As my hands explore his body, he remains absolutely still except for that stare. It follows my every move, my every breath. After what feels like millennia, I'm finally ready to meet his gaze. And it cuts through me. I ball my hands into tight fists to keep them from shaking, and then rest them on his hips to steady myself.

He leans down and I pull back, shaking my head no. A raised eyebrow from him. I run my hands back up his body until I'm grazing the flips of hair at his neck and my fingers luxuriously thread their way through the tangle of his dark golden hair. He sighs. A deep, shuddering sigh, and his eyes close for the tiniest and most beautiful of moments. And then I pull him into me, the warmth of his mouth fast on mine. The buzzing of the alarm is gone. All I hear are Lincoln's quickening breaths as he backs me up against the mirrored wall of the elevator, his hand skimming down my body, coming to rest at the crook of my knee as he pulls my leg around him, closing the space between us to beyond infinitesimal.

"Attention! Be advised! The fire department is on their way!" The staticky, urgent voice finally breaks through. Lincoln leans away from me and I find myself being pulled closer as he scans the elevator buttons for a way to stop the voice. Stop the fire department. He takes his hand from under my shirt and reaches across to the talk button.

"No need for all that. We're all fine here. Just a curious son who likes to press buttons." Lincoln's voice is breathy. It's all I can do to focus on the long, taut muscle in his neck that disappears beneath the collar of that blue oxford cloth shirt.

"Well, all right, sir, but let's try to get it going again, huh?" the disembodied voice says.

"I'm trying, mate," Lincoln says, his fingers tightening around my knee as he brings my leg in closer to him. He dives into me for another kiss as the voice whines on about valuable time and money. We finally both come up for air wearing the same annoyed, then resigned, expressions. A quick shake of his head and Lincoln depresses the red stop button. The elevator thunks back into its ascent. We disentangle ourselves and begin tucking in shirts and smoothing down fabric. I can feel the color in my face staying at blush red. The elevator slows and the doors ding open at my floor.

I rest my hand on his chest and step out of the elevator alone. My eyes are fixed on his until he disappears behind the closing elevator doors.

"Um . . . hello?!" Sasha is standing in the hallway in her pajamas holding a soda from the vending machine, her mouth hanging open. I can't speak yet, so I just shrug as I begin rummaging through my purse for my room key. "Wha . . . I mean . . . how? Who was he?" Sasha asks, following me down the hall.

"I don't know . . . I met him at the hotel bar," I say, my mind finally slowing down enough to piece a sentence together. I slide my room key into the slot, get the green light, and open the door. Sasha follows me in.

"Tonight? You met him tonight?" Sasha asks, cracking open her soda and sitting down in the desk chair.

"Yeah," I say, taking off my jacket.

"You're still all flushed, you know."

"I know. I can . . . I know," I say, feeling my face with the back of my hand. I'm embarrassed. I feel . . . wait. It's the same exact feeling that happens when I fear I'll get caught reading a romance novel. It's that blush. I kick off my heels and just stand there, letting my head fall onto my chest. I pull my long brown hair out of its twist and start to feel normal. Ish. I can still feel him . . . everywhere. I clear my throat, trying to regain some level of composure . . . if only temporarily. "I'm super tired and we have a big day tomorrow, so . . ." I walk toward the door to my room and Sasha follows, crestfallen.

"That's all I get?" Sasha asks, as I pull open the door.

"For now. I just need some sleep," I say, managing a smile.

"An early breakfast then," she says. "Where I'll get more de-tails?" Sasha steps out into the hallway. I nod. "He was cute. Seemed really into you." She cinches her robe tightly around her body.

"Yes, well," I say, letting the thought hang while I have an entire conversation with myself about what just happened—what I *did*—in that elevator. What came over me?? " Seven A.M. then?" Sasha nods with a sheepish smile and walks across the hall to her room. We close our doors with a polite wave.

I unzip my skirt, step out of it, and hang it up in the closet along with my shirt. Bra goes in the drawer, panties go in the laundry bag, makeup gets washed off, hair gets combed out, teeth get brushed, contact lenses get taken out, and glasses get put on. I can't look at myself, but hotels have a way of forcing you to look at your own reflection. In my apartment I have a system so I'm never caught off guard with my own reflection.

But hotels are lousy with mirrors in oddball locations whose goal, it seems, is to make me look at every angle of myself whether I want to or not. Every time I meet my own gaze I blush, still in disbelief at what I did. And then there I am again, and is that the sort of person Lincoln Mallory finds attractive? I lost myself in that elevator and all these mirrors are reminding me that I'm still me . . . forty-year-old-bodied me. *She ain't a beauty, but hey she's all right.*

As I plug my phone into the charger by the bed and set the alarm for six A.M., my mind is still swirling—the root of the maelstrom deep in my gut. I take my glasses off, turn out the lights, pull the covers up over my shoulders, and settle in on my side.

A flash. Him. His touch. I breathe. Flip onto my back. The warmth of his mouth, his body pressed against mine. I lay my arm across my forehead, eyes wide open in the pitch black. Those dark blue eyes fixed on mine in a way no man has ever looked at me. I flip over on my stomach, and the sensation of his fingers tightening around the crook of my knee sends tingles all over my body. I swallow. Hard. I flip the pillow over and the coolness of the other side calms me down. The tangle of his dark blond hair running through my fingers and I'm on my other side again, back where I started. I feel like a raw nerve. My brain is sharp and attuned.

My brow furrows and I pull the covers up tight around my shoulders. I want the darkness to surround me. Hide me. Cover me. Protect me. Something.

Incalculable.

I haven't felt this alive for as long as I can remember.

6

By the time Sasha and I meet for breakfast the next morning, just a few minutes past seven A.M., I've concocted untold thousands of narratives for how last night happened and how either a) I will continue to spiral out of control until I've been turned into some sex slave and only Liam Neeson's very specific skill set can save me, b) I will be be crushed when it turns out that I am not, in fact, in a romance novel and real life doesn't work like this, or c) Lincoln Mallory checked out this morning and I missed my chance at . . . and then my mind goes blank . . . missed my chance at whatever this is . . . was . . . I don't know. We order two breakfast buffets and everything seems to be settling back into the real world as I grapple with which toppings to put on my oatmeal.

"It doesn't even sound like a real name. Lincoln Mallory," Sasha says, biting into a chunk of cantaloupe.

"I know," I say, leafing through today's schedule. Helen Brubaker's workshop is today and both Sasha and I have been enrolled. We have some judging responsibilities in the early evening before we have to attend the . . . sigh . . . Pirate Booty Ball. I can't help but wonder how many times I'll be asked if I'd like to walk someone's plank.

"And you said he was British?"

"Yeah," I say, closing the schedule and going back to the work e-mails now overloading my smartphone. A few from my assistant and many more than usual from Audrey.

"Do you just want to eat breakfast alone or . . . ," Sasha says, no longer eating.

"What? Oh, I'm so sorry. I would have liked to see Preeti last night, is all. Either at the Con or here. I just want to make us . . . well, you know. Okay. I'll stop," I say, tapping out some final instructions to my assistant and setting the phone down.

What I want to say? I hate that Sasha saw me so unguarded. Hell, I hate that I was so unguarded, whether Sasha saw me or not. I've had to work twice as hard to get half the respect my mostly male colleagues get. Community college plus night classes doesn't come close to the pedigrees of most of the people I work with. And now I've gone and given them ammo to brush me aside. Turns out, vulnerability isn't just something that shall set me free—it also makes me a target. I must keep my head. Or decide that I can trust Sasha if I can't. Or don't want to.

I continue, "I just want today to go well, you know? I still haven't pieced together exactly how to involve Helen Brubaker and whether it's going to be a direct tie-in at all." I start in on my oatmeal, making sure to have brown sugar in every spoonful. "And that really bothers me."

"No, I know. It's like we came down here with this super-specific plan and the minute we got here it kind of all blew up," Sasha says.

"Exactly. I'm getting more and more confident that Lumineux is going to want to use the campaign we've designed for them. What I'm getting nervous about is whether it'll still be our campaign by the time we get to that point. Plus, I know we'll get the spokesman. That's for sure. And maybe that's the tie-in, that he's Mr. RomanceCon or whatever. But there's got to be something we can do with Helen and the actual book. Or maybe it'll just be the inspiration." I shake my head and take another bite of my oatmeal.

"Do you think she'll sign our copies of her book?" Sasha pulls her well-worn copy of *Be the Heroine* from her workbag and sets it on the table.

"Oh, I'm sure she would, but . . ."

"We can ask her, right? I mean, everyone in the workshop will want her to sign them," Sasha says, her voice growing desperate.

"Maybe we play it by ear?" I ask.

"Yeah, I know we have to keep it professional. Speaking of . . ." Sasha waggles her eyebrows at me and I know exactly what she wants to talk about: Lincoln.

"As I said, I don't know anything about him," I say.

"Didn't look like that."

"It's all of this. It made me do it. I was all hopped up," I say, feeling my face flushing once again. "I'm so embarrassed."

"You went to a fourth of a Greek-themed party, where from what I heard, all you got hopped up on was dipping various things into a chocolate fountain. And embarrassed? Why would you be embarrassed? Maybe you just liked the guy," Sasha says.

"Maybe," I say.

"Why is that bad?"

"I don't know. It just feels . . . bad. Not wrong bad, but different bad."

"In romance novels that's kind of the whole deal. Different bad is good. Different bad is hot. The sexy stranger who makes your wild side come out? I mean, for not reading any romance novels you're sure—"

"It's not like that," I say.

"I'm just saying be open to it, and not in a nasty way, just—"

"No, I know. *Open* open." My therapist's words come rushing back. "But it was a one-time deal, so . . ."

"That's a quote in every romance novel ever. So . . . good luck with that."

"Or it could just be *bad* bad and I'm trying to rationalize my way into doing whatever it is, anyway."

"That's true, too," Sasha says, poking at her scrambled eggs.

"He said that . . . ugh, it shouldn't matter what he said, but—"

"What?"

"He said that I was nervous about the campaign because I lacked confidence. That the most powerful thing someone can do is make you believe you only have the one good idea," I say.

"Well, isn't that kind of like what you were saying Audrey was doing to me? By acting like she can never remember my name?"

"Maybe. Yeah. I'd forgotten about that. Wow, that's exactly right," I say. We fall silent.

"My grandmother used to say I had this light in me . . . she said things like that." Sasha pushes away her plate and sits back in her chair. "And then when I got to be a teenager that light just went out."

"Happens to a lot of women, I think."

"So maybe this is about that. I think people—weak people or whatever, I don't think they're bad people necessarily—I think in order for them to feel brighter they have to convince others they're not as bright."

"And then we turn our own light out," I say to myself.

"Right. Look, if Audrey pulls something, we'll figure it out. It's not like we don't see her coming."

"We'll Marple her," I say.

"We'll what?" Sasha asks, laughing. I explain the Anna Wyatt Marple Theory to Sasha as quickly as I can as if I'm giving her directions to the bathroom.

"But that's not this."

"What? Of course it is."

"No. It absolutely is not. Audrey knows we're a threat. She doesn't think we're harmless old ladies at all," Sasha says. I'm about to say something. "Charlton does. Definitely. Probably Chuck, too. They think we're all idiots, but Audrey? No way."

Just then Lincoln comes striding into the restaurant. He has a brief conversation with the woman at the front desk, and she whips her hair over her shoulder and laughs coyly at something he's said. I feel a combination of jealous and ridiculous. Flirting with random women equals business as usual for Lincoln Mallory. She pulls a receipt from the little machine and he signs it, saying his farewells to the newest love of his life he scans the buffet and our eyes meet. Every hair on my body stands on end as my mouth runs dry. He stops and slides his hands in his pockets as if he's gazing at a painting in a museum. The buffet line shifts around him, and the growing crowd diverts and detours, people threading their way to the buffet with excuse me's and odd looks.

Lincoln doesn't move.

Until he takes his hand out of his pocket and motions for me to come over to him with an authoritative curl of his finger.

"Excuse me," I say to Sasha, taking my napkin from my lap and setting it on top of my half-eaten oatmeal. Sasha follows my gaze and I notice her cartoonish double take as I walk toward Lincoln.

"I need to see you again," he says. I look from him to the throng of people moving through the buffet line and wonder how he can seem so unaffected by it all. I open my mouth to speak and he interrupts me with "And don't say you're seeing me right now." That was pretty much verbatim what I was going to say, and all I can do is smile. "I must apologize, I would have come to your table, but I wasn't sure how much you wanted your work colleague to be privy to."

"Privy to? We're not animals, Lincoln. Let me introduce you," I say, taking his hand in mine and walking over to the table. It's a casual move—fueled by my bravado to be *so okay with this, woo-hoo*—but it catches even me off guard. I didn't mean to take his hand; I was just leading him over to the table. But there it is. We're holding hands now like two elementary school sweethearts on the playground. And as if it's all new to me, my fingers tighten and loosen around his like I don't quite know what intensity level I want to display right now. I settle on the level that just feels right as we near Sasha, who has been watching it all. "Sasha Merchant, this is Lincoln Mallory. He's here in Phoenix on business. Sasha is doing the artwork on our ad campaign." Sasha stands, extending her hand. Lincoln lets go of mine as he takes Sasha's.

"A pleasure, Ms. Merchant," he says.

"And also with you," Sasha says, her face flushing immediately.

"I'll walk you out," I say, moving Lincoln away from the table.

"Am I allowed to get breakfast first?" Lincoln asks, eyeing the buffet line.

"Yes, of course. I'm so sorry." I stop and face him. "About last night—"

"I didn't think people actually said that," Lincoln says, pouring himself a cup of tea into a to-go cup.

"Right? And yet here we are," I say. Lincoln laughs and it cuts through a bit of the tension.

"Fair enough. What if we just got dinner? Tonight?" Lincoln asks.

"I have . . . I have a Pirate Booty Ball to attend later tonight," I say, my entire being deflating with each word. Lincoln's mouth curls into a smirk. He waits. "It's a party at RomanceCon. A themed party. With pirates and—"

"And?"

"Booties." The word is pulled from my mouth by sheer force.

Lincoln just nods. "As you do. That actually works perfectly. A surprise field trip after your . . ."

"Booty Ball."

"Yes. Quite. If you would, love." Lincoln hands me his tea and I take it. "Cheers." He pulls his wallet from his inside jacket pocket and takes his business card from its soft leather folds. He pulls a pen from the same pocket, turns the business card over, and writes a phone number. He slides his wallet back into the jacket pocket, then the pen, takes his tea from me, and hands me his business card. "That's my mobile. We'll talk later." One last smile to me and he ambles out of the buffet, grabbing an apple on the way out, tossing it once in the air.

We're just finishing up when my phone rings. Audrey. I show Sasha the name and she makes a face.

"Audrey, hello," I say, faking enthusiasm.

"Anna," she says, her voice silken and easy.

"What can I help you with, Audrey?" I ask. Sasha rolls her eyes.

"I just wanted a progress report from Team Lumineux," she says.

"How thoughtful," I say. Sasha is scrolling through her phone and I can see something give her pause. She's scrolling and reading. A shake of the head and she looks up. I furrow my brow and she shows me her phone. As Audrey twitters on into the phone about how great we're doing and how lucky Holloway/Greene is to have us and Lumineux Shower Gel this and Quincy Pharmaceuticals that, I read an e-mail from Charlton to everyone announcing how proud he is of Chuck, who just brought in the account of a billionaire playboy who owns three separate sports teams.

And now everything makes sense. If I thought the heat was on before, Chuck signing this huge account has just lit the fuse.

"We'd better be heading off to the conference, Audrey. Thank you so much for checking up on our account," I say, hitting the word *our* with territorial flare. While I understand Lincoln's point, I am far from giving up on Lumineux. If Audrey wants to steal this idea, she's going to have to do just that. I refuse to make this robbery a comfortable situation for her. This time? I'm not turning off my own light.

"Yes, well. You're welcome," she says.

"You championing and supporting the work of other women means the world," I say.

"Of course."

"Best to you, Audrey," I say.

"And you," she says. We hang up.

Sasha and I are silent. Shaking our heads.

"Dammit," I say.

"Yep," Sasha says.

We drive to the conference hotel in silence. While Sasha is in the bathroom, I find an open corner of a sofa in the lobby. We have just thirty minutes before Helen's workshop. The lobbies, restaurants, and hotel hallways are filled with cliques of women laughing and talking. They're animated and joyous, like a bunch of kids who still believe in Santa Claus. I feel like an outsider. What a shock.

All of us were romance novelists when we were younger. I kept diaries and built fantasies. Every boy was a hero and I thought I was worthy of that lingering gaze across a crowded room. I was the princess in the tower and the kick-ass heroine who battled the bad guys. I slew dragons and kissed knights like I meant it. I not only allowed myself to get swept off my feet, I expected it. And it was never about fearing I was valuable only if someone liked me. It was the purity of knowing that this life was meant to be shared and that I had the right to someone amazing.

So what happened? How does that same little girl then settle for "You know, he makes a good living and my parents really like him," which are the exact words I said about Patrick weeks before I married him?

Patrick O'Hara was the right kind of partner. Every box was checked. He was whip-smart and curious. I will always love a man who asks questions. We were friends first. I thought I was happy. Patrick was always a good man, thoughtful and considerate. He was never cruel. But as our marriage eroded we both became versions of ourselves that neither of us were proud of. *Bratty* is the word that comes to mind as I think back on us now. Because our needs were so far from being met, we devolved into tantrumming toddlers who never respected the other's wishes in any meaningful way. In the waning months of our eleven-year marriage, we became more like feuding siblings than beloveds. Fighting about what was fair and that you got that so I get this and you said that so I get to feel this for this amount of time and on and on, stopping just short of putting a line of duct tape down the center of our home.

There are moments I miss him, but now I realize I miss the promise of him. What I thought married life would be. Who I thought I'd be as a wife. What I thought it would be like to finally set down roots. Be a family. Have a home of my own. A home I could stay in for longer than eighteen months.

I pull out my phone and begin sending a text to Allison. And then I delete it. How do I even . . . Do I just say it? Do I even know what there is to say besides "Hey, screw the yearlong Time-Out, I just made out with a complete stranger in the hotel elevator. P.S.: I love the movie *Ladyhawke*. LOL." Jesus. I exit out of the texting screen and tuck my phone back into my purse.

Somewhere along the line—probably in the septic tank that was my adolescence—I stopped believing I was the hero of my own story. Or that my story was worthy of a hero at all. I settled because that's all I thought I deserved. The Lincoln Mallorys of the world became those I dabbled with in the same way I learned not to splurge on sweets or any of the finer things. Moderation in everything and when I did allow myself to indulge—whether on a big meal or an expensive piece of clothing—the guilt that set in within seconds made it never worth it in the end. In choosing to be good, cautious, and efficient, I talked myself right out of amazing.

In becoming someone's anyone, I became no one's only one.

But then I think about the chocolate fountain at the Opening Night Bacchanalia. I was hungry so I dipped and ate and reveled in the opulence of it all. I felt no guilt. However, the nausea that followed probably speaks to my inability to moderate my own newly found freedom. About a lot of things. Hm.

I pull Lincoln's business card from the depths of my purse. Of course all this introspection is based on knowing pretty much zero about Mr. Mallory and is absolutely because I can't think about Audrey and her looming interest in the Lumineux campaign. But that's why this is so jarring. It's not about Lincoln at all. It's about why I deny myself everything in the name of knowing what's best for me. As if I'm not strong enough to handle it if the waters get a bit rough for a change. I've always known I've had problems with trust, but I've never asked the biggest question of all: Do I trust myself? And why do I need my life to be so very calculable?

"You gonna call him?" Sasha asks, walking up to where I'm sitting.

"I think so," I say, tucking the business card back into my purse.

"I mean, why not, right?" Sasha asks, scanning the now crowded lobby and excusing herself to a pack of ladies on their way to one of the many workshops just down the hall. "We should probably get going." Sasha motions to the crowds of women heading to where all the conference rooms are in the belly of the hotel. I stand and we join the throng.

Signs on easels announcing craft workshops, publisher spotlights, social media how-tos, and author talks stand sentry in front of every door as far as the eye can see. Getting into Helen's one-day workshop was definitely a perk of this ad campaign. Our two spots are highly coveted by the women who are scrambling for something else to do on the first morning of RomanceCon. While Helen is not in charge or connected with RomanceCon in any way, she is certainly this year's biggest draw. Which is exactly why we're here.

Sasha and I settle into a couple of seats in the very back row on the aisle. She and I both pull out our notebooks. There are about thirty women in this smallish conference room. Decanters of water, tea, and coffee are set up in the back along with various nosh—muffins, fresh fruit, etc. . . . I set my notebook on my chair and head to the back for some much-needed tea.

"Mrs. Brubaker would like a word," one of Helen's assistants instructs me as I'm pouring hot water into my paper cup. This assistant is a wiry young man who looks like he spends most of his life pushing his glasses farther up his nose. I nod and finish, finding the lid to the cup and following him out into the hall. I motion to the assistant as Sasha gives me a concerned look. I'm taken into an anteroom just off where we were and am met with an entirely new level of luxury. I imagine this is what people call a green room. Beautiful white couches and fresh flowers line a room anchored by an exquisite Persian rug. Helen Brubaker lounges on a silvery-gray chair over in the corner and motions for me to approach. This is the closest I'll ever come to meeting the queen.

"Anna," Helen says, motioning for me to sit on the couch just next to her.

"Mrs. Brubaker. I'm very much looking forward to your workshop," I say, holding on to the paper cup that is slowly burning my fingerprints off. I quickly scan the side table. No coaster. Dammit. I switch it to my other hand. And back again.

"So, we're thinking breakfast tomorrow morning, is that right?" Helen looks up to her assistant and he nods, tablet in one hand and smartphone in the other.

"That would be great. Thank you so much for taking the time."

"My assistant will give you the details," Helen says.

"Thank you. I look forward to it," I say.

"It's time," the assistant says.

"Thank you, Hector," Helen says to the wiry young man. She stands. I follow.

"A piece of advice, Ms. Wyatt?" Helen says, stopping the herd of Team Brubaker in its tracks. I brace myself. "When something is burning your damn hand, say something." She eyes my tea and then makes eye contact with me.

"Yes, ma'am," I say. Helen waits . . . a cocked eyebrow. "Something is burning my damn hand."

Helen laughs and I am supplied with a fresh cup of tea in a real teacup within seconds.

"Now that wasn't that hard, was it?" Helen asks with another slap on the back—which I am ready for this time and make sure not to spill the hot tea on my damn hand. I follow behind Team Brubaker back into the workshop. The span of, say, twenty feet between the green room and the workshop room all of a sudden feels like a gauntlet. Fans want autographs, their books signed, and pictures of Helen Brubaker or with Helen Brubaker. Her assistants and team control the mob as much as they can, but the distance that took me less than a minute to walk is now going to take Helen Brubaker more than fifteen. I wend my way through the horde and head back into the workshop.

"We've got a meeting," I say, settling back in next to Sasha.

"Are you serious??" Sasha asks.

"Tomorrow morning. Her assistant is supposed to get me the details," I say, finally taking a sip of the tea. This is definitely not the same tea that I got from the workshop.

"Any word from Preeti?" Sasha asks.

"Not yet," I say.

"Okay, well. If nothing else, this Brubaker meeting is a good sign." Sasha is doodling in her notebook: the workshop room, the chairs, the shoulders and heads of the women in attendance.

"That's really good," I say, nodding toward the notebook.

"Oh, thanks. I'm just bored," she says.

"When I'm bored I doodle arrows and stars, so . . ." Sasha laughs and continues doodling. The women she's drawing look like every woman we know. Different sizes, different hairstyles, different ages. Everything that I noticed about the gala last night. And what Sasha has captured gives me another piece of the puzzle.

"What if the woman in our ad was just . . . and I know this is going to come off as revelatory . . . what if she were just normal?" I ask, pointing at the women in her doodle. "Like these women."

"Real," she says.

"Right."

"I like that," she says, looking from me back down to her sketch.

"Of course, the guy has to be phenomenal," I say, knowing how hypocritical that is.

"I'm comfortable with that," Sasha says with a sniff. I laugh and am just about to continue speaking when the door to the workshop room is swung open and Team Brubaker pours into the small space. The hubbub outside infests the quiet workshop room and then is just as quickly silenced when the door is closed by conference volunteers.

Team Brubaker settles itself in the front of the conference room. Helen's smoky laugh fills the room quickly as microphones are tested, papers are straightened, and bottles of water are kitted with straws. As they busy themselves, I set my tea under my chair and pull my phone out of my purse to text Ferdie.

So, I think I met someone. Don't know much about him, but . . . I don't know. I stare at the rambling, everywhere text for a second and add, *I know this is out of nowhere, but as you're well aware I'm starting mid-thought, so . . .* I hit send before I think better of it. I also know that Ferdie won't be up for hours, so I feel safe in just . . . his text swoops back into my screen.

you've been gone a daym.

hahahahahaha

minus m, Ferdie corrects. *why not see where it goes?*

My fingers hover over the keypad. How to begin. My fingers zip and flash over the letters, unleashing the kraken of reasons, when Ferdie's text swoops in.

Stop. Erase whatever screed you just typed.

My fingers pull up from the keypad. Another text from Ferdie swoops in.

Erase it. I'll wait.

I delete everything I just wrote.

Fine, I text in its place.

see where it goes.

He's not . . . I'm not sure . . . I think he might be a player, you know? I get a player vibe from him. And I kind of attacked him in the elevator. I mean . . .

The conference volunteers buzz and move around the room. I'm running out of time. Ferdie's text swoops back in.

you're not attack in the elevator kind of kid.

I know.

you're not you and this might be good, Ferdie texts.

Good for you maybe, I text back.

finding people who fall for your bruce wayne side is easy. finding people who fall for the batman side is hard.

What. Are. You. Talking. About.

Attacking someone in elevator is your batman side. real you. bruce wayne is cool billionaire, you know . . . ordering salad and laughing at his jokes. Fake. Everyone falls for that.

right, I text, feeling my face flush again. Every time.

So, let him in the bat cave a little.

That's not a double entendre is it?

No. A moment. *And gross.* A pause. A terrified, now-that-I've-talked-about-it-with-Ferdie-this-is-real pause. *And now you're overthinking it.*

ahahahahahahah, I text back.

"Welcome to the *Be the Heroine, Find Your Hero* workshop

with the one and only Helen Brubaker!" the moderator announces. The workshop erupts in applause.

Gotta go. Thanks, I text to Ferdie.

no problemo, he texts back. I slide the phone back into my purse and pick up my notebook, which I set under my seat, next to that damn tea.

Helen Brubaker's workshop is nothing short of amazing. It's a roller coaster ride on a clear day with your hands raised high into the air. It's a church revival and you've got the tambourine. It's that first cup of tea in the morning and there's a breeze coming through the kitchen window. She is beyond clever and makes me yearn for a time when women bonded around a kitchen table or a fire instead of just liking one another's photos on social media. My notebook is lousy with notes with not an arrow or star to be seen because there is no time for doodling. Helen ends the session with the bombshell that the publisher made her add the line about "finding your hero" to the title of her book.

"Frankly," Helen says in that raspy voice of hers, "finding your hero doesn't deserve top billing. I'm a huge Nora Ephron fan. That's where this whole idea started. Be the heroine of your life, not the victim." Sasha nudges me and I smile. See, I gesture. See?? "Nora said that and it got me thinking. And then it got me writing. Living passively versus living actively. That's what's at the heart of my book, no matter what the title would have you believe." I hear myself mutter a "yeah" as if I'm intoning an "amen" in church. Living passively versus living actively.

More pieces of the puzzle come together for the Lumineux campaign. How can we make women feel powerful enough so they don't just read the book? How can Lumineux embolden women to become the heroines of their own stories in real life? Can it even do that? Can I?

And on that note:

The Pirate Booty Ball.

7

I'm standing, once more, on the fringes of the party, holding yet another club soda with lime. Preeti Dayal, the Lumineux executive, stands next to me. She's said maybe two words since she arrived earlier this afternoon. I've been trying not to loom. I don't think it's working. Sasha is on the dance floor with Helen Brubaker. I'm still on a high from the workshop and am on the verge of doing something very stupid with Lincoln Mallory after this party ends.

"Did you know that eighty-five percent of people who buy books are women?" Preeti says, scanning the room. Tonight, the cover models are swarthy rogues. Ryder Grant, last year's Mr. RomanceCon, is chatting up Sasha now that she's stopped dancing in the safety of Team Brubaker.

"Not sure of the number, but that sounds about right," I say.

"As true as any of those statistics are," Preeti says.

"Well, whatever the number, the gist is that a lot of women buy books," I say.

"And most of those women are buying romance novels," she says.

"That's definitely true," I say. The women here are dressed up in their eye-patched, parrots-on-shoulders best. One of the cover models approaches Preeti and me. I think this one's called Josh. With pitch-black hair and piercing blue eyes, he's not as gym-fit as the others; he's more lumberjack-fit. Like he could actually lift something besides a dumbbell. Unlike Blaise, who is just wearing a tiny pair of red-and-white-striped short shorts with a gold codpiece (?!), Josh is wearing—

"You're the Dread Pirate Roberts," I say, smiling up at him.

"It's my daughter's favorite movie," he says with a shrug. "I kind of had to."

"It's fine if you want to make up a daughter and not admit that *The Princess Bride* is your favorite movie," I say. Josh and Preeti both laugh. "Josh, right? This is Preeti Dayal; she's the executive in charge of the Lumineux campaign."

"Nice to meet you," Josh says, clearly a bit taken off guard by Preeti's position and what she could do for his career. I can see him getting flustered, and I'm relieved when a couple of fans politely ask if they can take their picture with him. "Excuse me. It was a pleasure." Josh shakes our hands once more and gets absorbed back onto the dance floor.

"It's like he's not even real," Preeti says, taking a large gulp of her soda.

"I know," I say.

"Why am I surprised that he has a daughter?" Preeti confesses.

"No, I was, too. I think I imagine them in their little Ken

Doll boxes, and they're only taken out to go back and forth from the cologne store to the gym or something," I say.

"Standing in front of whatever fan they can find on the way," Preeti says, laughing.

"Clothes being ripped from their oiled-up bodies," I add.

"Leaving a wake of orgasming women behind them," Preeti says. I throw my head back and laugh.

"Secret babies abound," I say. Preeti laughs, barely able to catch her breath. We stand there laughing for several minutes, just enjoying each other's company. We watch as the dance floor fills up with women.

"God, I haven't danced in years," Preeti says.

"Maybe at a wedding a few years ago," I say, trying to sort through my memories of the last time I danced. Sad. Preeti and I are quiet. "Shall we?" I say, only realizing a bit later that those were Lincoln's exact words.

"When in Rome," Preeti says.

"That was actually last night, but . . . ," I say, smiling.

"Why not, right?" Preeti and I set our drinks on the table and walk out onto the dance floor, where Sasha has finally disentangled herself from Ryder.

"Hey!!" she says, raising her hands into the air. "Oh my God!! I can't believe you're out here!" she yells over the thumping music. The colorful strobe lights swoosh and whip around the dance floor. Everyone is hooting and hollering to the beat. Helen Brubaker shimmies her way back over to our little corner, her two assistants behind her.

"Well, well, well. Look who decided to start having some fun," Helen says, looking from Preeti to me. We both laugh and nod like the party poopers we are.

It starts with some embarrassing rhythmic swaying. Maybe some shoulders. Maybe a foot shuffle here and there. Then there's some premier dancing face and a flurry of very incisive pointing. There are squeals of joy when that one song I haven't heard in forever bumps on. And then I whip out the lasso. Maybe a little sprinkler. And now the hips are in action. The head is down and I'm feeling the beat and the smile can't be wiped from my face. Preeti's blazer is now a scarf around her neck and Sasha has backed up into Helen, who's thrown her head back and is laughing.

I haven't had this much fun in years.

By the time we catch our breath, I'm sweaty from dancing and my face hurts from laughing.

Sasha, Preeti, and I are in line at the bar for something that will whet our whistles.

"I'm starting to see what all the fuss is about," I say.

"I told you," Sasha says. Helen sidles up beside us. Sasha attempts to hide her absolute glee.

"You know, I'm not much of a romance novel reader, either," Preeti says in hushed tones. "And I don't mean to bring the party down, but it was when my mom was going through her chemo that I started even noticing them as something other than . . . well, other than unimportant. They were the only thing she read."

"I'm so sorry," I say.

"May I ask . . ." Helen trails off.

"She's in remission now and she hasn't stopped reading those damn books. She said they made her happy and anything that can manage that during those circumstances? Well . . . needless to say, I stopped making fun of them." Preeti gets a little choked up as she ends her thought more abruptly than she expected. Helen smiles, passing her a tissue. We get to the front of the line and order our drinks, thankful for the distraction. "It's why I think I was more open to your pitch, if that isn't getting too personal."

"No, it's what happens. Why we're on the right track with this campaign. It demands that each woman who comes in contact with it gets personal," I say, loving the turn this conversation has taken. If Preeti makes this campaign personal to her, she will champion it to the higher-ups at Quincy. This is a good sign. Helen tells us she'll see us tomorrow morning and vanishes out of the Booty Ball.

"Well, I just love them," Sasha says, shrugging. We gulp down our drinks and spend the next few minutes talking about how great Helen's workshop was, taking in the general splendor, and trying to forget how Hector the Bespectacled Assistant's dancing was oddly arousing. "Well, I'd better be heading back to the hotel. We've got a big day tomorrow," Preeti says, setting her empty mineral water down onto one of the passing trays. I check my watch. It's way past nine P.M. I can't believe the time. My stomach drops as I remember Lincoln and his invitation for a post–Booty Ball field trip.

"Where are you staying?" I ask as coyly as I can.

"The Biltmore," Preeti says.

"Oh really? Wow, us too," I say.

"Shall we caravan back then?" Preeti asks, fishing her valet ticket out of her purse.

"Sure," I say, giving Sasha a wink as we walk out of the still-hopping Pirate Booty Ball. Sasha and I follow Preeti's rental car through the streets of Phoenix.

"Ryder Grant slipped me his hotel room key," Sasha says, pushing the air-conditioning vent toward her.

"Of course he did," I say, slowing down behind Preeti at a red light.

"I don't want our guy to be someone who does that," she says.

"Our guy?"

"Our Lumineux spokesman. I don't want him to play this hero and then slip women he barely knows his hotel room key."

"Is this about our guy or your guy?" I ask, ever so carefully.

"What? It's about Lumineux. This is . . ." She trails off. "Not about Lumineux at all." She heaves a long, weary sigh. "All of this stuff . . . it's screwing me up. That workshop, all this talk about being your own heroine. Do you know how much I would have given to have a guy like Ryder Grant want me? I mean, wasn't I just saying that he was hot a few days ago?"

"You were," I say.

"I'm so crazy," she says.

"You know who's not crazy?"

"Who?"

"People who think they're crazy." Sasha allows a small smile and I can tell she doesn't believe me. "I don't know . . . I think we just need to be kind to ourselves," I say. "Clearly we've fallen into an alternate universe where up is down and . . ."

"I'm saying no to Ryder Grant," Sasha adds, pulling his room key from her purse as proof. "And I know that's not even his real name. Ryder Grant. Come on."

"What would happen in the romance novel version of this?" I ask, trying to change tactics.

"Ryder Grant would turn out to be—"

"This isn't about Ryder Grant."

"Right."

"Be the heroine," I say, and then I roll my eyes at my own ridiculousness.

"No, you're right," Sasha says. I don't make her say it. I don't make her map out that turning down Ryder Grant was exactly the moment she started to respect herself. Or at the very least it was a moment of note. But I'm all hopped up on Helen Brubaker workshops, Booty Balls, and field trips with Lincoln, so I want to make it as sweepingly epic as possible and believe a medal is in order because I keep my grand theories to myself . . . for once.

Sasha walks in front of me as we sweat our way into the Biltmore lobby. She tosses Ryder's room key in the bin just outside the hotel. Preeti is waiting inside with her husband, whom she introduces to us. He's lovely, of course. They say their good-byes. We'll see her tomorrow, she says before turning for the elevators. Once she's gone—

"Is it okay if I did that because I don't trust myself? That I would totally cab it over there later on tonight if . . . no, *when* I got lonely?" Sasha says as we walk farther into the lobby. The air-conditioning surrounds us, as does the din from the raucous hotel bar.

"Yes. It's more than okay," I say, reaching out to her and giving her hand a squeeze. She smiles.

"I'm going to go watch bad television and order room service," she says.

"That sounds like a perfect evening, actually," I say. She nods. As she's walking away I pull my phone from my purse. "Sasha?" She turns around. "I'll knock on your door just before seven A.M. tomorrow morning? Apparently we're dining in

Helen Brubaker's suite tomorrow," I say, referring to the just received e-mail from Hector the Bespectacled Dance Machine.

"Oh, sure. Cool," she says.

"Right? Nuh-night," I say.

"You're going to text him, right?" Sasha asks.

"I don't know," I say. Sasha is dumbstruck. "I might just call."

"Oh, thank God," Sasha says.

"Don't stay up too late," I say. She just smiles and manages a
weary wave.

I stand in the lobby, flipping my phone around in my hands.
I pull Lincoln's business card out of my purse. Again. I flip the
card over and dial. My fingers are tingling and this terrified
numbness pings throughout my body, settling in my toes. I swallow. And swallow. Blink my eyes. It's like I'm giving myself errands to run around my body so I won't—

"This is Lincoln Mallory." Vomit.

"Hey, hi. It's Anna. Anna Wyatt from the other night. From
the . . . um . . . from the elevator? And the apple . . . breakfast
time—"

"I'm going to stop you there, love. I know who you are even
without the reminder of apple breakfast time," he says. His voice
is even better than I remember it.

"I apologize for my late call," I say, still not having taken a
breath in now going on nine minutes.

"I assumed you were busy at your Booty Ball." Lincoln Mallory saying *booty* will go down in history as one of my favorite
things in the world.

"You still hungry?" I ask.

"I've already eaten, but I did manage to get something for
dessert."

"And what's that then?"

"It's a surprise," he says. My face flushes. "When your Booty Ball ran long—a sentence I never thought I'd say, quite frankly—I had to strike out on the field trip on my own."

"So you're holding this dessert hostage."

"You make it sound so devious."

I scan the lobby. The hotel bar. The kiss. I close my eyes.

And leap.

"What's your room number?"

"409."

"I'll be right up."

"Cheers," he says.

"But just for the dessert."

"I do like a woman with her priorities in order." Silence. "Anna?"

"I didn't know if you'd hung up," I say.

"I hadn't."

"Right."

"But I will now."

"Sure. Okay," I say. Silence. "Hello?"

"It's never not funny, is it?"

"I mean . . . ," I say, unable to keep from laughing.

"Why don't you walk toward the elevator while I stay on the line," he says.

"Yes. I like multitasking," I say.

"I feel like we're solving a crime together," Lincoln says as I finally get to the bank of elevators and press the call button. Businesspeople with badges around their necks are taking over the entire lobby and hotel bar area. The elevator dings and the doors pull open. I climb inside and press the button for the fourth floor.

"The phone might cut out, though. Elevators are never very . . ." The elevator doors close. "Hello?

"Still here," Lincoln says.

"Oh wow, go Arizona Biltmore."

"They should really put that on their website. Come one, come all—we have excellent elevator reception," he says. I laugh and the elevator slows. And all of a sudden my surroundings come into focus. I step out of the elevator. "Other way." I turn around and there he is. He's leaning out into the hallway from his room. I wave and mouth "hi," still on the phone. I walk toward him. Another blue oxford cloth shirt, but this time there are suspenders involved. And he's in the process of rolling up one of his shirtsleeves, the phone tucked between his shoulder and neck. I swallow. He's barefoot. I stand directly in front of him, my hand now cramping because I'm gripping the phone too tightly. "Can we hang up now?" he asks.

I tilt my head back and just sigh. I push him back into his room and it's a blur. The door slams behind us. The phone is dropped, the purse is dropped, my mind whips back to whether or not I hung up and is this going to be the longest long-distance phone call ever or the shortest? Or . . . And then I'm underneath him on the king-sized bed and I can't get his suspenders off fast enough, which does nothing except pull them down around his shoulders and kind of trap his arms to his body for a few hilarious seconds. A panicked thought about my workhorse nude-colored bra and then the thought is gone. Who cares about that bra—Lincoln sure doesn't. My fingers run through his hair once again and I get lost in his smell—this oaky clean, outdoorsy scent that I didn't even know I missed.

"You're trying to remember if you hung up your mobile, correct?" he asks, his voice breathy. He leans his body on one of his arms and pulls back from me.

"Yes. Goddammit, yes. And maybe a little bit about the dessert," I say, sliding my hand up the side of his body—the blue shirt underneath my fingers. He laughs and gets up. He kneels at the foot of the bed and as I leap up he gives my ass a smack. Which makes me giggle like a teenager. I find both of our phones, various items of clothing hanging off me. "They're both still on!" I hold them up in the air, shutting them both off.

"Well, hurry up and get back over here," he says, untucking his shirt and pulling it off. Which is when I see them. He stands and drops his shirt to the ground, standing in front of me bare-chested. His entire upper body is scarred and mangled, shrapnel wounds and burns clearly from an explosion on his left side. "Afghanistan." He lifts his left arm up and turns to the side. "An IED. Do you know what that is?"

"Of course," I say, holding both of our cell phones. Resigned, he begins to put his hands in his pockets, but before he can I've dropped our phones on the desk and pushed him back onto the bed once more. The relief in his face almost brings me to tears. He flips me over easily and I'm underneath him once again, his smell infusing my everything. "Yes," I whisper once more.

Yes.

I wake up to a slant of light and distant tapping. A slow, blinking awakening gives way to a panicked oh-my-God-what-time-is-it start within milliseconds.

"It's early yet. Not to worry," Lincoln says, sitting in front of his open laptop in nothing but his boxers, holding a steaming cup of tea. I'm in Lincoln's hotel room. Shit shit shit. I'm in Lincoln's hotel room. I fumble around on the bedside table trying to find my phone, but my dried-up contact lens eyes thwart my search. "It's over here. I plugged it into my charger." Lincoln sets his tea down, unplugs my phone, and walks it over to me. I thank him, all the while trying to hide my early-morning crustiness: mood, breath, everything. He sits on the side of the bed, and the quiet of a still sleeping hotel surrounds us. Insulates us.

"I'm not quite awake yet," I say, looking at the time: 5:43 A.M. I have to be in Helen Brubaker's suite by seven A.M. Flashes of last night besiege me in swirls and waves and my body reacts— flushing, tingling, and immediately feeling embarrassed. Who was I last night? Even now, as I hitch myself up in bed, my hand effortlessly rests on Lincoln's hip, a few fingers on fabric and a few on his now goose-pimpling skin. The same skin that's burned and scarred by a history I have yet to ask about.

I think about leaving his hotel room and I die a little, but at the same time there's the comfort of a reunion with what's familiar about myself. Because within these walls, around this man, I am unrecognizable. No thought. Just want. Lincoln leans down and is just about to kiss me.

"You've already brushed your teeth," I say, sitting up in bed.

"I have," he says. Closer. Closer.

"So, that's officially cheating," I say, my fingers idly threading through his morning tangle of hair.

"How is that—"

"You're all minty and I'm still the little stinky engine that could. Pass," I say, landing a kiss on his neck before getting out of bed. The warm bed. His warm bed. He stops me, taking my hand in his. It takes me about two seconds to realize that I am standing there completely naked. I remember when I was little some of the neighborhood kids dared me to go on the high dive. Eager to make friends, I obliged. I climbed the ladder, terrified, but I was so distracted with the newness of it all that I walked the length of the platform, reached my arms over my head, latched my thumbs together, and dove right off the end headfirst without thinking. They hadn't dared me to dive, just jump. I remember swimming up to the surface of the water, not realizing what I'd done. Why I dove. It was just . . . instinctual.

Up until this moment, I had yet to dive off another platform.

"Not fair," he says, his eyes licking over every inch of me. And then it's just me and this feeling again. I'm not my body or my résumé or the new kid in school—I'm just me. And it feels like uncontrollable falling.

"When I emerge from that bathroom, I want to know what you've done with that dessert you promised. And?" Lincoln stands. "It better not be metaphorical for . . ." I scan his body and then back to his eyes. "You know." I punctuate with an arched eyebrow.

"I am not a man who trifles with the clarity of what dessert means," he says, then takes a sip of his tea.

"Good. Good," I say.

I grab my purse, underwear, and bra from the floor and go into the bathroom, closing the door behind me. I don't turn on the light. Not yet. There is a night-light on the far wall, and that's about the level of illumination I can take right now. I put on my bra but then realize I've grabbed a pair of already-worn underwear and quickly shove it into my purse, hoping Lincoln doesn't think I'm a dirty underwear–wearer. I find a gray

T-shirt of his on the bathroom counter, smell it—sighhhhh—and put that on instead. I dig through my purse for something, anything to help . . . help with all this.

"Lumineux should come up with some kind of morning-after survival kit is what they should do. Just Be . . . Presentable," I say, finding an almost empty package of tissues in the bottom of my purse, which I use to wipe away last night's mascara. I also find a single peanut M&M, which I pop in my mouth. "Kind of hypocritical, though . . . Be you, only better." I scan Lincoln's toiletries.

"Who are you talking to in there?" he asks from outside the bathroom door.

"Myself," I say, as if that's completely normal and I'm not absolutely mortified right now.

"Ah," he says, and I hear him walk away. I am clearly rusty at this whole dating game. I take a little of his toothpaste and use my finger to give my teeth a cursory brush.

Is this bathroom getting smaller? I finally look at myself in the mirror, illuminated by the night-light in this ever-shrinking yet noise-amplifying bathroom. I look . . . different. I lean closer. I feel lighter, but . . . that uncontrollable falling feeling is still here. I shut the water off and walk back out into the hotel room.

"It's sweet potato pie," Lincoln says, motioning to the Styrofoam takeaway container with two forks sticking out of it. I quicken my pace. "It's from Mrs. White's Golden Rule Cafe. I found it . . ." Lincoln trails off, thinking. "Last year? Year before? I don't know. I needed to find something in Phoenix besides golf and room service." He motions for me to try the pie. "Nice shirt." He hands me a cup of tea and I take a careful sip.

"Thank you. The whole walking-around-naked thing was getting a bit . . ." I make a face.

"For you maybe."

"No one's stopping you from stripping down," I say. He smiles. "Now . . ." I take a bite of the pie. "Oh my God."

"I know," Lincoln says, taking a bite.

"Mrs. White is a genius," I say. We stand there, hovering over the pie, taking orgasmic bites for untold minutes. The morning haze seeps in through the gauzy curtains. We finish the pie too soon and it takes everything I have not to lick the takeaway container it came in.

"And what does the day hold for you, Ms. Wyatt?" Lincoln asks, sitting back down on the side of the bed.

"We're meeting Helen Brubaker at seven A.M. at the conference hotel. She's the woman who wrote that book I was reading at the bar," I say, finding my skirt and sliding it on. Lincoln motions for me to turn around and I oblige. He zips me up, tapping the top of the zipper when he's done. I turn back around, a little uncomfortable that I'll apparently be breakfasting with Helen Brubaker whilst ever-so-classily going commando. "That *Be the Heroine* book?"

"Sure," he says.

"You know it?"

"Yes, of course," he says, not elaborating as much as I'd like. I take another sip of tea.

"So, we thought, how can we tap into that audience for the Lumineux campaign? There was something about that book—*is* something about that book—that women are really connecting with and we came up with—"

"If I may?" Lincoln asks, standing. "It's quite urgent."

"Sure," I say, pausing.

"You've brushed your teeth, you've had pie . . . ," he says, stepping closer.

"Yes," I say, staying put.

"No longer the—how did you put it—the stinky—"

"Little stinky engine that could," I finish.

"The stinky engine that could," he repeats. I smile just as Lincoln leans in and kisses me. The smile on my face is at once both spontaneous and inconvenient, as it precludes me from really diving into him. And yet I can't stop smiling. He pulls away from me with a smile of his own, tucking one of surely a thousand rogue hairs gently behind my ear. "Please. Continue." Lincoln picks up his tea and sits back down on the side of the bed.

"The book is empowering women to be the heroines of their own stories." I take his gray T-shirt off, find my shirt flung over the back of a chair, and begin to button it up.

"But it's to find a hero, though, right? So is *empowering* the right word?"

"I know, I thought the same thing."

"Seems like bollocks to me."

"I know. That part of it is bollocks."

"Do you even know what *bollocks* means?"

"It's not good, right?"

"No, it's not good."

"But Helen—"

"We're calling her 'Helen' now?" Lincoln asks.

"Ha, no . . . I mean, I would never to her face. Mrs. Brubaker said that she didn't even want the hero part in the title. That the publisher made her do that," I say, becoming newly defensive. "I think the book could have just as easily been a self-help book rather than a dating guide." I pick my cup of tea back up and settle in next to him on the bed.

"Still based on romance novels, though?"

"Yeah, I know," I say, uncomfortable with being anything but clinical about the books—and their content—even now.

"I don't have a problem with romance novels."

"This coming from the man who went to . . ."

"Oh, every posh school you've ever heard of."

"Eton?"

"No, the other one."

"Did you, Lincoln Mallory, wear a boater hat?"

"They're officially called Harrow Hats, thank you very much. And yes, I did. When forced. Which is how I know that the pompous wankers who look down on romance novels and the women who read them are actually full of shite. You know, having been one myself," he says.

"Been. In the past tense," I say.

"Ah yes, on top of being in Alcoholics Anonymous, I'm also a proud member of Wankers Anonymous." I can see him realize what he's said. It's slipped out and he can only avert his eyes. "So, to recap: you've just shagged a posh, ex–boater-hat-wearing git who was happily off his face for far too many years after being blown up overseas."

"Try finding a meeting for that," I say, and Lincoln throws his head back and laughs. "Although I think you'd find a very different kind of meeting if you actually did attend Wankers Anonymous. Because I do know what *that* is." Lincoln laughs again. "Anyway, Helen said she'd meet with us. Which is really great." I check the clock. It's 6:15 now. Lincoln also checks the clock and I can see him deflate just a bit.

"And how does she fit into this whole thing?"

"I don't know yet."

"Does she have to fit in?"

"I would hope so."

"But it's the book that's the inspiration, right?"

"Right. The Just Be campaign that we're pitching is so women can connect to that empowerment."

"Just be. That's good. That's really good."

"Thanks. Speaking of . . ." The last thing I want to do is leave this room. There's this rumbling fear that I won't be able to have this again or something. That whatever we have is fleeting and of its moment. And when I leave . . . the moment will have passed. But it's not every day that Helen Brubaker has you over for breakfast. "I should be going. It's another long day with another ridiculous themed party tonight." I rest my hand on his thigh and lean in close to him.

"A few parameters on these last few moments, if I may?"

"Sure," I say, flustered.

"One. I'm going to want to finish anything you start." He eyes my hand on his thigh. A crooked smile and his eyes are once again fixed on mine. "Two. I would love to see you again after your . . ." He trails off.

"Mermaid Bash."

"Naturally."

"That'd be nice."

"And three. This isn't farewell."

"No," I say, and I can hear the relief in my voice. Like out in the world and not just inside my own head.

"No," he says. I slide my hand to his back and pull him into me. He lets me. I'm beginning to get used to him. His body. His kiss. His smell. Something about this terrifies me. Why wouldn't it? We're in this weird alternate universe at some random hotel in Phoenix with none of our usual responsibilities or stresses or any dishes to do or any reality for that matter. And as I get lost in him once more, the time ticking away, I worry about what the real world will do to us. Or more aptly, the version of me in the real world. What will I think of all this come check-out time?

What will he?

8

"Mrs. Brubaker is on a phone interview right now. If you would."
Hector leads us into another room in Helen's lavish hotel suite.
The room is fitted out with urns filled with coffee and hot water,
fresh flowers, and an entire breakfast spread. We are obviously
one of several meetings Helen has this morning.

"Thank you," I say, entering the room and eyeing the Fortnum and Mason loose-leaf teas still in those beautiful Georgian
blue tins. Hector closes the door behind us.

"Are you kidding me with this?" Sasha loudly whispers, pulling her phone out of her purse and taking several pictures of
herself with the elaborate spread.

"Are you taking a picture with a platter of strawberries right
now?" I ask, cringing as she snaps the photo. "Why don't I just
take a picture of you?"

"No, I got it," Sasha says, now in front of the beautiful spray
of fresh peonies in the middle of the table. Pursed lips, raised
eyebrows, doe eyes, aaaand snap. Sasha looks at the picture, gri-
maces, and deletes it.

"I can't with the selfies," I say, making myself a much-needed cup of tea. "Don't post those anywhere. I know that's asking the world of you. Not to document one second of your life for your thousands of friends." I put air quotes around the word *friends*.

"For someone who didn't come back to her room last night, you should be in a much better mood," Sasha says, sliding her phone back into her purse.

"How did y—"

"I'm right across the hall," Sasha says, pouring herself a cup of coffee. She scans the condiments. "No soy? Come on, Brubaker."

I set my tea on the side table, tuck my purse and workbag next to my feet, and finally settle in on the tufted white couch, which is overrun with silk pillows. Sasha settles in next to me, knowing to leave the floral wingback chair for Helen when she arrives. I am trying to ignore Sasha. Because you *would* think someone who didn't come back to her hotel room last night would be in a better mood, and yet here I am. Cranky and picking on a poor twentysomething who has the audacity to show how excited she is about something.

"So you're really not going to dish?" Sasha asks, now gathering various fruits on a small plate for herself. I sip my tea. Fortnum and Mason, Royal Blend. A thing of beauty. I inhale its fragrance as I try to gather my thoughts. I am exhausted but amped—my entire body is buzzing. But whereas I thought I'd be scattered and elsewhere—namely in Lincoln Mallory's bed—I am more focused than I've been in months. I feel alive.

"It's just a fling," I say, and the words cut through me, choking in my throat. Another sip of tea.

"You slept with him?? You naughty little hellcat, you," Sasha says, pointing a strawberry at me emphatically.

"Shh!"

"Well, did you?"

"Hellcat? Really?"

"I know, right? I was like . . . did I really just say *hellcat* right now, but . . ." Sasha dissolves into giggles as she picks through her plate of fruit, finally settling on a piece of pineapple. "Don't change the subject."

"I've worked very hard to get to this point in my career, and something like this?"

"It's just a fling. Like you said."

"It can give people a reason to call my professionalism into question," I say.

"Well, they'd have to find out first, right?"

"Right."

A beat.

"Wait, you think I'm going to say something?" Sasha can't help but burst out laughing. "Who would care? That's . . . I actually can't breathe—" Sasha begins choking on her piece of pineapple and takes a long sip of her coffee. "You're the only one who talks to me at that office."

"I . . . what?"

"In order for me to spread any kind of rumors about you, I'd have to have . . . I don't know, made friends first? And seeing as how you're my only friend . . ." Sasha sips her coffee again. What was once funny has become a bit melancholy for her. "The women hate me and the men just want to . . . well, you know." She can't look at me. We are silent. "P.S.? I would never say anything. I'm not like that."

I look up at her. She finally makes eye contact with me. I nod. She smiles. And I start talking.

"I guess I just . . . I'm not a fling kind of person," I say.

"It sounds kind of amazing," Sasha says with a sigh. "Strait-laced businesswoman lets her passion get the best of her for a night of wild abandon with a hot British stranger." Sasha gestures broadly as if she's seeing the romantic comedy poster now. "But is it more than she bargained for as—"

"We're not in a romance novel. As much as—"

"As much as it sounds like you are?"

"Yeah, but here's what I know. All of those romance novels—and granted, I've only read a handful—all of the trials and tribulations the couple goes through are worth it in the end, because we're promised that they're going to live happily ever after. Right?"

"Right."

"But that's not how real life works. I've been married. I walked down the aisle with my dad in his dress blues to a man who wept when he saw me in my wedding gown. What they don't tell you is that even with that . . . you can still just fall out of love."

"But he wasn't your guy."

"What?"

"That first guy?"

"Patrick."

"Patrick? He's not The One."

"There's no such thing as The One."

"No, I know. I'm not delusional. I think there are several Ones. It's kind of based on how much you want to better yourself or how much you love yourself. Like stops on a train? If you keep going, your Ones get better. You just got off at the wrong stop with Patrick."

"So, this hot British stranger? This is what? The guy that I send to the store for tampons a year from now? I mean, because *that*? Is true love," I say.

"Yes! Exactly. Things have to start somewhere. It might as well be in a hotel in Phoenix," Sasha says, eating another strawberry.

"I don't know. You know, I'm too embarrassed to even tell my friends back home about him?"

"Why? It's wonderful," Sasha says. Her use of the word *wonderful* makes me kind of love her in that moment.

"I don't know. It feels . . . I told my brother about it—"

"Ferdie?"

"Yeah. He said that I had to . . . wait, let me get this right. That everyone falls for the Bruce Wayne version of us, but what we want are the people who love the Batman side."

"Wow."

"I know. And I knew I was doing that—you know, playing a part—with the men I was dating. Even with Patrick to a point. But I never knew how much I did that with my friends. I don't think even they see the Batman side of me," I say, unable to look at Sasha.

"Yeah, I get that."

Hector pokes his head in and tells us it'll be another ten minutes and to get comfortable.

"It just got me thinking." I pause. A sip of tea. Sasha waits. "I was over at a friend's house—a dear friend, I might add—for this nerdy book club that we do. We're reading Shakespeare in order. I've known Michael forever. And his wife, Allison, for going on . . . what is it, six years? She's lovely. They're both lovely," I say. I take another sip of my tea as Sasha offers me a mini-muffin. I take it and thank her. She takes a croissant for herself and proceeds to pick at its buttery layers. "I had to go to the bathroom, if you know what I mean. Like *go* to the bathroom. I'd started putting flax oil into my morning smoothies . . . it was a whole thing." Sasha's eyes get wide. "I ask to use the bathroom, they say yes—of course—and I am all over the place. A wreck. I do my business and it flushes—because I'd convinced myself it wouldn't, even though there was never a problem with the plumbing before. I wash my hands, trying to waft the smell of the soap around the bathroom. There's this tiny window, and I try to open it—but never noticed before that the window was levered. So, all of Allison's perfumes—which were lined up neatly on the sill—go tumbling onto the marble counter. And I get the 'Are you okay?' from just outside the bathroom. I yelp out 'Yes!' And now I'm panicking. I use some of Allison's lotion to try to, you know, offer another option in the scent column. I finally leave the bathroom and join them in the living room. I sit down. And Allison asks Michael if he could change that lightbulb she was talking about earlier."

"No."

"Where's the lightbulb, he asks."

"No."

"In the bathroom."

"Noooo."

"And they both stream back into the bathroom and are back there for what feels like *hours* as I just sit all alone on their couch with my little glass of bubble water and . . . my hands are shaking, my face is all hot, and my heart rate is through the roof. They come out and never say a word." I take a sip of my tea and Sasha finishes the croissant that she nervously ate during the telling of my story.

"I would have died."

"I know, but it's things like that that let me know I'm not only guarded around the men I'm dating, it's everyone," I say.

"No, I'm the same," Sasha says. We are quiet. Haunted.

"And this is after a year on Time-Out."

"Time-Out?"

"Oh, that's right. You don't know about that." I fill Sasha in on the 'Thunder Road' story, the yearlong Time-Out. She plows through another croissant during the telling of it.

"So before Hot British Stranger, you hadn't had sex in a year?" Sasha asks.

"It'd been longer than that," I confess.

"What . . . wait . . . wh—" The door to the room pulls open just as Sasha begins to speak. Helen Brubaker strides in with a cup of coffee from Starbucks and Team Brubaker at her heels.

"So, let's talk turkey, girls," Helen says, settling into the large, floral wingback chair.

"You have thirty minutes until your prizewinners," Hector says, tablets and phones and headsets abounding.

"Is this for the photo op or . . ."

"No, you're assisting two aspiring romance novelists with their pitches," he says.

"Ah, sure. Okay. Give me a five-minute warning," Helen says, taking a sip of her coffee. A coffee which, I notice, has the word *soy* written on the side of it. Sasha's eyes narrow. Hector closes the door behind him and we are alone with Helen.

"Thank you for making time for us this morning," I say, setting my tea on the large coffee table.

"You're welcome," Helen says. A beat. And then . . .

"Your book is exactly what women need right now. What I

need right now. The audacious idea that we should all be the heroes of our own stories? And the boldness to suggest we should put ourselves first," I say, coming forward on the couch just enough.

"Thank you," Helen says. This is a different version of Helen Brubaker. And it's terrifying. This is the businesswoman.

"It's inspired us. Professionally. Personally—"

"But don't you think all this is below you, Ms. Wyatt?" Helen asks.

"I absolutely did—"

"Like yesterday," Helen interrupts. "Do you know how many times I've defended the books I write to people like you? Explained that it's actually a fallacy that anyone could write a romance novel if they just lowered themselves for the weekend it'd take them to spit one out? That the relationships and people you read about in the books that are deemed 'important' are actually the same ones that I write about? The same ones my readers have and find within the pages of my books?"

"I know." Helen is legitimately pissed. As she should be. I all but insinuated her entire life's work was garbage. She winds through example after example and I realize that we'll be lucky if we get our allotted thirty minutes. This entire meeting is slipping through my fingers, and if I don't do something our time here at RomanceCon could be cut short, because if Helen Brubaker doesn't like you, no one does. I want people to remember my name, but not for this reason. I look up at Helen with the realization of what I have to do. Of course, she misinterprets it.

"It's the look of surprise when there's something truly meaningful found in the pages of a romance novel that gets me every time. That we're actually intelligent women and not drooling, wanton cat ladies."

"Cookie-cutter. That's what I hate," Sasha adds, trying to salvage the meeting.

"Cookie-cutter. Formulaic is one of my personal favorites. Of course, when a man writes about love and relationships it's worthy of a ticker tape parade or a Pulitzer," Helen says, sipping her coffee. "But when we do it it's unrealistic. Because I don't know about you, but I know countless pretty—but don't know it, of course—oversexed, yet virginal, college students who not only lust after their English professors but will get in line behind several other women for the honor of doing so."

"A miserable ending with unlikable characters doesn't make you deep," Sasha adds, edging closer to me. Nudging me to say something. Do something. My face feels hot. I know what I have to do.

"Amen," Helen says.

"You want to truly understand a culture? Just record what they read when they think no one is looking," Sasha says.

"Oh, that's good. I'm going to use that one," Helen says, tapping the thought into her phone.

"Thanks," Sasha says. They both turn to me.

The room falls silent.

"I was wrong," I say, flustered but not thrown.

"Damn right you were," Helen says.

Silence.

"So what happened?" Helen asks. A breath. And then the truth. Or at least whatever sliver of the truth I'm starting to understand.

"For me, it was easier experiencing pleasure secondhand," I say.

"How do you mean?" Helen asks.

"I wanted people to know I was reading the right books and listening to the right music . . . that I was up on what was being talked about by the right people. That brought me pleasure." Silence. A beat. "That I was better than the unwashed masses."

"There it is," Helen says.

"Right. The fact that I intimidated people made me happy," I say. Helen nods. "I was caught up in displaying my accomplishments because I'd come from such humble beginnings. It was like porn for me if I told you about some book and you'd never heard of it or even better, couldn't get through it because it was too hard. Ahhhh. I get all hot and bothered just thinking about it." Helen laughs.

"I appreciate your candor, Ms. Wyatt," Helen finally allows. The entire energy in the room is shifting. All I have to do is keep talking. Keep plumbing the depths. Keep telling the truth of the long-buried hidden shame of that Judy Blume book and being "found out."

"And it was safer. I didn't actually enjoy most of those books. I certainly wasn't undone by them. Except *Jane Eyre*. I could read that book every day until I die and never grow tired of it," I say, swooning.

"Oh, me too," Helen says.

"Love that book," Sasha says.

"So pleasure was always . . . at a distance." I look up at Helen and she's listening. Surprised. Her whole demeanor has changed. As she and Sasha splinter off into a side conversation, I can't help but think about last night with Lincoln. How the pleasure I felt at times was almost painful, it was so desperate and overwhelming. Close. How I almost shut it down time after time because I was on the edge. I think about how I felt after I pitched the Just Be campaign to Preeti that first day. I didn't want to get my hopes up. I didn't want to get my heart broken by being told no.

Feeling joy and happiness and pleasure secondhand meant the loss I'd inevitably feel when they were gone would be secondhand, as well. For me, it was about playing the odds or not playing the odds. Continuing to let Lincoln get as close as he did, allowing myself to tumble over the cliff happily with him time after time after time means I'll feel the loss of him firsthand. I want to feel that freedom, but . . .

I chose Patrick even knowing that—in Sasha's words—he wasn't The One. But he was the guy everyone wanted. And that brought me pleasure. With Patrick there was no edge. There were no cliffs. And that's what got me off . . . because he certainly never did.

I decided I wanted the car account because that's what everyone else wanted. I was told it was important. It would legitimize me in a world of advanced degrees and dynasties. Have I made it, you'd ask? And all I'd have to do is trot out that car account and you wouldn't even have to ask what college I went to or how many ladies products I'd slung in my day. But something is changing. I don't want the car account anymore. I want Lumineux. I want Lumineux because it's important to me. Whether everyone thinks so or not.

"Ms. Wyatt?" Helen asks as I realize I've fallen into quite the reverie.

"I used to go on these road trips by myself and make these elaborate playlists and I'd sneak these songs on there that I'd argue were for fun, you know? They were on my 'workout mix,' if you know what I mean." Helen and Sasha both nod, laughing. "But then that'd be the song that I'd turn up the loudest. It was the song that made me the happiest out on that open road. But I'd only allow myself one of them, even with no one else around. Who does that?"

"Women do, honey," Helen says. "We tell ourselves it's because it makes it more special, but that's not it at all."

"At all," I repeat.

"What do you think would happen if you made a whole playlist—is that what you call it? A playlist?"

"Yes," I say.

"A whole playlist of every song that—" Helen searches for the word.

"That's a guilty pleasure?" I offer.

"See, now why does pleasure have to be guilty?" Helen asks.

"I don't know," I say, honestly dumbstruck by her question.

"I don't think that it does, Ms. Wyatt. What would happen if you made an entire playlist with just songs that made you move and dance and smile?"

"My fear?"

"Yes."

"That I'd get stupid," I say honestly.

"No way," Helen says.

"I'm sorry?"

"There's no way. It's not about that at all," she says.

I'm quiet. Helen and Sasha wait.

"That people wouldn't like me," I say finally.

"That they wouldn't take you seriously, you mean."

"Right. That I wouldn't matter. I've tried to play one of these songs to certain groups of people—"

"Friends of yours?" Helen asks.

"In a sense. I got flak for it. My stock goes down, if you will," I say. "Well, went down. I've been cleaning house of a lot of friends as of late."

"Sounds like they weren't really friends to begin with," Helen says.

"I agree, but sadly it doesn't mean that those voices aren't still pinging around in my head," I say, thinking about how I haven't even told Allison and Michael about what happened with Lincoln yet.

"I spent far too long trying to be perfect and I hardly recognized myself," Helen says.

"I think what your book is really about—for me, anyway—is that it's okay to show people all of you. Not only okay—but empowering. The root of where our story is. Our real story, anyway. The imperfect, the intense, what you think is ugly is actually what will set you free. What makes you the hero people will root for. You've given permission to women—all women—to be . . . human."

"Thank you," Helen says.

"Broken people make the best heroes," I say.

"They do indeed," Helen says.

"The Just Be campaign will celebrate that. Real women in real situations without the noose of the impossible standards advertising usually strangles women with. The perfect house, the joy of cleanliness, the well-behaved kids, all the while keeping impossibly thin, of course," I say. Sasha passes over some of her beautiful artwork.

"Wow," Helen says. "May I?" I hand her the stack of Sasha's sketches. She's done even more since the pitch, using the inspiration of the women at Helen's workshop. "These are beautiful."

"Thanks," Sasha says, unable to hide her absolute delight in the compliment.

"And how do romance novels fit into all of this?" Helen hands back the sketches. "Thank you for these. You have real talent."

"Thank you," Sasha says again. I can't help but smile. She is almost bursting.

"If you look at Sasha's drawings, they are an homage to the romance novel tropes . . . with a twist. We're here for Mr. RomanceCon and I think that will add a bit of humor to the campaign, which it needs."

"I agree," Helen says.

"But it's the sweeping epicness that romance novels capture that we want to infuse into the Just Be campaign. The shower is an oddly sacred place for women. It's usually one of the only places we get any peace and quiet. And so are romance novels. They are an escape. And not in a bad way. In the best way possible." I think of Preeti's mom and find myself getting oddly emotional. "It's hard being a woman. Especially being everyone else's idea of what a woman should be. What we want is to make it okay to just be you. All of you. And to know that that's not only good enough; it's downright heroic."

"Well hot damn, Ms. Wyatt, you are good at your job. I'm about to run out right now and buy stock in whatever it is you're selling," Helen says, leaning back in her chair. "I had every intention of shutting this meeting down after I gave you the business for calling romance novels crap."

"I know."

"I had my speech all set up and now . . . here we are." I wait. "But I still don't see how I can help," Helen says.

"You've started this revolution, Mrs. Brubaker. We just want to be a part of it," I say. Lincoln's words weave themselves into the tight tapestry in my mind. His words. My words. "We just want your stamp of approval."

"My endorsement, you mean," Helen says, back in businesswoman mode. "Oh, well now I just feel—"

I cut in, "No. What I want is something much more valuable."

"Oh?"

"I want your counsel."

"My counsel?"

"Mrs. Brubaker—"

"Helen, please. Jesus."

"Helen, what I'm . . . what *we're* looking for is a mentor." Helen sits back in her chair again.

"Hm. I have to be straight with you, kiddo, I did not see that coming."

"Me either," I say, laughing. Sasha nervously laughs, inching closer to me on the couch.

Helen is quiet. Nodding. Her eyes flick between Sasha and me, Sasha's sketches and my entire Just Be proposal laid out before her. She takes a sip of her coffee.

"I need to think about your proposition, Ms. Wyatt."

"Anna. Please," I say.

"Anna. Your talent—both of your talent—is undeniable. If Lumineux doesn't go with this campaign they're moronic. I'm confident they'll choose you, in the end. But, you're right, what you're asking for is far more valuable than my endorsement—it's my time and energy you want. And I'm old enough to know that those are the most valuable commodities in the marketplace."

"I know," I say. Helen sets her coffee down on the table and stands. We gather our things and stand, following her lead.

"This isn't a no. I'll give you an answer before the conference is over on Sunday." Helen extends her hand to me and I take it. "You're an impressive woman, Ms. Wyatt."

"Thank you. And so are you," I say.

"Oh, I know. After far too many years, I'm finally quite in touch with just how impressive I am," Helen says, giving me a quick wink, and I can't help but smile.

"Ms. Merchant," Helen says, now extending her hand to Sasha. Sasha lunges in to take it with a wide smile. "What a talent."

"Thank you, Mrs. Brubaker," Sasha says, her voice bubbling over with excitement.

Helen walks over to the door and opens it up. The din of the outer rooms of her suite hits us immediately. Team Brubaker bustles around the room on phones and computers. They all look up as we appear. The women who are here to run their pitches by Helen stand as soon as she enters the room. They look terrified. One looks like she's about to cry. I know the feeling.

Sasha and I thank Helen again and are quickly spirited out of the hotel room.

"Ummm," Sasha finally says.

"I know," I say.

"Where did all that come from?" Sasha asks as we walk toward the elevators.

"I was losing her," I say, still in a haze. "I had to do some-thing." We push the call button and wait. I pull my cell phone from my purse and scroll through various work e-mails, acting like I'm not looking for some communication from Lincoln.

"Well, it worked . . . kinda. What's with the mentor stuff?" she asks, as the elevator dings open and we step inside.

"There's nothing she can do for us when it comes to the cam-paign. Her endorsement would pull focus from what we're trying to do, which is to establish Lumineux along with *Be the Heroine,* not in the shadow of it. So, having her connected to the campaign would actually do it a disservice," I say.

"Oh . . ."

"I know. I just got that this morning," I say. "It was really bothering me. I couldn't figure out how she'd fit in and then it dawned on me. She doesn't." The elevator dings open and we start walking through the packed lobby toward the valet.

"And the mentor thing?"

"It was worth a shot," I say, digging out the valet ticket from my purse. "I'm kind of in love with her."

"Right?" Sasha slumps down on the bench just outside the hotel as we wait for our rental. "I didn't know any of that stuff," she says.

"I've been thinking about all that this past year. Didn't quite expect that I'd have to unload it in a business meeting at seven o'clock in the morning, but . . ." I trail off, sitting down next to her on the bench.

"Ryder texted me late last night," Sasha says.

"Of course he did. I doubt he's experienced much rejection."

"I didn't text back," she says.

"Wow, that's huge."

"I know, right? I mean, don't get me wrong, I love that he texted. I love that I got to *finally* be the one that let a late-night text just hang there. God . . . I've been on the other end so many—too many—times," Sasha says. The valet brings our car around and we climb in, thankful that the air-conditioning is already on full blast.

"You should really be proud of yourself," I say, speeding toward the Biltmore and my bed and maybe some sleep and a much-needed shower.

"I thought of that book. And what Helen said in her workshop. And maybe it's about being here or whatever? But it was just so clearly the right thing to do. Even though . . . man it would have been fun," Sasha says. I clear my throat. Why am I embarrassed that Sasha knows perfectly well what Lincoln and I got up to last night? "That was your cue." I look over at her as we slow down at a red light. She's smiling. "And if you say you don't kiss and tell I swear . . ." Sasha balls up her little fist and raises it as high as one can in this tiny car. My face flushes bright red just thinking about last night.

"I don't know what to think," I manage, unsure as to why these ten-minute drives to and from the conference hotel have become an unofficial confessional for Sasha and me.

"You don't know what to think? About what?"

"There's the me back in D.C. and then there's whoever this Phoenix person is . . . where you know more about me than friends I've known for decades and I think I'm falling in love with a British gentleman I've just met and I'm unloading my feelings—like deep things that it's taken months in therapy to excavate—in some suite in front of Helen Effing Brubaker while eating a mini-muffin and with no underpants on, for crissakes,"

I say, pounding on the steering wheel. Sasha is about to say something, but I continue. "I feel outside of myself and I know that it's good and I know that my therapist will call this some kind of breakthrough, but right now it just feels like I'm coming apart at the seams."

"You're falling in love with Lincoln?" Sasha downright swoons.

"That's . . . of course that's all you took from that," I say, turning into the Biltmore's long driveway.

"That and you're not wearing any underpants."

"I just feel like I'm coming undone and . . . I'm scared," I say, slowing down behind a white Bentley at the valet of the Biltmore.

"I get that," Sasha says.

"I know you do," I say, trying to offer her a consoling smile. The valet opens my door and Sasha and I trudge into the lobby once more. We fall into a contented silence as we ride the elevator up to our rooms. Sasha looks over at me nervously a few times as we walk down the long hallway, and I act like I don't notice. She slides her key into her door and turns around, about to say something. "I'm so proud of you for the Ryder thing," I say. "That's really huge."

"Thanks," she says. A beat. She wants to say something more, but then just smiles. I open my hotel room door and can barely form a thought, I'm so exhausted.

"Lunch?"

"Sure. I'll knock at around one?" Sasha asks.

"Sounds good," I say.

"Then the meet-and-greet thing?" Sasha asks.

"Oh, that's right. Yes. Okay," I say.

"The title of Mr. RomanceCon depends on our getting to

know these men, Anna," Sasha says, trying to lighten the mood.

"I'm sure it does," I say with a wave. Sasha smiles and my door closes behind me. I begin to shed—purses, workbags, clothes, high heels. I turn on the shower and once it's hot enough, blissfully climb inside. There is something magical about a hotel shower. Maybe it's the water pressure or the promise of not having to clean up after yourself, but I can't remember my shower ever feeling this good.

My mind is blank as I let the hot water pour over me. I am far too exhausted to unpack all the goings-on since I arrived in Phoenix not even forty-eight hours ago. And it's not last night with Lincoln or my emotional download with Helen or my nervous breakdown in the rental confessional with Sasha or even the Lumineux campaign itself.

It's me.

I'm finally changing after whatever this last year was— training montage, Time-Out, hiatus, cleaning house. This is me finally admitting that I have had to change one thing: everything. And that everything changed around me so a life that was once familiar is now . . . completely unrecognizable. I shut the water off. A smile begins to spread across my entire face.

My life is becoming everything I hoped it could be.

As quickly as it came, my smile disappears, and I'm gripped by fear. The quiet surrounds me. Reminds me. Suffocates me.

Such a quiet life. My life, my childhood was so quiet. My mother would go back to her studio and paint and my father was off saving the world in the army. I knew what love was because I could see that they felt it for each other. I'd like to think that I learned not to care, but that would mean I understood what it meant to be loved in the first place.

No, mine was a very progressive freezing over. It just made

sense. We would move every eighteen months, and it wasn't practical to form any attachments. And then that which made sense just became the way life was. The way I was. By the time Ferdie came along, my heart didn't work like that anymore. It didn't swoon. It thought about things. It weighed and measured. It used reason. Because it had to, after having gotten so beaten up in the beginning.

As I grew older I learned that when I fell, I got up. If the wound bled, I washed it and put a bandage on it. I tucked myself in at night and soon came to enjoy the ritual of it all. I had Cheetah the stuffed animal to read to and fell asleep looking at the glow-in-the-dark stars on my bedroom ceiling that I took with me to every new house. I thought I was content. That I'd made a life for myself.

A life lived secondhand with everything at a safe distance.

As the years went on, it was order that I counted on. Control. Things being in their place made me happy. I think about my birthday; my inability to think of something to wish for as that candle flickered. Maybe that was the beginning. The moment the old way was no longer enough.

Over the past year, I've chipped away at the mythology of my beliefs to discover that love is not reasonable or measured. It undoes you. It's in the imperfections in each other, in ourselves, where we find our humanity. It's in our dents and scars where the deepest connections are made. Real love resides in the parts of me I think no one wants to see. And as someone who survived because everything was perfect and in its place, I know it's that fact alone that sends a chill down my spine.

"Broken people make the best heroes," I repeat to myself as the steam dissipates.

9

I desperately try to smooth out the indentations on my cheek from the pillow as we take the elevator down to the lobby. We're venturing out for lunch. Amid all this undoing and break-throughing, some authentic Mexican food will be just the balm we need. We are going to go to Asadero Norte de Sonora—a little hole-in-the-wall I found online. I plan on eating my feelings with a side of salsa.

Sasha is texting someone as we descend. When I ask if it's Ryder, she says no. And that's that. Her fingers burn across her keyboard. Wait. Then another flurry of texting. A scoff here and a stifled laugh there and I know that whatever conversation she's having is not a good one. I'm beginning to think Ryder isn't the only man in her life. The elevator dings open, we walk out of the lobby, and the blistering-hot Phoenix summer day hits us both like a ton of bricks.

"Oh my God. Oh my God," I say, shoving my valet ticket into the poor young man's hand.

"It's a thousand degrees—why would anyone . . ." We walk right back into the lobby and watch for our car from the safety of the hotel's air-conditioning. While I would love to breathe actual fresh air, for a change, I do not want to incinerate my lungs in the process. We're waiting for our car when I see Preeti sitting at a corner booth of the hotel restaurant.

"Isn't that Preeti?" I ask, bringing Sasha's attention up from her phone.

"Huh? Oh . . . yeah, looks like," Sasha says, her eyes returning to her phone.

"We should probably say hi," I say.

"Yep," Sasha says, not looking up. I tell the hostess that we're just going in to say hi to a friend who's already in the restaurant. She is immediately suspicious. We cross the expanse of the restaurant—and as if the patrons weren't loud and distracting enough, there are televisions mounted on every wall, in every corner of the establishment. Baseball games, golf, and shows about baseball and golf drone on in the background as people choose to ignore whoever they're dining with to follow along with the subtitles. We finally approach Preeti's booth over in the corner.

"We just wanted to come say hi, check in on you," I say, standing at the end of the table. Preeti is just about to open her mouth when the person she's dining with speaks.

"Ah, Anna. So wonderful to see you," Audrey says, sitting across from Preeti. She ignores Sasha completely, of course. Sasha immediately looks up from her phone and the heat of her laser stare could set the side of my face on fire any minute.

My brain runs through the options:

1. Drag Audrey's smug body out of that booth and shove her right out into the Phoenix heat where she'll most certainly burst into flames.

2. Lick Preeti Dayal and claim her as mine like I did with my food when Ferdie was slow to learn sharing.
3. Grab Sasha and squeeze both of us into their two-person booth come hell or high water.

I take a deep "cleansing" breath—only in quotations because it's the least cleansing breath I've ever taken—and decide on:

"What a lovely surprise."

"Isn't it, though?" Audrey asks, sipping her white wine. I can feel my shoulders creeping ever higher.

I look back over at Preeti. "Well, we'll leave you to it. Catch up with you at the meet and greet then?"

"Sounds like a plan," Preeti says. I can't read her. Does she want to be dining with Audrey? And even though I can't believe it, of course Audrey flew out here to piss all over the Lumineux campaign and make it hers. She's got nothing else going on and certainly has no idea how to find her own clients. Before I pass out from the held breath of sheer rage, I say my farewells. I nudge a speechless Sasha out of the restaurant, her phone pinging and vibrating in her hand. We walk right past the hostess, through the lobby, and out into the blazing-hot sun, where our stupid rental car awaits.

"Didn't know if you guys had changed your minds," the glistening valet says. I tip him some unknown amount of money and then laugh maniacally at his "joke" for way longer than is socially acceptable. He hurries to shut the car door out of self-preservation.

"I can't believe she's here. I can't believe she's here," Sasha says.

"We still have two hours until the meet and greet. Let's just stick to the plan and go to that Mexican place I was talking about," I say.

"Now you're talking," Sasha says. She texts one final thing and shuts her phone off, throwing it into her purse. I don't know what's going on, but I do know that whatever that moment was, it was a victory for her.

"This is because of that e-mail about Chuck. She's getting more and more desperate to bring in a big client," I say, pulling up the address to Asadero Norte de Sonora on my phone. I hand the phone to Sasha and we start on our way.

"But not desperate enough to actually go out and get her own clients, though," Sasha says, slumping over in the passenger seat.

"No, this is bad. I've never seen her act like this," I say. Sasha stifles a contemptuous laugh as her entire demeanor changes. Slumped over in that passenger seat, she looks like a tantrumming teenager, telling you juuuuuust leeeet it gooooo, Moooooom. "No. I'm serious. She's always been . . ." I trail off, searching for the right word.

"Bitchy?" Sasha blurts, and then tells me to take a right at the light.

"No, she's . . . imperial. So blue-blooded that her rarefied existence makes it almost impossible for her to understand how anyone—anyone normal, that is—lives. So, how can she advertise products for the rest of us?"

"She can't," Sasha answers.

"I mean, her idea of 'keeping it real' was this one traumatic time she had to fly first class rather than take the family's jet. And she talked about that like it was Nam," I say. Sasha leads me through the streets of Phoenix as I try to figure out where we stand now.

"Where I come from? We call that bitchy," Sasha says.

"No, this is worse. Bitchy I can handle. I mean, we all survived seventh grade." Sasha nods. "This is going against everything she's ever stood for . . . Do you know she was the one who saved my job a few years ago?"

"What?"

"I'd finally been promoted to a full-time agent. One of the other ad agents was yelling at me about some messenger he said he'd sent—of course he hadn't. But I was the low man on the totem pole and this was going to be my fault whether I liked it or not."

"Sounds about right," Sasha says.

"Audrey glides in and asks the guy to join her in the hall. It was so cool. She politely excused herself and I could hear her giving it to him just outside the office. He hadn't sent for the messenger. He was blaming me. This wasn't how we did things at Holloway/Greene and on and on. He slinked away and she walked back in and I'll never forget, she was wearing this beautiful gray, just-clingy-enough cashmere dress that I didn't even know how someone would dare try on, let alone look as resplendent in as she did . . ." Sasha repeats the word *resplendent*. "Anyway, she came in, stuck her hand out, and said, 'We haven't been formally introduced. I'm Audrey Holloway.'"

"Wow," Sasha says.

"I know."

"So, what happened?" Sasha asks, guiding me to make a left at the next street.

"I guess Chuck Holloway happened," I say. Sasha is quiet. Shaking her head. A deep sigh. Then—

"What are we going to do?" Sasha asks.

"We land Lumineux," I say.

"But—"

"It's our campaign. First? We don't forget that." Sasha nods. "So we continue working. We stay the course. There's nothing we can do about Audrey." Sasha is about to put up a fight, but I cut in. "There really isn't. In the end, she's our boss. All we can do is make sure that we are an integral part of this campaign and that we continue to make an impression on Preeti," I say.

"It should be . . . it should be right up here on the . . . right. Right there." We smell the restaurant before we see it. Wafting barbecued deliciousness. We find parking on a side street in front of an abandoned grouping of buildings behind an archway that says A LI'L BIT OF HEAVEN.

We walk the short distance, through the makeshift parking lot and into the inconspicuous reddish box of a building with the simple sign that reads ASADERO NORTE DE SONORA.

"What does it mean?" Sasha asks.

"Barbecue from the North Sonora region . . . ish," I say, not wanting to get into the complicated translations of the word *asadero*.

"It smells amazing," she says. We walk inside and seat ourselves at one of the few tiled tables. The waitress comes over and smiles.

"Coke, please," I say.

"Me too," Sasha says. The waitress walks off and I let myself inhale. I'm already calming down. Getting out of that hotel was for the best. The waitress returns with two heavy bottles of real Mexican Coke and two plastic glasses filled with ice. She also sets down a basket of chips, a bowl of salsa, a bowl of guacamole, and two other bowls of what look like watered-down pinto beans.

"*Frijoles charros,*" the waitress says, responding to my confused look. She then mimes that we eat it like we would any other soup. I smile and she waits, pulling out a pad of paper.

"Are you ready to order?" I ask Sasha. She nods no. The waitress smiles and indicates that she'll be back in a few minutes.

"They don't speak English here?" Sasha whispers.

"Why should they?" I ask, motioning to the pictures on the menu. "We can just point." I dig into the chips and salsa. Oh my God. Then the *frijoles charros.* The spices and the broth and the flawlessly cooked pinto beans . . . it's just what the doctor ordered. And then I take a long swig of Coke right from the bottle. "Perfection." The ranchero music blares in the background as people from the neighborhood come in for takeout, their children playing with the vending machines filled with useless toys that seem priceless to all kids everywhere. The faux painted orangish walls are decorated with pictures and randomly hung landscapes of what is probably Sonora. Sasha digs into the *frijoles charros,* and before I check back in with her, she's finished the bowl and is now drinking the last bits of it.

"Oh my God," she says, swiping her finger on the bottom of the little bowl for anything she's missed. "That? When you're sick? I can't even deal with that right now." Sasha takes out her phone and snaps a picture of the finished bowl. Then the real Coke in its iconic bottle. Then the restaurant itself. "Smile!" she says. I oblige and she snaps a picture of me. She looks at the photo. "Super cute." She takes that opportunity to scan her texts. A look of annoyance, then she does that same pushed-back-shoulder thing she did the first day I met her at Holloway/ Greene when she strode through the bull pen. She looks up and tucks the phone in her purse with a shake of her head. She takes a giant bite of the salsa and immediately chokes on the heat of it, desperately gulping down her Coke.

"It's hot," I say, taking a chip heaped with salsa and happily letting it incinerate my mouth.

"You're not kidding," Sasha says, laughing. I can't help but join her as Audrey's presence at the Biltmore begins to fade away in the haze of Sonoran barbecue. For now.

The waitress takes our orders and I check the time. We'll make it to the meet and greet at the Irish Cultural Center in plenty of time. We'll let Audrey have her little lunch with Preeti, where she'll no doubt charm her with that patrician air. But she'll know absolutely nothing about Lumineux and the Just Be campaign, and certainly nothing about romance novels and RomanceCon. People need time to reveal themselves, so that's just what I'll give her. Let her hang herself, Anna.

My eyes dart around as I piece things together. Try to figure out Audrey's move. Replay the scene. I'm sure Audrey will just say she's in Phoenix to make sure Preeti knows that she is important and that our agency will do its utmost to serve her and Lumineux. We're all on the same team, I can hear her saying now.

Another swig of Coke. A sinking feeling in the pit of my stomach. The pieces come together quickly in my mind and the realization hits me.

"Audrey doesn't just want Quincy," I say, finally seeing her desperation.

"What?" Sasha says, saying thank you in terrible Spanish as the waitress sets down our steaming plates filled with delicious food.

"She wants Lumineux."

"Yeah, I know," Sasha says.

"No, she wants Lumineux all to herself," I say.

"But—" Sasha packs a flour tortilla with carne asada and closes her eyes in ecstasy as she eats.

"Lumineux is right now. Audrey needs something immediately to convince Charlton that she's the right Holloway for the job. Quincy is too far away and still pie in the sky. Lumineux? We've done all the work and it would . . . it could tip the scales. If we stay on the Lumineux campaign . . . it's like what you said. We're not Miss Marple. We're a threat and Audrey knows it. She's got to get us out of the picture as soon as she can so she can hold Lumineux up as her very own hard-won trophy," I say, shredding my chicken and putting it into a flour tortilla along with some of the salsa.

"But it's not even ours yet," Sasha says with her mouth full.

"I know. But we have something she never will," I say. Sasha stops eating. Waits. "It was our idea, so not only do we have the inspiration, we have the knowledge that there's more where that came from," I say, calling back Lincoln's words.

"We're not just this one idea," Sasha says.

"No."

"So we Marple them. Our version of Marpling, anyway," Sasha says.

"Exactly. We Marple them," I repeat.

Sasha and I talk about the campaign and our morning meeting with Helen as we eat our lunch. The conversation is easy—drinking Cokes and shoving salsa-laden chips in our mouths midsentence.

"My grandma loved Agatha Christie. She used to watch the TV movie versions all the time," Sasha says as the waitress brings us more chips.

"She did?" I ask, realizing I know absolutely nothing about Sasha outside of work.

"All the time. She got me into reading, too. She's the one who had the romance novels," Sasha says.

"She sounds awesome," I say.

"She had this terrible orange lipstick that she used to let me wear. She'd dot it on my lips like this." Sasha pokes at her lips with her index finger and then smiles, letting the memory infuse its joy into the telling of it. I don't want to ask the inevitable question, as Sasha is speaking about her beloved grandmother in the past tense. "Of course, I'd always say how bored I was."

"You were little."

"Yeah, I just wish I could go back now and sit and listen to her talk, you know?" Sasha says.

"How long has it been?" I ask.

"A little over five years. I was at NYU when I got the call," she says, her voice sliding into a more robotic tone as she tries to keep the emotion at bay. "My grandma raised me; my parents were . . ." Sasha trails off, searching for a tiny word that can explain a lifetime of hurt. "Not around." A small smile to me and I can see her trying to control the swell of emotion.

"I'm so sorry," I say.

"Yeah, me too," she says, managing a small smile. "I think she's why I love romance novels. They remind me of her. I found this whole stack of them in her crafting room and I just dove in. It felt so naughty. The first one I ever read was about this gorgeous doctor with long blond hair who could only be herself at her country house where she kept all of her beloved horses."

"Sure."

"And I can't remember all of the details, but this serial killer was trying to come after her and of course she was denying her feelings for the rough-and-tumble guy who was in charge of her horses."

"As you would."

"So when the serial killer came after her—at her country house, no less! It was her sanctuary!—well, the two of them finally admitted their feelings for each other and battled the serial killer together. That's the thing about romance novels."

"That true love is your best weapon against serial killers?"

"No, ladyhawke." I bark out a laugh, shooting chips everywhere, and Sasha crumples in laughter.

"Ladyhawke," I repeat, still laughing.

"Well, the one and only Helen Brubaker lays into you just this morning and you still can't get over yourself," Sasha says.

"Well, I can't help it; it just sounds so ridiculous. Gorgeous blond doctor! She loves horses! He's hot and ready to protect her! And feminism wept as he swooped in and saved her with his magic penis. I mean . . . come on!"

"Not enough shape-shifting wolves for you?"

"It was a curse and he was the captain of the—"

"This is your problem," Sasha says, cutting in. She takes a giant sip of her Coke, as the salsa has choked her up again. She continues, "Yes, romance novels are extreme. The situations are turned up to eleven and everyone is beautiful without dieting or exercise and the sex is always amazing, but when I strip all that away what I get is that all of this"—Sasha motions to everything around us, and I'm assuming she means the world and our existence and not this particular Mexican restaurant—"that all of this is nothing without love."

"I know you're right," I say, my face flushing. Again.

"Thank you."

"In theory."

"In theory?"

"Whenever I think about what will remain of me after I'm gone? My legacy, I guess. It always hinges on what I did, not who I loved," I say.

"Oh, I *know* that."

"I can't ever seem to work the idea of having both in my life. I troll the music blogs for bands no one has ever heard of and listen to pop stars. Read *Jane Eyre* nightly and cuddle up with the newest cozy mystery series. Take over the world and love someone greatly."

"Yeah, I have a hard time with that, too," Sasha says.

"It's like once you start talking about love, people seem to write you off. Like you don't get—"

"What's really important. Yeah, I know."

"So, when you talk about romance novels and great love, I immediately jump to I'm barefoot and pregnant and I've lost my edge and I'm telling people that *we* loved that movie and oh my God, *we* stayed at the cutest little B&B in Williamsburg and all of a sudden I've forgotten how to be just an I. And who's to say that gorgeous blond doctor couldn't have bested that serial killer on her own, you know?"

"Because she was in the bathtub trying to have a moment to herself and—"

"I don't know why anyone takes baths anymore. I really don't," I say. "Oh, is there a serial killer after me? You know what I need? A nice long bath. I can't with these people." I motion to our waitress for our check.

"You okay?"

"No!" I yell. Sasha is quiet. Maybe she's smiling. She's definitely smiling. I just keep shaking my head and I feel like I'm sitting on Michael and Allison's couch again as they go into that bathroom and change that stupid pooey lightbulb. The flush of vulnerability tingles throughout my body as I remember my night with Lincoln. The waitress brings our check and I hand her my credit card, trying to keep things moving and not dwell on not having heard from him so far today.

"You can be great and have great love, you know," Sasha says.

"Can you?" I ask, my eyes flaring.

"God, I hope so," Sasha says.

"And is that who you're constantly texting? Your great love?" I ask, eyeing her still buzzing phone. Sasha looks completely thrown and I feel terrible instantly.

"He's not my great love," she says, unable to make eye contact with me.

"So why are you—"

"I . . . How do you . . . Helen's workshop the other day? I'm not doing any of that," Sasha says, ripping her napkin into millions of tiny pieces.

"Sasha, I—"

"No, it's true. I've read her book cover to cover a thousand times, highlighting and putting little stickies everywhere. But every time . . . every time, I'm right back to my old tricks again," she says. The waitress brings me back my card and the receipt. I sign it and tuck the card back into my wallet.

"Is this about Ryder?" I ask.

"No."

An awkward long moment.

She spins her watch around on her tiny wrist and checks the time. "We'd better go." She grabs her purse and stands.

"Sasha," I say, standing. She turns around and her eyes are just beginning to well up. "You deserve someone amazing."

"Do I, though?" Sasha continues walking out of the Mexican restaurant without another word. She is quiet as we drive to the Irish Cultural Center—which turns out to be a beautiful gray castle inexplicably in the middle of downtown Phoenix. She is angry and red-faced as we brave the thousand-degree heat, trying to find parking in the back lot. She becomes melancholy as we find the open bar in the stunning barnlike room where the registration table is. And she's downright wretched as she orders her first glass of wine from the open bar. Great. We're early.

I look out from the raftered barn and see a group of people actually braving the tables set up on the outside patio.

"Give Arizonans a mister and they're fine," Ginny Barton says.

"It must be—"

"It's about 103 degrees. It was 112 degrees earlier today. I was getting worried," Ginny says, sipping her lemonade. She winks. "Spiked." And she toasts me with her now much more interesting lemonade. "Map of Ireland." Ginny motions to the patio and sure enough, there's a map of Ireland in the cobblestones. "If you go up to one of the libraries, up there?" She motions to the larger building, spilling a bit of her lemonade in the process. "You can really get a good look at the map."

"How does this place exist?" I ask.

"Isn't it something? You must take a look around; it's the genuine article," Ginny says, in a full Irish brogue. "P.S.? I hear they sell British candy and real Irish tea right over there." Ginny points to a little gray cobbled cottage just across the patio.

"Real Irish tea, hm?" I ask. The live band positioned just next to the large black fireplace at the end of the barn begins playing gorgeous Irish music and the entire scene brightens. A line of alabaster-skinned girls with their arms tight to their sides begin dancing for the revelers, and we're all swept away to the Emerald Isle just like if we were in a romance novel.

I am pulled from my Irish dream as I see Sasha order another glass of wine right after downing the first one. I scan the room for Ryder Grant and find him "wooing" some poor woman over in a corner of the barn. I focus back on Ginny.

"Have you spoken with each of our cover models yet, Ms. Wyatt?" she asks.

"I've spoken with Josh at the Pirate Booty Ball and had my picture taken with Colt at the kick-off," I say.

"Five more to go," Ginny says, offering up an impossibly toned brown-haired gentleman whose black T-shirt looks like it's approximately five sizes too small.

"Billy," he says with a cool head tilt. Do I . . . do I head-tilt back?

"I'll leave you two to it," Ginny says.

"Anna," I say, extending my hand. He takes it and then . . . holds it? Are we . . . He takes my hand in both of his and . . . smolders at me for what feels like hours.

"*A* for Anna, *B* for Billy. *C* for . . ." He trails off, unable to come up with a *C* word. I've got a few. I pull my hand away. Quiet. He's just nodding. Pursing his lips, narrowing his eyes, and nodding.

"So, have you always wanted to model—"

"It's more of a calling, you know," Billy says.

"Well, it's great that you're fulfilling—"

"Yeah, I was hot and modeling called me," Billy finishes, laughing.

"Your passion," I finish, trying to wipe off the confused and annoyed look I'm sure I have on my face right now. "So, which covers would I know you from?"

"Romance novel covers," he says.

"Yep. I . . ." Deep breath. "Would I know any of the books?" I ask, scanning the room. Help. Helllllllp.

"Probably," he says.

"Good. Very cool," I say, noticing gratefully that there are books scattered on tables throughout the meet and greet. "Are you on the cover of one of the books here?"

"Oh. Yeah. Here." Billy spins around and plucks a bluish book from among the many stacked on a nearby table. He hands me the book and I can hardly believe it's the same guy. "Cool, right?"

"Yeah, you look great," I say. And he does. Without the inconvenience of him opening his mouth, Billy is, of course, stunning in photographs. He looks like an all-American boy I would have definitely looked twice at in some catalog or magazine.

"That chick was super hot," he says, pointing at the lovely woman he's ravishing on the cover of the book. "That dress of hers just wouldn't stay up, if you know what I mean." He winks at me. I couldn't be less turned on. But. *But.* This is casting. This Billy guy would appeal to a large cross section of women, especially in the Midwest, and would look great in the Lumineux ad campaign, but *oh my God,* he's an idiot.

"Well, I won't keep you all to myself," I say, looking at the crowd of people at the meet and greet, none of whom are clamoring to speak to Billy. I have genuine Irish tea to buy and a drunken associate to monitor.

"Oh, well, hey. You're welcome," he says, and again he takes my hand in both of his. "You know, I'm just going to throw this out there. You're a nice-looking lady, so . . . I want to let you know that I am very open to making an impression on you and your vote, if you know what I'm saying." He pulls my hand closer.

"You've made quite the impression on me, I assure you," I say, trying to pull my hand back.

"No, I mean . . . an *impression* impression," he says, giving me a look that makes me want to take a shower right now.

"That won't be necessary," I say, finally freeing my hand.

"You know I'm talking about sex, right?"

"Yep."

"I have sex with you and—"

"Yep. Loud and clear."

"You vote for me."

"I am trying to save you a shred of dignity, Mr.—"

"Billy."

I heave a long, weary sigh. "Mr. Billy." He steps closer. "I'm not interested and now you're being officially creepy." He stops and begins to speak, but I stop him. "Nope. Thank you for your time and I wish you all the best of luck. Billy." I find Sasha in the crowd and am making a beeline for her when Ginny stops me once again. She presents me with Jake, the cocoa-skinned, once–shirtless fireman. I spend several delightful minutes talking with him, and the conversation couldn't be better. After making idle chatter about juicing, I'm happy to find out that Jake and his partner, Richard, are planning on getting married back in Manhattan on Valentine's Day, and he's mad with wedding planning. We talk about *An Affair to Remember* and florists and centerpieces some more, and I joyfully wish him well as he is pulled into a group of giggling publishing ladies who'd like a picture.

As I'm learning the ins and outs of carpentry from Lantz, which is actually quite fascinating, I see Preeti and Audrey walk into the meet and greet. I look past Lantz's broad shoulders and find Sasha in the crowd. She's kept her distance from me all afternoon, but with Preeti and Audrey's entrance she immediately walks over to me. I introduce her to Lantz and then politely extricate us from *This Old House* so we can get our bearings.

"Have you actually tried to talk to these guys?" Sasha slurs. Oh, no.

"How many glasses of wine have you had?" I ask, watching as Preeti separates from Audrey to fall in with a couple of the publishing ladies over by the bar.

"I don't know . . . fourth—maybe two?"

"Okay. So, you can't talk to Preeti in this state. We're going to go into the bathroom, and I'll tell them that you're not feeling well. Something about the Mexican food," I say.

"Why hasn't hot British guy texted you? Has he and you just haven't told me? Are you . . . you have . . . And there it is I said it," Sasha slurs.

"Okay, honey. Let's get you in the bathroom," I say. I walk Sasha into the bathroom, and thankfully there is a small anteroom just inside. All the little Irish girls' clothes and bags are strewn everywhere. I manage to get her onto the love seat, and she slides down just enough that her little dress hikes up. I set my club soda down on the side table and pull down her skirt. She makes a *woo-hoo* noise as I do this.

"He hasn't, has he? So, maybe, *maybe you* are just as screwed as I am! Ha-*ha*! I don't mean that. *Shhhh,* I don't mean that. Hey. *Hey.* I don't mean that," Sasha says, trying to cradle my face in her hands.

"I know, sweetie. I know."

"But Anna. *Anna.* Why hasn't he, though?" Sasha is now whispering. This is a secret apparently.

"I don't know. I don't know," I say, honestly. It has occurred to me that I haven't heard from Lincoln all day. Of course it has. But I rationalized this radio silence, thinking he's here on business and has probably been busy. Just as I have. "I'm supposed to go to his room after tonight's party."

"He's going to tell you he has a girlfriend," Sasha says and mimes zipping up her zipper. "But after." More whispering and then she nods conspiratorially. "I'm not a hero." She pulls herself up into a standing position and puts her arms akimbo. "Superhero of nothing!" Sasha yells.

"Honey, I need you to sit down," I say, wrangling her back into a seated position.

"We're nice and '*you ain't a beauty, but hey you're all right,*'" Sasha says, cracking herself up. "It's such bullshit. It's okay to say bullshit, because Helen Brubaker says it, you know. You *are* a beauty, Anna. Hey . . . you know . . . do you think Helen likes us? Do you think she can tell I don't do her book?! *Do you think she can tell that I'm bad at it??*" Sasha crumples onto the armrest. "Did you know . . . did you know what I do to make men like me?"

"I imagine being gorgeous, twenty-five, and an awesome

person probably has something to do with it?" I say, craning my neck to see if anyone's coming. The coast is clear.

"I text 'em naked pictures." She is holding out her phone to me as proof. "That's where it happened. That's where the naked was. Who does that??" She slumps over on the love seat and just repeats, "I do. I do. I do."

"That's in the past, Sasha. Sasha?" She's starting to pass out, the blinks becoming longer and longer. "I need you to stay awake. Stay with me."

"Lumineux Shower Gel! *Bing boop bop,* naked pictures in your you-know-what," she says.

"You okay in here?" Josh says, walking in.

"Ladies only, Mr. Hot!" Sasha says. The Mr. Hot thing makes me laugh. I can't help it. Sasha touches my face and laughs with me. I can't with this one.

"She's had a bit too much to drink. It's the heat. She was thirsty and . . . ," I say, trying to pull her skirt down again, as her whole "Ladies only, Mr. Hot" line was accompanied by an elaborate arm movement that pulled her dress up a bit too far.

"Can I help?" he asks.

"I have to get her out of here before our boss sees her like this. I can make up a story about her being sick, but I can't do that if—"

"He sees how drunk she is," he finishes.

"*She,* but yeah . . ."

"Right. Sorry. There's got to be a back way; let me see if I can find something," Josh says, walking back out into the raftered barn. Sasha is about to pipe up and I quiet her.

"Don't even make a back way joke right now," I say.

"*I totally was. Oh my God.*" Sasha crumples into laughter and then is just as quickly crying, falling onto the floor like a tantrumming child.

"I swear to God, Sasha Merchant. You get up off this floor right now," I say, standing over her. "Enough is enough. Sit your body down on that couch." Sasha gets into a kneeling position and pulls herself up onto the couch. "Do you have a game on your phone?"

"A what?"

"A game. Solitaire, Scrabble . . . something like that?" I ask.

"I have this word puzzle thing that—"

"I want you to play that game right now. In order to get the prize that I have in my purse you have to beat at least five levels," I say, patting my purse with no prize in it.

"Five levels?" she asks, pulling her phone out and turning it on. "Where'd you get that prize?"

"At the store," I say.

"The Prize Store . . . okay, five levels and I get it?" She pulls up the game on her phone.

"On your marks." Sasha sits up straight and looks up at me with this . . . childlike wonder that just breaks my heart. "Get set." She straightens up and lets out an excited squeal. "Go!" And Sasha is off and running, focused—however drunkenly—on the task at hand. I look out into the raftered barn, and the meet and greet is now going full tilt. I have got to get Sasha out of here and be back as soon as I can—with Preeti and Audrey here I can't risk anything.

"Okay, we can take her out through the kitchen," Josh says, appearing again in the small anteroom. His blue gingham shirt is casual, but specifically chosen to accentuate an upper body that is distractingly muscular. His black hair is mussed without any product and his ice-blue eyes would make any woman swoon.

"Sasha, can you pause the game? We're going to take you back to your room," I say.

"Imma pause it so it won't count against my prize," Sasha says with a wink, trying to close down the game.

"Sounds like a plan," I say. She nods, closes out the game, and thinking she's sliding her phone into her purse, drops it on the floor next to the couch. She looks from me to Josh and then back at me. I pick up her phone and put it in her purse. Sasha stands, wobbles over to me, and in an impossibly loud whisper asks: "So how do you know Superman?" She looks over at Josh and then back at me with raised eyebrows. And then a knowing nod. "He thinks we don't know who it is."

"I get that a lot," Josh says.

"*Pfffflt,*" Sasha says, pushing him away.

"Okay, hold on," he says, sweeping Sasha up into his arms, and it's all I can do not to swoon myself. In his arms, she seems as light as a feather. Sasha's face is hilarious—like she's a little kid on a Ferris wheel . . . well, a drunken kid on a Ferris wheel. She wraps her arms around him and kicks up her feet.

Josh walks her out of the anteroom and through the kitchen, exiting through a back door right out into the back lot where we parked. I follow closely behind. Josh has done his best to answer Sasha's litany of questions regarding his time on Krypton and whether or not he's ever thought about cheating on Lois Lane. By the time Sasha is loaded up into the passenger seat of our rental, she's almost asleep, her head lolling against Josh's chest. He pulls the seat belt across her and clicks it into place.

"That was a good prize, Anna Wyatt," Sasha slurs, nuzzling

the headrest. I'm just about to ask her which prize as she points at Josh. "Felt like a carnival ride." Josh can only smile as she tries to applaud him. Is it clapping when one arm is trapped under her body and she can't figure out how to get it loose? She gives up after a while.

"Get some rest," I say.

"You get some rest," she says.

"Is she going to be okay?" Josh asks.

"She'll be fine. Hungover, but fine," I say, finally starting toward the driver's-side door.

"How are you going to get her from the car to the hotel room?" Josh asks, turning back.

"You're right," I say.

"Come on," Josh says, hopping in the backseat.

We drive the few minutes back to the Biltmore and I plead with the valets to let us keep the rental there while we run Sasha up to her hotel room. We try to make excuses for her, but everyone knows what drunk looks like. Her slurring, angry proclamations followed by snickering giggles, elaborate pointing, and unintelligible noises that insinuate that everyone is in on a very tawdry inside joke aren't helping Sasha in the least.

The elevator ride and the long walk down the hallway are painless as Sasha fights to stay awake. I dig through her purse for her hotel room key, for which I get called "Thiefy Barnaby," which is hilarious, and when I laugh, Sasha begins cradling my face again as she becomes overjoyed that she made me laugh.

Josh lays Sasha down on the bed, and she immediately kicks off all the covers, turns over on her stomach, and puts the pillow over her head.

"She'll be fine," Josh says, trying not to look as Sasha's little dress that has ridden up once again. He clears his throat and walks toward the door. I find a bottle of aspirin in the bathroom and fill up a glass of water. I put both things by her bedside along with a garbage can. I leave a note telling her to text when she's awake.

As we're leaving, I hear her saying something, muffled and still under the pillow. I tell Josh to hang on, and I walk back over, pulling the covers up over her as I ask her what she was saying.

"Thank you," she says, pulling the pillow up so she's looking right at me.

"You're welcome," I say, letting her moment of clarity warm the cockles of my heart.

"Don't tell Josh I just farted," she says at full volume. Josh barks out a laugh and Sasha joins in.

"I won't," I say. I tuck the blanket around her. "Get some sleep." She nods. Josh and I walk out of Sasha's hotel room and can only laugh. "Can you hold on another second while I switch out of these heels real fast? This is mine." I motion to my hotel room just across the hall.

"You mean stay in air-conditioning a bit longer and not stand out in that heat listening to Blaise tell me about his workout routine?" He motions for me to continue on into my room and I laugh, sliding my key into the door. I flip off my heels and switch over to my flats. Sighhhhh, so much better.

"Okay, thank you so much. I just couldn't stand in those heels anymore," I say.

"I changed out of mine earlier," he says, and I laugh.

We step out into the hallway and come face to face with Lincoln.

10

"Hey," I say, overwhelmed and immediately happy upon seeing his face.

And then I follow his gaze to the gorgeous man coming out of my hotel room with me.

Oh. Noooooo.

"Lincoln Mallory, this is Josh. Josh . . ." I trail off, realizing I don't know Josh's last name. An arched eyebrow from Lincoln and he extends his hand.

"Lincoln Mallory."

"Josh Fox," he says, and I can't even look at Lincoln right now. Of course Josh's last name is Fox.

"Cheers, mate," Lincoln says.

"Nice to meet you," Josh says. A moment as the three of us stand in the hallway. Quiet. A cleared throat here. An elevator ding there. A housekeeping cart trundles down a distant hallway. "I'll meet you in the lobby then?"

"Yes, I'll be down in five minutes," I say, and Josh says his good-byes to the world's most awkward situation ever.

"One of the cover models, I assume," Lincoln says, crossing his arms across his chest.

"Sasha got drunk at this meet and greet. We had to bring her back to the hotel room before Audrey and Preeti saw her," I say.

"I don't know who any of those people are," Lincoln says, checking his watch.

"Preeti is the VP in charge of the Lumineux campaign and Audrey is my boss who's flown in from D.C. trying to steal the account," I say, watching him. He reacts to my rattled-off information, popping out of his momentary icy chill.

"Oh," he says, flustered.

"Are you . . . do you have to be somewhere?" I ask, my eyes flicking to his watch.

"What? No, I . . ."

A breath. I would be reacting the exact same way if I found him coming out of his hotel room with some model. I step closer to him. A smile. I missed his face. Too much, if you ask me. Another step closer and I can see him thinking. He lets his arms fall and finally I see his face softening.

"Is it time to go to your room yet?" I ask.

"Not quite," he says. I let my head fall onto his chest and allow myself to breathe him in. Just . . . stop the spinning of the day for a moment. I close my eyes as he wraps his arms around me, bringing me closer. "How did your seven A.M. meeting go?" His voice rumbles in his chest, and it pains me to speak. I don't want to break the silence of listening to his breath. I turn my head to the side—splitting the difference—and speak.

"Helen Brubaker wanted nothing to do with me and rightfully so. I had to come clean with why I'd insulted romance novels and—"

"This was a business meeting?"

"I know." I lift my head up and pull back from him just a bit. The dark blue eyes are waiting for me. We don't know each other well enough to navigate the Josh thing. Or something. But I feel myself backing away from whatever openness I had just seconds ago. "It worked out in the end."

"Good . . . Good." That something inside of me takes root and I take another step back from Lincoln, hating that I was so naively familiar with him.

"Okay, I'm off then." I manage a smile as I dig my phone out of my purse, desperate for something to do other than panic and wish my time in Phoenix were over, and could I just go home now, please? Another smile and I press the call button for the elevators. The elevator dings open and I force myself to walk in.

"Anna," Lincoln says, throwing his arm between the closing elevator doors. He walks inside and the doors close once more. I push the button for the lobby. I can't look at him. "I hadn't heard from you. I didn't know if we were still on for tonight."

"Oh, well then, the way to confirm those plans would certainly be to not contact me all day and then be distant and offputting when I do finally see you." The elevator opens and we step out into the lobby. I find Josh by the front doors and give him a wave.

"Finally see you and you're coming out of your hotel room with a man that looks like that," he says.

"I don't care about him, Lincoln. At all," I say, my voice exhausted. Lincoln purses his lips and just nods. "I have to go," I say, walking away without turning back around. Josh and I drive back to the Irish Cultural Center making terribly forced small talk. How hot it is. How he got into modeling. His daughter. I am in full denial. Luckily, the hellish turn with Lincoln made me forget, however briefly, that Audrey has had ample time all alone with Preeti. So, yay.

"See you in there," Josh says, as we park the car. I nod and give him a weary wave. I shut the car off and take a second, the blistering heat sitting on the top of my head like I'm under a heat lamp. I am walking toward the meet and greet when the phone rings.

"Anna Wyatt," I say, knowing exactly who it is without even looking at the screen.

"This is my formal apology," Lincoln says.

"Go ahead then," I say.

"I'm sorry." I like that Lincoln doesn't elaborate or get lost in a maze of buts and excuses for why what he did was actually okay. A simple *I'm sorry* is the most beautiful thing in the world.

"Thank you," I say.

We are quiet.

"As I plan on kissing you first thing tomorrow morning, please do bring what you'll need to stay the night this time?"

"I can do that," I say, my face flushing red at the prospect of another night with him.

"I should be back from the gala at around nine thirty. Does that work for you?" he asks.

"Gala?"

"My clients are putting it on for charity and requested I attend," he says.

"Does your gala involve getting wet down under at a mermaid bash?" I ask.

"Sadly no."

"Pity." I hear the Irish music and the murmur of a bustling party.

"I'll call when I return," he says.

"Okay." We are quiet.

"I'm going to hang up now, Anna."

"Yep . . . got it," I say. Waiting.

"It's just never not funny. Cheers," he says, and this time I hang up the phone first.

I walk back into the barn and see Josh immediately. He smiles and walks over.

"By the time I got back, I'd convinced myself that the RomanceCon authorities would be waiting to kick me out of the competition," Josh says.

"Then you got back . . . ," I lead.

"And Blaise picked right back up at his biceps like I'd never left," he says, smiling.

"I think we're going to be okay. Thank you again for . . . Sasha," I say.

"No worries," he says, putting a hand on my upper arm.

"Aren't you going to introduce us?" Audrey asks, sauntering up behind us. Josh lets his hand fall from my arm, but it's too late. Audrey saw it.

"Sure. Audrey Holloway, this is Josh Fox, one of the men vying for Mr. RomanceCon."

"Pleasure to meet you," Josh says, extending his hand. Audrey takes it as if she's the queen of England herself.

"I'd be willing to break a few rules for you, too," Audrey says, giving me a sly wink. A beat as we weather her lazy insinuations.

"Yes, ma'am," Josh says. Audrey is just about to start speaking when he says, "I'd better get back to it. Nice meeting you, Mrs. Holloway." Josh smiles, excusing himself and folding into the ever-growing crowd at the bar.

"I know he's a lot younger than you or me, but he doesn't have to treat me like I'm his friend's mom," Audrey says.

"He's a nice enough kid," I say, asking the bartender for a club soda with lime.

"White wine," Audrey orders when the bartender looks to her. We get our drinks and turn around to take in the festivities.

"So, you going to tell me why you're here, or . . ."

"I'm here to support you and the Lumineux campaign," Audrey says.

"Uh-huh," I say.

"What?" I just look at her. I wait. "Fine. I just want to make sure you're staying focused—" I follow her gaze toward Josh. "And that Holloway/Greene is going to be well represented when we go back in for the final pitch."

"What happened to you?" I ask.

"What do you mean, what happened to me?"

"Audrey. Please think about what you're doing." She is quiet. Takes a sip of her white wine as I wait. And wait. Do I say something else? Do I remind her of her championing of me just a few years ago? That we may have never been friends, but I thought we were at the very least in the trenches together. An exasperated breath and then—

"And it's *Ms.* Holloway," she says, and I can actually see whole parts of her ice over.

"Yes, I imagine it is."

We are quiet. I take a sip of my club soda as she starts and stops what is no doubt a legion of new insults directed at me for my effrontery. In the end, she just sounds like an old car sputtering down the street.

"Amazing news about Chuck," I finally say. Audrey's entire body stiffens. I sigh. A bored little sigh and continue, "The king is dead. Long live the king." Audrey whips her head around and lasers in on me. I turn, looking her straight in the eye. "Take your shot, Ms. Holloway. I dare you." And then I smile as easy as I can, finally ending with clinking my glass into hers. "Lovely seeing you."

And I walk away. Into the throng. And I don't look back.

The meet and greet continues. I endure an entire conversation about aliens and alien abduction with Tristan, ending the evening's festivities with Blaise, who is actually quite business-minded. He has a website and plans on starting a modeling agency just for cover models after he ages out. He's married and has three kids, one more on the way. His wife is a costume designer and she's made all the outfits he's worn throughout the pageant. The golden codpiece was apparently Mrs. Blaise's idea. Audrey slinked off about an hour after our little run-in. I'm half waiting for a strongly worded e-mail dismissing me from Holloway/Greene. But luckily—or unluckily—since Chuck has been on his little roll, Audrey just doesn't have the power to fire me. Now, if she manages to steal Lumineux and lands Quincy, I'm screwed.

The crowd waves good-bye to the models so they can get ready for tonight's Mermaid Bash. As the Irish Cultural Center empties out, Preeti makes her way over to me and we fall into easy conversation. We are in agreement about the contestants:

Josh is the definite front-runner. We both agree that while Billy is clearly in second place, his personality is so gross that it takes away from everything else.

"Being our spokesman is more than just being a pretty face," she says.

"That's what Sasha said."

"Sasha is right," Preeti says, smiling.

"Did you know that Blaise's wife is the one kitting him out in all those outfits?" I ask, my voice dipping to a whisper.

"No. That is not true," she says.

"Yes. The golden codpiece? Her idea," I say.

"No."

"Yes. Because it highlights his—"

"Don't say it."

"His best asset," I finish. Preeti laughs. "I mean, was there a sketching process? Fittings? Is it papier-mâché?? *I want answers, Preeti.*" She can only laugh as I continue on with the obvious questions about the Blaise marriage. Before I know it we're caravanning to the conference hotel and straight back into the Silver Ballroom for the Mermaid Bash.

Once again, Preeti and I set up shop by the food in the back of the ballroom. We're "underwater" tonight, and all the women are sporting red wigs and shells over their breasts. The men are bare-chested (again) and draped in netting, while some have gone the extra mile and are spending tonight's celebration constantly posing with a trident. How they got those through airport security, I'll never know. Josh stops by on his way toward the dance floor.

"Another one of your daughter's favorites?" I ask. He stands before us dressed as a perfect replica of Prince Eric from *The*

Little Mermaid—with his jet black hair and blue eyes, a loose-fitting white shirt, a red cummerbund, and blue pants are all he needs to complete the look.

"She gave me her doll," he says.

"Although Prince Eric walking around with a doll replica of his beloved is—"

"A little disturbing, yes. I'll give you that," Josh says, laughing. He excuses himself and is absorbed into the throng.

"He's a sweet kid," I say, once he leaves.

"Sweet kid? That's an oddly asexual comment for such an attractive young man," Preeti says, eyeing me. I laugh. I didn't even realize.

"I feel weird ogling him. I feel weird ogling all of them," I say, honestly.

"No, I know," Preeti says.

"So, I devolve into saying weirdly genderless comments about them, apparently." Preeti laughs. The flush is back and I'm trying to hide that Judy Blume book under my bed again. Trying to shove my sexuality anywhere but where people can see it. Stay professional.

"I found myself telling another woman that *that* one?"— Preeti points to Lantz and his ridiculous broad shoulders— "Had real appeal and would, quote unquote, 'make women want to get lost in his ginger curls.' No, I don't know what it means, either." Preeti blushes and I laugh.

"Maybe it's a good sign that we're having trouble," I say.

"I think you're right."

Preeti excuses herself for another glass of wine, asking if I'd like another club soda. I jump at the chance, and as she walks over to the bar I can't help but feel hopeful. Marpling Audrey is going well. She's back at the Biltmore seething about Chuck, and I'm making Preeti laugh as she gets me another drink. Whatever Audrey thinks is going to happen with this account, bottom line is it's all about what the client wants. And right now, the client wants to know if I'd like another drink.

I'm fine.

I'm at the Mermaid Bash in Phoenix, Arizona, and when not challenging my boss like some frat boy in a Viking hat and being besties with a twenty-five-year-old pinup girl who just got soooo drunk, guuuuuyyysss, I'm spending my nights with a British stranger revealing more about myself than I did with my ex-husband in eleven years of marriage.

I'm fine.

Preeti comes back with our drinks, and we fall back into easy conversation, but when I go to take a sip of my club soda I notice my hands are shaking.

I'm fine.

I remember my mother would always ask me how I was doing when she came in after a long day painting. And I'd say, "I'm fine." She would smile blithely and return to her studio calm and happy, secure in the knowledge that I was content.

Fine.

I was never fine. I came to loathe *fine*. And then I got really good at actually being fine. I wanted to scream at her. I wanted to cry and laugh and tell stories about my day and perform the elaborate plays I'd written with Cheetah for her. I wanted to hug her and I wanted her to brush my hair like the moms in the TV shows did for their daughters. I wanted her to be nosy about my business so I could say, "*Butt out, mooommm.*"

No, this isn't about Lincoln. Or Sasha. Or Audrey. Or Lumineux. It's about me. About me being brave enough to let people get close, without a guarantee of happy epilogues and hand-in-hand walks into the sunset. Trusting I can handle it, even if things don't work out.

Of course, I know this already. Everyone does. It's the gist of 99 percent of the quotes on social media walls. Be brave and let go and let people in and love with your whole heart, blah blah blah. We all know what's good for us. The stumbling block is whether we believe we deserve better. The sad truth is that most of us are far too happy with settling for fine because that's the most we think we're allowed.

We know there is such a thing as greatness; the hitch is we don't think we deserve it.

Preeti and I make our rounds. Talk to the ranks of the League of Romance Novelists. Helen Brubaker is doing some television thing, so she's absent this evening. I'm kind of glad. After the proper amount of time, Preeti and I exchange exhausted looks. We say our good-byes and walk out to the valet together.

As we're waiting for our cars, I'm hoping she'll bring up her lunch with Audrey. Something. A progress report, what they talked about, how Audrey is half the woman I am and isn't it hilarious that she thinks she's going to horn in on this campaign! *High five!* The valet brings her car first. She says good-bye, and I can feel waves of desperation infused with competitiveness and laced with territorial rage bubbling up inside me while I airily wave to her as she drives off into the stultifying Phoenix heat. I drive to the hotel in silence. I don't even know where to start at this point.

Exhausted, I happily pull in to the Biltmore. The hotel looks particularly gorgeous at night all lit up.

I'm walking in from the valet when my phone rings. Ferdie.

"Hey, hold on a sec. Let me get into the lobby," I say, weaving my way through the crowd at the entrance to the hotel.

"Yeah, all right," he says.

"Is everything okay?" I ask once I'm out.

"Yeah . . . yeah, it's fine," he says.

"Ferdie."

"I mean, I'm in jail, but—"

"What?? Come on," I say, walking farther away into the lobby.

"I wasn't even going to call you, but you know the whole one-phone-call thing," Ferdie says.

"What happened? What did—"

"What did I do?"

"Yeah."

"What do I always do?"

"Fighting," I say, resigned.

"Yeah, there's a bunch of us in here. It won't be anything."

"I thought everything was going so well," I say, hating that I thought for even one second that Ferdie was out of the woods.

"It is," he says.

"Don't act like that. Don't be shocked that I'm upset," I say.

"It's not a big deal."

"To you. Which is my concern. I'm hoping you're just nobly downplaying this so I won't worry, but oddly I don't think that you are," I say.

"Look, I called. I drank too much and said some shit. I'll be out in the morning," he says. I am quiet. Shaking my head in the lobby of this stupid vortex of a hotel in Phoenix—a city I will never return to, thankyouverymuch. "Anna. Anna, I'm sorry okay?"

"No, you're not. You're just not."

"I am, I feel really bad," he says.

"But you don't, though. Whatever this life of yours is? It's working for you. If you wanted to make a change, you would."

"Oh, like you?"

"Don't do that. Don't turn this around. We're talking about you." I can hear the clicks and beeps of another call coming through on my phone. I check the screen. Lincoln. I don't answer.

"Yeah, we always talk about me."

"Yeah, we do, don't we? I am so tired of worrying about you," I say.

"Well, no one asked you to."

"Oh, so this call is supposed to what? Make me feel awesome?"

"I was just checking in."

"Next time could you check in from a job? Or how about the house of a nice lady friend that isn't named Jade and doesn't accessorize with bongs and dream catchers? Come on, Ferdinand. You're better than this," I say.

"No, Anna. I'm not. That's where you've always been wrong."

"Look, I get back Sunday night. We'll talk then."

"Fine."

"Can you stay out of trouble until then?" He is quiet. "Ferdie?"

"My time's up. Hey, have fun in Phoenix," he says.

"Ferdie. *Ferdie.*" He hangs up and I feel like screaming.

"Motherfu—" I say, hanging up. I'm however many thousands of miles away and . . . it doesn't matter. How much longer am I going to have to worry about my little brother? I thought this new gig reffing hockey would do something. Would make him happy.

I feel so lost. Angry. I've been good my entire life. A hard worker. A good friend. And over the last year, I've taken my life down to the studs, asking the big questions and . . . a text from Lincoln comes through. I throw my phone into my purse. No. *No.* I survived parents who couldn't have cared less and grew up with nothing to hold on to but myself and my anvil of a brother, constantly drowning me in worry. And work. I had my work. And I loved it. Because if I worked hard in school, I got good grades. If I turned in assignments I got a gold star. It was fair.

But now Audrey—oh, sorry, *Ms. Holloway*—wants to swan in and take the credit and get the grade I earned? It's not fair, but work hasn't been fair for a very long time. Relegated to the pink ghetto of only repping products for women, because God forbid I could sell something as out of my league as breakfast cereal or a running shoe. Several years ago at a huge advertising conference a couple of men from my office and I were asked to speak on some panels. I was over the moon at the prospect. Was it going to be about planning a big campaign, how to work with the art department, seeing an idea through to fruition? Nope. Those panels were for the other two men from the agency. Three other women and I were put on a panel called "Ladies Who Sell."

I feel my phone vibrate in my purse. Lincoln.

I can't.

As the lobby buzzes and moves around me, I am still. Paralyzed with anger. My parents are luxuriating in their Friday night, free from the knowledge that their one and only son is in the drunk tank again. I can hear Dad now preaching about personal responsibility and it'll do Ferdinand good to spend the night in jail and tough love this and man up that. And Mom would just be so overwhelmed with it all and disappear into her studio with just a string of French words and Dad would tell me, "Now look what you did to your mother."

I begin to pace around the lobby, trying to downplay the muttering. I can't help but talk this out. I have to get to my room, but I can't be trapped like that right now. The only thing keeping me sane is that I'm in public, ugh, *I'm in public.* I fold my arms across my chest and the intensity, the anger, and the unfairness of it all are momentarily contained. How . . . do I go home tonight? Will another opportunity be ruined by—

I look up to Lincoln walking across the lobby toward me, wearing a tuxedo with his bow tie untied. As he nears, he begins to take in how off the rails I am. His expression goes from confused to concerned to a tad bit scared in seconds. And yet he continues walking toward me. I have a thousand things to say to him. I'm fine! It's okay! Let's grab dinner! My brother sucks! Nothing is fair!

But Lincoln just walks over and pulls me into him, wrapping his arms tightly around me without so much as a word. And I just cry. And cry. Cry as he holds me and tugs me in closer and soothes me with a *shhhhh* with the lobby buzzing around us and people staring and the baseball game playing on the TV in the background and Audrey getting credit for my work and Sasha passed out and Ferdie in jail and my parents don't care and I'm all alone . . . I'm all alone . . .

"It's going to be all right," Lincoln says.

11

I don't want to talk about it as I follow Lincoln to his room. And I don't want to talk about it as I free him from his tuxedo. I don't want to talk about it as he strips me of my sensible business casual attire. And I don't want to talk about it as we fall into each other again with an intimacy and a tenderness that now seem frightfully commonplace between us. I don't want to talk about it as I take a shower later that night and I don't want to talk about it when he joins me. I don't want to talk about it as I sneak back to my room for my pajamas and toiletries wearing just his bathrobe and with a wet head from the shower. I don't want to talk about it as we order enough room service for a small army and I don't want to talk about it as he takes me again while we wait for the food to arrive. As I sit on his unmade bed in pajamas I thought no one would see, Lincoln lets me not talk about it. For a while.

"Tomorrow's the last day of the conference," I say, dipping my chicken fingers into a swampy barbecue sauce.

"And you leave . . ." he says, wiping his face after taking a giant bite out of a hamburger.

"Sunday morning," I say.

"I leave Sunday morning, as well," he says.

"Oh."

"Yeah."

We are quiet as we eat from a selection of food that would please any seven- or eight-year-old, with the dark cloud of real life hovering over both of us.

"What do you have on for tomorrow?" he asks.

"Nothing until the big pageant," I say.

"So we can just stay here until then," Lincoln says.

"Here as in . . ."

"This room," he says, taking a sip of his water.

"And then what?" I say, even though I hate it. I can't not say it. It's the elephant in the room and I can't stand it anymore.

"Hm," Lincoln says, his mouth full with hamburger.

"You can't keep shoving that hamburger in your mouth all night," I say. He swallows.

"And why are you so keen to have that conversation and yet perfectly comfortable not talking about what was so disturbing to you earlier?" He shifts in his chair.

"What?"

"You heard me," he says. He takes another giant bite of his hamburger.

"Nice. Very nice," I say, just as the sound of his chewing fills the room. I'm just about to start talking again when he takes another giant bite. "Fine. My brother called and . . . and he was annoying. Little brothers, right?" My voice clunks and hitches over what isn't said as if my answer has been redacted by some government agency. Lincoln takes the napkin from his lap and politely wipes his mouth. He sets his hamburger down on the plate.

"You're going to have to do better than that, love," he says.

"Whyyy?!" I ask, flopping down on the bed. "Can't we just . . ." I try to look sultry in my droopy, stained pink tank top and men's blue-striped pajama bottoms, and my hair up in a ratty topknot from the shower.

Lincoln yawns.

"It's my fault. It's my fault he's a screwup," I say. Out loud. For the first time.

"Who's a screwup?"

"Ferdie. My younger brother," I say. "By nine years."

"How is it your fault?"

"Because I essentially raised him, so I mean, I'd love to blame my parents, but . . . it was me," I say, unable to look at him.

"That is not your fault." His voice is solid. It's not a question and he's not confused.

"But—"

"I don't need any further information. I don't need to know how it was that a ten-year-old Anna Wyatt couldn't properly raise her baby brother. Have you ever thought that it was you who got him this far?"

"To a drunk tank in Georgetown?"

"Is that where he is?"

"I'm assuming so. It's where he was the last time. And the time before that." I gesture and the time before that and before that and before that . . .

"Is it the drink?"

"I know what you're going to say next, but—"

"Do you?"

"The whole AA thing."

"The whole AA thing?" he repeats.

"Ferdie's not an alcoholic," I say.

"Well, congratulations to him then," Lincoln says.

"I didn't mean to—" My eyes drop to his chest. The scars and the dents, the burns and the rebuilding of tissue. "I'm sorry."

"The first step is admitting you have a problem."

"Wait, so I have to do that for him, too?"

"Of course not, but he may not be the only one who has to come to this realization."

"He's my brother," I say.

"And he'll remain your brother, but—"

"But what?"

"But maybe he's not simply the loser you fear he is. Maybe he's an addict."

"Oh, so now he's an addict?"

"You tell me."

"He's addict adjacent."

"Hm," Lincoln says, shaking his head.

"He's all I've got," I say. This rush of emotions swirls inside me. I have no idea where they come from or how I can explain them. But I feel as though if I started crying right now I'd never be able to stop.

"Well, he's not all you've got," Lincoln says.

"You know what I mean."

"I don't think I do." I walk over to him, closer to the chocolate flourless cake he ordered. I lean over and kiss him. Another kiss. "This argument is fast becoming oddly arousing," he says, pulling me onto his lap. He wraps his arms around my waist.

"And yet you're still attempting to get out of talking about what was bothering you earlier this evening." He kisses me. And I feel him smiling. I pull back from him.

"I have no idea what you're talking about," I say, leaning back to reach for the fork.

"Will you stop at nothing?" he asks.

"I don't want to talk about sad things anymore," I say. I cut into the cake and bring the bite over and feed it to Lincoln. He lets me. He chews and swallows. But once he's finished, he stops my hand from feeding him another bite.

"I'm trying to get to know you," he says. I stand, take the cake, and go back over to the bed. Lincoln watches me. I take a bite of the cake.

"Why?"

"Just start bloody talking, woman."

"We have one more day, Lincoln. Why—"

"That may be, but—" His face changes in those seconds.

"So you agree with me. That we only have one more day." Lincoln is silent. He refuses to take the bait. "You know how you think about talking about one thing and then it becomes this tangle of cords you can't find the end of?" I say, taking another bite of the cake.

"Very well acquainted."

"If I talk about what was upsetting me earlier, it's everything. It's always been everything," I say.

"I get that."

"There was this great quote in an Agatha Christie mystery once that—and I'm paraphrasing—that everyone always acts like the murder is the first thing to happen, but it's actually the last."

"So, our lives are analogous to a dead body."

"No, you know—"

"I'm just trying to make a joke so I don't let on how much that one statement completely resonated with me."

"As you do," I say. Lincoln laughs. His smile fades.

"Because then I'd have to ask why was I in Afghanistan in the first place," he says. "What came before." He brushes his hand over his scars. "You know what I used to say to women when I was . . ." A long sigh and he looks up at me as if he's thinking, why not. "When I was done with them?" I shake my head no. "They'd ask me about what happened in Afghanistan and I was probably pissed and definitely didn't want to talk to them about it. I would just say—oh my God, this is mortifying— I'd just say, 'All of my scars are on the outside.' The worst." I am quiet. Trying not to laugh. "No, please. Feel free. Who says that?" I'm just shaking my head. "I may have said baby. 'All my scars are on the outside . . . *baby*.'"

"Yeah, I said it with the baby attached in my head," I say.

"You would have to." He has something else. "I was shirtless all the time, by the way. Just all the time. That way, they'd be so focused on the scars, never on me. They were always so cautious with me. Let me get away with anything. Not you." This catches me off guard.

"What?"

"You weren't cautious with me. For the first time in a long time I felt . . . like me. Normal. I don't know why I'm telling you that. It's just . . . something I was thinking about."

"No, I understand it completely, actually," I say.

Lincoln pulls the napkin from his lap and drops it on the tray of food. He crosses to the bed, tucking in next to me. He rests his head on my lap and as he speaks I wind his hair around my fingers. He sighs, settles in close, and continues, "So what came first. Unlike your brother, my younger brother was everything right with the world. He was exactly like my father. Which meant that there were now two monsters in my life. After university, I was to follow in my father's footsteps and join his army regiment, where I would become just another Rupert who was biding his time before he took over the family's estate."

"A Rupert?"

"It's what people call posho wankers like my younger brother and me . . ."

"I can only listen to this story if I know for sure your brother survives," I say.

"Oh, he does. He's far too dreadful to be any kind of war hero, I assure you."

"That's a relief," I say, and Lincoln laughs.

"Thing is, I liked it . . . in Afghanistan. It was the first time I felt like I belonged. That what I was doing was important and I was actually good at it. The other lads in my regiment, once they realized I wasn't a total—"

"Rupert."

"Yes. They began to accept me. And then I had to go and get blown up." My hand clutches back with his words, and I'm stunned and hesitant, even though I don't mean to be. "Please don't stop, Anna." His voice sounds so soft in that moment. I wind a dark blond curl around my finger as he continues, "We were in a convoy. It was routine. There hadn't been a strike or any kind of violence in days. We were talking about football. Arguing about football, really. And—" He shudders. Turns his head away from me. His entire body is tight. I can't see his face.

I don't know what to do. So, I do what he asked. I keep going, twirling his hair in my fingers. And I feel him settle just enough. Soften. Another shake of the head. He clears his throat. "Only I survived."

"Oh, Lincoln," I say.

"And I shouldn't have. The three others . . . they were better men. Kids. Married. Just better all around. I woke up in some hospital. They said I was out for almost three weeks . . . I had to be in this whole contraption to keep from getting infections . . . the burns and the skin grafts and the surgeries. And the whole time I'm thinking . . . why me? I'm a useless piece of rubbish and here I was. Alive. I didn't deserve to be." I feel a tear soak through my pajama bottoms. And another. And another. "So, I drank." He sniffles a bit, wiping his face and sitting up next to me, his dark blue eyes rimmed in red, his face blotchy and creased in pain. It breaks my heart. I swipe a stream of tears away with my thumb, letting my hand linger on his face. He tilts his head into my hand, closing his eyes. A deep breath. "Your turn." He manages a raised eyebrow and a smile through all the guilt and erupting grief.

"That's—"

"Not fair? Maybe." He tries to smile again, but I can see that he's completely tormented with what he's shared. I'm thinking he's sick of telling people he's fine about as much as I am. "I've shown you mine, now you show me yours."

"It's not anywhere near as heroic or . . ."

"I've been laid bare before you, darling. Please," he says. And then a little glint.

"You're so full of it."

"Oh, absolutely and yet . . ."

"Fine."

A beat. He waits. I take a deep breath. And just start talking.

"My father was a colonel in the army—never made general. Which was the perennial subject of our family dinner discussions. My mom is a painter. French Canadian—never had any interest in mastering English. To this day. Which meant that even within the nomadic military community we were weirdos. Which she never cared about, but—"

"So, you're fluent in French?"

"Oui."

"You want to open with that next time," Lincoln says, brightening up a bit. I smile, but then, just as it did in the shower that day, it disappears as quickly as it came. "Hey, come on. What could go wrong? We're just two complete strangers sharing our deepest, darkest secrets in a hotel room in Phoenix mere hours before we both check out." The tears are immediate and I crumple into sobs, hiding my face in my hands. "Oh God, I'm sorry. I'm so sorry." Lincoln pulls me into him, wrapping his arms around me, tight . . . tighter.

"We're doomed," I say, drooling through my sobs.

"What?"

"We're doomed. You can feel it, too, right? You know it," I say.

"What I know is that you will go to any length not to talk about yourself," he says, bringing my face up to meet his gaze. I laugh. Throw my head back and laugh. It feels . . . so good. Lincoln smiles . . . the furrowed brow giving away his worry or pain. Or both. I breathe. Try to regain control. Talking myself back to the relaxed place I return to when I get upset. Or feel lonely. Or have any emotion at all, really.

"I was by myself a lot as a kid. I don't even remember when I stopped . . . just stopped. Trusting, asking, loving . . . it just happened along the way somewhere. I don't have some tragic story—I'm not a war hero like you. I was just a lonely little kid. And then I became this." I shrug and can't look at him. "A dead body waiting for some amateur detective to stumble over her." I sit back from him a bit and really think about this. My hands whip up, and it's as if I'm holding a ball of energy between us. "The idea of really letting go—whatever that even means? I don't think I know what that is, because if I knew what that was, I'd have tried to do it."

"I don't think it's some kind of checklist, love," Lincoln says.

"Well, why not??"

"It doesn't work that way."

"I've been to therapy. I've been on a yearlong hiatus from dating. I've cleaned house of faux friends. I've made smoothies with flax oil in them and started drinking green juice. What else do I have to do?" Lincoln can't hold in his laughter. "I know. The green juice? Not as bad as you think it's going to be. But you know what? There was this moment." I lean into Lincoln, excited. "I was taking this pilates class. I know. Just stay with me. I tried everything over the last year to help fix myself. Everything. And I'm stretching out my back and the instructor takes his fingers and gives my spine a quick little massage. He gets down to my sacrum."

"Your what now?"

"This. Your sacrum," I twist him around and put my hand at the base of his spine. Lincoln nods. "And I howled out in pain. I turn around and the instructor says, 'Ah, I was wondering where yours was.' 'My what?' I ask. 'Where you hold all your pain.' Just like that. Where you hold all your pain. Like he was talking about where I keep my produce or my reusable bags for the grocery store."

"Sounds like a prat."

"Maybe, but what got me? I thought I'd grown out of it, that my adult brain knew how my parents acted—how icy they were and just . . ." I look away from Lincoln. "How they . . ." The tears. I stop. A breath. "How they didn't love me. At all." I look up at him. And he's just there. He doesn't look like he feels sorry for me or that I'm some sad little match girl. He's just there. Listening. So I continue, "I understand—however abstractly—that that's on them. So, I thought all that pain—I had it all figured out of course—would just evaporate. But apparently it doesn't. It just sank down into my sacrum where it waited for some yahoo to knead his fingers into it and then smugly report that, you know, he knew it was there the whole time." Lincoln laughs. "That's what scares me. That this is just how I am. Like directions. If I don't know how I got here, how am I going to know how to get back?" I bite the inside of my lip, hoping it'll stem the tide of tears trying to push its way up and out. It doesn't. Now I'm crying and the inside of my mouth is bleeding. Lincoln pulls me into him and I hold on to him. "How am I going to get back?" I ask again.

"I don't know . . . I don't know . . . ," he says, rubbing my back. "And we're not doomed." I let out a strangled laugh and pull away from him. Looking straight at him.

"Come on. We can barely handle three days in a hotel," I say.

"D.C. and Manhattan aren't that far apart," he says.

"What are we going to do? Date?"

"Sure."

"Uh-huh. So, you're comfortable with this level of intimacy. Just, like . . . all the time."

"Are you?" he asks.

"You're answering a question with another question."

"Of course I'm not comfortable with this level of intimacy all of the time," Lincoln says. He looks over at me and waits.

"Neither am I."

"Right."

"So what do we do?"

"I don't know." Another look over at me and then he lets his head fall into his hands. "I don't know, love." He drags his fingers through his hair and finally looks up. "I'd like to say that I've been . . . careful? Is that the right word? No. Shut down. That I've been shut down since the accident, but that's not true. The accident just slammed the door shut. Tight. Maybe I thought I could handle you . . . this . . . us? Because I knew or rationalized that it was only going to be temporary, if I even thought about it at all, which I'm really good at not doing."

"Why am I relieved?" I say, almost in a whisper.

"What?"

"I don't think it's good. I mean, in the way that everything with you is terrifying and whatever it is that you just said made me relieved."

"And that's not good?"

"No, because that means I think I'm off the hook."

"Off the—"

"Right. That—"

"No, I know." Lincoln looks away from me. He shakes his head. "I'd screw it up." He manages a smile. Pain. A shrug. Another shake of the head and then an ironic laugh as he finally settles. In the end he can only get up from the bed in shame. I stop him. "Any relationship—I mean, if you can call anything that I've had a relationship—doesn't last more than . . . a few weeks? Maybe a month?" he says.

"See now that's where I've got you beat. I, at least, had the ability to shut down and endure a loveless marriage for eleven years. And you call yourself dysfunctional."

"Are you trying to beat me at being emotionally unavailable?"

"What?"

"You are, aren't you? You are actively competing with me to be more hopeless."

"I'm just . . ." I can't help but laugh. "I mean, can you blame me for wanting something good to come of it?" He laughs.

We are silent. He takes a few steps toward the bathroom, his hand falling out of mine. Something about it feels . . . intentional. A chill runs through my body. He doesn't turn around as he begins speaking.

"I can't have you hate me." He turns around. The night-light from the bathroom illuminates him like a low moon. He lets his head fall. His arms akimbo. He shakes his head. "I don't think I could survive that."

"What are you on about?" I say, and he laughs.

"You've been hanging out with me too long."

"Aye, matey!"

"And now you're a pirate," he says. I begin inexplicably singing a confused, rambling medley of songs from Mary Poppins that were almost ruined by Dick Van Dyke's terrible cockney accent. And somewhere around "Step in Time" I notice that Lincoln isn't laughing anymore.

"The other women. Every woman, really. I've disappointed. Why couldn't they understand that it's because I like them that I had to stop dating them?" He laughs. "What was that quote . . . one of the Marx brothers?"

"Groucho." He nods and I can tell it hurts him that I know exactly what he's talking about.

"Groucho," he repeats. "That he'd never want to belong to a club that would have him as a member."

"Right."

"I never wanted to date someone who would have the poor judgment of falling for me. I mean, I know exactly how worthless I am; why didn't they?" A mean little laugh crumbles into a layer of him that breaks me open.

"Fools. Every last one of them," I say. Lincoln laughs. "Thank God I had the sense to steer clear." I reach for a glass on the nightstand and gulp the stale water, hoping it will mask the wobble in my voice as I try valiantly to keep from crying.

"This has to stay temporary. It has to. Or else you'll end up hating me."

"I hate you now, so . . ." Only half true.

"Good."

"Good." I want to scream. I want to . . . well, anything else except have Lincoln Mallory telling me we only have mere hours left together. Instead, I walk over to him in the dim light of that hallway. Up close, I now see the tears streaming down his face. I am calm. Eerily calm. I take his face in my hands, brushing his golden curls back.

"I think we should just look at the next however many hours we have together as the only thing that's for sure. I know I want to spend the entire day in bed with you. I know I'm tired of talking about sad things. You make me happy—so happy," I say, and then I kiss him. "Happier than I've ever been. Right here and right now and . . . I don't want to think about what happens when we have to leave this bed."

"I feel the same."

"I know you do."

"Anna, I—"

"Don't. Just don't," I say, stopping him with a kiss.

12

And that's exactly what we do.

After I get word that Audrey has returned to D.C., I can only think that coming to Phoenix was merely a portion of her plan. She'll go back to the agency and Sasha and I will brace ourselves for whatever the next wave is. Helen Brubaker is attending the giant signing with all the authors and Sasha is still hungover and dead to the world—I have nothing to do but languish in Lincoln's hotel room until the pageant that night.

We sleep soundly in each other's arms as the sun comes up, and then I wake up just long enough to find that I'm curled up and facing away from him, my arms hugging the pillow. Lincoln is snoring away on his side, his fist notched into the crook in his neck, thumb tucked into his hand like a baby. The morning rolls into lunchtime and Lincoln is up and telling housekeeping to skip us, but he's taking the mints they offer him as a consolation prize. He presents me with one in a low morning growl, flipping it to me as he flops back into bed, pulling the covers over him. As the heat and bright sun of high noon break through the drapes, I shuffle over and pull them closed, falling back into bed and into Lincoln for what are fast becoming more and more desperate sessions with each other. We can feel the countdown getting louder.

"I'm bloody starving," he says, crouching down next to me by the bed. "I'm going to get something from the machines. Any requests?" He cinches his bathrobe around him, his flips of dark blond hair everywhere. I grab my glasses from the nightstand and hitch myself up.

"Something from the machines?" I ask, still blinking myself awake.

"Yes, darling," he says.

"What time is it?"

"We're going to need to prioritize in these last hours, my love." He kisses me. "Food. What do you reckon?" he asks, taking money out of his wallet on the nightstand.

"Everything," I say.

"Good. Kettle's on," he says and he's out the door.

A beat.

The silence settles in around me as the chill of . . . the void begins to creep in. I swing my legs over the side of the bed, find my pajama bottoms, and lace my arms through the spaghetti straps of my tank top. I scrape my hair up into a ponytail, wrapping the tie around and around my tangle of hair. I check my phone. Nothing from Ferdie. I let my head fall into my hands as I realize how completely exhausted I am. From everything. Exactly how long have I been in Phoenix—a month? Month and a half? A decade?

But this is how it's going to be when he's gone. And not just at the machines for food. Isn't this why I decided to marry a man like Patrick—to avoid this exact moment? A moment that feels like I'm on a speeding train and can only watch as the blown-up bridge in front of us gets ever closer. Utterly helpless. How do I go back to my life after experiencing what I have with Lincoln over the last few days? Is the training montage over? Is that what this is? Me stepping into the ring? Even now the pangs of loss begin to tighten their grip around my heart.

I will drink tea. I stand and pour myself a cup, laughing that Lincoln Mallory actually travels with an electric kettle. I remember my own words:

I want to be happy and not feel guilty about it. I want to be curious without being called indulgent. I want to be accepted regardless of what I look like, what I do for a living, my marital status, whether I have kids, or whether you think I'm nice enough, hospitable enough, or humble enough to measure up to your impossible standards. I want purpose. I want contentment. I want to be loved and give love unreservedly in return. I want to be seen. I want to matter. I want freedom. I want to be . . . I want to just be.

Ninety percent of that list has nothing to do with Lincoln and everything to do with me. So why does it feel exactly the opposite? Maybe I just already miss him.

I think about Helen Brubaker and her question about what would happen if I made an entire playlist with just the songs I enjoyed. Even if I'd previously labeled them fluff. Why did I believe I had to ration out the good stuff to myself into bite-sized nuggets, apologizing to those who caught me indulging as if what I was doing was so wholly shameful? Of course I know. I dig into the deeper recesses of my mind to uncover a childhood with very little good. So I rationed it like it was sugar during wartime. Always careful. Always mindful. Never reckless.

Until now.

What do women want? Let's start with what I want. I want to feel like I deserve greatness. To demand the best all the time. I lift my head up and grab the hotel pen and pad of paper on the bedside table and write.

>   *JUST. BE.*
>   *Lumineux:*
> ~~*Because luxury should be something*~~
> ~~*every woman deserves on a daily basis.*~~

No.

> ~~*Because luxury is something every woman deserves each day.*~~

No.

>   ~~*Women deserve luxury every day.*~~

No. Almost.

>   ~~*Because luxury is for every day. . .*~~
>   ~~*each day. . .*~~
>   ~~*on a daily basis.*~~

No. Come on. Think.

>   *Lumineux:*
>   *The everyday luxury all women deserve.*

YES.

YES.

YES.

I look at what I wrote. That's it. That's the missing piece. It's one thing to convince women it's okay to luxuriate in romance novels and long hot showers with a fresh-smelling shower gel. I want this ad campaign to give women permission to sink into these things without all the baggage. Wanting to be happy does not make us bad people. Allowing ourselves to feel pleasure should not make us feel guilty. We are not being selfish if we don't always put your needs first.

We are women. And we can be the person we want to be, not the version you wish we were.

We'll repackage Lumineux. Beautiful and simple, stark whites and deep blues. A modern font with few words. No pink. No sparkles. And absolutely no glitter. Women are, although this may upset the applecart, neither idiotic nor little girls.

I text Sasha to see if she's up yet. She replies that she is. I suggest we meet before the pageant and head down together. She agrees. I balance the cell phone on the armrest of the chair, idly spinning it around as I blow on my tea. I take a deep breath and look at the time.

Four forty-three P.M.

The pageant starts at seven P.M. That leaves me with just over two hours with Lincoln until . . . until who knows.

Thing is? We both know. This isn't that scene in a romantic comedy where the audience wishes the two main characters would just talk to each other. Tell the truth! Tell him you love him, they yell to the movie screen. Sometimes you can have the most honest conversation of your entire life and the timing still isn't right to fall in love with someone. At least that's what I'm telling myself right now. I finally take a sip of my tea.

The door clicks and Lincoln tromps in with an armload of snacks and drinks. He dumps it onto the bed with a ta-daaaaaaa and an oddly executed curtsy. I watch him as he scans the candy. A brush of his chin as he thinks, and I can't help but smile.

"It's an embarrassment of riches," he says, running his hands through his muss of hair. He plucks a bag of roasted peanuts from the pile and rips it open. "I need protein." He pours the bag of peanuts into his waiting mouth.

"It's almost five o'clock," I say, my voice calm and low. Lincoln chews and swallows the peanuts, washing them down with a newly purchased bottle of water. I'm just about to start speaking again and he nods no. Another gulp of water.

"You'll come back here after the pageant," he says. I am quiet. He crosses the room, kneeling down in front of me. He takes my cup of tea, sets it on the bedside table, and takes my hands in his. "Just come here after the pageant." He squeezes my hands.

"Okay." He pulls me in for a kiss. It's . . . urgent. Desperate.

"Good," he whispers, so close to my face. Another kiss.

"So, I'll go get ready for tonight then. Now that this isn't . . . you know." I can't say it. Another kiss and I wriggle past him, my hand brushing his shoulder as I pass. I walk into the bathroom, grab my toiletries, and come back out into the room to find him sitting in the chair I just vacated. His bathrobe is cinched tightly around him and he just sits there.

"Hurry back," he says, his voice tight. I nod, looking down at myself. The same droopy pink tank top, the oversized striped-blue pajama bottoms. The clothes I wore yesterday are in a pile by the closet, and I pick them up, nestling them in the crook of my arm. He stands and walks over to me. "Here." He motions for me to hand him over everything. I oblige. A shake of the head and an "I mean . . . come on, love." He takes everything and dumps it on the bed next to the snacks. He tidies and zips up my toiletry bag, folds my clothes from yesterday, and stacks them underneath the bag. He turns around and takes me in. He walks over to the dresser and pulls a blue V-neck sweater from the drawer. "You can't go out like that. Up." I raise my hands high and he threads the arms of the sweater onto mine. I pop my head through the neck and he pulls the sweater down over my body. It smells of him, that'll be one of several things that break my heart tonight. A kiss. And I just look at him. I try to stay rational about this . . . everything. I smooth a hand over the cashmere and the softness of it starts to break me open. "Just come back after the pageant." His voice is quiet, pleading. Whether he's begging me to return or begging me not to lose it right now, I don't know. Probably both.

"Okay," I say. I curl my fingers around the lapel of his bathrobe, and I am immediately taken back to those first few minutes in the elevator less than three days ago. And unlike before, when his eyes were surprised, confused yet wanton, today his eyes are just . . . sad. But the stillness. This man has a talent for stillness. I pull him into me and let myself burn up in those moments. Letting go. Giving over. Losing myself.

"And just like that, you're going to be late," he says, and we're on the bed once more, laughing and happy. Apparently he's just as comfortable with being in denial as I am.

* * *

I'm getting out of the shower back in my own hotel room when I hear a text come through. Ferdie? No. Lincoln. It's a picture. Of him surrounded by empty candy wrappers with just the words *Look what you made me do.* I laugh. Time ticking away. I pull my towel off and finish drying myself. I carry the towel to the bathroom and hang it on the hook on the back of the door.

hahahahahahaahah, I text back to Lincoln. I realize that this is the only picture I have of him. The only thing to remind me that he was real.

I switch screens and text Sasha that I'll knock on her door in fifteen minutes.

what??? TOO SOON TOO SOON! I smile and throw the phone back on the bed.

I put on the bare minimum of makeup and put my hair up into some passable updo that doesn't look like a style called "bedhead plus unwashed." I spray on a little hair spray and finish getting dressed in the one moderately formal dress I brought to Phoenix—an orange, belted shirtdress with a nice pair of espadrilles I pull from the bottom of my closet. I throw my pajama bottoms, the dingy tank top, and Lincoln's sweater into my purse along with whatever basic toiletries I'll need for tonight. I don't have time to think about tomorrow morning. Flights and airports. Saying good-bye or asking questions with no answers. I shake my head, grab my hotel key, close the door behind me, and walk across the hall to Sasha's room. She opens the door in just her bra and panties.

"Come in, come in . . . ," she says, pulling me in and closing the door behind me. "You're early." It's barely 6:15.

"We're supposed to be there by six thirty," I say, walking over to the desk and settling in the chair. "How are you feeling?"

Sasha's notebook is on the desk, opened to the notes she took during Helen's workshop.

"I'm okay. I've taken too many antacids and maybe some Gas-X and definitely too many aspirin. I've tried to stay hydrated and of course I've already taken my hangover cure," Sasha says, stepping into her slinky black dress. She walks over to me and I zip her up.

"Hangover cure?"

"Doritos Nacho Cheese and a Coke," she says, hurrying into the bathroom, where she finishes putting on her makeup.

"Is that the official hangover cure?" I ask, scanning Sasha's notebook.

"It should be," she calls out.

Underneath Sasha's doodles of a wedding cake topper, I find what Sasha has entitled "The Rules of Romance." They are as follows:

1. Everyone deserves to be worshipped.
2. There's a hero inside all of us.
3. The hero and heroine are fine on their own but know they're better together.
4. Risk your heart, it's worth it.
5. Always believe in a happy ending.

I can feel the emotion rising in my throat, a particularly violent kind of joy. At the bottom of the page, Sasha has drawn a sunset and a couple walking hand in hand toward it. I brush my hand over her little drawing. Always believe in a happy ending.

"It looks so easy," I say.

"Whaat?" Sasha calls out from the bathroom. She walks out, putting an earring on. "What?"

"The happy ending thing," I say. I point to her notebook. "The Rules of Romance."

"Oh. Yeah." Sasha's entire body deflates just enough for me to become concerned.

"What is it?" I ask.

"I know we have no time and we're going to be late, but I have to tell you something," Sasha says. My stomach lurches. Has Audrey told her we're off the campaign?

"Okay."

"It was Chuck. Chuck Holloway? That's who I had that date with and that's who I've been texting," Sasha says. She breathes. "So go ahead. Tell me I'm terrible. But you know what? You don't even have to! I know I'm terrible. I was looking at those rules last night or this morning, I don't know, it's been kind of a haze, but I wasn't doing any of that. I wasn't doing anything in Helen's book; I wasn't even doing anything from the romance novels that I say I love. Nothing. And there I was talking to you about how you should do this and 'well, in romance novels that means that,' and I was the one who was going behind your back with the villain!"

"The villain?"

"Yeah. I mean, if this were a romance novel, wouldn't Chuck Holloway totally be the villain of my story?"

"Him tricking you to his apartment would make a pretty good argument," I say.

"I know, but I told myself—lied to myself, really—that I should be flattered. He'd gone to all that trouble just to go on a date with me. Wasn't it romantic?"

"No. No, it is not."

"No, it is not," Sasha repeats. "It's creepy."

"Not for nothing? If you take a scene or relationship out of a romantic comedy and put it into real life, though? A lot of it? Creepy."

"Right?"

"Oh, absolutely. I can see why you liked him."

"He was funny."

"I can see that."

"He'd been flirting with me for months before he made his move. I thought it was cute. What I was texting about in the elevator—remember?"

"I think so," I say. I absolutely remember and it's been killing me.

"A girlfriend of mine who still works at the club where I used to run the coat check said he'd been playing the same old line on another of the waitresses there. This time he was going on and on about how smart she was and how she could totally come work for him and . . . well, basically all the same stuff."

"Oh, sweetie. I'm so sorry."

"Me too. I'm pissed that it took something like that for me to see it. Like . . . what if I'd never found out? Am I really not able to police myself? You know what I mean?"

"I think you're being a bit hard on yourself."

Sasha flounces off to the bathroom and calls out, "I should have known."

"Sasha, you're not the bad guy in this scenario. Chuck is. It's not a bad thing that you're a romantic. It really isn't." She walks out of the bathroom and steps into her stiletto heels, grabs her glittery clutch, and motions for me to head out. I stand and follow her out of the room.

"You're sweet, but it kind of is. Because I'm a romantic with a self-esteem problem. Which means I build romance novels around losers. All they have to do is show up and I fill in the rest."

"Join the club," I say, as we rush down the hotel hallway.

"I was thinking about your 'Thunder Road' story," she says.

"Oh?"

"I think I need a Time-Out, too," she says. "Because you're right, it's not a bad thing that I'm a romantic. I just need to stop falling for the villain. Because right now? I'm the poor girl that gets shot jumping in front of some loser as he holds the hero and heroine hostage, you know what I mean?"

"I think I do."

"Aww, you finally speak romance novel," she says. I can't help but laugh and, oh my God, it feels amazing. It's so needed.

In the elevator, Sasha looks at herself in the silvery reflection of the closed doors and couldn't be less impressed with what she sees. She is quite literally the most beautiful woman I've ever seen in real life. And like a lightning bolt, it hits me. I finally get what we're trying to do with the Lumineux campaign.

I remember when Sasha and I were back in D.C. and I had one of those green drinks that I'd started drinking. I felt very smug and noble touting the beauty of cold-pressed this and four-times-the-vegetables that and "it really should be in a glass bottle, but . . ." When Sasha asked me about it, I insinuated that she should drink them, not because they're healthy and she's healthy and everything's great, but because something was lacking in her diet and the juices would "fix" things. That's what we do in advertising. We're the frenemy who makes you feel just bad enough that you'll reach for our product to fix you. Sure, you're passable, but with this? You could be perfect. For now. And this tactic works like a charm because it mirrors how we women communicate with the people we call friends. How many times have I sat across from someone who "meant well" and been shamed into trying some new exercise program or cleanse or makeup or salon treatment?

That's what's at the root of Helen Brubaker's success. She doesn't make women feel lacking in any way. Hers is not a dating book based on how you can change yourself to best ensnare some low-hanging fruit. No. *Be the Heroine* is a phenomenon because it finally does the one thing women have been waiting for: it respects them.

"If you think you need a Time-Out, then . . . I trust you," I say, as we step out of the elevator and make our way through the lobby. Sasha just looks at me. Brow furrowed. Her mouth opens and closes as she stops and starts several sentences. I say, "You know what's best for you, so . . ." Sasha's eyes narrow. I give our ticket to the valet.

"So you think I should?" Sasha finally asks.

"I can definitely say that my Time-Out changed the trajectory of my life."

"I want that. I want a new trajectory."

"Then there's your answer," I say, as the valet brings around our car. Sasha is quiet as we drive to the conference hotel. She's elsewhere. That makes two of us. She spins her cell around in her hands and has taken to reading passing signs for Phoenix businesses out loud. We pull up to the conference hotel, valet our car, take the same escalators up, up, up, and—

We are met with every kind of rendition of gangsta/gangster one could imagine. Women in 1940s garb with plastic tommy guns next to B-boys and super 1980s break-dancers with clocks around their necks and a few flappers here and there. One thing is for certain: this is the night everyone went all out.

"Why are you not more mad about the Chuck Holloway thing?" Sasha asks.

"I don't know. It's in the past and . . ." I stop. We're threading through the crowd, winding our way back into the Silver Ballroom.

"And?" Sasha asks, pulling her black dress down a bit.

"And you're my friend," I say.

"I am?" Sasha asks.

"Yeah," I say.

"Why am I crying?" Sasha asks.

"I don't know, but . . ." I realize I'm a bit misty-eyed as well. "I feel like I'm seven years old or something."

"I feel like we've been in Phoenix forever," Sasha says, pulling a tissue from her glittery clutch.

"Me too."

We crane our necks to see which of the doors is unlocked as the crowd of gangsta women begins to line up for tonight's festivities.

"Anna?" Sasha says. We try a couple of doors. Locked.

"Yeah?" A single door on the far end of the hallway opens and Ginny Barton peeks out. She motions for us.

"You're my friend, too." I smile at her as we hurry toward Ginny. We squeeze past her and she slams the door behind us.

The ballroom has been transformed. Rows of chairs fill the room awaiting the horde of women who gather just outside. The stage is done up just as it was the night the contestants were announced; their banners still hang from the rafters. Conference volunteers bustle around the room with chairs and placards and headsets and clipboards all while garbed in full gangster regalia. There is no sign of the contestants. Probably backstage primping.

"Thank you for coming; it's quite crazy here," Ginny says. She then offers an answer, a direction, and a nod to three volunteers asking three different questions. Ginny is wearing a beautiful fringed silver dress right out of the 1920s, her curly brown hair tamed with a sparkly headband and accented with a large white feather at her temple.

"Everything looks amazing," I say, taking it all in.

"We didn't dress up," Sasha says, stating the obvious.

"Don't you worry about that," Ginny says, giving Sasha a maternal pat. Sasha softens.

"Exciting night," I say.

"It is, indeed," Ginny says. Sasha gives me a look. Exciting night? I just shrug. Not all my material is going to be revolutionary.

A harried volunteer. And another. A quick sound check. A lighting check. Another emergency, another fire to put out, and Ginny scans the room for anything else that needs her attention. Sasha and I are hovering. Droolingly hovering.

"Ms. Dayal is already at the judges' table along with Mr. Grant. If you could," Ginny says, motioning for us to join them.

"Oh, right. Okay, good luck tonight," I say.

"And you," she says and is off to open the doors. "I'll join you as soon as we let everyone in." Sasha and I make our way to the judges' table, which is situated on risers right in front of the long walkway extending from the stage. Sasha slows as we near the judges' table. Ryder.

"This is where I used to have to slink up here. But now?" Sasha motions for us to climb the stairs to the judges' table. I oblige her. The volunteers at the base of the steps check our badges and wave us on. I grab the cold metal handrail. Sasha's shoulders are back, her head held high. "Hey, Ryder." A little wave, a hair flip, and Sasha slides into her seat. Ryder can only shift in his chair and check his phone. I settle in next to Preeti, letting Sasha take the seat at the far end. Sasha can't stop smiling.

"I've got to admit, this is all very exciting," Preeti says. The room quickly fills with costumed, excited women streaming into their seats, ready for the show. The ambient music thumps and pulsates just below the growing din. Groups of women pose for photos, explosions of laughter dot the room, and the strobe lights whip and move around the ceiling. This is like nothing I've ever seen.

"They do put on quite a show," I say, scanning the judging sheets in front of me. The different categories and criteria are both elaborate and quite scientific—especially for judging something like "beach bod," which is an actual category I'm supposed to be the expert on. As the sound in the room builds, Ginny joins us at the judges' table and settles in next to Ryder. The feather on her headband hangs over him like a question mark, tickling the top of his head. He has no idea what it is and keeps waving away what he thinks is an annoying fly. It's amazing.

"Welcome to Mr. RomanceCon!" Helen Brubaker's voice rings throughout the Silver Ballroom like a bell. She appears through the silver lamé curtains wearing a phenomenal ball gown. She holds up a hand as she settles in behind the podium and the ballroom shushes into silence.

"Ladies? Are you ready?"

The entire Silver Ballroom erupts in *Yes!!*

"Then let's get to it."

And the ballroom falls into blackness as the opening chords to Joe Cocker's version of "You Can Leave Your Hat On" kicks in.

I hear Preeti gasp.

"Oh my God," I say, as the silver lamé curtains open to reveal seven silhouettes.

13

Seven men. In 1940s-style suits. Fedoras tilted. With their backs to the audience. My mouth drops open. I hear Sasha dissolve into giggles next to me. Preeti scoots her chair closer.

A spotlight. Colt turns around.

A spotlight. Blaise turns around.

A spotlight. Tristan turns around.

A spotlight. Billy turns around.

A spotlight. Jake turns around.

A spotlight. Josh turns around.

A spotlight. Lantz turns around.

The women in the audience go crazy, and I can't wipe the smile from my face.

As the song continues, this quickly becomes a number one might see in Vegas or at The Naughty Kitty. Jackets come off slowly, fedoras are whipped into the audience, and suspenders get lusciously pulled down broad shoulders.

"But I thought the idea was to leave their hat on?" I whisper to Sasha as a fedora hits the judges' table and falls into the crowd below. She laughs. Now shirts are unbuttoned and peeled down muscular arms to reveal bulging biceps and oiled-up chests and and and . . . The expertise among the contestants and their ideas of come-hither dancing cover the entire spectrum. For men like Billy and Blaise (hahaha), it comes down to how fervently they thrust their crotches at the audience. AT THE AUDIENCE. AT! THE! AUDIENCE! For men like Colt and Tristan, it's your basic hot guy dancing. No rhythm, but looka this bicep and looka this six-pack and whaddaya think of this, though . . . aaaand thrust. Jake and Lantz actually look like they're having a good time, dancing and playing to the audience. I do love a man who can dance. And then there's Josh, who just looks kind of embarrassed, fumbling with his clothes and oh, did taking off my shirt reveal an incredible body? Sigh . . . This ole thing? And that's why he's the favorite. He's Lewis Carroll's snark. He's the elusive unicorn. He's the guy who's model-hot but doesn't know it. Although he *did* sign up for the pageant in the first place. So . . .

The song comes to an end and the men are all standing on the stage in various stages of undress. The crowd goes wild.

Right then, Helen Brubaker walks out in front of all seven men, her eyes flicking over every inch of them with an arched eyebrow and a crooked smile. She's now dressed in a beautiful one-shouldered, floor-length black gown. And the diamonds. Oh my God, the diamonds. The spotlight finds her and the men retreat backstage for the next phase of the pageant.

"Welcome to the final night of RomanceCon! You all look amazing," she says, shielding her eyes from the bright spotlight to take in the audience fully. "While our seven handsome contestants get ready for their next event, I want to introduce the judges who have the unenviable task of choosing just one of those luscious men as Mr. RomanceCon. And this year, the stakes are even higher. The winner of tonight's Mr. Romance-Con has the opportunity of becoming the newest spokesman for Lumineux brand shower gel!" The crowd oohs and aahs, building to a crescendo. Preeti beams. "Our first judge is a face you will happily recognize. He's graced over one hundred covers of some of your favorite books and was last year's Mr. Romance-Con. Mr. Ryder Grant!" The crowd cheers as Ryder stands up, waving to the crowd, blowing kisses, and holding his arms up like some kind of prizefighter. And yes, now he's kissing his biceps. I can't. "Next to Mr. Grant is our esteemed League of Romance Novelists president, Ginny Barton!" Ginny stands and waves to the crowd. "Don't you look lovely, Ginny!" Ginny blushes and sits back down. "Next to President Barton we have our esteemed guest from Lumineux Shower Gel herself. She confided in me that it was her mother's love of romance novels through a very trying round of chemo that turned her on to the genre." The crowd reacts with awwws and applause. "Mrs. Preeti Dayal from Lumineux Shower Gel." Preeti stands and the crowd applauds. "She's in remission now, yes?" Preeti nods, getting choked up as the crowd's applause swells. Sniffling, she sits back down next to me and I smile at her. "And finally we have our two Mad Women, in charge of the Lumineux campaign. Coming to RomanceCon in search of a spokesman was their brainchild: Ms. Anna Wyatt and Ms. Sasha Merchant." I am beyond thankful that she introduced us together. The crowd applauds us. Sasha and I stand and wave, and it finally hits me how big a deal this is. The sea of women out there is bigger than I ever expected, and seeing them all together is overwhelming. I look over at Sasha and I can see that the moment is hitting her in much the same way. She looks at me and smiles, and I can't help but smile back. We sit down again, situating ourselves back at the judges' table.

"It looks like our men are ready for round two already. Contestants vying for Mr. RomanceCon are always known for their stamina," Helen purrs. The crowd hoots and hollers. Preeti laughs and I can only shake my head. "As you know, Mr. RomanceCon has to master a lot of different looks on some of your favorite romance novels." The large screen at the back of the stage begins to flash with various romance novel covers. And for each the crowd goes wild. Helen walks us through different plotlines of these novels for each cover: "They have to be warriors. Earls. Rakes. Cops tortured by their past. And the doctors who help those in need. They're single fathers. And cowboys. They are the undead. Those who battle the undead. Werethis and werethat. They must embody royalty from a time in the not-so-dystopian future and then breathe life into those who mean to start revolutions against royalty from a time in the not-so-dystopian future. They are your heroes."

The men appear in tuxedoes and stand in a straight line that stretches across the front of the stage. Helen announces that the contestants will be asked questions submitted by the women of RomanceCon.

Colt's role model is his father, a rancher who works the land and is still married to his mom after thirty years. He taught Colt what it meant to be a man, Colt says. Something he hopes to pass on to his son. Aww.

Tristan says that "the everyday" inspires him. When Helen asks what he means by that he rambles on about simplicity and Buddhism and the silence of meditation and then we're maybe touching on aliens and how there's something bigger than us out there but it's spiritualism and his dead grandmother and maybe he had a dream about her and now he's talking about being a light-bringer and we all have a light inside of us. A smattering of applause as Tristan smiles and waves, thinking he's inspired everyone into silent awe.

Jake says the worst thing that could ever happen to him would be to lose his mother. He gets choked up and the entire ballroom clutches their pearls as we sniffle along with him while he talks about what a force his mother is and how she keeps him grounded and taught him what love is and then he makes a joke about her being immortal and everyone laughs through their tears. He smiles and steps back into line with the rest of the men with a single tear adorning his impossibly beautiful face.

Blaise sees himself running an empire a year from now. An empire built on romance novels and cover models and maybe some costume design because his wife is clearly a genius and he views himself as a modern-day Renaissance man. Helen asks him what man from the Renaissance is his inspiration and Blaise stumbles through his answer of "all of them" and "you know, bits of everything from everyone of all time periods and then some from modern-day guys, too, maybe." A round of applause and Blaise steps back in a confused haze.

Helen asks Lantz how he thinks he can improve on his personality and he just laughs. "What can't I improve on, right??" And everyone laughs with him. He runs his hand through his reddish-blond overgrown tangle of hair and then thoughtfully brushes his scruff of a beard for a few seconds. Both of these things are really bringing home this whole log cabin, pioneering spirit thing. He looks like he should be on the outside wrapping of some paper towels. Maybe we've got a bit of a dark horse here in Mr. Lantz. He winds through how life is all about curiosity and humility; knowing that you don't know anything is the best place in the world to be. And it's like we're all Team Lantz now. Until Josh ambles up to stand with Helen. The pitch-black hair and the piercing blue eyes I can see from here. The broad shoulders all contained in a finely tailored tuxedo. It's almost too much. Almost.

"Well, goddamn," Sasha mutters just next to me. I nod.

"Agreed," Preeti says next to me.

Josh is asked if being sexy has a negative connotation. Preeti leans over and says that that's a really good question. I nod in agreement.

"That's a really good question," Josh says, and I look over at Preeti. She gestures that she and Josh are clearly of the same mind, and I laugh. "I think sexy is negative only if it's the only thing about you. I'd be a total hypocrite if I argued that being thought of as sexy, however uncomfortable I am with it, is somehow a burden to me. Come on." The crowd laughs. "But if that's all you are? I mean, that's what leads to old dudes in red Corvettes trying to pick up on girls half . . . not even half—a third their age. If you don't know or value that there's more to you than being sexy . . . I don't know, that just feels sad to me. So, my official answer is being sexy is only negative if you think that's all you have to offer."

The crowd applauds. And swoons. And throws panties. And we might as well just pack this whole thing in now. Sasha looks over at me with an "Are you kidding me?" face. I nod. I know. I know. I hear Preeti sigh next to me.

And up walks Billy. I would not want to follow Josh. Helen

asks Billy what makes him fearful. It's a good question. Jake made us swoon with what he feared most. This is a real opportunity to get us on his side.

"What makes me fearful. So . . . scared? What am I scared of? I mean, bears, right? Gotta go with bears. Sharks maybe?"

Is that . . . I begin to laugh, thinking that Billy has just made an awesome joke and now he's going to launch into his hidden fears and . . . nope. He's walking back to the line of men with his hands in the air as if he just naaailed it. Helen just . . . the look on her face is priceless.

The men are excused and Helen presents the romance novel award winners from earlier today. Applause and short but sweet thank-you speeches from the authors. Fans show their support from the audience as we grade the formal wear/Q&A and pass our ballots to the conference volunteers. The stage goes black once again.

The opening chords kick in to Lady Gaga's "Bad Romance." Sasha nudges me and I whisper, "They'd have to, right?" She laughs.

The contestants are now in swimsuits. The women in the audience are on their feet and dancing along with the contestants. Each man presents himself to applause with a combination of dancing, thrusting, and flexing, given his personality. And, of course, Blaise is wearing a Speedo. I mean, I'm thankful there's no dance number in this portion of the pageant; I can't begin to think about Blaise and that tiny Speedo and any sort of crouching or bending over.

The contestants retreat again to more costume changes as we judge and pass our ballots to the conference volunteers once more. Helen takes this time to unveil the date and theme of next year's RomanceCon. The crowd goes wild again. I know every-one already hates that we all have to leave tomorrow and return to real life. A flash. Real life. I have to leave tomorrow. Lincoln. A breath as the announcements and applause mute around me. What am I going to do? I can't . . . I can't leave with nothing. I have . . . I have to figure something out. I have to . . . The entire room falls into blackness and just the banners that hang over-head are illuminated.

The music kicks in—it's the kind of epic music used in movie trailers, and it's perfect. The men stream out onto the stage in the costumes from those same banners now spotlighted high above us. Fireman. Steampunk dirigible captain. Mr. Darcy. Undead loverboy. Scottish rake. Sexy gladiator. And cowboy. They really are those romance novel heroes come to life. The spotlight hits Jake in all his fireman hotness as the music thumps. He steps forward as the crowd hushes. He walks across the stage, and conference volunteers step forward and quickly dress him in a suit and tie, and he strikes a pose as a businessman. Then con-ference volunteers shift some of his clothing and add a badge and an overcoat, and Jake hits another pose, absolutely becom-ing the tortured cop. The crowd is riveted.

"This is really cool," Sasha says, leaning over.

"How are they doing this?" I ask.

"Totally amazing," Sasha whispers back, our eyes focused on Jake, who's now becoming a small-town doctor with every in-tention of healing his next patient.

Each contestant goes through this same gauntlet, showing just how versatile he can be in the characters he must portray on these covers. How it's not the clothes, it's the stance and the tilt of a head and a narrowed eye and a furrowed brow that makes the character come to life. It's fascinating to now know these men a bit and see how personalities come through. As the last man hits his pose in the last vignette, Helen bids them adieu once more. We hand in our scorecards to the waiting conference volunteers and the board of the League of Romance Novelists will tabulate the final scores.

The men are presented once again in clothes that they've chosen—which range from jeans and cowboy boots to a tailored suit to something that looks like a crushed velvet . . . is that an ascot? Come on, Mrs. Blaise. Helen is handed an envelope and the drumroll fills the room.

"Thank you so much for joining us, and I have so enjoyed myself at this year's RomanceCon!" The crowd applauds. "Cocktails will be served in the hallway outside, just so the hotel staff can transform this room into the 1940s dance party that will take us into the wee hours of the night. Gentlemen, won't you join me at the front of the stage?"

The men step forward.

"Our second runner-up and the man we all want to bring home to Mom, even though his is immortal: Jake!" Jake steps up and accepts a boutonniere pinned to him by conference volunteers. I applaud. Great choice.

"I really liked him," Sasha says. I nod in agreement.

"And our first runner-up and the man I know to turn to when anything in my house needs fixing, Lantz!" Lantz is in shock. I love it. He absolutely came from behind. I love that Billy got shut out. Lantz steps forward, his entire face flushed, and he can't stop waving at the audience and thanking Helen. He goes over and stands next to Jake, and they adorably wrap their arms around each other in a bear hug.

"And this year's Mr. RomanceCon, with a shot at becoming the new spokesman for Lumineux Shower Gel. The man we hope will walk through several lakes in a loose-fitting white shirt: *Josh Fox!!*" The crowd is standing as Josh steps forward. Confetti and balloons fall from the ceiling as the music kicks in. Helen shakes his hand and leans in to say something. He nods and nods, just smiling at her as she talks. He says, "Yes, ma'am" as she pins the boutonniere on him. He laughs as she talks to him, taking forever with the pin and his lapel, and he's just standing there being patient with her. She pats the flower and the conference volunteers present him with a sash that says MR. ROMANCECON—he bends over so they can slip the sash over his muss of pitch-black hair. The music erupts and the other contestants gather around Josh, congratulating him. The crowd applauds and, after several minutes of celebration, begins to stream out of the ballroom, happy and ready for a night of dancing.

"He's perfect," Preeti says.

"I know, right?" Sasha and I say in unison.

"And you know . . . the top prizewinners are so different, we can actually use all three for different markets," Preeti says. I just smile and don't point out that Preeti is already talking about what she plans to do with our campaign. I can only hope that this excitement spills over into Monday's pitch and that leads to us landing Lumineux. And then: Quincy Pharmaceuticals.

"That'd be amazing," Sasha says, leaning over me. "They're all so great."

"Thank you so much for judging. I think we got a real winner," Ginny says, standing up from the judges' table.

"He is going to be perfect," Preeti says. Ryder exits the judges' table without anyone saying good-bye. Sniff.

"This has been lovely, President Barton. Thank you so much for making us feel welcome," Preeti says, extending her hand.

"Oh, it was our pleasure. I look forward to working with you in the future," she says with a warm smile. She picks her way carefully down the stairs and joins the streams of women heading out to cocktail hour, kicking playfully at a few balloons in the process. The hotel staff and conference volunteers are already clearing chairs as the DJ begins to eye the judges' table for where she'll set up her turntables.

"We should probably . . ." I motion to the steps. "So, we'll see you on Monday."

"Monday," Preeti says.

"I'm looking forward to it," I say, extending my hand. Preeti takes it and is about to say something. Again. Then a nod. A smile. A squeeze of my hand. Then Sasha's. "Make sure to bring all three of them with you."

"All three?" I ask.

"Why not? To visualize the scope of your campaign," she says.

"The scope, huh?"

"At least that's what I'll tell my husband," Preeti says with a wink and disappears into the river of women exiting the ballroom.

"Are you going to stick around?" Sasha asks. "Or . . ."

"Or," I say. This feeling is swirling in the pit of my stomach. It's making me agitated. Anxious.

"And how is or?" Sasha asks.

"I don't know," I say, and the tears begin to well in my eyes without any warning.

"Wait . . . don't cry . . . come on," Sasha says, pulling me into her. I say nothing. There are no words. I let myself cry on Sasha's shoulder and she just talks to me. About romance novels. Stories. Love. Hope. Time. Letting go of butterflies. Swans. This one ballad that can get her crying no matter what. What's the name of it? It was her grandmother's favorite. What's the name of it? Something. Bette Midler. "The Rose," she squeals. "The Rose," she whispers. And then she's humming it. And now she's singing it. Every time it makes her cry. Her entire body rumbles with the passion of Bette Midler. She raises her fist to the rafters as she sings, "And you think that love is only for the lucky and the strong." She gets me laughing as she lets her voice whisper the next few lyrics, crouching with the intensity the song deserves. She never lets me go. She cries with me. She gives me a tissue and doesn't mind that I get snot on her little black dress. The ballroom empties out and it's just us and the hotel staff and conference volunteers. The DJ tests out the sound system, and her music fills the room.

Sasha and I finally stop clutching each other like long-lost siblings reunited after decades apart. A nod. A smile. We leave tomorrow morning. The shuttle leaves at eight A.M.

"Mrs. Brubaker would like to see you," Hector the Oddly Arousing Assistant says, appearing out of nowhere.

"Oh . . . thanks," I say, as Sasha and I try to collect ourselves. We follow him up the stairs, backstage, and find Helen, who's now dressed in full flapper garb. Her assistant is fitting a beaded headband tightly around her now pin-curled hair. Another assistant hands us two copies of *Be the Heroine*. We thank her. I look at Sasha. She's thinking the same thing. Consolation prizes for saying no to our request for her counsel.

"Oh, don't be all pouty. I'm saying yes," Helen says, thanking her assistant as the headband is set perfectly in place.

"Really?" I ask.

"Hector will e-mail you from my private e-mail address," Helen says. Hector nods. Sasha opens the book. It's signed. She looks up. Beaming.

"Thank you so much," I say.

"Now, I don't know how this is going to work, but I do know that if I get a call from you and all you want to do is talk about how your boss doesn't understand you and ask me to act like your mom or something—"

"I can assure you that is not what we're thinking this is, either," I say. Sasha is speechless, clutching the book to her chest.

"I know. I know you don't," Helen says.

"Thank you so much," I say.

"You're so great," Sasha says, and Helen smiles.

"Okay, so I'll see you when I see you then," Helen says.

"Looks like," I say. Helen gives me a wink and walks out into the swarm of women already enjoying cocktail hour.

I open the book. Helen has written:

Anna:
Change doesn't happen just because we think something
is wrong. Change happens because we think something
is wrong and then don't stop fighting until it's right.
Don't stop until it's right, Ms. Wyatt.
We're all counting on you.
Your mentor,
Helen

Sasha and I walk out from backstage, through the transforming ballroom, and into the cramped and busy hallway. One final smile. Sasha stays behind at the cocktail hour and tells me she'll cab it back to the Biltmore. I make my way to Lincoln.

I now know what I must do.

14

I walk through the Biltmore lobby in a haze. Climb into the elevator, push the button for Lincoln's floor, and stand back from the doors. I'm not ready. I'm not ready. I get out on his floor. I can hear my labored breathing inside my head. My heavy footfalls bringing me close . . . close . . . closer to him. My belt cinches at my waist. Squeezing me tight. I undo it, looping it up and throwing it into my purse in a panic. My dress falls loosely around my body. His door. I turn to it in what feels like slow motion. I put my hand on the doorjamb and lower my head. A deep breath. I raise my head and knock.

I hear him just inside, his confident steps nearing the door, and everything in these last moments becomes precious to me. I want to save the sound of him walking toward me under glass. He opens the door, pulling it wide open. Come in. I walk under his arm easily and enter the room. I cross to the far window. I turn around and he's by the door.

"You Marpled me," I say.

"I beg your pardon?" he asks, putting his hands into his jeans pockets.

"You Marpled me. I didn't see you coming. And now I'm sitting in some well-appointed salon as you unmask me as the murderer," I say.

"This is in refer—"

"The Anna Wyatt Marple Theory: No one ever noticed her observing, chronicling . . . working. No one ever noticed her at all."

"Not to be confused with us being the dead bodies of our own story?"

"No, and apparently I make a lot of Agatha Christie references," I say. A smile.

"Anna, I—"

"If someone doesn't perceive you as a threat, how will they see you coming? They won't. I won't. I didn't. I never saw you coming."

He is quiet.

"You've unraveled me," I say. Lincoln is still. "You're so good at that."

"What?"

"Stillness."

"Only on the outside, love."

"Hm," I say, feeling the first tear stream down my face. I can see Lincoln fighting the urge to come to me, comfort me, soothe me. But he knows he can't. Not about this. *Temporary.* The word cuts through me. I take his blue V-neck sweater from my purse and lovingly place it on the bedside table.

"You're not staying the night."

"No."

"Smart." He shakes his head. Hurt. Angry. Frustrated. He manages a smile. "Smart," he repeats.

"It doesn't feel smart," I say.

"Well, at least you're not a coward."

"Lincoln—"

"Earlier today? I thought I was this white knight saving you from this terrible fate. Stopping things before we got in too deep—"

"Too late."

"Too late," Lincoln repeats. A smile. A painful smile.

"And I think I might be as big of a coward as you are."

"We truly are soul mates then." He laughs and then stifles a sob as he brings his fisted hand up to cover his mouth. "I'm sorry."

"Me too." I cross the room toward the desk. "But . . . but I can't leave with nothing." I find the pen and pad of hotel paper among the beginnings of his packed clothes and write. I tear off the slip of paper and walk over to him with it. I let my head fall onto his chest and feel his hand instantly on the back of my head, his other arm wrapping around my waist, pulling me close. Closer. He kisses the top of my head. Desperate. Urgent. Insistent.

"It's going to be all right," he says, his voice rumbling in his chest. And I just shake my head no. As the ice of the last forty years melts, the tears finally come. I pull myself away, the now crumpled piece of paper in my heated palm. I fold the paper into his hand and close his fingers around it.

"It's a Hail Mary, I know."

"Hail Mary?"

"Oh, that's right. American football reference. Sorry. Um . . .

a last resort? Look it up, it's actually perfect for whatever this is I'm about to do."

"You have my full attention."

"Here's the address of this little Italian restaurant in D.C. we went to for my birthday this year. I didn't know what to wish for. Isn't that weird? I should have known then." The tears choke me up and I let my head fall again into him. He can only wrap his arms around me and wait. Helpless. I make myself look at him. Those dark blue eyes. He's in pain. I put my hand on the side of his face and he leans into it. His eyes closing. A deep breath. He calms. "Come to dinner. It's all there." Lincoln opens his eyes with a deep breath. He unfolds the piece of paper and reads. My birthday. The time. The name and address of the little Italian restaurant in D.C. He looks up from the paper and the anger and frustration have transformed into . . . sadness. A desperate sadness.

"This is a year from now," he says.

"That's usually how birthdays work," I say. He laughs. And I smile. Lincoln carefully folds the paper up, pulls out his wallet, and tucks it into its leathery folds. He looks at me again. Pleading. He looks down at me with this . . . pain. "Lincoln." I close my eyes and just breathe. I put my hands on his chest and force myself to push away from him. Make myself leave. I stand in front of him and he kisses me. And in those moments, I am as raw and naked as I have ever been. I whisper, "And if I don't see you again, loving you will have been the bravest thing I've ever done." And Lincoln lurches forward, desperately pulling me into him.

I don't remember walking away from him. And I don't remember—won't remember—what he looked like in those last desperate moments. The hallway. The elevator. If I slept. The wake-up call and the zombie-like shuffle to our shuttle in the wee hours of the next morning. Sasha fell asleep on my shoulder as we waited for our flight and I tried Ferdie again. And again. And again. Nothing.

So, I keep busy. I talk to business affairs while we're at the airport and tell them what Preeti said about bringing all three men to the pitch meeting. They give me the green light. Once we're on the plane, I send e-mails to all three of the winning contestants' representation requesting that they join us in New York for the pitch meeting at Quincy Pharmaceuticals. Even though it's Sunday, flight arrangements are made, hotels are booked, and congratulations are extended. We're all set for tomorrow's big pitch.

And every time I think about what I've lost, maybe forever, I just let it come. The tears. The emotion. All of it. I sit in the first-class seats that I upgraded us to sometime this morning and just sob. The flight attendant offers me tissues and the businessman across the aisle just looks concerned. And the bundle of used tissues that I stuff into the netted compartment on the back of the seat in front of me grows. And grows. And grows. I'm trapped in this steel tube hurtling through the air away from Lincoln, and I can't stop crying. But the scary part? It feels good. And soon—somewhere over the Midwest—it starts becoming less about Lincoln and more about me. My past and my childhood and my parents and who I am and most of all, who I had to become to survive it all. The bundle of tissues grows. And the flight attendant brings me more tea and I can't stop crying.

"You sure this—" Sasha asks, looking up from the drawings she's finalizing for tomorrow.

"This is good. It's good," I say, sniffling and sniffling. Sasha thanks the flight attendant for another bundle of tissues. She passes them over to me.

"What if he's an earl? Or a prince? Oh! Oh my God. What if you're pregnant and then? A year from now at your birthday dinner? You present him with his secret baby love child and he's all 'And now you are my queen and this is my heir.'" Sasha's voice becomes reverent and whispery. "He places a tiny crown on the baby's head." Of course she acts this out and then in a booming voice with the worst British accent of all time, she says, "'Come with me and we shall rule everything the light touches.'" Sasha's arm sweeps in front of her. Thank God we're in first class; she wouldn't have nearly enough room to be so dramatic back in coach.

"First, that's *The Lion King*. Second, what am I, *Teen Mom*? We used protection. And third, what kind of unhinged martyr would be all—yeah, I'm carrying his child, but you know what's going to work out best? If I shoulder this whole pregnancy thing on my own and then spring the baby on him way down the line when I'm properly filled with just enough resentment that it would be completely disastrous."

"So you're saying he could be at least an earl," Sasha says. I sigh, balling up another tissue, stuffing it in with the others. "You should have stayed the night. You should've—"

"And then what?" I ask.

"Then he sweeps you up and asks you to marry him, sobbing that he's never before loved—"

"I was in that hotel all night. He never knocked on my door to sweep me up and beg me to date him, let alone marry him. So, this isn't—" The emotion builds and I can't help but get caught up in it once more. "It wasn't just me," I finally squeak out.

"I know. I know it wasn't," she says. She smiles and goes back to her drawing. "But the secret baby would have been an awesome reveal." I look over at her. She's said it almost to herself. As she chooses different colored pencils and with her tongue sticking out just so, she looks like a little kid sitting there. The same little kid who found that stack of romance novels in her grammy's crafting room all those years ago. I tear up (of course) and smile. I can't help it. After everything she's been through with men—on the cusp of her own Time-Out—she still believes. In the happy ending and being swept up by heroes and . . . love. She still believes in love.

Do I? Did I ever?

That's the saddest part. When I think about me as a kid . . . searching for it. Waiting for it. Hungry for it. Just as I learned to write in cursive and spell three-syllable words, I learned to live without love. The bundle of tissues grows to epic proportions as I sniffle through several more work e-mails and maybe watch a few cat videos just to balance things out. It's all such a blur.

Sasha and I fly into JFK since our meeting is first thing tomorrow morning and I'm happy to be busy and tromping through Manhattan. This is where Lincoln is. And then I'm crying in the back of a cab and Sasha is telling the cab driver—who couldn't care less—some sob story about why I'm hysterical. By the time we check in to yet another hotel I am finally calming down.

Before we meet for dinner at the hotel's restaurant, I excuse myself to put yet another call in to the ice rink where I met Ferdie less than a week ago.

"Hi, is Ferdinand Wyatt there? He reffed a game last Tuesday," I ask the put-upon woman who has the unfortunate task of answering the phone.

"Who?"

"Ferdinand Wyatt? Ferdie Wyatt?" I ask.

"Oh, Ferdie. No, you know what, he's been AWOL all week. He was supposed to ref a game tonight, but nothin'," the woman says.

"Oh . . . okay, well, if he does happen to check in—" And the woman hangs up. "Dammit." I can only shake my head and make plans to ambush him at his apartment when I get back to D.C. Of course, Lincoln's words come back to me. That it doesn't help Ferdie to fix things . . . but I just need to know he's safe. Alive. And then I'll back away. Maybe. After checking to see if he has groceries.

Baby steps.

15

It's Monday morning.

The Lumineux waiting room. I half expected Audrey Holloway to be waiting here for us. And when she's not it's the least calming revelation in history. She's waiting. Biding her time. This campaign belongs to Sasha and me. It's ours because we have come to embody it. With everything I've learned and cried about and excavated over the last week, it all comes back to this.

Just Be.

Sasha and I sit in the corner with Jake, Lantz, and Josh, who look even more unbelievable in this everyday environment. A few businessmen sit on the other side of the waiting room. I catch each one of them looking at the three men, trying to flex nonexistent muscles and, finding themselves wanting, going back to scrolling their smartphones. Sasha is quiet. She is tight and elsewhere.

We stopped for bubble water and I had antacids ready for her before we got our first cab. But I know—from firsthand experience—how rocky the terrain is at the beginning of a Time-Out. It's not much better a full year into it, truth be told.

I think about what Helen wrote in my book that change doesn't happen just because we think something is wrong. Change happens because we think something is wrong and then don't stop fighting until it's right. It was a cruel wake-up call when I realized just because I had become aware of the blind spots in my life, that didn't mean that I automatically got some secret key that'd take me to the next level. No. It sucked. For a very long time. Every day. There was a reason I went under-water. My parents are never going to be who I want them to be. Ever. The glimmers I think I catch sight of every now and again are just that—glimmers. They're not the promise of depths I've yet to uncover or tips of some love iceberg I am on the verge of crashing into. They're aches from a phantom limb that never existed.

So, now I know. They're never going to be the people I want them to be. The thing about living in a fantasy world is that anything can happen there. In this fantasy world my parents could turn around one day and gift me with the love I've always wanted. And my childhood could be erased and replaced with the happy one I always dreamed of. Now, with the cold truth of who they are out in the open, comes the task of resetting the bones that were broken and learning how to walk again.

Learn how to walk so I can run.

By the time we reached the waiting room this morning, Sasha was off the rails. She showed me the back-and-forth she had with Chuck Holloway late last night. All in text, of course. She was questioning everything as we took a cab over to Quincy this morning. Maybe he's the one. Maybe he's the one I was supposed to be better for.

"I just heard myself say that," she said and let her head fall against the window of the cab. "Be better for." The words are barely spoken, but the breath of them fogs the cab window. "I just want someone to love me, not want to possess me."

I know there's nothing I can do for Sasha as she begins to see her life in the light of day. But I try. I reiterate that Chuck's in the past and whatever he thinks he gained from trying to play her didn't work and the joke's on him and and and . . . but I can tell she's not buying it. Because it's not about Chuck at all. Just like it's not about Lincoln and it's not about my parents. It's about us.

Time ticks by. Slow. Slower. Slooooooweerrrrr. I try to make idle conversation, but everyone is nervous—including the contestants. If we land this campaign, each one of their lives will dramatically change. Booking a gig this big—to become the spokesman for a product—is something every one of them has been waiting for.

The door opens and Preeti emerges. I can't help but smile. She came out to get us herself.

"Ms. Wyatt. Ms. Merchant. Gentlemen," she says, making eye contact with each one of us. We stand and follow Preeti through the same hallways we did when we first made the Just Be pitch.

We file into a much larger conference room. The number of executives, if it's at all possible, has multiplied once more. No all-glass walls this time. In addition to the executives actually in the room, there are also a few watching from laptops and screens; it looks like something out of a science fiction novel. The executives are milling and talking, refilling coffee cups and grabbing pastries from the large buffet table placed just under the picture window with the Manhattan skyline just behind it. Sasha sets up her artwork on the two easels at the front of the room, turning them around so we can unveil them at the right time. I notice her hands are shaking.

When Josh, Lantz, and Jake enter the room, the executives fall silent. They find their seats and a few even manage to close their mouths. And I forget about Phoenix and Audrey Holloway and "Thunder Road" and drunk tanks and hockey rinks and Lincoln and cowardly white knights.

I'm on.

"Last time I was in this room, I asked the eternal question: What do women want? Well, I went out and found it." And the room breaks into laughter as the three men just stand there. Swoon-worthy and every woman's fantasy. I command the room. The pitch. The speech. The practiced gestures. Ten minutes and thirteen seconds later and I've got everyone on the edge of their seat. If they're not riveted to what I'm saying, they're staring at one of the men. And if they're not staring at one of the men, then they're ogling Sasha's artwork. The redesign of the brand. The social media campaign. The revolution we mean to cause. We're going to change until it's right.

It's sweeping.

It's grand.

It's epic.

And then the unveiling:

JUST BE.
LUMINEUX SHOWER GEL
THE EVERYDAY LUXURY ALL WOMEN DESERVE.

And the executives applaud. They actually applaud. A few stand. Including Preeti. And I finally breathe. And smile. A demure bow. A "thank you for your time" and we are being shown out into the waiting room.

"We're going to give you your answer today. We'll deliberate and let you know. Please, have a seat in the waiting room," an executive says, closing the waiting room door behind him. And it's like a gut punch. My smile fades, Sasha's face drains of color, and the three men just sit down on the long couch.

"You did great," Josh whispers, leaning over.

"Thanks," I say.

"It couldn't have gone better, I don't think. Right?" Jake says, scooting in closer to the conversation.

"I mean, they applauded," Lantz adds.

"I can't believe they're just going to blurt it out right here. I mean . . . just out in the open like that," Sasha says.

"We're going to be fine," I say, trying not to vomit. "We're going to be fine."

And we wait.

No one takes out a smartphone.

No one picks up a magazine.

No one speaks.

The waiting room is silent except for the receptionist who's answering the phone and transferring the hundreds of calls that come into just her small corner of Quincy Pharmaceuticals on a minute-by-minute basis. I look around. Hands clasped. Everyone looks straight ahead. Just when I think I have my nerves under control, I feel my face redden, my stomach drop, and my mind launch into a whole new assortment of emotions.

I did my best.

I gave it everything I had.

But that doesn't stop me from replaying every moment, every second, every word of the pitch meeting.

After a full hour, the door opens. Four executives walk out, along with Preeti. Sasha and I stand. I breathe. Breathe. Hold it together.

"Ms. Wyatt. Ms. Merchant?" A tall, gray man in an expensive suit speaks. The men stay seated behind us. "That presentation was—well, it was like I was finding religion or something. Ms. Dayal was right to take that initial meeting." I look over at Preeti and she's beaming. I can't help but smile. Sasha whispers a reverent thank-you, and I'm afraid she's on the verge of one of her curtsies. She fights the urge this time. "We are excited, Ms. Wyatt. We haven't been excited about Lumineux in a very long time. Congratulations. The account goes to Holloway/Greene. I look forward to working with you. We'll contact you this week and get things going." I can hear the stifled cheers from the men seated behind us. Sasha lets out a sort of half cry, half squeal . . . then a sniffle. I look over and she is very quietly and elegantly crying.

"Thank you, sir."

"Now get to work," the executive says with a wry smile. I nod and thank him again. I am barely holding it together. He scans the waiting room and each cover model gets a "well done" and a hearty handshake from the tall, gray man. I shoot one last glance to Preeti, and she looks as if she's a proud parent watching her child at a Christmas pageant.

The quartet of executives say their farewells and walk back through the waiting room door. Leaving us by ourselves. The men high-five each other, shaking hands and giving congratulations all around. The minute the door closes, I turn to Sasha and pull her in for the biggest hug.

"We did it," I say. She just nods. Over and over again. Repeating my words. We did it. We did it. Sasha and I break apart and it's hugs all around. Jake scoops up each one of us. Lantz is all hearty handshakes, and Josh is near tears with gratitude and thanks.

"Let's get out of here before we really embarrass ourselves," I say, and everyone agrees, laughing and texting their respective partners, families, and representation. I take Sasha's hand and we're down the hallway, down the elevator, and through the lobby. She's sniffling and just keeps saying, "I can't believe it . . . I can't believe it."

"Have you two ever thought about opening your own agency?" Jake asks, as the bustle of New York moves and flows around us.

"Sure, who hasn't?" I say. He looks at me. Pointedly. "Now? You have got to be kidding me." I can't help but laugh. I look around for a place for us to raise a glass. Something to mark the occasion. I see a restaurant—just next to my favorite bakery—on the other side of the street and decide to make our way over there. "We just landed our biggest account. This is going to change everything at Holloway/Greene. They can't shove us back into the pink ghetto now. No, Lumineux first, Quincy next," I say.

We did it. After a lovely celebratory brunch, I take an early train back to D.C. We were supposed to return tomorrow, but I decide to take this extra time to see what's going on with Ferdie before the madness of the Lumineux campaign really takes hold.

On the return train trip I send an e-mail to Helen letting her know we got Lumineux and then another e-mail to Ginny Barton thanking her for her hospitality and letting her know we landed the account. I then e-mail Charlton Holloway with all the details and the timeline for the campaign. We'll be launching in October. I'll debrief him when I return to the office tomorrow morning. And then I'm sketching out ideas and writing copy and thinking up social media this and hashtags that and billboards and commercials and then—quite miraculously—I just stop. Close my laptop. Order a nice cup of tea and some shortbread cookies. And allow myself to bask. I'm just smiling, watching the landscape speed by. Work is back to being fair again. Finally. Something makes sense. Sasha and I came up with the best campaign and we landed Lumineux.

It's odd finally seeing myself as the seasoned warrior that I've become. The panning shot of the soldiers as they ready themselves for the onslaught and now I finally see that I'm the one with the scar running down half her face and that these eyes . . . ohhhh, these eyes have seen some horrors. And that that's a good thing. Age. Wisdom. Being forty. I like it here. I take a sip of my tea and can't stop smiling. I earned here. This cup of tea. These shortbread cookies. This landscape speeding past me. The Lumineux campaign. I also know that it took what it took to get me here. That if I would have gotten a big campaign like Lumineux any earlier I wouldn't have believed I deserved it. Or I would've believed that I deserved it for reasons other than my own talent and skill.

Timing.

I think about Lincoln and me. Was I just putting off the inevitable by inviting him to my birthday dinner or was I giving us a chance to actually become something real? Something unhurried. I don't know. But I do know that I'm not done believing in us yet. Like I said to Hannah at my birthday dinner, I was so ready to be with the wrong kind of men that I realized how unready I was for the right one. Lincoln is the right one. Just not right now.

Maybe that's what growing older does; it puts things into perspective. Love. Success. Self. Every day it feels like I battle the illusions of my past—unlovable, unwanted, insignificant. These are the fishhooks from my childhood that get snagged into my adult life's tapestry. And they yank. And they catch. And they try to pull at who I really am. And on the good days, I can pluck them out and toss them aside, but on the bad days, I can only talk about how scared I feel and that the fishhook hurts and maybe, because I don't have the strength to, could a friend lend me a hand and dig it from my flesh for me? And so it goes. Day in and day out. No automatic key to the next level. I must take this step by step. Floor by floor. Every day the fishhooks dull just a bit and every day I get a bit more skilled at unwinding them from myself.

And once again, by overthinking something, I've thought myself right out of feeling pleasure firsthand. Fishhooks? Jesus. Just . . . why can't I just sit here and drink this tea and bask? Smile. Let the joy wash over me.

I always love watching that part in the Olympics when the athletes are on the podiums, medals around their necks, and the first notes of their national anthem are played as their flag ascends into the heavens. Everything they've done has led up to this moment. And to watch them run through the gamut of emotions, tears, a smile, taking in the crowd, trying to sing along with the song, disbelief, and then this panic that the moment—

the moment—is almost over and have I felt it enough, have I properly chronicled every second of it so that I can relive it . . . and then the song ends and the athletes come out of the haze and just wave their hands over their heads in thanks.

The power of a moment. To just allow it to happen. Experience it firsthand. I guess with all my theories on fishhooks and the wisdom of age, that one still eludes me.

16

I climb the three flights to Ferdie's walk-up and prepare my speech. I'm not going to butt in, but if we could I'd like to have a conversation about what he thinks he's doing with his life. He's thirty-one years old now. And then maybe we'll talk about some of this . . .

The landing in front of Ferdie's apartment is overrun with garbage and his door is open. My stomach drops. I race up the stairs and push open the door.

Tinfoil on the windows with an old bedsheet nailed up as "drapes" for good measure. Pizza boxes everywhere and just . . . darkness, trash, and hopelessness permeate the entire apartment. And there's Ferdie. He has a black eye and several other cuts from whatever barroom brawl landed him in jail however many nights ago. His knuckles are bloodied and I'm sure I don't want to see what the other guy looks like. Ferdie's sitting in that old leather club chair that used to be Dad's, surrounded by empty beer cans, beer bottles, fifths of scotch, bongs, and pipes, and on the coffee table in front of him is what looks like the remnants of a line of cocaine.

I clap my hand over my mouth and finally see it.

Ferdie's not a loser. He's an addict.

He hasn't woken up. I walk closer to make sure he's alive. Check his pulse, realize quickly I don't know how to check pulses, and then just put my hand on his chest to see if he's breathing.

"What . . . what are you doing?" he slurs, bringing his head up.

"Checking to see if you're alive," I say.

"And am I?"

"Just barely," I say. He laughs a little, his head slamming back against the chair and he's out. "Ferdie? *Ferdie??*" Nothing. I check his breathing again. It's there, but . . . slow. I pull out my phone and dial Michael at work.

"Well, hello, stranger. How was Phoenix?" Michael says.

"It's Ferdie," I say. I hear my voice. It's panicked. Not my own. I'm usually so calm in these situations, but this isn't just another day. Things have changed. I've changed.

"What's happened?" Michael asks, shifting gears instantaneously.

"I think . . . he needs help. I'm here at his apartment. He called from jail while I was in Phoenix and apparently he's been on quite the bender," I say, taking in the mayhem around me.

"What can I do?" Michael asks, without hesitation.

"Didn't your nephew have to go to rehab a while back?"

"He got hooked on Oxy . . . or that was one of the things he got hooked on," Michael says.

"I think I need to get Ferdie into rehab," I say. Out loud.

"Okay," Michael says.

"But it's not one of those country club places with the limos and all that, is it? Where it's just—"

"No, this place was good. It was in Virginia. This place—" I can tell Michael is sifting through papers, probably trying to find the name of the rehab. "Here it is. The Recovery House. Hilarious, that I couldn't remember that name. Okay . . . let me call and see if they have a bed. I kept in touch with the main guy over there. Let me call you back."

"Okay."

"Anna. He's going to be okay. Do you hear me?"

"Yes."

"Okay. I'll call you right back." Michael hangs up and I just stand there. Everything in me wants to clean up Ferdie's apartment before Michael gets here. Protect him. Protect us. I don't want anyone to see what . . . what's become of him. Do I want to hide the truth or the illusion? Which version of Ferdie . . . shit. I sit on the arm of the old leather chair and Ferdie absently rubs my back. And it's that simple thing that breaks me open. I cry quietly while my little brother's mitt of a hand tries to soothe me—even in his drugged-up haze.

What I wouldn't give for my walls now. What I wouldn't gi—oh no, of course. Of course. Now I see it. I was never the only Wyatt trying to distance myself from feeling things firsthand. I used ice, walls, and control. Ferdie used booze, drugs, and numbness.

I lost myself in becoming a winner just as sure as Ferdie lost himself in becoming a loser. Becoming these labels meant we didn't have to be us. Human. Vulnerable. The kind of kids parents don't love.

I wipe away my tears, set my purse on the filthy floor, and stand. Pace.

I find his backpack by the door, empty it of all the weirdo detritus he's always accumulated (what grown man needs a single rubber ball and two combs?), and pack what I think he'll need: T-shirts, boxers, jeans, and a sweatshirt. I walk into his bathroom, trying not to lose it as the filth and the . . . just the hopelessness of it all overtakes me. Did this apartment look like this the night of my birthday dinner? Sure it did. So, he came home to this? Why . . . why didn't he ask for help?

Because he's a Wyatt. It's not like I asked for help, either. Jesus. I pluck the toothbrush from the cup, grab some tooth-paste, deodorant, and the glasses he never wears and tuck them into the outside pocket of his backpack. And why exactly am I making a mental note to get him a toiletry bag for Christmas? Because I can't stop being me on a dime, that's why. I walk back out into the main room and Ferdie is up doing another hit from a bong as big as my arm.

"When did you get here?" he asks, sitting back in the chair, the smoke coming out in little rings. Rings. Rings.

"A few minutes ago," I say, putting his backpack over my shoulder.

"Oh," he says, blinking back into beautiful oblivion. My con-versation with Lincoln. Is it the drink, he asked? I so easily laid everything firmly on Ferdie. No, it's not the drink. It's *him*. I am always so quick to believe that it is us who are inherently flawed. My phone rings.

"Hello?"

"Okay. They've got a bed. Here's what we're going to do.

Ferdie's too big for just you, so I'm going to drive over there and we'll load him up together."

"Thank you . . . Thank you so much," I say.

"Don't worry about it. But here's the complicated part. It's not like Ferdie has medical insurance, and Recovery House costs a lot. Most of it up front. It's a six-month program."

"Six months?"

"It's the least amount of time this particular place offers," he says.

"Okay."

"Can your parents chip in at all?" Michael asks.

"Probably not," I say.

"I know. Look. I'll start over there; we'll get him loaded up while he's kind of out of it and then figure out the money stuff as we go. Okay?" Michael asks.

"Okay. Michael, did you——"

"I knew he smoked a lot of pot, but I don't know. It's Ferdie. He's always been kind of a goof."

"I know."

"He'll always be that little brat with the skateboard, you know?"

"I know." I smile.

"Okay, I'm on my way. I'll tell Allison what's going on." He gives me all the information for the Recovery House, the phone numbers, how to transfer the money . . . everything. We sign off. I whip Ferdie's backpack onto both shoulders and hold my phone until I'm positive it's going to break. I walk into the tiny galley kitchen—dishes, more pizza boxes, more empties, roaches skittering around the counter. I ball my hands up into fists, taking it all in. How can he live like this? I turn around and face the refrigerator. One single picture hangs underneath a magnet for the local Chinese takeout place.

Ferdie and me.

I brush my fingers over the photo. I must have been about thirteen and he was no more than four or five. He's in those damn Underoos he never took off and that oversized pith helmet he got at the Natural History Museum. Dad bought him that dumb thing. The only thing he ever bought him and Ferdie just . . . he treasured it. I've got a pink shirt tucked into purple corduroys, an outfit pulled together with a rainbow belt and the whitest Keds any child ever had. It's a grainy photo, ripped at the corner. I pull it off the fridge and tuck it into the backpack. The pith helmet. I have to ask at least. I dial.

"Richard Wyatt."

"Hi, Dad. It's Anna," I say.

Silence.

"I signed a really big client today," I say.

"Would I know it?"

"Lumineux Shower Gel," I say, proudly.

"Never heard of it."

"Yet!" I say jokingly.

"What?"

"You haven't heard of it, yet," I say.

"Is this why you called?"

"Well…" My voice stutters.

"What?" I can feel my face flushing.

"Is this why you called, Anna? Honestly. To tell me about

some shower gel I've never heard of?" I swallow. Steady myself.

"No."

"Well, what then? I have to get—"

"Dad, I need to ask a favor."

Silence.

"Ferdie needs to go into rehab."

"Oh, please."

"Dad—"

"Ferdinand has been nothing but a disappointment to your mother and me."

"There's a bed open at a rehab in Virginia. They'll take him tonight, but—"

"Ferdinand isn't a little boy anymore."

"I know that. I know, Dad. He needs help."

"What he needs is to take some responsibility for his life. Show some control. Know when to say when."

"I think it's a little more complicated than that, Dad."

I hear Dad heave a long, weary sigh into the phone. I can hear Mom in the background. She asks him who's on the phone. He says it's me. A long silence and then she launches into a list of errands she needs him to run and to get off the phone already. Stop wasting time, she tells him.

Stop wasting time.

"Dad, please," I say. "He'll pay it back. Every penny. I'll make sure of it."

Silence.

"Dad?"

"This is it, Anna. This is all I'm doing. And he has one year."

"To get sober?"

"To pay back the money, Anna. Jesus." I give him the information. All the numbers. All the amounts. He is quiet.

"Thank you," I say.

He doesn't say good-bye. He doesn't say anything. I hang up my phone and just stand there. In the real world where my parents are who they are and there are no phantom limbs and no glimmers. That is my dad.

Michael arrives within the hour. I still have Ferdie's backpack on both shoulders.

"Jesus," he says, walking into Ferdie's apartment. It takes everything I have to not apologize, start tidying up, and/or make excuses for Ferdie.

"I know," I say, just letting it sit.

"Okay, the car is double-parked downstairs. Did you talk to your folks?" Michael asks, stepping over various empties and pizza boxes to where Ferdie is.

"Yeah, Dad said he would wire the money," I say.

"Really?"

"It wasn't pretty," I say.

"What you need, son, is to cut that hair o' yours!" Michael says in an exact Richard Wyatt impression. He stands straight up at attention. "I don't know how you two stood it." Michael takes the bongs, the pipes, the pot, and the cocaine and bags them up. "Everything illegal we should get rid of just in case Ferdie doesn't come back here." Always the lawyer.

"Where would he go?"

"If he's lucky he'll go to a sober living house after he spends six months at Recovery House," Michael says.

"Hey, man. What are you doing here?" Ferdie asks, his head bobbing and his eyes blinking open.

"I got the car downstairs; you want to go for a drive?" Michael asks.

"He's not a dog, Mic—"

"Yeah, sure, man. Sounds like fun," Ferdie says, getting up out of that stupid, old chair. He sways and after a few tries we're down the stairs and heading out of the city and into Virginia in rush-hour traffic.

Ferdie is in the backseat, his arm extended over Michael's baby seat. He finds a plastic bag of Goldfish crackers and starts eating those.

"I got the Lumineux campaign," I say to Michael.

"You did?"

"Yeah. This morning," I say.

"Oh, wow. That's so huge. Congratulations," Michael says.

"What about the guy you met in Phoenix? The one who likes your Batman?" Ferdie asks, leaning forward through the two front seats like he used to do when Michael and I were teenagers.

"The one who likes your Batman?" Michael repeats.

"She attacked him in an elevator," Ferdie says, digging his hand between the baby seat cushions for more crackers. He finds plenty and, of course, he eats them.

"Lincoln Mallory," I say.

"That is not a real name," Michael says.

"It is. And he's British," I say. Ferdie's crunching fills the car.

"I know it's been a while for you, but making up an imaginary—" Michael says, laughing.

"No. He was real." And I sigh.

"You just swooned."

"I did not."

"This is bad. You haven't swooned since . . . who was that boy? With the swoopy black hair—he swam, right? Oh, you loooooved him."

"His name was Cam and he was my betrothed secret lover."

"You never said one word to that boy." Michael laughs.

"I know. Not one."

"No, wait. You did actually," Michael says.

"Don't. Don't say it," I say.

"Shanks," Michael says.

"It was half sure, half thanks." My head falls into my hands. "Morrrrtified."

"So, this Lincoln Mallory," Michael urges.

"I invited him to my birthday dinner," I say. Michael finally gets off the highway. I'm thankful that we've passed the time laughing and talking. I don't know how this is going to go once we get there.

"Like a year from now birthday dinner?" Ferdie asks.

"Yeah," I say.

"I don't get it," Michael says, making turns on one lush Virginian street after another.

"I'm not ready for . . . I have other things to clean up

before . . . you know," I say, motioning back to Ferdie. Michael nods.

"And you'll be ready in exactly one year?" Michael asks.

"Well—"

"It doesn't work like that, Anna. You can't schedule when you're going to start living your life," Michael says.

"Yes, you can," I say, and Michael just laughs.

"So, no pressure on your birthday dinner then," Michael says, pulling into a parking lot behind a nothing building that looks more like a strip mall than a Recovery House.

"He said he was saving me."

"From what?" Michael asks.

"From him."

"Ugh, that's such a line," Michael says.

"I use it all the time," Ferdie says.

"Well, you would," I say.

"Right?" Ferdie says, laughing.

"I'm fine with it either way," I say.

"Liar." Michael turns off the car. I smile and turn around to face Ferdie.

"We're here," I say.

"Oh cool. Where's here?" he says.

"This is the Recovery House. Ferdie, I think you need help." Michael gets out of the car and walks into the rehab facility.

"What?" Ferdie asks, leaning forward.

"You need help," I say, twisting around. Ferdie leans his head through the front seats and rests his mop of hair on me.

"Don't leave me," he says, pulling my hand to him.

"I'll never leave you," I say, kissing the top of his head.

"You're going to leave me here. You're going to leave me here," he says. His voice is exhausted. He looks so tired.

"You need help," I say again.

"I know. I know."

"These people can help you," I say. Michael comes out of the facility with what looks like two orderlies. Ferdie crumples in tears.

"You don't love me anymore," he says, and the sobs come out of him like he's a tired baby at a grocery store. He's rubbing his eyes and just . . . crying. I step out of the front seat. Tell the men to give me a second. I open up the back door and tuck in next to Ferdie in the backseat. He crumples into me.

"What did I always say to you? Right before bedtime?" I ask.

"I'll eat you up, I love you so," Ferdie says. I nod.

"It's you and me, right?" I ask. He nods. "You and me." I make him look at me. Those big brown eyes. Just like mine. "Say it."

"You and me," he repeats.

17

The flower arrangement on my desk is from Helen. I can't stop staring at it. The card is short and sweet. *You kick ass.* And she signed it with just an *H.* Michael finally dropped me off at home at around ten thirty last night. I had just enough energy to put on my pajamas, plug in my phone, and fall into bed. Which means I'm processing what happened yesterday in the early morning hours before Holloway/Greene opens. On the day after I landed my biggest account and checked my little brother into rehab.

As the Lumineux e-mails stream in and the scent of the flowers wafts, I replay what the check-in counselor at Recovery House said. Ferdie is going to be on lockdown. No cell phone. No communication with the outside world. He'll be attending meetings and earning his keep. I can come see him when he gets his thirty-day chip. That's the longest Ferdie and I have gone without speaking. A knock on my door.

"I knew I'd find you here," Sasha says, stepping into my office and sitting down in one of my client chairs with a steaming cup of coffee. "Isn't it amazing? She sent me one, too," Sasha says, eyeing my flower arrangement from Helen.

"They're beyond," I say, eyeing my phone. As if it will somehow telecommunicate with Ferdie.

"You okay?" she asks.

A beat.

"No," I say honestly. I look up at her, through the wafting beautiful flowers and the afterglow of a job well done, and I'm just exhausted.

"Do you want to talk about it?" Sasha asks.

"My brother. We had to check him into rehab yesterday," I say. I clear my throat and can't stop shaking my head. "He'd tried to get sober before. Never told me about it. He'd go cold turkey for however many weeks. He even checked himself into a place once. Told me he was going to a hockey camp. Why wouldn't he tell me?"

"This happened yesterday?" Sasha asks.

"He called when we were in Phoenix. From jail. Fighting. Always for fighting," I say.

"In Phoenix? And you didn't say anything?"

"I know. So, I went to check on him after brunch. It was so bad. It had gotten—"

"So, you did a good thing. He's in the right place, now," Sasha says.

"The counselor told me that—I mean, she was nice about it—but she said I was his prime enabler. *Enabler.* They use words like that there. I didn't help, I enabled. Lincoln said I wasn't helping him by constantly fixing everything. He was right," I say.

"You were just trying to love him," Sasha says.

"I know, but I need to learn how to love people without trying to control everything," I say.

"Yeah, well," Sasha says.

"Michael—he helped yesterday, we've known each other forever—thought my idea about inviting Lincoln to my birthday dinner was more of the same. Me trying to control everything," I say.

"What? He doesn't know what he's talking about. That's romantic. It's—"

"It's super controlly," I say.

"Maybe, but—"

"On precisely this date at this time for this function you will present yourself to me and we shall both be ready on precisely this date at this time and at this function to be in love exactly the way I've always imagined and then we'll walk off into the sunset that I've timed to happen just when I blow out my candle and know exactly now what to wish for that will make me happy and the question I've struggled with for exactly one year will finally be answered to my satisfaction," I say.

"That's bananas. That was so cool what you did. *Pfflt,*" Sasha says.

"That's the thing. It sounds really cool and all romance novelly, but in reality it's me trying to be the boss of everything yet again, so I wouldn't . . . you know, I thought I did it because if I gave him this sweeping epic option he couldn't say no. He could see the error of his ways and not be afraid or something," I say.

"No, I get that," Sasha says, deflating a bit. "I really wanted it to be awesome."

"Me too," I say.

"So, what do you do then? Do you call him or just . . . wait?"

"I'm beginning to think I do whatever feels completely wrong. I have to let it go," I say.

"Let it go? What . . . I mean, how does that work?"

"Just like it sounds. I let whatever is going to happen, happen. Just like with Ferdie. I can't go down there and make sure he goes to his meetings and I can't—" I choke up. "I can't make sure he's okay all the time. Every day. I can't keep protecting him. That counselor was right. I never let him grow up. It's hard not to jump from there to it being my fault."

"It's no one's fault," Sasha says.

"That's what the counselor said," I say. "But, see, if I blame myself for it then I get to control it and then . . . I can fix it! Oh my God, it's everywhere?!" I say.

"Isn't the first step admitting you have a problem?" Sasha asks.

"It is."

"Well."

"My name is Anna and I'm addicted to control."

"Hi, Aaaaaanna," Sasha says.

We're quiet.

Sasha continues, "But Lincoln still might come to the birthday dinner, so . . ."

"I know, so it's perfect. I wait around for a year for someone who may or may not show up. I don't have to date or anything in the interim and then if Lincoln doesn't show up I've had a year to ready myself for it," I say.

"The good thing is that we've got Lumineux launching in October, so every day until then is going to be packed with awesome. Letting go will be a little easier," Sasha says.

"Hope so," I say.

"Audrey is being oddly quiet," Sasha says.

"Oh, I know," I say.

"She was CC'd on all the Lumineux e-mails and never responded." Sasha cranes her neck toward the door.

"We have to be ready. There's another play."

"But Lumineux is ours now."

"One would think," I say, crossing my fingers.

"Well, I'm not going to let Audrey Stinkpants ruin today. We are awesome and this campaign is going to be awesome," Sasha says.

"Speaking of, I'm off to see the elder Stinkpants," I say, gathering myself.

"Charlton?"

"He wanted to debrief on the Lumineux pitch," I say.

"You want me to join you?"

"Nah, it'll be fine," I say. Sasha looks immediately relieved. I stride through the office to a smattering of congratulations, but mostly what Sasha and I did at Lumineux yesterday is off everyone's radar. It's not the big car account. It's not that billionaire that Chuck brought in. No one cares about Lumineux. Yet.

"Anna Wyatt to see Mr. Holloway," I say to his ancient, terrifying secretary.

"Right this way," she says, rising from her chair and leading me through the gorgeous mahogany doors and into Charlton Holloway's corner office.

"Ms. Wyatt here to see you, sir," she says.

"Yes, thank you, Nora," Charlton says, giving an efficient nod to the woman who has taken care of his professional life for decades. She closes the door behind me and I take a seat in one of the chairs across from Charlton.

"Congratulations, Ms. Wyatt," Charlton says, signing a letter and setting it aside.

"Thank you, sir," I say.

And then he's quiet. I cross my legs. Quiet for a long time. I recross my legs, the leather of the chair now the soundtrack to the quietest meeting on record.

"We're waiting on one more," Charlton says, signing another letter and setting it too aside.

"Oh, sure," I say, breathless. Which Holloway child is it going to be? A quick knock and I turn to see Audrey sighing her way into Charlton's office. I eke out a smile.

"My apologies," Audrey says.

"Oh, we're fine. I was just congratulating Ms. Wyatt here on Lumineux," he says. Charlton Holloway has yet to look at me. He's signing letters with a pen that costs as much as a year's rent.

"Yes, very exciting," Audrey says.

"Thank you," I say, looking at her. We make eye contact and then she slides her gaze back over to her father.

"Shame about the rumors, though," she says.

"The what now?" Charlton says, still not looking up. I don't lean forward in my chair. I am calm. *I am calm, goddammit.*

"You know me, Daddy. I hate to gossip . . . ," Audrey starts.

"But . . . ," Charlton leads, finally setting down his pen and looking at us for the first time.

"But as one of the few women in this office, I believe it is my duty to protect and stand up for—champion, if you will—the other females at Holloway/Greene," she says, her hand at her breast. I plaster a smile on my face, remembering to breathe. I don't move. I can't. The stupid leather chair will give away any imperceptible shift.

"Audrey, I have another meeting in ten minutes; please stop babbling and just spit it out," Charlton says.

"While I think the spokesman who was selected for Lumineux is gorgeous and women everywhere are going to fall in love with him, I wouldn't want it to get out that he and Ms. Wyatt here had a bit of a fling during the conference," she says.

"I assure you—"

"I know, Anna. It had nothing to do with him winning, but other people might not be as open-minded as I am," Audrey says.

I say nothing. This is her move. I knew it was coming. I dared her to take her shot. And here it is. And it's a doozy.

"It's not like other execs haven't dipped a toe in, Wyatt," Charlton says with a newfound respect that's more disturbing than if he'd been horrified.

"Mr. Holloway, I can assure you that I behaved in a professional manner at all times during the conference," I say, my voice even and level.

"That doesn't sound like any fun at all," Charlton says.

"Well, just to be sure we've dodged the bullet, I'm willing to join the Lumineux team and support Anna in any way I can," Audrey says.

"Sure, sure. Go ahead," Charlton says, picking back up his pen.

"Thank you, Da—"

"Won't have to worry about one of those beefcakes coming on to you, eh, Audrey?" Charlton laughs and I watch Audrey. With new eyes. How is she any different from Ferdie or me? Audrey tries to hold her head high, but I can see her deflate centimeter by centimeter as I sit here. I look away.

"Will there be anything else, Mr. Holloway?" I ask.

"No . . . you're good, Anna. And congratulations, again. On Lumineux and whatever his name is," Charlton says, waving his hand around as if Josh's name is somewhere in the ether above his desk. I stand and smooth my skirt. A nod to Charlton and a nod to Audrey.

"What was his name, Anna?" Audrey asks.

"The Lumineux spokesman's name is Josh Fox," I say with a smile. "They're over the moon with him and the two runners-up, Lantz Kelton and Jake McCall. We're very excited to get started," I say, my voice a monotone.

"As am I," Audrey says. A nod to Audrey and I will myself to move. Move. Step. Walk toward the door. Another nod to Nora the Terrifying Secretary and I pick up my pace toward Sasha's office.

"It's just lazy," I say, slamming her office door behind me.

"What happened?" Sasha asks, setting down her pencil.

"She insinuated that because of my . . ." I shake my head and set my hands on my hips.

"Hey. Sit down. Come on. Just sit down," Sasha says, half standing. I look at her. Imploring. "Just . . . sit." Sasha leans across her desk, pointing at her client chair. Another point. I sit.

"Audrey was there," I say.

"At the meeting?"

"Yeah."

"What the fu—"

"She insinuated that Josh was crowned Mr. RomanceCon because he had a fling with me," I say.

"What? Are you . . . Wow. That is . . . masterful." Sasha slumps back down in her chair.

"The sick part? Charlton? Unfazed," I say, waving my hand violently in the air. "Almost made him respect me more."

"What?"

"I know."

"Why would Audrey—"

"I'm sure she got the idea when Josh and I came back from taking you to the hotel. We arrived together at the party."

"Oh my God. I'm so sorry," Sasha says.

"What? No way. Don't even. I'm not saying that it was anything worthy of . . . no. Wait. I'm just saying that's probably when she got the idea." Sasha gives me a look. Begging me to tell her the truth. "I mean it. She was going to do something. This? Actually isn't that bad."

"So what does it mean for the campaign?"

"She wants to be on the team."

"That's it?"

"That's it."

"That's totally not it," Sasha says.

"Nope. Not at all," I say.

She smiles and we dive into all the Lumineux new business. We've already been allotted a support team of three for the campaign—along with Audrey, who will do no work and spend the entire time trying to ingratiate herself with Lumineux. As the morning wanes, Sasha and I get ready for our first Lumineux meeting, and she's right. I think about Lincoln and Ferdie a little less as I funnel it all into this campaign.

Audrey is a no-show at the first meeting. I'd be angry, but I'm relieved. We can get to work and she won't be in the way. I'm finishing up with one of the copywriters when I get a knock on my door. It's just after five P.M.

Chuck Holloway. At my door. The copywriter scurries out, and before I can say or do anything, Chuck walks into my office and closes the door behind him. Other than my brief sojourn at The Naughty Kitty lo those many days ago, Chuck and I have had very little interaction. Well, other than my knowledge that he's an entitled sexual predator and that his mere existence motivates Audrey to try to ruin my career. Outside of that? Smiles in the hallway and CCs on e-mails. I look up. Why did he close the door? I've had about enough of this Holloway sibling rivalry.

"Congratulations are in order," Chuck says, sitting in one of my client chairs.

"Thanks," I say, pressing send on an e-mail and then giving Chuck my undivided and highly suspicious attention.

"Did you ever see *From Dusk Till Dawn*?" Chuck asks, apropos of nothing. A moment as I recalibrate my expectations for this conversation and . . .

"I have no idea what you're talking about."

"It's a movie."

"Yep."

"It's a Quentin Tarantino movie," he says.

"It's late, Chuck. Thanks so much for your—"

"Okay, what about *Johnny Be Good*," he says.

"Nope. I . . ." I close down my computer and reach for my purse. "I really must—"

"Look, I'm trying to make a point."

"It sounds like you're trying to make a point without actually making that point. Am I going to have to read between the lines or . . ." I settle back into my chair and wait.

"Quentin Tarantino can't act worth shit."

"Oh, good. In between the lines it is."

"Anthony Michael Hall played a great nerd," Chuck says like he just gave me the coordinates to the Holy Grail.

"That's fascinating."

"You have to know what you're good at, is my point."

Ah. And then it hits me.

"This is about Quincy," I say.

"What you did with the Lumineux campaign, I could never have done that," he says.

"For a lot of reasons, over and above me being a lady," I say.

"No, I know that."

"Do you? Or do you think my knowing how to pitch that shower gel had nothing to do with talent and expertise and everything to do with getting my period or something?" I say.

"Ugh." Chuck takes a moment. "I just need you and Sasha to be ready for Pop and me to make a tough decision," he says. Pop. And. Me.

"It's not sounding like it's going to be a tough decision for you at all," I say.

"You're a—"

"What am I, Chuck? Someone who reels in the big fish so you can take your picture with it?"

"I don't get it."

"Right, because it's not a Quentin Tarantino movie."

"Look, I'm not trying to be disrespectful here. I'm appreciative of what you've done with Lumineux. But as far as Quincy goes—maybe that's more our deal than yours."

"It's only anyone's deal at Holloway/Greene because I brought it in. In its DNA it's my deal," I say.

"Sometimes you gotta pass the baton, you know what I mean?"

"No."

"It's a track-and-field—"

"I understand the reference, Chuck. What I don't understand is how—according to you, at least—all of a sudden I'm out of my depth with something I created."

"We're talking potential. Scope."

"You can't give me one day? One day of basking in this thing?" I ask.

"It just got me thinking," he says.

"About Tarantino," I say.

"Well, yeah," he says.

"Sure."

"This is a compliment, Anna. I'm saying you wrote *True Romance*. You're capable of *Inglourious Basterds*. You're going to win an Oscar," he says.

"But just not for acting," I say.

"Right. *Right!*" He's on the edge of his seat and I'm having flashbacks to the Queen Elizabeth/Bloody Mary conversation. For two people who are completely at odds and hate each other, Chuck and Audrey sure are eerily similar.

"That's . . ." I shake my head. "That's . . . ugh. That's not fair," I finally say, sifting through several four-letter words that spring to mind a lot quicker. Chuck looks taken aback.

"It is, though. And you know it. Holloway/Greene is a team," he says. I laugh.

"A team," I say.

"Let us take it from here," Chuck says.

"You're essentially telling me that I'm only good at coming up with ad campaigns for women's products."

"No, I'm saying you're great at it. And that's not an insult," he says.

"How is this not an insult?"

"It doesn't feel like it is."

"Okay, does this make it clearer? The big accounts we have. The car account. That breakfast cereal. The brokerage firm. That terrible superstore chain. Even that goofy car insurance company. These are the accounts we tout on our website, right?"

"Well, yeah."

"The ones that, when you're at a party with your dad and somebody asks you guys which ads your agency has done, you say those, right?"

"Sure."

"So, those are the important accounts," I say.

"Well—"

"And those are the accounts that, using your reasoning, I'm not capable of representing," I say.

"Wait . . ."

"Ergo, I am—and the accounts I now have and hope to have in the future are—less important," I say.

"No, you're twisting my words."

"This isn't about Tarantino or Anthony Michael Hall."

"Wait, what?"

"You can't have already decided this. Give me a chance to prove to you and Mr. Holloway that I can not only handle a big campaign like Lumineux, but that I'm the only person who can actually bring in Quincy. I deserve a place on the team. Sasha deserves a place on the team," I say.

"I try to give you a compliment and somehow—" Chuck

labors to get up out of his chair, burdened by my lack of under-standing. "This is why everyone says women are crazy." Chuck opens the door and starts to back out as if he's unexpectedly found himself in the bear pit at the zoo. "*True Romance* is a really good movie." And he closes the door behind him.

I want to scream. But I can't because I'm in public, so I end up half growling, half yelping, which does nothing to assuage my . . . can you even call it a mood when it resembles more of a hurricane?

The closed door. The air-conditioning thunks on. The bus-tling office just outside. Be the heroine of your life, eh? What if my life sucks and it was only this façade of a life that was actually good in any way? The fantasy world and the fake personality and the friends who . . . no no no: I have dinner with Hannah tonight. I'd been putting it off and—I check the time. I'm meet-ing her at six P.M. at a sushi place around the corner.

I pull my blazer off the back of my chair with what can only be described as a maniacal laugh, try to wipe away any tear rem-nants (a skill at which I'm excelling), and pack up my laptop. I stop off in Sasha's office on the way out.

Her office is overrun with art. Every inch of her walls is cov-ered with it. Paintings, drawings, and comics are framed, pinned, and hung in any way she can devour them. The deep reds and browns of her office envelop me, and I get pulled deeper and deeper in.

"Hey, you," she says, looking up from her desk, almost drag-ging herself away from what she's working on. My workbag falls off my shoulder and thunks into the crook of my arm. Instead of hiking it back up I just lean down so it'll hit the floor. "You okay?" she asks.

"I have dinner with a Slow Fade friend tonight. We were going back and forth and it's just so fake at this point. But I feel so guilty for not wanting to be her friend anymore that I was all *oh my God, let's get sushi, yayyyyyy!*" And I let the workbag drop and just throw up my hands. "When . . . who says that?"

"Not you," she says.

"And Chuck all but said that we aren't going to get the Quincy pitch if it happens," I say.

"What?? First Audrey and now this?"

"I know," I say.

"What did he say?"

"That I need to know what I'm good at," I say, putting air quotes around the statement.

"Are you serious?" Sasha asks.

"Yep. I asked that he let us prove that that Quincy pitch is ours, but I don't know," I say.

"I honestly don't know what I ever saw in that man," Sasha says.

"He's handsome, rich, and can be charming when he wants to be," I say.

"Oh, yeah. That." Sasha laughs. "Lumineux is going to be huge. I don't think Chuck is going to have a choice but to let us pitch Quincy, and Audrey didn't even show up to today's meeting. We got this," she says. I let out a slow, meandering whine. "Do you want company at your Slow-Fade dinner?"

"No. Thank you. And I don't care what people say, it's harder to break up with your friends than get a divorce," I say, putting my workbag back over my shoulder. "All Holloways are crazy." I turn to walk out of Sasha's office, my hand on the handle. I turn back around. "Thanks."

"Don't mention it," Sasha says. A smile, a dramatic weary wave, and I'm off.

I walk to the little sushi place. In the waning summer days of D.C., the humidity and thunderstorms allow summer to end with a bang and not a whimper. In an odd way, I'm happy to be going to dinner with Hannah. Going home after the day I've had, after the week I've had, feels a bit overwhelming right now. The silence of my apartment feels tight on me. Especially now that Ferdie is . . . *away*. Maybe it'll be good to just talk about nothing for a while.

I walk into the sushi place and the staff loudly greets me. I immediately see Hannah waving over in the corner. I motion to her and the hostess smiles. And I try to smile. Hannah stands up and we hug. She's always been such a good hugger. We settle at the table, as I put my workbag at my feet and drape my purse over the back of the chair. Hannah immediately presents me with a gift.

"What's this?" I ask.

"I forgot to bring your gift to your birthday dinner, so sorry. So here it is!"

"Oh, you so didn't have to," I say. I read the card and it's lovely. And I'm feeling more and more guilty about my Slow Fade by the minute. "Thank you so much." I tuck the card back into its envelope and dig through the tissue paper, my fingers curling around an object. I pull it out. It's a coral-colored journal, with a fountain pen and a scarf that's perfect for me. "It's beautiful."

"I know how you love coral," she says, ordering a pot of jasmine tea. I actually hate the color coral. Hannah suggested that I'd look good in coral however many years ago and now she makes it a point to get me something coral for every occasion. I own nothing coral except what Hannah has gifted me over the years.

"It's so thoughtful. Thank you so much," I say, carefully putting the gifts back in the coral tissue paper inside the coral gift bag. "It's so good to see you!"

"You too. I'm so glad we could do this," she says.

"So, how's everything? How are the kids?" I ask.

"Oh, they're so great. Almost back in school, thank God," she says.

"It's fifth, third, and . . . please don't tell me James is already in kindergarten?" I ask. The waitress comes over and drops off the pot of jasmine tea and a couple of menus with little pencils for us to mark off what we'd like. I scan the list, checking off sushi roll after sushi roll.

"Can you believe it?" Hannah asks, scanning the menu as well.

The hostess seats a woman and a little girl a couple of tables over from us. Hannah and I both notice them. The woman asks to be moved to another table. That table is dirty, she sighs. (It's not.) No . . . not that one, either. The woman's expression looks like the hostess vomited all over herself and just left it there during their entire interaction. The woman and the little girl finally deign to sit in a booth by the window. The little girl doesn't even look at the hostess while the woman manages a snotty thank-you that is more insult than actual thank-you.

"Is that . . . is that child wearing a fedora?" I ask, my voice dipping to a whisper.

"And that's the real deal, too. That's a Goorin Brothers," Hannah says, leaning closer across the table.

"How do you buy a—"

"At least a hundred fifty dollars," Hannah says.

"No."

"Yes."

"For a six-year-old?"

"You should see the kids at James's preschool. Real Uggs and jeans that cost hundreds. They dress better than I do," Hannah says. The woman is wearing her own fedora, placed just so on the very back of her head. She has a loosely done side braid that trails down her back. She's wearing a stylish maxi dress, and from her pinky lipstick to her vintage boots, she drips with the height of hipster fashion.

"You know they keep chickens," I say.

"Oh, absolutely. And she's really getting into canning. You know, keeping it real," Hannah says, pounding her chest with her fist.

"The little girl's name is either Holden Caulfield, all one name, or possibly Soirase," I say.

"And she corrects everyone when they pronounce it wrong," Hannah says.

"Um, it's *SHER-sha*?!" I say, in my best hipster affected accent.

"Everything in her house is in mason jars," Hannah says. I laugh.

"And the husband—"

"Who's really into modern Danish furniture," Hannah says.

"Only uses those old-timey suitcases when they travel," I say.

"They use them for dressers as well," Hannah adds.

"And he plays the banjo in the evenings," I say.

"Because, um, they don't haaaave a TV," Hannah says.

"But they are reading little Simonetta Jinx the classics—starting with *Finnegans Wake*," I say.

"Simonetta. Jinx." Hannah laughs. And on we go. For another hour. We talk about everything and nothing.

And it's fine.

Fine. There's that word again. But there's a difference. Not everyone in my life has to be this wildly intimate, super intense, wholly authentic experience. I had a blast with Hannah. It was light and it was fun and we kept it totally on the surface. And that's fine. That's what she wants. Who am I to judge her or say that that's a bad thing?

Let it go.

Let this friendship be what it is.

And maybe someday work up the courage to tell her how much I loathe coral.

18

But I'm not fine the next day or the next. Or the next week or even the week after that. It could be partly due to my overachieverness. I'm doing everything I can to change and be all in and be the heroine of my own story and level up and let go, and I still haven't gotten that gold star yet? I'm just beginning to see that the gold star *is* the act of unraveling.

This. Enrages. Me.

If vulnerability were a person, its picture would be taped to a bull's-eye with a thousand darts in it right now.

I've thought about calling Lincoln no less than one thousand times. And that embarrasses and surprises me. I see something funny and I want to tell him. Something happens at work and I want to tell him. I want to talk about missing Ferdie and how nervous I am about going down to Virginia tonight to watch him get his thirty-day chip. But mostly I just want to hear that quiet snoring of Lincoln's as I fall asleep and wake up to him telling me the kettle is on. And when I think about that? I realize how stupid it is to be happy with "fine."

I have too many questions and not enough answers. And not even, oh, give me some time and I'll figure it out. No. It's give me some time and I'll get even more confused.

Here's how I know I'm on the right track. I'm wildly uncomfortable and everything feels wrong. That's my answer these days. That's me "living authentically."

I pull into the Recovery House's parking lot in my rented car and find a spot. I'm early so I scroll through the ten or so e-mails that came in since I left the office. We're heading into New York next week to—my phone rings. Preeti.

"Hello," I say, stopping just short of saying hi or hiya or something less formal.

"Anna, hi," she says, finding the perfect balance of casual and formal that eluded me. "We're all set for next week to shoot Josh and then we'll have Lantz that Tuesday and then finish up with Jake on Wednesday."

"Yep, we're all set," I say.

"I know you know this. I think I'm just—"

"No, me too."

"The art Sasha sent over is breathtaking."

"I know. She's amazing," I say.

"It's like she has this Norman Rockwell thing going on, but then it's just . . . not."

"I know."

"And the ideas you sent over about social media and how we can disseminate the campaign are with our digital department now," she says, obviously going through her checklist for the day.

"Oh, perfect," I say, watching people stream into the meeting. I check the clock on the rental's dashboard. I've got time.

"I was talking to Audrey yesterday and she had some new

ideas about billboards and how we can play off the Just Be tag-line. They're pretty great," Preeti says.

"Oh, cool. I'll meet with her tomorrow and see what she's thinking," I say through gritted teeth. Of course, I've heard nothing about these ideas and had no idea that Audrey was communicating with Preeti. So glad she's part of our team.

"Our focus groups are through the roof on this campaign. I've never seen anything like it," she says.

"Really?"

"Yes, so now it comes down to execution, distribution, and consumption," she says.

"The hard part is over. We have a great campaign and a shared vision. I'm excited," I say, popping another antacid.

"Okay, I'll channel your excitement so I can steer away from nausea, which is the arena I'm currently in," she says. I laugh and we sign off. I send an e-mail to my assistant asking her to set up a meeting with Audrey tomorrow. You know, to hear her great ideas for billboards.

I power my phone off and slide it into my purse, and get out of the car into the humid Virginia evening. Fireflies dot the wooded area just behind the Recovery House as dusk falls. It's beautiful. I lock my rental and follow the people toward the side door where I'm assuming the meeting is.

I walk past a crowd of smokers and find what looks like any other meeting inside. It could be PTA or Junior League, same milling people, same terrible folding chairs, same smell of burned coffee and stale cookies sitting out at the back of the meeting room. Except for the smoke wafting in from outside and hanging in the air above us. It brings me to my knees. There's a haze from here to the podium, which, I'm guessing, sits at the front of the meeting room. My eyes begin to water as I dig through my purse for eyedrops. I put the eyedrops in and blink their lusciousness in. It helps for exactly one second. I turn around, wringing my hands and searching the room. Is Ferdie still even here? I mean, he could have left and be on another bender for all I know.

I walk over to where the seats are lined up in neat rows and sit on the aisle, my purse still on my lap. There are about fifty people in the room—either talking to someone, sitting down, or pouring themselves some terrible coffee. People are laughing. People are keeping to themselves. I notice a couple of other women who look like family members sitting on the aisles with their purses on their laps. I told Mom and Dad about this meeting. How we're supposed to come to support Ferdie when he gets his thirty-day chip. Dad hung up on me before I could give him the address.

A line of about ten people comes in to the meeting from behind the podium. Thinking that it might be the residents of the Recovery House, I pay close attention. There he is. He's in a white T-shirt and khakis, his hair is now all the way shaved off, and he is clean-shaven. And he's wearing his glasses. Tears spring up immediately as I realize I haven't seen Ferdie's face in more than just the thirty days. He's been hiding behind beards and facial hair and mohawks and bloodshot eyes and pulled-low hoodies for years.

He sees me.

And the smile. Oh my God. The smile. The light is back on. He's . . . there. I smile back, trying to hold it together (and failing). I wave, not knowing what the protocol is for these kinds of meetings. He motions for me to hold on a second as he goes off into the crowd. I'm having a hard time keeping myself together; the emotions are coming from everywhere. It's just so vast. I find a tissue in my purse and dab at my eyes, telling the woman next to me that it's all the smoke. She looks at me and just nods and smiles, letting me lie to her.

Ferdie walks over with the biggest man I've ever seen in my entire life.

"Anna, this is my sponsor, Ralph," Ferdie says.

"Nice to meet you," I say. Ralph's mahogany skin is set off by a shock of white hair. He wears glasses, too—but I think when a man like Ralph wears glasses people call them spectacles. I shake hands with Ralph and my hand disappears in his completely.

"Nice to meet you, Anna," he says.

"Sponsor?" I ask.

"Ralph's been in the program for—"

"Almost thirty-two years," Ralph adds.

"So, he's going to help me. Guide me," Ferdie says.

"I played professional ball back in my day, so Ferdie coming from his athletic background felt like a good fit. Plus, I'm the only guy bigger than he is," Ralph says, laughing. Ferdie smiles. "I'll give you two a minute," Ralph says, then lumbers away toward the coffee.

I lunge into Ferdie and he sweeps me up in his arms. Tight. Tighter than he's held me in years. He smells like soap instead of pot, and I nestle into the crook of his neck as he squeezes tighter and tighter. We break apart. I look into those big hooded brown eyes of his and they're just . . . they're bright again. How did I not notice how dull they'd gotten? He looks so young, so alive, so vital. He's taken off a good

fifteen to twenty pounds since we checked him in and he's
back to that titan I used to marvel at as he skated so grace-
fully across the ice.

"How are you? Am I allowed to ask that?"

"I'm good, and of course you're allowed to ask that," he says,
tucking a strand of my hair behind my ear.

"You look— —" And I start crying. "I'm sorry. I don't mean
to . . . I've been crying a lot lately and it's not . . . I don't want to
pressure you or make you upset. I'm . . . I'm just really happy to
see you . . . you look . . . you look happy and I just—" I pull him
in for another hug and I whisper in his ear, "I just love you. I love
you so much."

"I love you, too," he says. His voice is so smooth and easy.

"Okay, y'all, we're gonna get started," a wiry man announces from behind the podium. He has a rich Virginian
accent and his direction to sit and settle is like butter through
the smoke-filled room. I tuck into my row, not letting go of
Ferdie's hand just yet, and we sit. Ralph joins us, the chair
creaking beneath his weight. The wiry man continues, "Hi,
I'm Joe and I'm an alcoholic."

"Hi, Joe," the room answers. Joe winds through the rules of
the meeting before asking people to come up and read from *The
Big Book*. I look over at Ferdie.

"It's got the Twelve Steps and the Twelve Traditions in it. It's
AA's guidebook, I guess," Ferdie whispers. I nod, tuning back to
the young-looking girl whose voice is tight and shaking as she
mutters through her reading. By the fourth person I now know
to say hi back when they introduce themselves. Joe calls on
Ferdie. He lets go of my hand and rubs his sweaty palms on his
pants. Ralph watches him go.

"Come on over here," Ralph says, motioning for me to scoot closer. I oblige quickly. "I'm glad you came."

"Thanks," I say. "I'm sorry . . . my parents . . ."

"Don't worry about it. That's normal here," Ralph says.

"Hi, I'm Ferdinand and I'm an alcoholic and an addict." Ferdie's voice is shaking.

"Hi, Ferdinand," we all say back. Ralph passes me some tissues as the first tear pools in my eye. I thank him. Ferdie goes on to read a passage from *The Big Book*. When he finishes he walks back over to us and I shift over, leaving his seat next to Ralph vacant. I smile as he settles in.

"I hate that part," he says.

"Would anyone like to share?" Joe asks from behind the podium.

And person after person stands up and just talks. Bares their soul, really. Hi, I'm Beverly and I'm an alcoholic. Hi, I'm Terrance and I'm an addict. Hi, I'm Marcus and I'm an addict. And every time we say hi back. And every time we clap when they finish. They talk about life and pain and the want to use or drink. They talk about the people they've let down and the promises they've broken. They talk of never fitting in. Hi, I'm Marilyn and I'm an alcoholic. Hi, my name is Sun and I'm an addict. Hi, I'm Carly and I'm an addict. They talk about getting a job and finding love again. They talk about seeing their children and feeling overwhelming guilt for the mistakes they've made. They talk about when tragedy struck and they were too high to help. They talk about the guilt they live with day in and day out. Hi, I'm Kyle and I'm an alcoholic and an addict. Hi, my name is Sara and I'm an alcoholic. Hi, I'm Lydia and I'm an addict. They talk about what they've had to do to get drugs. And they talk about who they hurt to get them. They talk about what got them here and the scars and the life before. And some people are funny and some people can barely get out a sentence. And some people just sob as they retell horror stories, the shame of it finally loosening its stranglehold on them word by word. Some people have just used or drank and are back and some people have over thirty years, but goddamn life gets hard sometimes.

And it's raw. And it's brave. And it's vulnerable.

And it's intense. And it's sad. And it's painful.

And I realize I'm crying. Not because I'm sad. And it's not fear or vulnerability or dread or pain. It's hope. I look over at Ferdie and . . . do I really get to have my brother like this? Bright-eyed and present?

Ferdie stands up.

"Hi, I'm Ferdinand and I'm an alcoholic and an addict."

"Hi, Ferdinand," we all say.

"I get my thirty-day chip tonight." A smattering of applause as Ferdie nods. "Why do I feel like I don't deserve it, you know?" He stops and lets his head dip. He takes off his glasses and rubs his eyes. Ferdie looks down at me, tears streaming down his face. His voice is a whisper. "I'm sorry. God, I'm so sorry." I just sit there. I don't want to enable. I . . . "My dad used to take me on the ice when I was little and he'd make me shoot goals at him. He'd never let one pass. He was all over that cage. And I didn't care, because my old man never gave a shit about me except for when I was shooting on him in that goal. I didn't care that nothing ever went in, you know? But he used to heckle me. Just the worst shit. And I still lapped it up. I'd be happily shooting away, he'd block it and call me some name, and on we'd go. Until one day, I thought . . . what if I actually tried? I mean, maybe that's what he wants. Maybe that'll make him . . ." Ferdie's voice chokes. He wipes his eyes and finally puts his glasses back on. "Maybe that'll make him love me." A smile and a cruel laugh. "So, I shoot on him. And I score. And I score. And I score. And he's all quiet and I think he's just in awe, you know? That this is going to be the moment I've been waiting for. So, then I'm showing off and skating all these patterns and scoring. And scoring. Our time is up and the team is lining up along the rink. And I skate over and I've got the biggest grin on my face. And I start in with some line and he just punches me. He . . . he broke my nose. I remember how cold the ice was. On my back. And I hated that I was crying. I hated it. I mean, it's not like it was the first time he'd hit me. Dad threw his hockey stick at me, but it missed. Which just pissed him off even more and I . . . the sound of it skittering across the ice . . . it's just . . . there. Right there. I knew enough to stay down. I was maybe twelve at the time. He skated off the ice and never came back. Not to a game. Not to shoot around. Nothing. And we never talked about it. I finally got up off the ice and all the kids and the parents and the coaches were just standing there staring. I picked up his stick, and do you know what I said as I passed them?" Ferdie crumples up and rests his hands on his hips. The room is so quiet. "I wonder if the concession stand is open yet, right?" And he laughs. "The poor kid I said it to was like, 'I don't know, man.' Blood was everywhere. And right then, I never wanted to feel that again. Shit, I never wanted to feel anything ever again. Since I've been here that's all I've been doing and I am so tempted every day to just drink it away. Go back to that sweet numbness where I can't remember the sound of that hockey stick skittering across the ice or what it felt like to get hit by my dad for being proud of myself.

But then I think about"—Ferdie's hand clasps around my shoulder—"real love and how safe it can feel. I think maybe I've got a shot. Thanks." Ferdie sits down and Ralph pats his leg and tells him he did a good job. Calls him son.

Ferdie looks over at me and I shake my head . . . I'm sorry I'm crying. I'm sorry I'm almost hysterical, I try to get across. And he smiles, pulling me in. I tuck under his arm.

"Okay, it's time for birthdays," Joe says. He counts back from twenty years. A gray-haired woman in a pressed pantsuit stands up at eighteen years. Fifteen. Ten years. Five years. Three years. And at a year a handful of people rise and Joe presents all the people who are celebrating a birthday with a cake. We clap and the cake gets swept off and cut and set out on paper plates next to the terrible burned coffee.

"Okay, nine months . . . six months . . . ninety days?" Joe asks. A few people stand and accept their chips from Joe. We clap and they can't help but smile. This sneaking smile that just breaks my heart. They tuck the chip into a pocket or slide it onto a key ring with the others. Whatever they do with it, it's clearly a treasure.

"Sixty days?" Joe asks. One man steps up and Joe presents him with the chip. He has much to say. How he got here. How he's an inspiration. I hear Ralph whisper, "Well, he has it all figured out, doesn't he?" to Ferdie. And Ferdie smiles.

"Thirty days?" The people who appeared in a line from behind the podium all stand and approach Joe in the front of the room. Joe presents them each with a little chip. It looks almost like a poker chip from where I'm sitting. The men and women thank him and they smile. Hope. Fear. Stooped shoulders on some and others walk tall. Ferdie takes his chip and he just . . . holds it, lovingly curling his fingers around it as he walks back to us.

Ferdie settles back in next to me and shows me the little chip. There are words inscribed on it: TO THINE OWN SELF BE TRUE. I smile. I hand it back to him and he just cradles the damn thing. This from the kid who used to use state hockey trophies for shooting practice.

"I want to thank y'all for coming, and as we always do we're going to say the Lord's prayer and then end with the serenity prayer." Everyone in the room stands and starts folding up chairs, stacking them along the wall. I follow, folding my chair up and handing it to a gentleman who stacks it along with the others. Everyone gathers back into the middle of the room. I stand next to Ferdie on one side and Ralph on the other. Ralph takes my hand in his and I see that everyone is forming a circle, hand in hand. Ferdie's fingers curl around mine. Everyone starts speaking the Lord's Prayer as one. Then we begin the serenity prayer.

"God grant me the serenity to accept the things I cannot change, courage to change the things I can, and the wisdom to know the difference."

And then Ralph and Ferdie both take up my hands and shake them out with each word: "Keep coming back, it works if you work it."

We let go of our hands and clap.

As the crowd disperses and Ralph says his good-byes, I hold on to Ferdie. I won't get to see him until he gets his sixty-day chip. He has to go. I'm so proud of him, I say. I'm babbling. I'm crying. And he just sweeps me up again in his arms, squeezing tighter and tighter.

"I'll eat you up, I love you so," he whispers.

19

"Your assistant summoned me?" Audrey asks, knocking on my door first thing the next morning.

"Yes, won't you come in," I say, motioning to my client chairs. I'm brain dead this morning. I didn't sleep at all last night. How could I? All the pieces are finally coming together. Why we are the way we are. Trust and safe distances. Having surface relationships and never being vulnerable with anyone wasn't a choice for us—it was a necessity. Acting like we cared or looking to someone else for any kind of validation meant either getting our noses broken or being ignored.

But something feels different now. And it's not about blame. This is my life. Ferdie and I are adults. Just like Audrey and Chuck. I am not my story and I certainly don't want to sit around and spend the next forty years talking about how everything is my parents' fault. What's the saying—that would be time spent drinking poison and expecting them to die? I'm not going to give them even more power and walk around like I'm some remora feeding off a sad childhood.

But it does feel like we've finally taken a flashlight and looked to see what was making all those scary noises just outside our bedroom window. And while it's certainly not nothing, it's nowhere near as bad as what we dreamed up night after night trembling under our covers. By making the decision to face our demons, Ferdie and I have given ourselves a shot at a future. But once again, making a decision to face demons and actually facing those demons are two very different things.

"Well, what is it?" Audrey asks.

"I spoke with Preeti yesterday. She said you approached her with some ideas about billboards?" I ask. I take a long drink of my tea.

"Yes, about that—" I put a finger up. She stops talking. I have every intention of laying into her, but then . . .

"Let's hear them," I say. I'm tired of fighting.

"What?"

"Let's hear your ideas. She said they were good," I say. Audrey walks me through her ideas, and just as Preeti said, they're not bad. They're not great or anything we can use, but they're not terrible. "Those are good."

"Thanks," she says. I am quiet. I don't even have to say it. "I know what you're going to say, that I should have spoken with you before going to Preeti, but I didn't know how you would react and—"

"You've just seen how I reacted."

"Right."

"And how was it?"

"It was good . . ."

"But?"

"Oh, please," Audrey says.

"Oh please, what?"

"This meeting is an aberration. I didn't bring you those ideas because you can't not roll your eyes when I'm speaking," she says, and it's all I can do not to roll my eyes. "You almost did it right there."

"You've done everything you can to undermine me and you wonder why I don't rejoice at your ideas?"

"I've done what I've had to do. Just like you."

"I'm not your enemy, Audrey. Are you hearing that? I just want to come to work and do my job. Why is that, all of a sudden, something you find offensive?"

"I'm not threatened by you," Audrey scoffs.

"I never said you were." Audrey is quiet. "You want to be on our team? Be on our team. Roll up your sleeves and get to work. We'd be happy to have you," I say.

"I don't need you to welcome me to your team, Anna."

"Stop. Stop already. God, do you hear yourself?"

"Of course I hear mys—"

"We used to grab dinner after work. Do you remember that? Remember when we met that one client at that hotel and he was all nervous so he ordered—"

"Jam," Audrey says.

"I mean, maybe he thought it was going to be a fruit plate? But either way he spent that entire meeting eating a ramekin of jam with a fork like he meant to do it." Audrey laughs.

"Didn't even order toast," Audrey says, smiling.

"He was in too deep," I say. Audrey laughs and then the smile fades. "Please," I say. "We can do this. Let me be your ally. As you said, there are so few women in this office—"

"You don't understand," she says.

"Make me understand." She shakes her head and won't look at me. A deep breath and she throws her head high. She re-crosses her legs and her mouth settles into a hard line. "Audrey."

"Look. You don't need to worry. I don't want Lumineux," she finally says. The truth. For once.

"What?"

"I mean . . . really?"

"It sure doesn't look that way," I say.

"I think it's adorable what you guys have done, but Lumineux just . . . well, it's not really where I see myself."

"Finally. We agree on something," I say.

"Oh, relax," she says. Sasha knocks on the door.

"Oh. *Ohhhhh.* I'm sorry," Sasha says, her face draining of all color upon seeing Audrey.

"No, no. Come on in. Don't let me keep you," Audrey says, standing.

"Think about what I've said. Please," I say. Audrey just stares at me for a long moment. She looks at me as if I'm a busy street and she's trying to figure out how to safely traverse it to the other side. A breath. A resolution. Her head held high. And she turns toward the door.

"Excuse me . . ." Audrey trails off.

"Sasha. You know my name is Sasha," she says, her voice quivering.

"What?" Audrey asks.

"You do," Sasha says, crossing her arms across her chest.

"Hm," Audrey says and closes the door behind her.

"What was all that about?" Sasha asks.

"Preeti calls me and says that Audrey approached her with some ideas about billboards," I say, standing. "Tea. I need tea."

"Oh . . . sure." Sasha and I walk to get more tea. "What about the billboards?"

"Meh."

"So, why didn't she come to the group with them instead of going straight to Preeti?" Sasha asks as we wend our way through the outer office.

"From what I gather her reasons are twofold: one, apparently I roll my eyes whenever she speaks and, more importantly, two, her grand plan only involves Lumineux insofar as it can get her closer to scoring Quincy for herself," I say. Sasha makes a face.

"Oh, well, that's kind of good news then. I mean, on the Audrey spectrum of things, but still on the good end," Sasha says, as we finally get to the break room. I pull a tea bag from the cupboard and drop it into the mug Allison made me for my birthday. I pour in the hot water as Sasha tops off her coffee.

"That was pretty amazing what you said," I say.

"Right?? I felt like such a badass. *You know my name is Sasha,*" she repeats in what sounds like a slight Austrian accent.

"It was pretty great," I say, and Sasha beams. "And we'll just keep an eye on Audrey. It's all we can really do."

"We'll just be extra aware," Sasha says, putting her finger on the side of her nose along with an elaborate wink.

"Keep your friends close . . . ," I lead.

"Definitely." Sasha agrees, missing the opportunity. "So, we're going to be in New York, huh?"

"Yeah, Josh on Monday and—"

"Isn't that where Lincoln is?" I narrow my eyes at her. "And we know where he works, right?" Sasha asks.

"We do."

"I mean, who's to say that you couldn't just accidentally bump into him, you know? And . . . what's this? Oh, you know—it's just a picnic basket and maybe some red wine in it. I don't know. Is that a baguette and some cheese?" Sasha is, of course, acting this whole scenario out.

"And we're back to the romance novels," I say.

"Or maybe? He'll know you're in New York and find you," Sasha says.

"Running through the rain," I say.

"Oh my God. That would be awesome."

"Because calling me would be too—"

"Ugh, boring," Sasha finishes, not even looking up from taking a sip of her coffee.

"Sure."

"Leaves changing all around you, strolling through Central Park," Sasha says, now completely swept away.

And then we're on set in New York and it's beyond anything I could have imagined. As the crew hustles, Lumineux executives look on, and makeup fusses with Josh, all I can see is Sasha's drawings come to life and everything we've talked about finally there—right in front of us. *Just Be. Lumineux Shower Gel. The everyday luxury all women deserve.* I take a sip of my tea and try to bask. Try.

"It looks amazing," Preeti says, taking it all in.

"I know. It's exactly what we envisioned," I say. Sasha scurries over to the set and moves a textbook here and a dish drainer there. She stands back from the scene, her hand on her chin. She pulls the costume designer in and starts talking about what the kids are wearing. She keeps saying it's too hipster. It's too hipster. The costume designer takes the kids back and they emerge in much more appropriate attire. Of course, Sasha was right. She joins us once more.

"Yes, these are everyday people, but oh look the kids are wearing designer shirts? Come on," Sasha says, making a face.

"And the light? From the kitchen window?" I ask.

"I know. It should be duskier," she says.

"Exactly," I say. She takes off and is speaking with the lighting guys; I see her motioning to the window and explaining that this is supposed to be at the end of a long workday. The lighting guys are nodding and the light from beyond the faux kitchen window dims as night falls in our little made-up world.

The director we hired for the shoot starts barking orders and moving people around as the photographer stays quiet, shooting and looking at his product on the computer screen. They fuss and perfect and discuss. And we wait. And we sit. And I scroll through e-mails. And laugh with Preeti and gossip with Sasha and we pull out Sasha's initial sketches and then we get into it with the director about a detail we see differently than he does.

And Sasha is lamenting her Time-Out as she watches Josh move through the shoot like a very professional deer in the headlights. I think about what she said about accidentally happening upon Lincoln by his work. Maybe that's a compromise between waiting to see if he shows up to my birthday dinner and letting go. I'm beginning to think it's not the worst idea I've ever heard.

We huddle around the computer screen and watch as the photos of our campaign stream in. The lighting, the composition, the casting is perfect. And as the day continues there is less and less for us to do except sit back and let it sink in. This is happening, this is finally real, and it is everything we hoped it would be.

We crawl back to the hotel late that night and are up bright and early the next day with Lantz. And then we're back at it again on our final day with Jake. And each day it becomes more real and yet it's hard to believe that this is what I get to do with my days and with my life.

I'm good at my job. Really good. I think about what Jake said when we landed Lumineux. About Sasha and I opening our own agency. And now I think that maybe that's not as crazy of an idea as I once thought. If Lumineux is as huge as I think it's going to be and I move up the ranks at Holloway/Greene as I know I will, even with Audrey and Chuck's ridiculousness, I could have my own agency within five years, if I play it right. We can take on all clients and no one could cryptically school me on Quentin Tarantino's accomplishments ever again.

As we wrap on our final day, there is a buzz. We all know we've made something exceptional. What was once a concept has become something extraordinary. Lumineux executives are excited and, while we're all exhausted, all we can do is float back to the hotel on a cloud.

"Chelsea Market is right there," Sasha says, motioning to the beautiful brick building just at the end of the street.

"Oh cool, maybe we'll go there for breakfast tomorrow," I say, scrolling through my phone. We decided to stick around New York for one more day just in case there is an issue with the product or Preeti wants to meet, or, you know, Quincy wants to call us in and hire us on the spot for all its advertising needs.

"I'm going to meet some friends for breakfast tomorrow," Sasha says as we wait for the elevator.

"That sounds great." I look up from my phone.

"I used to model with them back in the day. It'll be great to see them again."

"That sounds perfect," I say.

"The perfect Time-Out activity. Drink?" She motions to the bar just as the elevator opens up. I nod. Why not? We walk over to the bar and settle in at one of the tables.

"A bottle of champagne please," I say.

"Well, well, well," Sasha says in what is probably supposed to be a French accent, but only sounds confused and a bit guttural. The waitress brings our champagne over and—*pop*—opens it tableside. Sasha and I just smile. We can't help it. She pours two flutes and sets them in front of us, resting the champagne bottle in a silver bucket next to our table.

"To Lumineux," I say, raising my glass aloft.

"To us," Sasha adds.

We clink our glasses together and proceed to spend the rest of the evening drinking champagne. Somewhere around midnight, Sasha starts in.

"So. Tomorrow. Chelsea Market," she slurs. "You are going to go over to Chelsea Market and buy adorable foods for your accidental meet-up with one Lincoln Mallory." Of course Sasha says Lincoln's name in a terrible British accent.

"I am?"

"Yes. You'll just . . . oh, hello . . . is this . . . is this where you work? I was just . . . passing by," Sasha says, acting the entire thing out.

"We've already talked about this. I'm trying to let go, remember?"

"This is kind of letting go. You're letting go of the original plan and coming up with a new one," Sasha says.

"That's letting-go adjacent," I say.

"Exactly. Letting-go adjacent," Sasha says, lifting her glass and downing it in one.

"I do miss him," I say.

"And just think. You could see him tomorrow," Sasha says. Who am I kidding? Sasha doesn't need to convince me of anything. I've been dying to see Lincoln since I got into New York. Hell, I've been dying to see Lincoln since I walked out of the Biltmore in Phoenix.

"Okay," I say. Another drink of champagne. "I'll do it."

"I wonder if you can rent a beach cruiser on such short notice," Sasha says, pulling out her smartphone.

20

I know it's a bad plan. I know it could end badly. I know all this. I'm haunted by this reality as I wander around Chelsea Market in search of "adorable food." But here I am. With a reusable bag slung over my shoulder and an actual baguette sticking out of the top. How can it be an accident if I've brought food? Shouldn't I be "coming from a meeting?" And why am I in Soho? I buy myself some tea and decide to power through. I want to see him. And yet . . . I want to see him without risking actually saying I want to see him. Oh, is that . . . is this where you work . . . hm. I'm just in New York and couldn't care less! (I love you.)

I hail a cab and give him the address for Mallory Consulting on Wooster Street in Soho. Soho, with its cobbled streets and high-end boutiques, of course that's where Lincoln's consulting firm is. My reusable bag filled with baguettes and I will fit right in. Cue maniacal laughter.

I scroll through my e-mails and am over the moon with the pictures coming in from our week of photo shoots with the

RomanceCon men. Preeti keeps sending me shot after shot with subject lines that range from "OMG" to "No, this is my new favorite" and on and on. I go back and forth with Sasha, sending her all the feedback we're getting as well as the front-runners for the photos we plan to use. Sasha is out of pocket this morning, except for a photo she just posted to Instagram of her and four impossibly beautiful women somewhere in Brooklyn. I can only imagine that it's going well. With all this Lumineux stuff, it's felt like the world has gotten smaller and smaller. Sasha meeting up with her friends means we're loosening up a bit. Getting back to our regular selves, albeit a tad rawer. Hopefully. Or not. My mind is racing. I'm trying to be esoteric about five models having coffee as if it's the beacon of normalcy that I've been waiting for lo these many months. I'll stop at nothing to get out of thinking about where I'm headed.

The cab slows down. I could just wave him on and go back to the hotel. And then what? Spend the next ten months waiting? On pause? I pay the fare and step out in front of a beautiful sage-green building, the words MALLORY CONSULTING in white block print along the bottom of one of the huge windows that line the front. A shiny black door has a gold plaque and a bell you can ring to be let in.

I immediately start walking down the street, looking in the boutiques and trying to lower my heart rate so I don't pass out in front of Mallory Consulting. The image of me having a seizure in front of his office, probably becoming incontinent as my little perfect baguette rolls down the street, isn't helping the situation.

I've timed my arrival right around lunch so I'll have a better shot at catching him stepping out for something to eat. Oh my God. What if he's meeting someone? What if he's having a torrid affair with his secretary or another consultant? What if he's married? The scenarios rack up as I pace back and forth in front of Mallory Consulting. I walk past his building and down the block again. The sounds of New York all around me, honking cabs and blaring sirens in the distance. But this section of Wooster Street is quiet enough that I can hear the rustle of the trees above me and the *rat-a-tat* of the tires along the cobblestones. The fresh smells and the tinkling music waft from the boutiques and cafés that pepper the classic, idyllic New York lane. I turn around and walk down the street once more.

Lincoln.

He's standing out in front of the building. Just standing there. Hands in his pockets. Head tilted. I recover from the shock of seeing him and can't help but smile. He's dressed more casually today—gray tweed pants and a gray cashmere sweater over a light blue oxford cloth shirt.

He's what's been missing.

I walk toward him, hitching my purse and the stupidest reusable bag in the entire world over my shoulder. My stomach immediately drops. I can't read him. Furrowed brow with the hint of a smile—but the hands in the pockets is never a good sign.

I stand right in front of him. I stop and start a thousand sentences. Everything I'd planned to say has left my head and now I'm just breathing heavily as I stand in front of Lincoln Mallory out in front of his office building. Wow, the bad ideaness of this whole thing really hits home. His face is—

"I'm in New York on business," I croak out. I clear my throat.

"This doesn't look like that little Italian restaurant in D.C. that you gave me explicit directions to," Lincoln says. That voice. I'd forgotten what he sounded like.

"No, well—"

"No," he says. He's . . . annoyed. Oh, no. He's annoyed.

"Okayyyy, well, this was a terrible idea," I say, walking to the curb in a fugue state and flinging my arm up in the air to hail a cab.

"Anna," he says, and dammit if Lincoln saying my name doesn't just roll through my body like a tsunami. I turn around, my arm still in the air. Oh, that's right, mister, I'm still hailing a cab. This is still happening. "My office is right there." Lincoln finally pulls his hand out of his pocket long enough to point to the large window just above the shiny black entrance to his consulting firm. Or what others might call "a front-row seat to watch Anna Wyatt psychotically pace and mutter to herself."

"Oh?" I ask, shocked that I can form words or say anything through the absolute horror of what's transpired here this afternoon.

"Was it twenty times?" he asks, his hand going back and forth.

"I'm starting to see why all those women hated you." I turn around. "You can just say you're not interested, you know," I say, and I am back at the curb with my arm in the air.

"Your arm is going to grow tired if you continue to insist on dramatically hailing cabs to punctuate your frustration," he says, folding his arms across his chest.

"How can you be so cavalier?"

"I'm being cavalier?"

"Haughty," I say.

"Do you plan on running through all the synonyms or—"

"I'm just—" I say.

"So the woman who told me to appear at her birthday dinner

in exactly one year is now calling me cavalier?" His folded arms. The tensing jaw. Lincoln is pissed.

"Yes," I say, clearing my throat.

"And this is where that folksy saying about pots and kettles comes in?"

"It was romantic," I say.

"It was Machiavellian," he says.

"What?"

"I wanted the messy conversation. I may not have been ready or . . . may not . . . no, I definitely wouldn't have said the right things, but I wanted to try."

"Don't you even try to rewrite history and portray yourself as the one who didn't explicitly say it had to stay temporary and you didn't want me—"

"No, I know. I know."

"This wasn't all me."

"I know."

"I was desperate. I had to come up with something, because the thought of not seeing you again . . ."

"This has nothing to do with me."

"It has everything to do with you!"

"No. It's your birthday dinner. It's your candle. It's your timeline. It was even your bravery that you commended yourself for in the end," he says.

"But—" Lincoln steps closer. It's then that he sees the baguette. He just shakes his head.

"I was a coward. I know that now; hell, I knew that the minute I said it," he says. He unfolds his arms and stands over me. So close. "But all this?" He motions to the adorable bag and all of its adorable contents. "Why didn't you just call me?"

"Why didn't you just call me?"

"I wanted to. So many times."

"Me too."

"I don't know how to do this," he says, unable to look at me. I hear him take a deep breath. I step closer. He reaches out and I want to tell him to stop. Don't make me remember what it's like when you touch me. Let me have the sweet oblivion of forgetti— He runs his hand down the length of my arm and takes my hand. I curl my fingers around his and the ache of it eclipses the horror of the last ten minutes. He wraps his other arm around my waist and pulls me into him. And I breathe him in—that oaky, outside smell of his. My arms remain at my sides, that stupid tote bag thunking and banging into my back. I push Lincoln back and throw the tote bag into the gutter of the perfect little cobblestoned street. I set my purse down between my feet. I look up at him. Finally. Those dark blue eyes. He's hurt. I lift my hand hesitantly as if I'm reaching out to pet a stranger's dog. Is it friendly? Will it bite? All these questions are also relevant in the scenario currently playing out on Wooster Street.

His mouth is a hard line as he watches me. I bring my hand up to the side of his face, the stubble tickling the palm of my hand. And as he always has, he closes his eyes and leans into my touch. And finally—a deep breath. His eyes open for the briefest of moments and before I know it, his mouth is fast on mine. The world blurs around us and when we finally part I don't know what to say. Do I tell him about how I'm trying to let go? Would that be anti–letting go? He straightens the collar of my blouse, patting it into place.

"I have to go. My lunch is rolling down the street," I say. Lincoln laughs.

"What do we do now?" he asks. And another kiss. I wrap my arms around him, his smooth leather belt just under my fingertips.

"I don't know," I say. "I don't think I'm ready." I look at the reusable bag in the gutter. "Clearly." Lincoln laughs. "But I meant what I said: loving you is one of the bravest things I've ever done."

"Before it was *the* bravest thing you'd ever done." I smile. And think of Ferdie.

"Things have changed," I say. Lincoln throws his head back and laughs. And then a smile. A beaming, proud smile that even I can recognize.

"Well, you're my person. I'll wait." He kisses me. "I'll be here when you're ready for messy," Lincoln says, my face in his hands. I kiss him and he holds me close . . . close . . . closer.

"I know," I say.

He takes my hand and we walk to the curb. He puts his arm in the air as a cab rumbles down the cobblestone street. It pulls over. He opens the door for me and pulls me in for one last kiss.

"Do hurry back, my love," he says. I run my hand down the front of his sweater, over the scars and the heart and the body and the man that I love. I nod. Unable to say a word, I get into the cab and he shuts the door behind me. The cabbie turns around and asks where to. I don't want to tell him. If I tell him he'll pull away from this curb.

"Where to?" the cabbie repeats. I mutter the name of my hotel and the cabbie situates himself behind the wheel. I stare out at Lincoln and his eyes are fixed on mine. He smiles as we pull away from the curb. Lincoln remains just where he is, watching me drive away.

The television in the cab blares.

I pick my fingernails.

. . .

A honk.

The cabbie talks on the phone.

I roll down my window.

Close my eyes.

Lean my head against the door.

Wind.

Wring my purse straps.

The leather creaks.

Creaks.

"This is it," the cabbie says.

Focus.

What?

What's happening with time?

The TV blares.

"We're here," he says.

The doorman of my hotel opens my door and I give the cabbie money. Through the lobby. Push the button. In the elevator with all the mirrors. Where's my key card? Key card. Down the hallway and slide key card. Green light. Drop my purse. Pull down the duvet, turn off the lights, and crawl under the covers.

And cry.

The next morning, Sasha sits down across from me on the Metroliner with two cups of tea and a muffin. I thank her and manage a smile.

"I'm so sorry," Sasha says.

"I'm not," I say, blowing on my tea.

Silence.

"You're too quiet," she says.

"I wasn't ready. So busy trying to find the wrong man . . ." I can't even finish the sentence. Hoisted by my own petard.

"But you don't have to be totally ready for these things," she says.

"No, I know. I learned all this stuff, but when I was put to the test I defaulted right back to my old ways. Kept trying to control everything. I'm not ready to step in the ring."

"Yeah, I guess so."

"I was so set on creating this perfect environment where no one would get hurt and . . . well, not no one. Me. Where I wouldn't get hurt. I knew if he walked through that door into that Italian restaurant—which I am never setting foot in again, thankyouverymuch—that he would be ready to love me in such a way that I wouldn't . . . oh my God." Crumbs shoot out of my mouth as I continue to speak with my mouth full. "It's Machia-vellian. *Machiavellian.*"

"I thought it was romantic," Sasha says.

"What am I going to do?"

"He said he wanted messy, so . . ."

"I don't know how to do messy."

"I think he just wants you to be—"

"If you say raw or authentic right now I am going to throw this muffin at you," I say.

"Real. I think he just wants you to be real."

"Do you think he wants me to Just Be?" I ask with a smile. And she laughs.

"I was totally going to say that," Sasha says, still laughing.

"We've been doing this damn campaign for weeks and I have no idea what it actually means," I say.

"Well, it's whatever . . . what is it you were saying? It's whatever feels totally wrong and uncomfortable," she says.

"Why can't I drop the act? Why couldn't I just let it go?"

"Because sometimes the act is all we've got, you know?"

"Oh, I know," I say. A beat. The landscape speeds by outside the train's window. "Why didn't I just . . . why wasn't . . . oh my God. It's changing the lightbulb in the pooey bathroom all over again," I say.

"It's the what?"

"Remember?" I ask, not wanting to open old wounds.

"Oh no . . . right. The lightbulb story."

"I need to be able to let him change the lightbulb," I say, my head falling into my hands at the mere thought of such horrific things.

"You're not going to g—"

"No. Oh God no. It's a metaphor. Can you imagine? Me swanning into Mallory Consulting and just . . . yes, hello. Lincoln? I'm here to use your bathroom," I say, hysterically laughing.

Sasha is wheezing laughing.

"Smell it! *Love me!*" I laugh.

"Oh my God." Sasha laughs. "I . . . I can't breathe." It feels so good to laugh. She pounds the little table between us and snorts, whipping her head back and cackling some more.

21

The Just Be campaign is a phenomenon.

It's not only put Lumineux Shower Gel onto shopping lists and into grocery carts around the nation, but the campaign itself has gone viral. And not just within the ad world. Women are posting it to their social media profiles and the tagline has become a call to arms. It's made people ask questions about their own lives in a way that transcends advertising or shower gel. It's become a movement.

I'm sitting on the Metro going to work and I see a woman take out her phone and snap a selfie in front of one of the Just Be placards. She's pointing at her hair—an amazing pixie cut, newly shorn. She looks happy. Proud. Excited. She did it. She finally cut her hair the way she's always wanted. I'm beaming at her as she looks at the picture and smiles. She's happy.

And this is not the first time I've seen something like this. Two women standing under a Just Be billboard with tickets to a Broadway show. A pack of teenage girls off on a great adventure caught taking a picture in front of a Just Be bus-shelter ad. But my favorite of all these beautiful vignettes was when I was behind a woman in line at my local coffee shop. She was on the phone talking with her friend and from what I gleaned, she was unhappy with her job. The usual stuff. But then she said she'd seen these pottery classes at this little studio by where her daughter goes to school. She'd always wanted to learn. I smiled, trying not to act like I was eavesdropping. And then she said, "I mean, Just Be, right?" And it took everything I had not to lunge into her for a hug right there.

It's become the subject of morning talk shows, and Lumineux has even come out with T-shirts—all done in that same simple, modern font with the words *Just Be* on them. It's been described as the antidote to all the airbrushed models in string bikinis eating cheeseburgers in front of luxury cars that women are bombarded with daily. Lumineux isn't about shaming women; it's following Helen Brubaker's lead and actually respecting them. Lumineux stands alone in its message among the long-legged models stepping off yachts and happy perfect homemakers dancing with their mops as their children carelessly track mud through their home.

Lumineux is our crowning glory, and Sasha and I are riding high in the days and weeks after the campaign explodes. There is no downside; even Audrey being on our "team" can't dampen our spirits. Charlton had to admit that Lumineux is an unadulterated success—women's product or not. He even put Lumineux on the website. Which means we are now officially "important."

Michael and I went down to Virginia to watch Ferdie get his sixty-day chip last week, and it was just as emotional and hopeful and wrenching as the last meeting. Watching Ferdie come back to life is nothing short of miraculous. We told Ferdie we were putting the Shakespeare book club on hold until he could rejoin us. He thanked us and then joked that he thought he was going to get out of reading *Hamlet.*

A knock on my office door. Sasha.

"So what is it you're going to be again?" she asks, settling into one of the client chairs in my office. Every year Holloway/Greene has a huge Halloween party instead of a holiday party. Of course, I think it's because Charlton would rather see his female staff in their slutty Halloween finest rather than bundled up in their holiday best, but that's just me being cynical. Ish.

"It's a surprise," I say.

"Okay, then I'm not telling you mine, either," Sasha says.

"But you're dying to tell me yours," I say.

"Totally," she says.

"Did you see that whole thing *The View* did on Just Be?" I ask, turning my computer around for her to see.

"Yeah, it was good, right?"

"Really good," I say, turning the computer back around.

"Oh, good, you're both here." Chuck ambles into my office, plopping down in the other client chair. Sasha situates herself farther away from him. He doesn't notice. "So, you both are coming to the party tonight, right?"

"Of course," I say. Chuck looks at Sasha and she nods yes.

"Good," he says, slapping his legs before standing. "Good." He walks out of the office without another word. Sasha and I stare at each other.

"Do you think—"

"It's got to be Quincy, right?" I ask.

"Clios haven't been announced . . . and even then Lumineux can't be nominated in this go-round anyway," Sasha says.

"Right," I say.

"It's gotta be Quincy," Sasha says.

"I don't want to get my hopes up, you know? But Audrey—"

"I know. I don't know," Sasha says. A smile. A squeal. She stands and rushes back behind my desk, holding her arms out. "We're hugging now. Come on!" I stand up and we hug. Of course, I'm still wary, but I let the moment whisk me away, even as Sasha starts hopping up and down—while still hugging me—to the words "Quin-CY! Quin-CY! Quin-CY!"

We finally break apart and she chants her way out of the office. Sasha twirls around in the doorway and struts to her office, hiding two middle fingers behind her back.

As I focus back on the work at hand, I don't think about fairness or messiness or getting my hopes up or what I think I deserve.

I just feel proud.

That proud feeling takes a bit of a beating later that night when I hail a cab dressed as Princess Leia, cinnamon buns and all. I try to hide the iconic white sheath with a trench coat, but then I just look like Princess Leia: Private Eye. And it doesn't help when some smart-ass chooses to yell, "Why don't you just use the force!" as I stand out in front of my apartment, hand in the air as the cab slows down just in front of me. And maybe I could have been classier than to tell him I wish he'd fall into the sarlacc pit. Which makes for an awkward beginning with the poor cabbie who just wants to know where he is taking me this fine evening, to which I joke, "Well, clearly not Alderaan."

Silence.

I clear my throat and give the cabbie the address of the restaurant in Georgetown. I pay the fare, finding myself in a gor-

geous restaurant that's been completely taken over by Holloway/
Greene's Halloween party.

The music is loud and people are on the dance floor already. A moment as I remember the parties at RomanceCon
and how great their dance floors were. A smile as I think
maybe I'll just join in later. Who knows? Candles and floral
centerpieces dot the outlying tables, and the costumes . . . oh,
the costumes. There are Ghostbusters and a Captain America
and Pink Ladies and police officers and nerds and ninjas, and
I'm half expecting spotlights to illuminate banners just over-
head as I pick my way through the crowds. As I make my way
through the party, everyone just laughs and points, telling me
my costume is awesome and to help them, Obi-Wan Kenobi,
he's their only hope. I smile and laugh back. This party is already better than however many of the ones I've endured since
I've been at Holloway/Greene.

"Wyatt!" Charlton says, appearing with a flute of champagne
and what looks like maybe someone's babysitter on his arm this
evening. "I didn't know we'd be having royalty attend our little
soiree this evening." Charlton bows and I give him a regal nod.
Charlton and I are on much better terms now that Lumineux is
a success. He hails a waiter, takes another flute of champagne
from the tray, and hands it to me. I thank him. I take in his costume and it's the bloody bare feet that give it away.

"John McClane," I say.

"Yippee-ki-yay, moth—"

"And you've said that . . . a thousand times tonight already?"

"'Come out to the coast, we'll get together, have a few laughs,'"
he says, jostling his child bride in the process. She smiles.

"You have no idea what that's from, right?" I ask.

"What what's from?" she asks. I look at Charlton and he just shrugs.

"And you're a . . . ," I ask.

"A nurse," she says.

"My kind of nurse," Charlton says, tugging on the poor girl's pleather nurse outfit that barely covers anything.

"Anna Wyatt," I say, extending a hand to the girl.

"Kayla," she says, taking my hand in a half shake, half maybe going to kiss my hand, and then we're just clutching each other's fingers for a few awkward seconds. I smile and pull my hand back, taking a sip of my champagne as I scan the room for Sasha.

"You looking for Sasha?" Charlton asks.

"Yeah," I say, always shocked that a man so tone-deaf is actually remarkably perceptive.

"She's over by the bar," Charlton says. I thank him, say my farewells to Kayla, and walk toward the bar, seeing Audrey dressed as Cleopatra. Of course. She gives me a royal nod and I wave back. I squeeze through the crowd and oh, is that your sword, and finally I'm at the bar and see Sasha.

Wonder Woman.

"Hey!" I say, approaching her.

"Hey!" she says, twirling around. "What do you think?" I hug her, saying that it's amazing. That's right. It's just Princess Leia and Wonder Woman hanging around a bar in late October.

And then we just stand there. Smiling and basking. I think we're both still stunned at the success of the Lumineux campaign.

"Lantz got booked by that outerwear company," Sasha says. "It's the whole—" And both of us mime "beard" at the same time.

"Did he really?" I ask.

"Yeah, that's what he said," Sasha says.

"Did he now," I say, sipping a poached glass of champagne.

"Just because I'm on Time-Out doesn't mean I can't plan ahead," Sasha says with a wink.

"Indeed," I say, smiling.

"And if he's the right guy? He'll be there a year from now," Sasha says.

"He'd be lucky to have you," I say. Sasha smiles, undoes her golden lasso, and says, "I can see if you're telling the truth, you know." I laugh and it takes her upward of twenty minutes to get the lasso back to how it was. "Did you get the invite yet?" Sasha changes the subject.

"To Jake's perfect wedding? Of course," I say.

"They're bringing him in for a soap opera next week," she says.

"Oh my God, he'd be perfect for that," I say.

"And then he wouldn't have to leave his beloved New York," she says.

"Right?" I laugh.

"I saw that Josh booked a movie. This is going to be so huge for him," Sasha says. I nod. Happy. I'm happy.

"Is this thing on?" We all turn to face Charlton as he hops up on what looks like a little stage for karaoke. The spotlight finds him and he momentarily shields his eyes. "This costume was awesome until I realized I had to use the public toilet with no shoes on." Everyone laughs.

"What's Chuck dressed as?" I whisper to Sasha. She fixes her gaze on her ex-flame. Then . . . confusion.

"Is it . . ."

"It's some Internet meme thing. No one gets it," a guy dressed as Inspector Gadget says.

"That's awesome," I say, pointing to his costume.

"This, everyone gets," he says. We laugh.

I situate myself next to Sasha and she takes my hand and gives it a good squeeze. I look over at her and we smile. We did it.

"Happy Halloween, people of Holloway/Greene," Charlton says. "Before we get too drunk, I want to thank everyone for coming out tonight. It's been quite a year for our agency and it's going to get even better." Sasha gives our joined hands a wiggle and I settle in even closer to her. "Tonight, we're starting a new tradition. It seemed more than fitting after the year we've had to mark the performances of a select few with a bit of an extra bonus." Chuck brings up two trophies and two pink envelopes. He stands just behind Charlton as he continues speaking. Sasha starts squirming.

"I know," I whisper. "It's going to be okay." She nods and nods and nods, but I can see her face tensing as we both take in the two trophies, which are not the Quincy campaign. Charlton is droning on about other campaigns and this and that. "This doesn't mean we didn't get Quincy. Those might not even be our trophies."

"The pink envelopes?" Sasha's voice cracks as she points to the ridiculous pink envelopes.

"I know," I say, trying to stay ahead of my emotions. It's not going well. I scan the room and find Audrey. She . . . she has no idea what's going on, either. Clearly.

"But tonight is about announcements and our brand-new Employee of the Year Award. It should come as no surprise to anyone here who this year's recipients are. The masterminds behind the monster Lumineux campaign, Anna Wyatt and Sasha Merchant! Come on up!" The crowd applauds and Charlton takes a swig of his beer as Sasha and I walk up to the little stage, the crowd parting like the Red Sea. "Leia. Wonder Woman." Chuck hands us each a trophy. Each trophy is topped with a businessman carrying a briefcase. "They didn't have ladies. Funny, right?" Chuck whispers. Hilarious. "And this nice little bonus should let you know the depth of our admiration." Chuck hands us the two pink envelopes. Sasha begins to open hers and when she sees that I am not opening mine, she clears her throat and smooths the tear over. "Thank you again, ladies. And let's all say it together." And the entire room intones: *"Just Be."* The crowd applauds as Sasha and I nod and thank Charlton before tucking ourselves back into the bar next to Inspector Gadget. I open up the pink envelope and, wow, the zeroes just keep going and going on what looks like a bonus check from the partners of Holloway/Greene. Sasha tucks the stupid businessman trophy under her arm and opens her own pink envelope. A huge smile.

Of course, this all makes me very nervous. Charlton continues.

"What Anna and Sasha accomplished with the Lumineux campaign was beyond anything we could have imagined here at Holloway/Greene. But more than anything else? Quincy Pharmaceuticals has finally taken notice."

The crowd goes wild. Sasha and I freeze.

"He'd better pull us back on that stage, I swear to God," I say, eyeing Audrey, who is inching her way to the stage. I motion to Sasha to look.

"No. *No.* This . . . this can't be happening," she says.

"I can't believe it. I thought—"

"We have a meeting with Quincy next week!" Charlton thrusts Chuck's arm into the air and the crowd goes wild— although around Sasha and me, the crowd is more measured, clapping and checking us, clapping and gossiping. Audrey looks as though she's about to erupt as she melts back into the crowd. "Yippee-ki-yay, mothe—"

"Why didn't we hear about this meeting?" I hear myself say from the back of the restaurant. Sasha tries to stop me as I pick my way through the crowd and toward the stage.

"Wh—" Charlton asks, shielding his eyes from the spotlight. He registers who it is and his face drops, but then . . . anger. And not because I'm undermining him. Nope. Charlton Holloway IV is pissed because I'm ruining his stupid party.

"Why haven't we heard about this meeting?" I say, now standing in front of the stage. It's in this moment that I get a shot of me in the mirror behind the stage and remember that I'm dressed as Princess Leia.

"It's the Halloween party, Wyatt; we'll discuss this la—"

"Charlton! Why didn't we hear about this meeting?"

"Why would you guys have?" Charlton looks to Chuck, who is just as confused.

"Why would we have?"

"Yeah," he says. A sniff. "I'm sending Chuck." And that's all I need. I pull myself up onto the stage, resituate my cinnamon roll buns while holding my stupid businessman trophy and the cloyingly patronizing pink envelope.

"Because you wouldn't have a meeting without the work Sasha and I did on Lumineux, that's why," I say. The crowd is quiet. The music plays in the distance.

"You're being emotional, and like Chuck said, this was a tough decision," Charlton says.

"Yeah, you two seem all broken up about it," I say.

"Look, we have big plans for you and—"

"No, this is bullshit. I'm done. I quit. I *quit*." I slam the trophy down on the stage floor and it hits with a hollow thud. And then I bring my white go-go Leia boot heel down hard onto it—shattering the stupid thing into a million pieces. "And you can find business*women* trophies; you just have to look a little harder." I hop down off the stage and take the bonus check out of that stupid pink envelope and throw the envelope at Charlton. The pink envelope floats to the floor as I make a show of tucking the check itself into the little white clutch that I thought would be the most Leia-like.

"Anna, come on. Calm down," Chuck says. I walk past Audrey. I stop. A moment. Her eyes are rimmed in red and there's nothing I can say or do to her that her own father hasn't already done. She forces out a smile. It's genuine. The first tear looses itself from her heavily made-up cat eyes, and she can only shrug. Chuck hops down off the stage and follows me through the crowd.

"Anna, come on," Chuck says. Charlton is standing on the stage. A spotlight on him in all of his *Die Hard* glory. I stand at the entrance to the restaurant. Everyone is quiet. Mouths hanging open. Watching me. I look back at Sasha. She is smiling. I smile back. I give her a wink.

"Yippee-ki-yay, motherfucker," I say, and walk out of that restaurant.

22

"Yippee-ki-yayyyyyy," I say again, shooting the rubber band that was wrapped around the sushi container Sasha brought by along with everything that was in my office at Holloway/Greene. The rubber band hits the TV screen and tumbles to the floor. It's early afternoon and I'm in my pajamas. I've been unemployed for three weeks.

I spend my days asking the one eternal question I can handle right now: How did it get to be three thirty P.M.?

I've gone from feeling like the heroine of my own story to feeling like a tantrumming baby who didn't get her way and took her toys and went home. It's funny how heroism can feel a lot like recklessness in the harsh light of morning. I've spent the last three weeks fighting with myself—mostly aloud—about whether I did the right thing. Why wasn't Lumineux good enough for me? Maybe I should ask for my old job back because the idea of going to work for another agency, another Charlton, another hustle, and another master key to the pink ghetto makes me sick to my stomach.

So, I sleep. I sleep and I take showers. I take showers and I walk. And as autumn tumbles in around me, I isolate. I take to wearing the same blue-striped pajama bottoms I wore in Phoenix and one of Ferdie's old hockey jerseys. At first I wear this outfit around the house and then I rationalize that if I wear this outfit at nightfall for one of my meandering walks, people won't be able to tell that it is essentially pajamas. Then I decide I can wear the outfit at dusk. Then I decide I can wear the outfit to the corner store in the afternoon when I need tea and maybe some of those brownie bites.

Then I decide I can wear the outfit when I make my task for the day procuring a *pain au chocolat* and a latte from the café down the street. It's ten thirty A.M. I sell that particular field trip by wearing a tank top underneath the jersey in place of a bra. If someone asks, I say to myself as I pull the café door open, I'll say I've just come from pilates. Today "pilates" is code for the depths of despair.

"Just the pastry and the coffee?" the girl behind the counter says.

"Yes, thank you. I worked up quite an appetite at pilates. Phew!" The girl takes my money and gives me change. I dump the change into the tip jar. Hush money. She smiles. I move to the side and await my latte, pulling a bite off the *pain au chocolat*.

"Anna?" Nope. I don't turn around. This is not happening. "Anna?" The voice again. A deep breath and I turn around. It's Nathan. Oh, that's fine. I don't like him anyway.

"Hey," I say with a smile. He smiles back and then scans my outfit. "Pilates." I clear my throat and take another bite of my pastry.

"Great," he says. The café buzzes around us as drinks are

called out and the music plays and people chatter at tables and all this happens while I'm wearing my pajamas.

"How are Hannah and the kids?" I ask.

"Oh, fine. I hear they're fine," he says.

"What?" I ask.

"Hannah and I are spending some time apart," he says.

"What? I had dinner with her . . . when was it . . . ," I say.

"I don't think she's telling many people. Or anyone, I guess. We're in couple's therapy, so . . . it's not like we're thinking it's permanent," Nathan says.

"I'm so sorry," I say.

"Here . . . this is bugging me," he says, taking a napkin and wiping my cheek. He shows it to me. Chocolate. Or . . . *chocolat,* if you want to be fancy about it.

"Thanks," I say, shocked that my appearance could actually be any worse. We are quiet. I don't know what to say. "I hope you guys can work it out."

"My parents were married fifty-two years," Nathan says.

"Oh, wow, that's—" I say.

"And they hated each other the whole time," he says.

"Oh . . . uh . . ."

"I don't want to be like that," Nathan says. We get jostled a bit as the crowd awaiting their coffees grows. Nathan continues once we settle back in next to the condiment bar. "They constantly said they stayed together for the kids. As if we didn't know they hated each other." I am quiet. This is the most Nathan has ever said to me. Ever. "We felt like it was our fault they were so unhappy."

"I'm . . . I'm so sorry," I say. The girl calls out Nathan's name and he excuses himself. I push back my headband and resituate my glasses, not knowing where else to put my nervous energy. Another bite of *pain au chocolat* and I've finished it before I even get my latte. I crumple the bag up and toss it in the bin. Nathan settles back in next to me with his steaming coffee. The name "Merthon" scrawled on the side of the cup.

"They get it wrong every time," he says, laughing. "Nathan. How hard is it?"

"Merthon is such a common name," I say. Nathan laughs.

"I don't want our kids to feel like I did," he says.

"I get that," I say.

"When my dad finally passed away, everyone was so worried about what Mom was going to do. Fifty-two years they were together." Nathan says these words like a swooning old lady. It's kind of adorable. I smile. "My brothers and I weren't worried, of course. Mom moved into a condo in Arlington and has been traveling the world with her girlfriends ever since. I follow her on Instagram," he says. I laugh and he smiles. He pulls his phone out of his coat pocket and pulls up her Instagram account. He flicks through photo after photo of a group of older ladies in visors and matching floral separates in front of various wonders of the world. "She's happy." He smiles again and his eyes crinkle up as he slides his phone back into his coat pocket. The girl calls out my name and I go pick up my latte. Nathan waits for me. I walk back over and show him my cup. It reads "Lana."

"Close," he says as we wend our way through the crowded café. He holds the door open for me and I walk through with a thank-you. "It was good seeing you, Lana."

"You too, Merthon."

"If you would, I'd wait for Hannah to approach you with this. If that's okay," he says.

"Absolutely," I say.

"I think she's embarrassed we're having problems," he says, taking a sip of his coffee.

"I won't mention it," I say.

"Thanks," he says.

"I wasn't at pilates. I quit my job," I say. Blurt, really.

"I was wondering," he says.

"Thanks for letting me lie to you," I say.

"No problem," he says.

Nathan and I say our good-byes, and I walk back to my apartment. I realize I've been happily numb for the last three weeks and after one random meet-up with Nathan, I feel . . . embarrassed. Annoyed. How is my plan to achieve oblivion going to work if people from my life keep reminding me that there's a world beyond my apartment?

I unlock my door, throw my keys down on the side table, and am happy to be back home. Safe. In the dim haze of late morning. Time-Outs and Thunder Roads. Phoenix and romance novels. Marpling and Machiavelli. Being the heroine and finding my hero. That's the thing. You hear these stories about people reacting bravely and decisively in the face of certain death or wondrous miracles. When something miraculous happened to me, I told it I wasn't ready.

I sip my coffee, tucking my foot underneath me on the couch as I've done every day for the last three weeks.

I had no plan when I quit that night. Talk about messy. And look what's happened. All the work I've done, everything I've changed, everything I've worked for equals me having no job, no hero, and no friends. Apparently when I let myself Just Be, things turn to shit.

I pull out my phone and take a picture of the wreckage surrounding me: takeout containers, empty water bottles, little aluminum candy wrappers, dirty laundry in the background, and a box containing everything that was in my office. My tube-socked foot is in the foreground.

Messy.

I text the picture to Lincoln. I tap out several clever things to say and then erase them all. The picture really is worth a thousand words.

Within minutes he texts back. The picture is of a drawer; it looks like the bottom drawer of his desk. He's taken the photo with the drawer open to reveal everything from five tape dispensers to several candy bars to a bottle of aspirin and several unsent thank-you cards. It's an absolute disaster. His hand is holding on to the drawer pull. He's wearing a black sweater with a stark-white oxford cloth shirt peeking out underneath. I smile, staring at the picture for a few more (okay, several) minutes. I finally set the phone down.

I flip the remote control around in my hand over and over, my coffee resting on my knee. The warmth of it feels good. I can feel my breathing begin to quicken as I see what my life has become. And not just in the three weeks since I left Holloway/Greene.

I set my latte on the coffee table, tuck the remote control into the sofa cushions, and stand. I scan the takeout containers and the dirty clothes on the ground. I look at the box of my belongings from Holloway/Greene still over by the door. Unopened. The mail piled up. The Princess Leia costume is on the floor right where I left it that night. And I stand there. Trapped in it all, the walls closing in around me. The walls that were so comforting now . . . I can't breathe. I bend over and put my hands on my knees as I try to catch my breath. What have I done? I whip off Ferdie's jersey and throw it into the corner. What have I done?

Is this how it ends? I step off the conveyor belt that my life had become and just . . . cease to exist? Without a plan and the trajectory and the hierarchy and the promotions and the gold stars for a job well done and the road more traveled—without all of that, I devolve into this?

Oh my God. I begin to pace.

It's not even my plan. You want to be good? You want to be happy? Do this. Live this way. Be this person. Follow these rules. Read these books. Think these things are important. Love this way.

I didn't have to think about how I felt or who I was or what I was missing because I was too busy checking off boxes on someone else's to-do list. It comforted me, and as I grew up, it came to define me. If I'm part of their plan, then I don't have to be left out in the cold again. If I'm part of their plan, I'm tethered to something bigger than myself.

Now I know why I chose to live that way. Someone else's idea of happiness was a lot easier to attain than a happiness I could not envision and didn't think I deserved. Truth is, I wasn't striving toward happiness. What did I want more than anything? To be someone the world had to acknowledge was important.

What would actually make me feel good or happy or meaningful to me versus something I'd been told was worthy of my legacy? Again, if I'm part of their plan, then I never have to be left out in the cold ever again. If I'm part of their plan, then I'm tethered to something bigger than just myself.

It goes back to what Helen was saying—what do I think would happen if I made an entire playlist of just the songs I was too ashamed to admit I liked? This feeling bubbles up inside me just thinking about making such a playlist. Shame. Its black sticky tendrils tug and pull as I imagine the freedom of doing it. That's what it is at the root of this: my own flawed humanity. I'm not cool enough, steely enough, or perfect enough. I poo in other people's bathrooms, for crissakes.

I feel like I should dramatically slide down a wall at this point in my complete breakdown. The heroine in a romance novel would definitely slide down a wall sobbing right now. I scan my apartment and there are no slide-downable walls in the bunch.

"I can't even do that right!" I scream. I slump into one of my dining room chairs. Okay. Okay. Come on.

My idea of success was to make partner at Holloway/Greene. It's firmly established and everyone's opinions of it are based on decades upon decades of highly regarded work. Making partner would mean that I embodied those things. People would have to respect me. Like leaving out that unreadable tome on your coffee table. Whatever you may think of me, I'm a partner at Holloway/Greene and am working my way through this Nobel Prize–winning masterpiece—so, you have to kiiiind of think I'm at least a little clever. Why did I think I needed to act like I was intelligent? I *am* intelligent.

I *am* intelligent.

I flatten my hand on my dining room table. Feel something real.

I've got to burn it down. Burn their plan down. Burn down the safe trajectory and someone else's idea of happiness. Throw what they think is important onto the raging fire. I have to stop trying to make myself fit into someone else's idea of what it means to be exceptional. The problem isn't that it wouldn't work. The tragedy comes when it does.

I stack the newspapers that are piling up on the dining room table. Stack them. Pick them up and toss them in the garbage. The full garbage. I take it out to the chute. I grab another kitchen bag and fill it with takeout containers and carry that out to the chute. I do a load of laundry. And another. I open the mail, pay the bills, and put the kettle on. I change the sheets and clean the bathroom. I open the curtains.

As night falls, I take a shower, put on actual clothes (including a bra), and walk down to the corner market for dinner fixings. As I meander through the aisles, I grow frustrated thinking about what the new plan is. My plan. What is it that I want? Right at this very moment? It's cheese. I ask the man behind the cheese counter for Midnight Moon and grab some crackers to go with it. I put a few bubble waters in my basket, along with the makings for my famous salad (knowing full well that I'll fill up on the cheese and call it a night).

I get a look of concern from a husband and wife and realize that I've been muttering "Burn it down" to myself as I've meandered around the market. Great. That's . . . that's fantastic.

I head back to my apartment, get back into my pajamas, and settle into my now clean surroundings with the cheese and crackers, the salad fixings nestled safely in the refrigerator, where they'll stay until they rot and I throw them away with a muttered "why do I bother?" I click on the TV, switching channels and stopping at this one show and that one for a while. Cheese. Bubble water. Mutter "Burn it down." More cheese. Change channels. Scroll through no e-mails. Daydream about Lincoln and replay our last interchange on Wooster Street over and over again.

Sasha texts me that Lumineux is not happy at Holloway/ Greene. Audrey screwed up a big meeting this morning. They wanted all different versions of the campaign for the international market and all Audrey did was pass off the same ones we used in the United States. And then Audrey tried to pin it on the team. That was when Preeti stepped in, telling everyone that wasn't what happened and pointedly asking Audrey if she needed time to collect herself.

It was the first negative experience Lumineux had with Holloway/Greene and one that made a Lumineux executive ask why I wasn't on the conference call. Sasha said he hadn't been told I quit. Apparently he was not happy. He finally said, "Please govern yourself more professionally in the future, Ms. Holloway. Ms. Wyatt was our point person on this account. Please let us not mourn her absence moving forward." Of course, I'm conflicted. Cheese. Change channels. Switch the laundry. Troll the Internet for news on Lumineux. The phenomenon still rolls on. I pat myself on the back. Curse that Lincoln doesn't have any social media that I can stalk him on. More cheese. I change the channel again.

Sixteen Candles.

I stop.

I set the remote control down, put my plate of cheese and crackers on the coffee table, and lean forward. I've watched this movie hundreds of times. But this time? I'm watching one thing.

Anthony Michael Hall.

The yellow oxford cloth shirt. *THAT? Is what the pictures are for.* Drinking the martini in Jake Ryan's kitchen. I'm smiling. Laughing. *"My clean, close shave?"* "He really was the best," I say in a reverent whisper. The iconic shot of Jake Ryan in front of the red Porsche. And as the movie comes to an end, I mouth the lines right along with them. *"Happy birthday, Samantha. Make a wish."* I swoon. The song. That plaid shirt. *"It already came true."* Sighhhh.

The credits. Anthony Michael Hall is literally called just The Geek. I think about Chuck's words. Could he have been right? I mean, it doesn't get much better than The Geek in *Sixteen Candles*—maybe Brian Johnson in *The Breakfast Club,* but no matter what anyone says, Anthony Michael Hall is not better in *Dead Zone.* This? This is his sweet spot. This is what he's good at. I click off the TV, still humming "If You Were Here" as I clean up my all-cheese dinner.

I'm great at advertising women's products. This is the truth. I rinse my plate and put it into the dish drainer. My hand stays curled around the plate. Wait. The water from the plate dribbles down my arm. I don't move.

I'm great at advertising women's products.

Why is that a bad thing? Why did I take it as an insult? I pull my hand back from the wet plate and absently dry my arm off with the dish towel. I turn around and lean back against the kitchen counter. I scan everything in my kitchen.

Women are the most powerful, influential consumers. From bath gel and toothpaste to real estate and automobiles, the power of the buy lies with women. They are the decision makers. As in charge as my own father thought he was, it was my mother who gave him the nod about which car we could buy. It was my mother who bought everything in the house—from the furniture to the milk in the refrigerator. Even the homes we lived in, my mother had the final say. And yet advertising insists on disrespecting, misunderstanding, and downright ignoring women.

I am great at advertising women's products.

I am also great at advertising to and for women.

Why is advertising products directed at women, for women, less important? Whose rules are those? Once again, why is that romance novel any less important than that slim volume of cryptic poetry you insist is groundbreaking?

It's not.

I walk over to my desk and find a legal pad and a pen. I sit back down on the couch and open up my laptop. Chuck wanted me to handle women's products for Holloway/Greene. What if I started my own agency specializing in just that: products for women, by women. I spend the rest of the night researching and writing notes and coming up with ideas and growing more excited and terrified as I sketch out a dream I never even knew existed inside me. A dream that's been waiting for me to be strong enough to believe in it. A dream that relied on me trusting myself. Acknowledging myself.

I look up at the clock. Three thirty A.M. My entire coffee table is littered with papers and sketches and complicated equations and information on 401(k)s and bank accounts and how much does that tiny office space cost a month?

I close my laptop. I flip the sheet on the legal pad and brush my hand over the clean paper. I take my pen and write in a black sharpie:

XIX

"*Nineteen*. After the Nineteenth Amendment," I say. Out loud. A deep breath. No tears. No doubts. This is the most right thing I've ever done in my life. This is what makes living a life of "fine" laughable. I'll open an agency specializing solely in women's products. And I'll be honored to do so.

Now.

I'm going to need Sasha. And I'm going to need Preeti.

23

Sasha sneaks into the restaurant in oversized sunglasses and a giant floppy hat the next day for lunch. She sees me and slinks over, sliding into the booth with a conspiratorial nod.

"'Ello there," she says, her voice breathy and is that . . .

"Are you speaking with a British accent?" I ask.

"Now you're just being daft," Sasha says, sweeping off her sunglasses.

"You know you actually stick out more with all that stuff," I say.

"Oh, I know. It's awesome, though, right?" Sasha asks, taking her hat off and primping her perfect black ringlets.

"You're ridiculous," I say, happy to see her.

"You look good. Out of those clothes," she says, setting her floppy hat on the table.

"I know. I should do a ritual burning," I say.

"Not of Ferdie's jersey, though," Sasha says.

"No, of course not," I say.

The waitress comes over and we order our drinks, promising

her we'll look at the menu and be ready to order by the time she gets back.

"I wish I could have recorded what happened at that meeting the other day. It was so perfect," Sasha says.

"What went wrong?" I ask.

"It was exactly like you said it would go down. She doesn't know the campaign like we do, so she doesn't get the ins and outs or the nuances well enough to tailor it for the U.K. or Germany or South America, and on and on. She just looked up where the product was going to be advertised—like geographically—and aside from translating it into that language, she just used the U.S. ads. I mean, take Lumineux out of the picture, she has no idea how advertising works. At all. And unlike me, she refuses to learn."

"Oof." However badly I want to be irreplaceable, I don't want Lumineux or Preeti to have to shoulder the cost and pay for Audrey's learning curve.

"Audrey was just shell-shocked. I don't think she had any idea what went wrong. Kind of felt sorry for her, truth be told. Then she called me Clara and . . . oh, look at that, sympathy all gone," Sasha says. The waitress comes back and is very disapproving that we haven't had time to look at the menu yet. Sasha and I make a point to scour the menu for what we want and are ready when she returns with our drink refills.

"So, I have an idea," I say, once the waitress leaves us alone.

"Oh?"

"What if we started our own agency?"

"What?"

"And all we did was women's products. That's our hook. Our thing," I say.

"Just—"

"Women's products."

"Anna, I—"

"With the bonuses that Charlton gave us for that Employee of the Year thing, plus 401(k)s and savings, it could work. Fifty-fifty. We'd be partners. The buzz we have on Lumineux could get us some meetings and then in four or five yea—"

"Anna, I—"

"If Lumineux is unhappy, we can meet with Preeti. I'm sure she would come over to us—at the very least get us a meeting. And that account alone could bankroll us while we bring in new clients. And I'm thinking? Why not New York? Ferdie is doing so well now and I think moving to New York would actually be a good thing. It'd prove that I trust him. That I'm—"

"Anna—"

"And we could meet with Helen. I sent her an e-mail yesterday—about quitting Holloway/Greene and my idea about the agency. I want to call it Nineteen. For the Nineteenth Amendment? Where women got the right to vote? And the logo would just be roman numerals. Just an XIX. It looks really cool. And you could design the logo and be in charge of the art dep—"

"Anna—"

"Don't say no. Please? Can you just thi—"

"Anna! I'm in. I was in twenty minutes ago," Sasha says.

"Really?" I say, standing up awkwardly in the booth trying to hug her, but really only grasping her arms and kind of touching her hair in the process.

"Are you kidding? It's the opportunity of a lifetime," Sasha says. "And I love the idea about just repping women's products.

That's genius. Oh, and Preeti? Has already asked if you're start-ing your own agency. So . . . we're so in."

"She has?"

"Yep. After the fiasco with Audrey she came to my office. Asked about you and, of course, I told her everything. She espe-cially liked that you did the entire thing dressed as Princess Leia."

"It's actually odd—or maybe it's just my survival skills kick-ing in—that I keep forgetting that fact," I say.

"Hard to, really," Sasha says, miming huge cinnamon buns on the sides of her head. "I'll give my two weeks, but in the in-terim why don't we set up a meeting with Preeti. She's still in town. You know what? Why don't we see if she's free for drinks later?" Sasha asks, pulling out her phone. She e-mails Preeti just as the waitress brings us our food. I dig into my lunch. Sasha has pulled a pen from her purse, pushed her meal to one side, flipped over her place mat, and is now doodling several versions of a logo design. As I eat, Sasha is lost in her design. After a few minutes I try to make idle conversation.

"Depending on what work we get initially, we'll have to think about hiring. A receptionist, interns, support staff. It's going to be—"

"Amazing," Sasha says, turning the place mat around with the logo. *The* logo. XIX. It takes my breath away.

"Oh, Sasha. It's perfect," I say.

"I know," she says, smiling. She folds the place mat up and slides it into her purse. "I'll dabble with it a bit. Finalize it." She pulls her lunch back over and digs in.

Sasha and I meet with Preeti that night and she's beyond ex-cited. She can work her magic over at Quincy and move Lumineux over to the newly formed XIX straightaway. She'll set up a meeting. She says it'll be easier for her to sell it because it's me at the helm and XIX will be in New York. Apparently, Holloway/ Greene being in D.C. has always been a sticking point for the Quincy higher-ups. And fortunately for us, Audrey's screwup will encourage Lumineux to jump ship that much more.

As I'm getting ready for bed that night I get a text from Lincoln. It's a picture of his computer keyboard covered in tea and he's giving it the V sign, which I quickly look up on the Internet and learn that that's basically the British middle finger. I cringe. Spilling tea on my keyboard. My worst nightmare. I walk into the bathroom and brush my teeth. As I'm looking at my hair in the mirror, I spy one single gray hair—right in front, of course. Before I pluck it out with a vengeance, I take a picture of it and send it along to Lincoln.

Two weeks later, with Sasha no longer at Holloway/Greene, we head up to New York early to meet with Helen. We've sent our business plan ahead for her to review. On the train ride I give notice on my apartment and start poking around to find a new one. My heart rate slows down. Because moving? I'm good at.

Do I schedule a dinner with Michael and Allison? Or is this just another aspect of being an adult? It's a two-hour train ride, we'll still have our book clubs and the kids' birthday parties, as well as the impending birth of their newest. And what about Hannah and Nathan? How does that work? Hey, let's have dinner and how's that separation I'm not supposed to know about going? I've got time, I'll figure those out. And Ferdie. I can't deal with Ferdie right now, because believing that moving to New York is treating him as an adult seems very far away. I still want to Bubble Wrap him and make sure he's okay, and I know that's called enabling now, but that doesn't mean it doesn't feel completely foreign to not do those things. It took everything I had not to clean out his apartment now that we know for sure he's not returning. He has to take care of it. *He has to take care of it.* But if I could just e-mail him this company's information that does this sort of . . . *No.* Walk away from the to-do list, Anna.

Sasha and I stand in front of Helen's drool-worthy brownstone on the Upper West Side. I hold the slip of paper with the address, my workbag slung over one shoulder, my purse tucked just underneath it. Sasha pulls me over and looks at the address again.

"Central Park is just—" I say, motioning to the beautiful park just behind us.

"I knew people lived here, I just didn't know *I knew* people who lived here," Sasha says.

We walk up to the imposing limestone face and brick façade, careful not to touch the Grecian columns and in awe of the triangular pediment looming large above us. We pick our way up the marble steps, taking in the elaborate topiaries adorning either side of the imposing brass door. There's a call button on one side.

"What time is it?" I ask.

"Nine twenty-seven A.M.," Sasha says, checking her phone.

"Okay," I say, pushing the call button.

"Yes?" the voice asks.

"Anna Wyatt and Sasha Merchant to see Helen Brubaker?" A buzz and I push open the heavy door. We step into the black-and-white marble-tiled foyer. Beautiful floral arrangements pepper the hallway as chandeliers twinkle and illuminate the room high above. To the left are a couple of French doors and a woman behind a reception desk. Sasha and I proceed with caution.

"Helen will be right down. Can I get you anything? Tea?" the woman asks.

"Tea would be lovely," I say. Sasha and I settle onto a white tufted couch. White. Everything is white.

"Do you take anything?" the woman asks.

"No, thank you," I say. The woman looks from me to Sasha.

"Nothing for me, thanks . . . thanks you. Nothing for me, thank you," Sasha says. The woman walks to the left of reception and into a little kitchenette.

"It's okay to ask for the beverage you want. It lets them know that you belong here," I say.

"I just feel so guilty, you know?" Sasha whispers. "Like who do I think I am, right?"

"It's okay to let her do her job, and you deserve to be here," I say.

"Okay," Sasha says, situating herself in her chair. The woman comes back with my cup of tea. Fortnum and Mason, just like in Phoenix. "If I could trouble you?" Sasha says. "I'd love a coffee."

"No problem at all. What do you take?" the woman asks with a smile.

"Soy milk and sugar, please," Sasha asks.

"Just like Helen," the woman says, smiling. Sasha beams.

"Just like Helen," Sasha repeats once the woman excuses herself to the kitchenette.

"Fancy," I say, letting the scent of tea calm me. I close my eyes and inhale.

"I hope I don't spill. Everything is white white white," Sasha says.

"Have you ever spilled coffee before?" I ask.

"What? No, of course not," Sasha says.

"So, there's no precedent. You're not a coffee spiller," I say.

"Right. I am not a coffee spiller," Sasha repeats.

"And if you do? It's white, they can bleach it out. You don't think that receptionist has one of those bleach sticks in her desk right this very moment?" I ask.

"Right. She totally does. They can bleach it out," Sasha whispers to herself. The woman comes back with a cup of coffee for Sasha. "Thank you ever so." The woman smiles, albeit a tad confused. I'm holding back laughter as I turn to Sasha. "I don't know. I'm out of my mind. I can't . . ." She blows on her coffee and I know her hands are shaking by the tinkling of the teacup on her saucer. Sasha laughs and I can see she's lightening up a bit as we sit and drink our beverages in Helen Brubaker's perfect white waiting room.

"We should do something like this. I love it. And we could totally do it on the cheap. A waiting area that's feminine. Flowers. Tufted couches. Tea in teacups."

"Right. It's so interesting because my worry was that it would seem unprofessional, you know? Like a girls' clubhouse, but I don't feel like that here," Sasha says.

"No way, it's the ex—" The woman's phone buzzes and a yes, ma'am, and a sure and a straightaway. She hangs up and tells us that Helen is ready.

"Follow me, if you will," the woman says, walking out of the reception area and down the marble-tiled hallway, under the sweeping chandeliers, and the smell of stargazer lilies and fresh-cut flowers wafts as we pass conference rooms and copy rooms and offices.

Two grand doors at the end of the hallway. I can hear Sasha's teacup saucer begin to chatter again. I turn around and just smile. A deep breath. The woman opens the doors and motions for us to continue in. I thank her and she clacks back down the hallway.

"Come on in," Helen says, coming out from behind her desk. The windows. The Persian rugs. The walls lined with filled bookcases. All you can hear are Sasha's and my clattering tea-cups. "Here. Put those down before you spill something." Helen gestures to a meeting area on the opposite side of her desk. It's situated in a little nook surrounded by bay windows with a lush patch of green just outside, a fountain bubbling in the distance. Little birds flit and bathe themselves as we situate ourselves around the table.

"Thank you so much for seeing us," I say.

"I'm your mentor. This is me mentoring," she says. The woman comes in and sets a pot of tea down in the middle of the table. She hands Helen a perfectly made cappuccino with a heart in foam on the top. Sasha and I shoot a look at each other. "I know. She spoils me." Helen takes a sip of her coffee, licking her top lip of foam with a dainty shrug. "So, you two are opening your own agency."

"Yes. I had this conversation with Chuck Holloway—Charlton Holloway's son and the next in line—where he said that I was great at marketing women's products. At the time, I took it as an insult."

"As you do," Helen says. Another sip.

"I wanted the important accounts. The ones on the website. The ones—"

"For men," Helen says.

"Exactly," I say.

"And now?" Helen asks.

"We changed the landscape with Lumineux. We took your lead and valued women instead of shaming and belittling them," I say. Sasha passes over her sketches of our logo.

"Nineteen. Nice," Helen says.

"We'll set up right here in New York and we'll make our mark as the agency for women, by women," I say.

"But a lot of those corporations are run by men," Helen says.

"And for that, it comes down to money. They want to make it and we can get their products into the grocery carts of the decision makers: women." Helen takes out the business plan I sent her. Sasha and I look at our own copies. Crunched numbers. Research. Forecasts. Outlooks. Helen flips through the business plan. I sip my tea, trying to stop my hands from shaking.

"I had a chance to review it; it's good work," Helen says, turning page after page.

"Thank you," I say, looking over at Sasha. She looks terrified.

"So, let's get down to the nitty-gritty. This isn't the adorable montage in a romantic comedy where you find a perfect office space in some quaint exposed-brick building that doesn't actually exist. There will be no line out the door. There will be no social life or life at all outside of starting this business. You both will live and breathe Nineteen. There will be no holidays or weekends. The buck that stopped with your boss or his boss or somewhere else up the pecking order now stops with you. From

the light bill to the ordering of tea to the hiring of staff to the
wooing of new clients to the firing of that one secretary who's
super nice but just terrible at her job to the attending of meetings
to the arguing with contractors to the paying of bills and more
bills and then more bills, it all comes down to you. And as partners, it will be fifty-fifty. Not Wyatt here talking as Merchant
passes over a beautiful drawing with shaking hands. You, my
dear, are going to have to step up."

"Yes, ma'am," Sasha says.

"Why are you doing this? Do you know the answer?" Helen
asks Sasha. I look at Sasha. I'm ashamed. Of course, I never
asked her that. Sasha sets down her teacup and slides forward in
her chair.

"When I was at NYU I used to have this vision. I was walking through an office and I was smiling and nodding to the staff.
Oh, hello, Miller. Nice day out, Webley. Have that on my desk by
the end of the workday, Glickman."

"You made up names for your imaginary staff?" Helen asks.

"Of course," Sasha says.

"Go on," Helen says, unable to keep from smiling.

"I was respected. I was respectable. I know I'm good at my
job, Mrs. Brubaker."

"Helen, please."

"Helen," Sasha says with a childlike squeal. "I know I'm
good at my job, *Helen*." A smile to me and I can't help but smile
back. "But that always seemed to come second or even third or
fourth to who I was screwing or who people gossiped about me
screwing or if my skirt was too tight or if these mean girls decided that I had slept my way to the top instead of earning it,
which I knew I did. I don't know. What finally got me? It's the

utter shock when people see how good I am at my job. They can't put it together, so they usually chalk it up to a one-time thing or that I had someone else do it for me. Anna sees me. She sees me." Sasha looks over at me and smiles. I smile back. "I want Nineteen to be the kind of office a woman like me can stride through."

"Well said," Helen says.

"Thank you," Sasha says, her voice easy.

"Okay. Location. I wouldn't get too precious about it. While Red Hook and Greenpoint and that Brooklyn business is really hot right now, you are going to have to think about your clients. Corporate America wandering around Bushwick is not what you want." Helen buzzes her receptionist. The woman appears through the grand double doors with a folder. Helen thanks her and the woman disappears. "I had my realtor look into a few spaces for you. I know. You're welcome. I centered on the West Village, the Meatpacking District, Soho, and I know everyone's talking about NoMad, but to me that's just depressing Midtown. But there are a couple of office spaces included because I had to play nice with my realtor. She's meeting you at the first place on the list"—Helen checks her watch—"in thirty minutes." She stands. "Now. In this folder is also a list of contractors and handymen and everyone I've worked with in the past." Helen hands me the folder. "Close your mouth, dear. This is mentoring." She walks out from behind the table. "Leave your teacups." Sasha and I gather our things and follow her down the marble-tiled hallway. "All of the places you will see today are within your budget. A few of them have the option of residential living space just over them or behind them. I find that works for me." Helen motions to the sweeping staircase, which probably leads to her home on the upper floors of the brownstone. "I will throw you an opening gala and invite everyone I know. We will throw it here or in your new space. Your choice. It will be a networking opportunity and you will need to have the staff and resources available to serve their needs." Helen has walked us out onto her front stoop. A black town car pulls up in front of her brownstone. "This is Marcus. He'll be your driver for today. I know, you couldn't possibly. Oh, but you will. And you're welcome." Helen extends her hand to me. Then to Sasha. We are speechless. "And I'm hiring you. Please have contracts drawn up as soon as possible and when you're properly attired, we will meet and talk about the exciting future of Brubaker Enterprises and Nineteen."

Stunned silence.

"Chop, chop. Marcus is waiting." Helen walks us down to the car, opening up the back door.

"Thank you," I say. Sasha mutters a stunned thank-you just behind me.

"You're welcome," Helen says.

"Why . . . I can't . . ."

"You're the good guys, Ms. Wyatt. That's why."

She tucks us into the backseat of her town car and we're off to meet with her realtor and I will never stop clutching this folder to my breast or holding Sasha's hand or how did this happen and . . .

"We're the good guys," Sasha says. She looks over and smiles.

"I guess we are," I say.

24

Helen wasn't kidding. For the next two months, Sasha and I ate, slept, and breathed Nineteen. I put all my worldly belongings in storage, making sure to snap a photo of the stacked chaos and sent it to Lincoln. My bed was a cot in the back of our new office space in the West Village—another photo to Lincoln. His response to that one was a photo of a ripped pair of tweed pants. Right down the back seam, his hand poking through. He accompanied the photo with the words "Walked around in these all day." I texted back that I would have loved to have seen that. I had to brush my teeth in the kitchenette and joined a gym so I'd have somewhere to shower. I snapped another photo of the delightful pair of shower sandals I bought at the local drugstore and sent that along to Lincoln, too.

With the construction going on around us, Sasha and I set up a makeshift office with card tables and folding chairs so we could handle the Lumineux campaign. We immediately felt the impact of not having the support staff we luxuriated in at Holloway/Greene. Our days were spent running errands and copying contracts and answering phones and what do you mean the toilet is backed up and when in the world is that pounding going to stop and oh my God, we're out of tea?

When the contractors finally finished my living space, I was able to move my stuff to the upstairs of the XIX offices. Sasha moved back in with an old roommate from her modeling days. She was excited about it, said that living on her own—especially during a Time-Out—felt a bit lonely. I know the feeling.

Ferdie and I spent Thanksgiving and Christmas together at the Recovery House. They have extra rooms for relatives and staff. And then I spent New Year's Eve seriously questioning my life choices while freezing my ass off sitting on that cot with nothing but a space heater, my constantly full e-mail box, and a picture Lincoln sent of himself, alone and still at work. He'd even bought a sparkly hat. I texted him back a picture of me with a couple of deflated balloons left over from the impromptu party Sasha and I had after we landed another client. They'd been rolling around the break room for days. In the picture I'm holding the sad balloons and wearing the jaunty faux fur trapper hat I'd started wearing to help with the cold.

The shame spirals are violent and come from out of nowhere. I really would have thought that after months of investing in XIX they would lessen. They haven't.

With the rush of seeing our letterhead for the first time also came the voices of who do you think you are? When we hired a receptionist, I felt the burden of her livelihood as I burned the midnight oil. A meeting with our new accounts manager and I knew for sure he thought we were amateurs. Sasha brought on a couple of new hires for the art department and immediately I tried to inappropriately impose sage advice on them. Pass the coffee? Don't you mean do unto others as you would have them do unto you, Skylar?

On my last trip down to D.C. to visit Ferdie, I met with a saleswoman I always liked from Holloway/Greene. I made her an offer she couldn't refuse. And when she accepted, it was all I could do to not kiss her full on the lips. Sasha brought in a few interns from NYU who looked like they should be playing Little League, and all I could think was how much more they'd be learning at a place like Holloway/Greene. See, I knew how to be a great employee. I knew how to bring in accounts for the bigwigs upstairs. I knew how to impress the professor. I knew how to serve the Holloways of this world. And I thought I would be the perfect boss right away, and I'm completely frustrated that I don't know how to be in this new life 100 percent and stride through XIX like I own the place (which I do). I thought not only that the training montage was over, but that the fight was going to be a breezy knockout. Why then do I still feel like a fraud when the little intern trembles as she tells me my three P.M. is here to see me?

It's the first days of spring with some shimmery snow still on the ground, and XIX is finally up and running. I grab my tea, pack up my laptop, lock up my apartment, and walk down the stairs to the office. I flick on the lights, turn on all the power strips and the kettle and the coffee maker and the copier, throw a random piece of paper into the bin, and clean a bit of dust off the conference table as I make my way back to my office. I see the light on in Sasha's office, so I dump my workbag and purse at my desk and, still clutching my tea, head in to see what has her here so early.

I poke my head into her office and am met with the same

dark reds and browns that she had back at Holloway/Greene. Art is everywhere. Covering every inch of her space.

"We're meeting with that little Disney actress today or her people, probably," Sasha says, not looking up.

"For her clothing line," I say, sitting in one of Sasha's client chairs.

"They sent me an e-mail late last night about there being more to it than that," she says. The difference in Sasha is noticeable. She has become that woman she envisioned striding through that office. Her voice is stronger, calmer. Her shoulders are always back and she hasn't done that thing where you say "excuse me" even though it was the other person who got in your way? Yeah, that.

"You should have said something," I say.

"You've got that big exit meeting with Ferdie today. Plus? I've got it," she says, looking up with a huge smile.

"I know you do," I say.

"They're thinking of a whole backpack line and school supplies and then that can go over to this new animated character they're auditioning her for. So, this could be huge." Sasha hands me the printed-out e-mail with all her notes on it.

"You're going in with Nick?" I ask, speaking of our new accounts hire.

"Yeah, and I thought I'd bring Skylar. Show her the ropes," Sasha says.

"That sounds great," I say.

"I saw that Preeti sent you over the numbers on Lumineux. Holy moly, right?"

"I know. It's unbelievable," I say.

"You're going back in to meet with them next week?"

"Yeah and hopefully . . ." I cross my fingers.

"I know. I mean, it sounds like that's what they're thinking," Sasha says.

"But I think we really have to stay with our mission statement and only represent the Quincy products that are targeted at women," I say.

"Agreed," she says.

"And we're both on the same page about being wildly happy that Chuck blew his meeting at Quincy, right?"

"Oh, absolutely."

"And if we were lesser people, we'd spend hours upon hours gloating and laughing."

"Thankfully, we're not lesser people," Sasha says. I smile and Sasha can't help but laugh as she shifts in her chair.

"Okay, I've got a train to catch. Plans for the weekend?" I ask.

"Work. Work. And more work," she says. I smile at her and say my good-byes. I'm just about to walk out of her office when . . .

"Does any of this ever get to you?" I ask.

"Any of what?"

"Nineteen. Being someone's boss. All of this. Do you ever feel like a fraud?"

"Every day."

"Really?" I ask.

"Yes! Are you kidding? Wait. You do, too?"

"Yes!"

"Wow, I thought you had it all figured out."

"I thought *you* had it all figured out," I say.

"Nope."

"Me either."

"Do you think Helen Brubaker ever feels like a fraud?"

"No way. Not at all." I laugh.

"Yeah, I didn't think so, either."

"Okay, the train. She awaits. Good luck with the Disney princess. Let me know how it goes," I say, turning to leave.

"Roger that," she says, calling out after me. I walk out through the XIX offices, into the newly fallen snow, and I'm back on the Metroliner speeding toward Ferdie and his exit interview.

"Anna? Come on back," Ralph says, later that morning. He lumbers down the long hallway and into a vacant office in the back of the Recovery House. "Any plans for the weekend?"

"Work, probably," I say. Ralph turns around and smiles. He motions for me to come in. Ferdie is there already.

He takes my breath away. Standing in front of me is the brother I remember from our childhood. He's been here for six months. Six months of sharing at meetings through tears and anger. Apparently, he and Ralph got into several shouting matches and one particularly Godzilla versus Mothra shoving match that ended with Ralph tugging Ferdie in for a monster bear hug, telling him that he knew he was mad, he knew he was mad . . . it's okay. Let it out, Ralph soothed. Let it all out. Ralph wasn't going anywhere.

I launch into Ferdie for a hug, and I love that I've gotten used to his new smell. The new smell is the old smell. He pulls me close and when we break apart he pushes up his glasses and just smiles. It's a hesitant smile, but something else is there. Ferdie is proud of himself. And now? There's no one around to punch that feeling out of him.

"Anna, thank you so much for coming down here today," Ralph says.

"My pleasure," I say, taking Ferdie's hand in mine as we sit across from Ralph.

"How's Nineteen?" Ferdie asks.

"It's terrifying and amazing," I say.

"I know the feeling," Ferdie says. I squeeze his hand tight. Tighter. We are quiet. I don't know who to look at or what's supposed to happen here today. So, I just look from Ferdie to Ralph and back at Ferdie. It's Ferdie who continues. "I've decided to stay on at the Recovery House. They've found a place for me doing intake and I can work up to being a counselor here."

"That sounds amazing," I say.

"Okay . . . cool," Ferdie says.

"Were you worried?"

"Well, you always wanted me to go back to school and all that," he says.

"I just wanted you to be happy," I say.

"Being here makes me happy," he says.

"When this facility evaluates someone for employment, they make sure that they're not using Recovery House as a crutch or a place to hide. We know that there's a big, wide world out there, and we need to have every confidence that our employees can make it there, too," Ralph says.

"Oh . . . . right," I say.

"That's the case with Ferdinand," Ralph says.

"I feel like I can do some good here," Ferdie says. "I mean, who better, right?"

"No one," I say.

"Ferdinand would work almost as an R.A., if you will, for the first few months and then from there—"

"If I wanted to pursue addiction counseling, I could go back to school for that," Ferdie says.

"It sounds great. It just sounds great," I say, smiling. Smiling. Smiling.

We are quiet. I don't know what else there is to talk about. Is this—

"Ferdinand wanted to broach the issue of your parents," Ralph says.

"Oh?" My stomach drops.

Ralph looks to Ferdie. Ferdie turns to me, taking both of my hands. I grow worried. Panicked. I have no idea what's coming.

"We've talked a lot about family in here. What it means and all that. I have you." Ferdie stops talking. Abruptly. He looks down. A deep breath. "But Mom and Dad? As it stands right now, they're not people I really want in my life."

"I totally get that."

"I plan on paying them back all the money. I'm forever in their debt for making this possible. But I can be indebted to them and love them from a distance. I think I thought that when I got 'fixed,' then all of a sudden my relationship with them would be better. But that's not how it works. It was never about me. It was never about us."

"I know. I . . . want to think that. I want to know that," I say, trying to hide my welling tears from Ralph. He slides a box of tissues over to me. I smile and act like I'm not totally crying right now.

"I think family can be a lot of things. And Mom and Dad

always acted like they were doing us a favor in loving us—or trying to love us, anyway. That it was such a burden, but that's not right," Ferdie says.

"I . . . I know," I say. Ferdie looks down at me, squeezes my hands, and waits for me to look up into those deep brown eyes of his. So clear. So bright now. He looks so young and alive. Unafraid.

"People have to love all of us, not just some of us," Ferdie says. I nod. And nod. I lean in close.

"The Batman side."

"Right."

"What if they're right, though? And there are parts of us that are unlovable?" I ask, my voice a whisper.

Ferdie pulls me in for a hug. And then he whispers in my ear, "They're not right, Anna. They're not right." He pulls me in closer and when we separate he holds my face in his hands. "It is a privilege to love you and to be loved by you. All of you." I nod as the tears stream down my face. Ferdie watches me. Do I get it, he wonders. I nod. I nod yes. I nod yes. He pulls me in for another hug.

"I'll eat you up, I love you so," I say.

I'm sitting in my rental car in the pouring rain. Ferdie's words echo and pinball around my mind, this car, the world. *They're not right.* There are not whole parts of me that are unlovable. Loving me, contrary to popular opinion, is not a burden. It's not my fault that my parents couldn't—*didn't*—love me. I was a kid. What could I have done that made me so unlovable? My secret fear, my shame, was that it was never anything I did; it was just me. All of me. That at my root, in my essence, I was so inherently flawed that even my own parents couldn't love me.

Why did it never occur to me, until now, that it was about them?

Because it was easier to think it was me. I could control it if it was about me. Or try to. I could get good grades, go to community college plus night classes, pull myself up by my own bootstraps, and land a fancy job in advertising, and I could squeeeeeze love out of my parents blue ribbon by blue ribbon. And if they were cold and detached, I could still work harder. There was always an answer! There was always another hill to climb! There was always another opportunity to thank my parents while standing atop another podium.

If it was about them, there was nothing I could do. It was beyond my control. I was helpless.

The rain falls.

They're not right.

They're not right.

They're.

Not.

Right.

It's time to step into the rings.

I pick up my phone and dial.

"Mallory Consulting."

"Hi, this is Anna Wyatt, is Mr. Mallory in?"

"No, he's not in. He's actually speaking at a small college upstate for their parents' weekend," the woman says.

"Oh, that's right. And which small college is that?" I ask, digging a piece of paper out of my purse along with a pen. The woman tells me the small liberal arts college in Poughkeepsie, and I thank her. I look at the clock on the dashboard. I input the address of the university into my phone's map. Five hours. Over three hundred miles. I could make it tonight and be there to meet him by morning.

I pull out of the Recovery House's parking lot and set my course for Poughkeepsie, New York.

And I'm stuck in the D.C. traffic. I don't have cash for the tolls and I have to stop and get money in some gas station whose bathroom is a porta-potty by the side of the flooding highway. I pull past Manhattan as night falls and it's another traffic jam and horns blaring and should I stop and get clothes for tomorrow or at the very least my toothbrush—no. I press on.

I have no good music, so I'm forced to listen to the radio all the way up. Pop song after pop song. And it's amazing. I turn up the music and, once the rain stops pouring, I roll down my window and sing along. I stop at a diner and have the world's greasiest cheeseburger and fries, sitting by myself in a booth by the jukebox. The waitress calls me hon and she's worried that I'm driving around after dark.

I roll into Poughkeepsie just after nine P.M. and find the nearest hotel. Full. Parents' weekend, they say. Sure, that makes sense. Onto the next hotel. Full. The night grinds on and I decide to stop and call around to the other local hotels. All I can find is a terrible twenty-four-hour fast food place that's full of obnoxious college kids, so I order a soda and sit in the parking lot calling around to find that no hotel has any room.

"This is why a plan is a good idea," I say, locking my doors, lowering my seat down, and pulling my coat over my shoulders. I turn onto my side, mess with the headrest like it's an actual pillow, and pull my coat up a bit more. The clock on the dash. The little

blue numbers illuminated as my windows fog over. 11:34. I turn
on the car and run the heater. Off again. Doze off. My eyes blink
open. 12:56. I run the heater again. I flip over on my other side,
pull my coat up. Doze off. 2:21. Is this the longest night ever? I flip
over again and wonder why sleeping on that stupid cot all those
months didn't make this one night any better. 3:01. Oh good.
Time is slowing down. Shift change as employees arrive and I
decide to go inside and use the bathroom at the fast food place. I
sneak back outside and try to resituate myself as I run the heater.
3:34. 3:56. I turn off the heater and flip over. 4:01. I close my eyes.
Keep them closed. My contact lenses are dry and my mouth is a
ball of cotton. My shoe got kicked off at some point and now it's
just hitting me in the shin every time I move. But if I try to get it,
the cold of the early morning will rush in as my coat falls off my
shoulders. I bend down and quickly resituate my shoe. Freezing.
I bring the coat up over my shoulder again. I'm now past tired and
have reached that lovely point where the exhaustion and cold is
just in my bones. This was a terrible idea. I couldn't have gotten a
hotel when I was back in D.C.? Stopped in Manhattan and
started this stupid trek first thing in the morning?

Of course not. I had to be dramatic. 4:37. More people start
pulling into the fast food parking lot. Then a few more. Headlights on my windshield as I feign sleep. At five thirty, I decide to
give up. I start the car up and head back to the diner on the edge
of town for breakfast.

It's in the diner bathroom that I see what evil spending the
night in that fast food parking lot hath wrought. The rearview
mirror had been kind. Black circles under my eyes, makeup
askew and worn out. I find some Lumineux Shower Gel sam-
plers in my workbag and use those to wash under my arms and

my face. I make a mental note to pitch Preeti a Lumineux Woman-on-the-Go bag for emergencies. That's twice in the last year I could have used it.

My hair is doing things I've never seen it do before, actually sticking straight out of my head in places—which I thought was physically impossible. I use the water from the sink and try to smooth my hair down, but now I just look like a drowned rat. Do I slick it back into a ponytail and look like the lunch lady who tormented me at school, or do I try to keep it down so I look like I've just run through some sprinklers after breaking out of the state pen? It's really a win-win. I decide to put it back into a ponytail. No, down. A braid? Maybe two ponytails? How about some cinnamon bun rolls on the sides of my head? That seemed to be quite effective. I dry my hair under the hand dryer in the bathroom and decide to keep it down. It's windswept, I tell myself. When I sit back down, the waitress looks terrified. Once she leaves, I throw the whole rat's nest into a ponytail.

Two cups of tea and a country breakfast later and I'm parking my rental car/sleeping compartment on the edge of the picturesque college's grounds. My silk blouse looked tasteful and amazing for yesterday's meeting with Ralph and Ferdie. This morning? It looks like I wadded up a napkin, cut out a neck hole and some armholes, then proceeded to squeeze my body inside it. My sensible pencil skirt is wrinkled and off-center, but it's the drool on my blazer that really brings the outfit home. I walk onto campus and see the white tents set up in what appears to be one of the main common areas. Students are beginning to mill around, and it's the coffee kiosk that has drawn the most interest at the moment.

I find a flyer for today's festivities and see that Lincoln is speaking this afternoon at a room just off the common area. Okay. I can see if any hotel rooms have opened up, go take a shower, fix my hair, and—

Lincoln.

"You know I meant messy in a metaphorical way," he says, his black overcoat pristine and his gray cashmere scarf lilting in the crisp morning air. I smooth my drool-stained blazer over my wrinkly napkin blouse and step closer to Lincoln.

"I eat all the movie popcorn before the trailers have finished. That TV show about the chemistry teacher that makes meth? I got through one season and then just watched the finale. I hate cats; I think they're smug for no good reason. I had an accident in my sleeping bag when I spent the night over at Tatiana's house when I was twelve and lied about it. I love sports being on in the background. It makes me feel not so alone. I didn't love my ex-husband and I almost canceled the wedding, but the invitations had already gone out. I love Taylor Swift. I do. I love her. I cry during any medal ceremony. My left foot swells up when it gets hot, and I'm positive it's because I secretly have diabetes. I bite my fingernails and have no intention of stopping. I think I'm smarter than most people and if someone doesn't think I'm funny, I am immediately suspicious. I think you are amazing. I knew it the moment I met you. You made me believe in The One and I know how cheesy that sounds, but it's true. It's you. It was always you. You're my person, too."

Lincoln pulls me into him, his mouth fast on mine, his arms wrapped around me. The warmth of him envelops me. That oaky, outdoorsy smell is everywhere. He pulls me in close, hugging me tight.

And in my ear he whispers, "You Marpled me too, love."

About the author

Read on

Insights,
Interviews
& More . . .

Meet Liza Palmer

Author photograph by Edwin Santiago

LIZA PALMER is the internationally bestselling author of *Conversations with the Fat Girl*. *Conversations with the Fat Girl* became an international bestseller its first week in publication and hit number one on the Fiction Heatseekers List in the United Kingdom the week before the book debuted. *Conversations with the Fat Girl* has been optioned for a series by the producers of *Rome*, *Band of Brothers*, and *Generation Kill*.

Palmer's second novel is *Seeing Me Naked*, of which *Publishers Weekly* says, "Consider it haute chick lit; Palmer's prose is sharp, her characters are solid and her narrative is laced with moments of graceful sentiment."

Her third novel, *A Field Guide to Burying Your Parents*, which *Entertainment Weekly* calls a "splendid novel" and *Real Simple* says "has heart and humor," was released in January 2010.

Palmer's fourth novel, *More Like Her*, received a starred review from *Library Journal*, in which they said, "The blend of humor and sadness is realistic and gripping, and watching Frannie figure out who she is and what matters is gratifying."

Kirkus Reviews called her fifth novel, *Nowhere but Home*, "a heart-wrenching tale told with true wisdom and brilliant wit. . . . An uplifting reading experience."

After earning two Emmy nominations writing for the first season of VH1's *Pop Up Video*, Palmer now knows far too much about Fergie.

Girl Before a Mirror is Palmer's sixth novel. ∼

Anna and Lincoln's Guide to Phoenix

I HAD NEVER BEEN TO PHOENIX. I haven't been to a lot of places, so this isn't really news in the Palmer household. But I wasn't setting *Girl Before a Mirror* a lot of places—I was setting it in Phoenix. I thought I could hide behind good research, but it remained plainly obvious: as Tina Fey says (ish), "I had to go to there."

So, if you're ever in Phoenix . . .

STAY

ARIZONA BILTMORE
2400 East Missouri Avenue
Phoenix, AZ 85016

I needed a solid location to set Anna and Lincoln. It had to be a character in and of itself. And that's exactly what I got in the 1929 Frank Lloyd Wright–inspired Biltmore. So I set my GPS from L.A. and drove. And drove. And drove. New Edition's "If It Isn't Love" can only energize you so many times. It was hot. That last loop into Phoenix rivals *Cannonball Run*. I needed food and a bed. I pulled into the Biltmore and I remember just sighing. It was nighttime, so it was all lit up—fountains, Italian café lights—people milling around. It was exactly the type of place two broken people would let their guard down long enough to fall in love.

EAT

ASADERO NORTE DE SONORA
122 North 16th Street
Phoenix, AZ 85034

Real Cokes. Spanish wafting all around.
It reminded me immediately of when
I used to visit my aunt Concha—the
smell of pinto beans lilting from the
kitchen. Tiled tables with a roll of paper
towels atop. Vending machines with
cheap toys and framed pictures of old
Sonora. I was in heaven. I spoke in
broken Spanish and the waitress, bless
her heart, acted like it wasn't terrible.
And then I ate. And ate. I can still smell
the barbecue even now.

MRS. WHITE'S GOLDEN RULE CAFE
808 East Jefferson Street
Phoenix, AZ 85034

Whenever I did research on Phoenix,
someone would always mention Mrs.
White's. The cobbler, they'd drool. The
cobbler though. After having more than
a bit of trouble with an ornery one-way
street (it was the street's fault, okay?),
I parked and headed in. The thing
about locals-only places? They know
you're not from there. The good ones,
though? Can't wait to find out more
about you. That's Mrs. White's. All the
way from L.A.? For our cobbler? They
hated to tell me: they were out. BUT.
BUT. Have you tried our sweet potato
pie? No, I whimpered. We'll get you ▶

some, honey. AND OH MY GOD. It was warm. And I may have cried a little. But I'm still going back for that damn cobbler one day.

GO

IRISH CULTURAL CENTER
1106 North Central Avenue
Phoenix, AZ 85004

I needed a location to set an event for RomanceCon. Something . . . epic. Maybe an Irish castle in the middle of Phoenix will do? I parked—oh my God was it hot—and walked through the gates, and it was . . . how does this place exist? Gray stone castles and little cottages and barns with raftered ceilings and libraries and kids learning Gaelic (programs you can find under the heading of "Wee Folk"). A wonderful red-haired woman with a smoky voice proudly showed me around, explaining murals and giant black fireplaces and flags, and I was transported. They have a little shop there. Sells tea and chocolate. Just sayin'. ⌣

Have You Read?
More from Liza Palmer

For more books by Liza Palmer, check out . . .

Read on

NOWHERE BUT HOME

The strategy on the gridiron of *Friday Night Lights* is nothing compared to the savagery of coming home . . .

Queenie Wake has just been fired from her job as a chef for not allowing a customer to use ketchup . . . again. Now the only place she has to go is North Star, Texas, the hometown she left in disgrace. Maybe things will be different this time around. After all, her mother—notorious for stealing your man, your car, and your rent money—has been dead for years. And Queenie's sister, once the local teenage harlot who fooled around with the town golden boy, is now the mother of the high school football captain.

Queenie's new job, cooking last meals at the nearby prison, is going well . . . at least the inmates don't complain! But apparently small-town Texas has a long memory for bad reputations. And when Queenie bumps into Everett Coburn, the high school sweetheart who broke her heart, she wishes her own memory was a little spottier. But before Queenie takes another chance on love, she'll have to take an even bigger risk: finding a place to call home once and for all.

MORE LIKE HER

What really goes on behind those perfect white picket fences?

In Frances's mind, beautiful, successful, ecstatically married Emma Dunham is the height of female perfection. Frances, recently dumped with spectacular drama by her boyfriend, aspires to be just like Emma. So do her close friends and fellow teachers, Lisa and Jill. But Lisa's too career-focused to find time for a family. And Jill's recent unexpected pregnancy could have devastating consequences for her less-than-perfect marriage.

Yet sometimes the golden dream you fervently wish for turns out to be not at all what it seems—like Emma's enviable suburban postcard life, which is about to be brutally cut short by a perfect husband turned killer. And in the shocking aftermath, three devastated friends are going to have to come to terms with their own secrets . . . and somehow learn to move forward after their dream is exposed as a lie.

MORE LIKE HER

LIZA PALMER

AUTHOR OF *Conversations with the Fat Girl*

Discover great authors, exclusive offers, and more at hc.com.